# INNOCENT'S WEDDING DAY WITH THE ITALIAN

## MICHELLE SMART

# BACK TO CLAIM HIS CROWN

## NATALIE ANDERSON

**MILLS & BOON**

First published in Great Britain 2023
by Mills & Boon, an imprint of HarperCollins*Publishers* Ltd,
1 London Bridge Street, London, SE1 9GF

www.harpercollins.co.uk

HarperCollins*Publishers*, Macken House, 39/40 Mayor Street Upper, Dublin 1, D01 C9W8, Ireland

Innocent's Wedding Day with the Italian © 2023 Michelle Smart

Back to Claim His Crown © 2023 Natalie Anderson

ISBN: 978-0-263-30688-0

08/23

# INNOCENT'S WEDDING DAY WITH THE ITALIAN

MICHELLE SMART

MILLS & BOON

For Mitchell.

May the world always be this exciting and loving
for you. xxx

# CHAPTER ONE

THE STRETCH LIMOUSINE was greeted in the piazza by dozens of cameras flashing manically. Since the announcement of her engagement, Rebecca Foley had avoided cameras like the plague. She'd known it would be impossible to avoid them today, the day of the wedding of the century. Italy's premier bachelor was about to get hitched, and she was the lucky lady he was pledging his life to.

While waiting for the driver to open her door, Rebecca looked at the empty space beside her where her father should be. This car she was about to be helped out of should be *his* car, the 1960s battered classic he'd been so proud of getting for a steal, as he'd called it, the year she'd set off for university. Each visit home had seen him proudly showing off all his painstakingly slow improvements. He'd died with the renovations unfinished. Leaving the car locked in a storage facility had been the biggest wrench for Rebecca when she'd made her move to Italy, harder than leaving the only real home she'd ever known.

She fisted her hands and clenched her teeth at the pang that ripped through her. Four years since the death of her parents and today the pain of missing them was as sharp as it had been in those terrible dark days. She'd never needed them more than she did right now.

The door opened.

The driver held his hand out for her.

It wasn't just the paparazzi capturing the bride's arrival outside the domed cathedral but hundreds of well-wishers too, all lining the cordons Enzo had paid the authorities to erect. Having oodles of money meant the barriers normal people faced could be circumvented. It was the greasing of his money that allowed the opulent car transporting her onto the public square vehicles were usually forbidden from entering.

Taking a deep breath, Rebecca straightened her back, fixed a smile to her face, put one foot in front of the other and prayed not to trip over her dress. Shouts of encouragement followed her into the famous Florentine cathedral.

She'd imagined this moment for so long. The wedding had taken months of planning by a highly specialised team. She'd envisaged Enzo's expression when he saw her in the fairy-tale dress of her dreams and, when he turned at the far end of the aisle to face her, it didn't disappoint. Every step closer to him brought that expression into clearer focus and brought him into clearer focus too.

Enzo Beresi. Self-made billionaire. A six-foot-two hunk of pure muscle injected with testosterone. An Italian success story. Dark brown hair worn stylishly messy. Always immaculate and dapperly dressed. The kind of man women salivated for and men wished they could be. Easy-going to a fault. Charming. Even-tempered. Ethical. Renowned for his charitable works. A liar.

Throughout their whirlwind five-month romance in which he'd proposed four weeks after their first date, Rebecca had constantly asked herself *why me*? Why had Enzo Beresi set his sights on her, a twenty-four-year-old primary schoolteacher, when he had the pick of the world's most eligible women? He could have had *anyone*. But he had chosen her. He had swept her off her feet. And Rebecca had fallen head over heels in love with him.

As she neared the altar, her father's sister, Rebecca's closest living relative, the woman who'd done so much to help her through the trauma of losing both her parents within three days of each other, appeared in her eyeline. She was sat in the space usually reserved for the mother of the bride.

Rebecca blurred her aunt out before the pain of the loss of her parents and the loss of her future grew too big to endure.

She reached Enzo.

His incredible body clothed in a dark grey tuxedo with a swallowtail jacket and dusky pink cravat, his translucent brown eyes sparkled. He mouthed the cliché that must come from every groom's lips. 'You look beautiful.'

He was so good. So believable. That gorgeous, chiselled face with its generous mouth and aquiline nose composed itself into an expression of adoration as he took her hand and drew her to him.

It sickened her that she could still react with such violent intensity to his touch. Sickened her that she could still want the man who'd never wanted her.

His insistence that they wait for their wedding night to consummate their marriage had not been the romantic gesture she'd reluctantly gone along with.

It had all been a set-up.

He'd never truly wanted her. He'd only wanted what marrying her could bring him.

At least she now had the answer to the *why me?* question.

Hands entwined, they turned to the priest. The five hundred–strong congregation filled with the rich, the powerful and the beautiful rose as one. The wedding service began.

All the months of planning and Rebecca had envisaged that the service itself would drag, that she'd be mentally urging the priest to get a move on and get to the good bit. She'd practiced her Italian until she could say her vows faultlessly. Sure, it was only two words—*I do*—but she'd wanted her accent to be perfect.

Now that she was living it, she found herself wishing the order of service to have the brakes applied. The closer they got to the moment, the quicker time passed and the more her heart threatened to burst from her ribs.

The priest got to the meat of it all.

They faced each other and clasped hands.

'Do you, Enzo Alessandro Beresi, take Rebecca Emily Foley to be your wife…?'

She was going to be sick.

He looked her in the eye adoringly and without any hesitation said, 'I do.'

And now it was her turn.

'Do you, Rebecca Emily Foley, take Enzo Alessandro Beresi…?'

She breathed in, looked Enzo straight in the eye and, in the strongest voice she could muster, loud enough for the entire congregation to clearly hear, said, 'No. I. Do. Not.'

Enzo's head jerked back as if she'd slapped him. The half smile froze on the tanned face that drained of colour. His mouth opened but nothing came out.

The only thing that had kept Rebecca together since she'd opened the package earlier that day was imagining this moment and inflicting an iota of the pain and humiliation racking her on him. Only there was none of the satisfaction she'd longed for. The speech she'd prepared in her head died in her choked throat.

Unable to look at him a second longer, she wrenched her hands from his and walked back down the aisle leaving a stunned silence in her wake.

It was only when Rebecca stepped outside onto the cathedral steps and into the Florentine heat that the magnitude of it all hit her.

Several hours ago, minutes before the hair stylist had arrived, the anonymous package had been delivered to the hotel with her name, suite number and *Urgent* written clearly on it, and the cloud of happiness she'd been living in had been torn apart. And now she felt it in the core of her being, an agony ripping through her soul.

She staggered down the steps. Suddenly, the amassed paparazzi, reporters and well-wishers, all busy chatting amongst themselves while they waited for the service to finish, noticed the bride had left her own wedding twenty minutes early. Before they could scramble into position, Rebecca hitched up the skirt of her silk and lace dress and set off over the piazza at a run, past the limousine waiting to transport the happy couple to the reception, past the ancient fountain which crowds of people were congregated around, oblivious to the gawps, deaf to the calls of concern. She had no destination in mind, just an overwhelming need to flee as far as it was possible to get from the man who'd ripped her heart in two. She would have run until the heels of her shoes had worn to nothing if she hadn't caught a heel in a cobble and gone sprawling like a child, landing palms down and coming within an inch of smashing her face on the ancient ground.

'Signorina?'

In a flash, a group of adolescent males whiling their day away admiring each other's Vespas and generally doing their best T-bird impressions, came to her aid.

A cloud of cheap aftershave enveloped her as she was solicitously helped back to her feet, her hands examined for injuries and the rips in the lace of her two-hundred-thousand-euro dress clucked over. She tried to say thank you as she wiped away the tears streaming down her face but her throat was still too choked. She did manage a form of laughter when shaking her head at a cigarette.

Was that what she'd come to? A damsel in such distress it seemed reasonable to offer her a cigarette?

In the distance behind her came a shout, rapidly

followed by more shouts. Those congregating inside and outside the cathedral were on the move. From the hollers, she guessed they'd spotted her. Her fairy-tale white wedding dress hardly made her inconspicuous.

She nodded at the row of Vespas and, her Italian deserting her, asked in English, 'Can I have a lift please?'

Only one face didn't respond with a blank look. 'Where you want to go, lady?'

She gave the name of the tree-lined avenue Enzo's villa was located. Six sets of eyes widened. And no wonder. It was one of the most exclusive areas of Florence. 'Please?' she beseeched. *'Per favore?'*

Looking over her shoulder at the growing crowd heading their way and catching her urgent desperation, the young men sprang into action. Before she knew it, Rebecca was on a Vespa, the skirt of her dress tucked as well as it could be between her legs, clinging tightly to a skinny young man she doubted needed to shave regularly, and then they were off. With the rest of his gang coming along for the ride, her saviour zipped through the traffic. The journey should have taken a minimum of twenty minutes but by treating the rules of the road as an old-fashioned inconvenience and tooting his horn at any pedestrian stupid enough to attempt to cross in front of them, they soon left the bustle of the city proper, and fifteen minutes after they set out, her saviour came to a stop outside Enzo's electric gate.

She jumped off the Vespa and punched the code to open it. 'Can you take me to the airport?' she asked as the gate opened. 'I'll pay.' She had cash in her purse.

Her saviour's mouth, open in stunned awe at the

sprawling whitewashed villa with its terracotta roofs, snapped shut. He smiled. 'Okay, lady.'

'Five minutes.' She held up her still-bleeding palm with fingers and thumb stretched out to stress the point, and ran up the drive to the front door. Before she reached it, Frank, Enzo's uber-professional butler, shot out of his adjoining quarters.

'What has happened?' he asked in careful English. Barely a day ago he'd carried her overnight bags and wedding dress to the car waiting to take her to the hotel she would spend her final night as a single lady in, and wished her the happiest of wedding days.

Fearing she would start crying again, Rebecca shook her head.

Concern writ all over his face, he opened the door for her.

Inside, she wasted no time. Kicking off her white shoes, she hurried through the vast ornate reception room, through the arch that led to the east wing, and ran over the terracotta-floored corridor to the cinema room. The walls were lined with original prints of advertisements for Hollywood movies from the fifties and sixties. She went straight to the one with a beautiful blonde flanked by two men in swimming trunks and removed it. She remembered how she'd laughed when Enzo had shown her the safe. Remembered too, the grin on his face when he'd put her passport in it a week ago. She'd thought it a grin of happiness that she'd finally moved in with him, even if they were sticking to separate bedrooms, at his insistence, until the wedding. If only she'd known it was because she was one step closer to giving him what he really wanted. Which wasn't her. It had never been her, and as she placed her eye to the retina scanner, memories of the day they'd met five months ago filtered like a reel in her mind.

Her aunt's fiftieth birthday lunch at a beautiful country hotel. The weather as cold and grey as the cloud that had cloaked Rebecca for three and a half years. Her dismay when she left the lunch party to find her car had a flat tyre. Hauling the spare out of the boot. Wrestling with the wheel nuts. The gorgeous man with the heartbreaking dimpled smile and the most amazing translucent brown eyes that danced with merriment, who'd jumped out of the back of a car worth more than her house and offered his help. *Insisted.*

The memories solidified as she remembered how he'd removed his long, dark brown overcoat and the jacket of a suit that clearly cost more than her entire wardrobe and handed them to her to hold for him. They'd carried the most amazing, woody scent. He'd then rolled his sleeves up and sank onto the cold, wet ground. Throughout his expert tyre change he'd kept up a steady stream of talk, all in the most gorgeous deep, velvet voice and with the most fantastic accent her ears had ever heard. When he'd finished, Rebecca had been mortified to find his expensive trousers and shirt were stained with dirt and grease.

'You must send me the dry cleaning bill,' she'd insisted through chattering teeth when she passed his suit jacket back to him. 'It's the least I can do.'

He'd slipped his arms into it, his eyes gleaming. 'Or,'

he'd said, 'you can join me in the hotel bar and we can defrost over a hot drink by the fire.'

She could still feel echoes of the jolt of excitement that had shot through her.

Even though she'd already checked his ring finger, something she had never done before, she'd handed his overcoat to him unable to stop her gaze from dipping again to his bare left hand. 'How is that repayment?'

'The associate I am meeting is running late and so I am at a loose end for the next hour. If you keep me company, I will be less likely to die of boredom.'

She'd grinned at his drollness.

His dimples had reappeared. 'You will be doing me a favour. One drink and we will be even.'

Her smile at this declaration was so wide that for the first time in over three and a half years, Rebecca had felt the muscles of her cheeks working. 'One drink. And I'm paying.'

He'd frowned and tutted. 'A gentleman never lets a lady pay.'

She'd raised her eyebrows in her best schoolteacher fashion. 'Did the turn of the twenty-first century pass you by?'

Amusement had danced between them and then they'd both started laughing, and to remember how it had been and the connection she'd felt with him right from the start and know it had all been staged, that he'd punctured her tyre himself…

The green light of the safe flashed and blinded the memories away. The reinforced door swung open.

Her heart wrenched to see her passport exactly where he'd put it, nestled on top of his.

Swallowing back another roll of nausea, Rebecca snatched hers up, pushed the safe's door shut, then raced back into the corridor, ran up the closest stairs two at a time, and hurtled to the bedroom she'd used since her first visit to the villa all those months ago.

How long did she have, she wondered, her mind racing as to where Enzo could be. Would he think to look for her here? Or would he go straight to the hotel she'd stayed the night at and which they and their guests were supposed to head to for the evening celebrations?

Grabbing her handbag, she dropped her passport into it next to her purse. Her phone was at the hotel but that couldn't be helped. She had enough cash to get to the airport and enough money in her bank account to get herself home.

About to leave the room, she caught sight of her appearance in the full-length mirror and almost crumbled. Her perfectly made-up oval face, perfect because it had been done by a professional makeup artist, was a mascara-streaked mess. Her large brown eyes were red-rimmed, her too-wide mouth pulled in tightly to stop the scream of anguish fighting to escape from it. The artful up-do the celebrity stylist had spent so long working on was gone, her honey blonde hair and ripped dress now giving her the look of someone who'd been dragged through a gooseberry bush backwards. Swallowing back the scream with all the strength her throat could muster, Rebecca yanked the clip holding what remained of the original do together. She was already out of the door before the rest of her hair fell to her shoulders.

As she hitched up the skirt of her ruined fairy-tale dress and flew back to the stairs and down to the ground floor, she imagined the shops at the airport. She'd be able to buy clothes to change into…

She skidded to a halt, the scream leaving her throat before her senses properly registered the man standing guard at the front door.

Rebecca's heart, already pounding from the exertion of tearing around the villa, slammed hard into her ribs.

Towering over her, Enzo's chiselled jaw was clenched. The colour had returned to his tanned olive skin but the designer messiness of his hair had lost the designer quality to it. The dusky pink cravat that had graced his strong neck in the cathedral had gone, the top buttons of his white shirt undone.

'Get out of my way,' she whispered, finding her voice.

His answer was to fold his arms across his broad chest.

It made her broken heart splinter that bit more to understand she must be seeing the real Enzo Beresi for the first time.

'I said get out of my way.'

His folded arms tightened, the muscles visibly flexing. His nostrils flared. 'No.'

A swell of rage punched through her. Launching herself at him, she pushed at him, trying to shove him away from the door. 'Get out of my way!' she shouted.

But he was too big, too muscular, too *substantial*. With an agility no man his size should possess, he held her arms to her sides and then twisted her around and pinned her to him so her back was pressed tight against his solid chest, his muscular arm trapping her to him.

'Stop that,' he snarled when she started kicking back at him and the heel of her bare foot made contact with his shin.

'Let me go!'

'When you are calm.' His breath hot in her hair, his velvet, accented voice calmed as if to display what he required of her. 'There is nowhere for you to run. I have sent your Vespa boys away.'

'Then I'll get a taxi.'

'And go where? The airport?'

'I want to go *home*.'

'You *are* home.'

'No.' She shook her head. Salt water spilled down her cheeks to remember the joy that had consumed her to imagine filling this beautiful villa with Enzo's babies and the blissfully happy life they would have together. 'No.'

'Why did you do it?' he asked, not loosening his hold around her. 'Tell me, Rebecca. Tell me why you did it.'

'Why do you *think*? And if you don't let me go this second I'm going to scream loud enough for the whole of Florence to hear.'

He spun her round with the same speed and agility he'd pinned her to him. Large hands gripping her shoulders, rage contorted the handsome features bearing down on hers. 'You dare play the injured party when you were planning to take your passport and run away from me without a word of explanation or goodbye?

When you have humiliated me in front of the whole damn world? I had to steal a Vespa to get here before you could run. Tell me why you did that to me. You owe me that much.'

'I don't owe you anything,' she cried, pushing at his chest. 'I know, damn you. I know exactly why you were marrying me. It was all a set-up!'

For the second time in less than an hour the colour drained from Enzo's face. He staggered, groping behind him for the door which he propped himself up against. His throat moved before he whispered, 'Rebecca...'

'Don't! I don't want to hear your lies. I know everything. *Everything*. You never loved me or wanted me. The only thing you wanted was my inheritance.'

# CHAPTER TWO

WATCHING ENZO COMPOSE himself was something that in ordinary circumstances Rebecca would marvel at, was something she *had* marvelled at. Never had she been in greater awe at this ability than the few times he'd come close to losing his control and making love to her as she'd pleaded for him to do. His breaths would be hot and heavy, his skin fevered, his arousal solid and visible through the clothes he always kept on, but always he would pull himself back. One long, deep breath through his nose and the passion that had blazed from his eyes would vanish and his composure would be assured.

At least she knew now how he'd been able to manage that side of things so well. While she'd been sitting there physically aching with need for him, it had been no real effort on his part to disengage his brain from his body's responses. His responses to her had been nothing but an automatic reaction. She could have been any reasonably attractive woman.

Back straight, his light brown eyes locked on hers. 'How did you find out?'

She laughed through the tears. 'Is that the first thing you think to ask? All you care about?'

'I ask because it's important.'

'A package marked urgent was delivered by a woman to the hotel reception for me. I don't know or care who the woman was.'

A swathe of emotions flickered over his darkening features. 'It was a copy of your grandfather's will?'

Another swell of rage pulsed through her from deep in her stomach all the way to the tips of her fingers and toes.

Once, over the course of a meal, Rebecca had mentioned that she'd never met her mother's parents because of an estrangement that had occurred before she was born. Only now did she make the link to his brief show of sympathy and then an abrupt changing of the subject to it being because it was something he already knew. Enzo knew her past better than she did.

He knew it because he'd been her grandfather's business partner and the man her grandfather had trusted enough to appoint as executor to his will.

That meant Enzo must have known about her parents too. The evening Rebecca had cuddled into him with her head on his chest and relayed how her dad had suffered a fatal heart attack only three days after her mother's death from blood cancer, a blow that had rocked the foundations of her world, a grief she'd never believed she would recover from, Enzo had stroked her back and murmured words of comfort and he'd *already known*.

'How could you do this to me?' Her anger was such that to hear the pain resonate in her voice only added fresh anguish, because it meant *he* could hear it too.

'All this time. All those lies. You told me you loved me and all you ever wanted was his business. Now let me go. It hurts to even look at you.'

Not an ounce of remorse flickered on his set features. *Nothing* flickered. His self-control was too strong. 'Remember all the press covering our wedding? They are already outside the gates. Leave now and they will eat you alive.'

'As if you care what happens to me.'

'I care.'

'Don't *lie*,' she screamed, losing control again and hurtling her handbag across the room. It hit an eighteenth-century eighteen-inch marble statue, knocking it off its plinth and sending it to the floor where it shattered with an ear-piercing shriek. The way Rebecca felt, she could make her way through the entire villa and systematically destroy every object he held dear, shatter it all into the same fragments Enzo had shattered her heart into. 'Every word ever exchanged between us has been a lie.'

Chiselled jaw clenched, he shook his head. 'No.'

'Another lie! I gave up everything for you and it was all a lie. You wanted an explanation as to why I humiliated you in the cathedral and now you've heard it. I don't want to spend another second in your company so get out of my way and let me leave. I never want to see you again.'

The clear brown eyes she'd gazed into with her heart filled with such love and hope held hers without expression before closing. His throat moved and his chest rose slowly as if he were trying to control emotions she now knew he didn't possess. And then he walked away from the door and crunched over the shards and splinters of marble to pick up her bag and hold it out to her.

Without a word, she plucked it from his hand and headed out of the door.

The moment her bare feet touched the marble steps, a cacophony of noise and light that rivalled the beaming sun engulfed her. Straight ahead, at the end of the driveway, behind the high electric gates, the press and paparazzi who'd lined the cordons outside the cathedral stood packed and jostling for position. The scramble of questions being shouted at her came close to being drowned out by the helicopter swooping in her direction overhead.

She stood there for the longest time, staring at the pack who, with one comment from her, had the power to bring Enzo Beresi down. His philanthropic, good-guy persona would be destroyed with just eight words.

*He was marrying me to steal my inheritance.*

The swelling of pain and rage shifted and hardened, and injected her spine with steel. She walked slowly towards the pack, barely blinking as the camera flashes grew stronger.

*He was marrying me to steal my inheritance.*

And then she stopped.

Rebecca knew what he'd done. She knew why he'd done it. What she didn't know was how.

She spun back to the villa.

The reception room was empty of life. Treading her way carefully around the wreckage of the marble statue, she found Enzo at the bar at the far end of the sprawling double-height living room that looked out over the vast, manicured grounds she'd imagined their children playing in. He was pouring himself a drink, his back to her.

The impulse to turn back around and leave like she'd intended was strong but she fought it. She deserved answers. She *needed* answers.

'I've changed my mind.'

Her words flew across the huge room and landed on him like an electric pulse, making his head snap back.

'I'm still leaving but first, you owe me answers,' she said stonily. 'I'm going to get changed and pack my things. While I'm doing that, you can pour me a gin and tonic and arrange for a car to collect me. When I come back down, we will have one last drink together and you will explain what it is you hate so much about me that you thought I deserved to be treated with such cruelty.'

Other than the movement of one shoulder, he didn't react to her stony words or turn around to face her, and for that she was glad. It meant he didn't see the tear trickle down her cheek. Wiping it away, she went back up to her room.

It had taken three women over an hour to sew Rebecca into her wedding dress. Using her nail scissors, she ripped her way out of it in seconds. Then she stripped off her underwear and stood before her full-length mirror.

What was it about her body that had repelled him into not consummating their relationship, she wondered miserably. She remembered the moment she'd told Enzo that she was a virgin. It was after their third date. He'd invited her back to his London apartment. He'd been so smooth. So suave. So flipping gorgeous. She'd already been smitten by that point. She'd accepted his invitation with butterflies like she'd never imagined existed loose in her belly, butterflies that had strengthened as they'd taken his private elevator to his penthouse. Then, when she'd crossed the threshold into an apartment more palatial than her wildest conjuring and he'd pressed her against a wall and started kissing her with such fervent desire, she'd responded with a heat so wanton and *vital* that she'd blurted out her virgin state before things went too far and she forgot to tell him later on.

He'd backed right off.

At the time, she'd taken him at face value, that her being a virgin meant they shouldn't rush things. Once she'd accepted his proposal his next excuse had been that he wanted their wedding night to be the most special night of both their lives. She'd taken that at face value too, had been *thrilled* at the romantic notion behind it, even if his absolute refusal to budge from it had driven her steadily insane.

'Good things come to those who wait, *cara*,' he'd often said with a cheeky wink that had always melted her insides. When she'd questioned why he'd never felt the need to wait for the legion of women who'd come before her, he'd answered with a simple, 'They meant nothing to me, not when compared to how I feel about you.'

That morning, she'd woken buzzing with excitement at marrying him and practically giddy with anticipation that, finally, they would make love, had even done an internet search to learn the minimum acceptable time to leave your own wedding reception so you could slope off to bed with your new husband. That was before the package had been delivered and her heart smashed into smithereens of course.

Enzo had used her virginity as the excuse he needed not to bed her, and now she studied her naked body and naked face and wondered what he'd found so repulsive about them that he'd grabbed the first excuse that had come along to back off from having to make love to her. She knew she was a little on the skinny side but she couldn't help that. And neither could she help her small breasts. Both were an inheritance from her mum. Not that he'd seen her breasts or the dark pink nipples that topped them. He'd felt them though. He'd even remembered to fake a groan before removing his hand from under her top. He couldn't be repulsed by her pubic hair because he hadn't seen that either, or even felt it. His hands had never roamed her skin below the waist. Gropes of her backside didn't count.

She supposed he would have forced himself to make love to her and consummate the marriage. Yes, he'd have wanted the consummation done as quickly as possible. He wouldn't have risked an annulment.

Even Enzo's impatience to marry her as soon as was humanly possible had been a lie. The biggest lie of all.

Unable to stare at herself a moment longer, she stood beneath the shower and, as the hot water sprayed over her body, tried her hardest to scrub the day and all of Enzo's lies off her skin.

\* \* \*

Clean and dry, dressed in faded jeans and a loose black V-necked top with elbow-length sleeves, what she could cram of her clothes packed in one of the carry-on cases Enzo had bought for her first visit to Florence, Rebecca left her room for the last time, leaving behind the array of designer clothing rammed in her dressing room, all of which he'd bought for her. On her dressing table amidst the array of perfumes he'd also bought her, sat her engagement ring.

She was glad she was doing it this way rather than running away as had been her instinct. It was cleaner like this.

She would force Enzo to explain himself and then she would leave properly, with her head held high and her dignity intact.

She had the rest of her life to fix her shattered heart.

The marble fragments had already been cleaned away. Rebecca put her case by the front door. Peering through a window, she saw a large black car with blacked-out windows parked at the front. Her getaway car. She was quite sure the driver would run over the marauding press if necessary.

Ankle boots placed ready by her case, she padded her way back to the living area.

Her gin and tonic was waiting for her on a small round glass table but Enzo had disappeared.

Taking a deep breath, she had a long drink of it and curled up on her favourite squishy round chair.

The composure she'd worked so hard to find almost shattered in sympathy with her heart at his appearance.

From the dampness of his hair, he'd showered too. His wedding suit had been replaced with a pair of faded jeans, and a V-necked black T-shirt. Like hers, his feet were bare.

A day ago, it would have sent a thrill racing through her that they had independently mimicked each other's clothing. Now it made her stomach clench painfully.

Gripping tightly to her glass to stop the tremors in her hands betraying her, she had another long drink. How could he have paid such attention that he knew exactly how she liked her gin and tonic, even down to her preferred number of ice cubes?

She was forgetting his big brain, she reminded herself. How else could a thirty-three-year-old be a self-made billionaire without an oversized brain? And smarts. He had that in abundance too. The kind of smarts that came from a different part of the brain to mere cleverness. It was a combination that had fascinated her from their first real conversation in the hotel bar on that cold winter day. She remembered it so clearly, right down to the crackle of the log fire they'd sat beside nursing their hot drinks.

Shy with strangers—unless they were small children—Enzo's open, gregarious nature and beautiful velvety voice had put Rebecca at an ease she'd never felt before. She could have listened to him speak for hours and she only realised she'd been watching the time pass with increasing trepidation when he'd asked if he could see her again and her delight and relief had bloomed like a flower under the bright rising sun.

But even then, even at that very first meet, had been the nagging question: *Why me?* This street-smart, clever, suave, gorgeous, rich man every woman in the hotel bar kept side-eying liked *her*? He wanted to see *her* again?

Deep down she'd known all along that it was too good to be true. If only she'd listened to that incredulous nagging voice all those months ago…

Enzo nodded at her glass.

She nodded back, finished her drink, put the glass on the table and pushed it towards him.

He stepped closer to take it. The crisp clean scent of freshly showered Enzo hit her. It was a scent that had greeted her so many times these last five months and which never failed to make her want to throw herself at him. Resisting that temptation since moving in had become a game, but it was no game now, and she curled deeper into the sofa and wrapped her arms around her calves.

Once he'd made them both another drink and warily placed her glass back on the table—she imagined the wariness came from him wondering if she was going to throw it at him—he sat on the edge of the two-seater sofa closest to hers, both feet on the floor, had a sip of his Scotch and then put his tumbler and a half-full bottle of Scotch on the glass table beside his seat.

Rebecca blinked away the memory created just four days ago when she'd laughingly said they would have to change the living room drinks tables when they had children. Glass tables and small children were a combination she'd thought best not tested. He'd laughed, and then turned his face away as if his mind had been captured by something else. Used to that strange quirk of his whenever she idly contemplated their future, she hadn't thought anything more about it, but now she knew the truth. He'd turned his face away so she wouldn't see the mockery behind the laughter.

She breathed in deeply, watching as he clasped his hands together and placed them on his lap.

His chest rose slowly before he looked at her and said, 'Rebecca, I know it is hard for you to believe but I never lied about my feelings for you.'

'Save your breath,' she dismissed. 'I'm not marrying you. My grandfather's business shares will never be yours.'

'I don't care about the shares.'

Genuinely amused at the blatancy of his lie, she laughed, then laughed harder to see him flinch. 'Does lying come to you as naturally as breathing? Don't answer that,' she added when he opened his mouth. 'I'll only assume it's another lie.'

'Rebecca…'

'And stop saying my name before you taint it for good.' He was the only one to call her Rebecca. To her parents she'd been Becs. To the rest of her family, friends, colleagues and distant acquaintances she was Becky. *Everyone* shortened it. Everyone except Enzo. She'd adored the way her full name rolled off his tongue. To hear it roll off his tongue now hurt immeasurably.

His lips clamped together and formed a straight line, the bones of his jaw virtually breaking the skin.

She'd bet no one had spoken to him like this in a decade. Maybe that was part of the reason he was an unconscionable bastard. He should have known better than to mess with a primary schoolteacher. They were pros when it came to dealing with liars, even if the liars were generally three and a half feet high and struggled to do their own shoelaces up. She'd never imagined those lying traits could continue so long into adulthood.

She shifted in her seat, reached for her drink, crossed her legs and faced him properly. Forced herself to look at him properly. Dispassionately.

'Here's how we're going to play it,' she said in her best teacher's voice. 'I'm going to ask you questions and you're going to answer them, clearly and concisely. Stick to the facts. Do not attempt to justify yourself unless I ask. If you have to think before you answer I will assume you're lying. Do not speak to me of *feelings* or *love*, and don't ask what I'm going to do about my share of the business but keep in mind that the way I'm feeling about you right now, I'm quite capable of taking advice as to how best to destroy the whole business with it.'

It had only dawned on Rebecca since taking her shower the power she held. At midnight she turned twenty-five and so would inherit half of her grandfather's business, whatever that was, although she supposed the clue was in the name, 'Claflin Diamonds'. She didn't have to suppose that this was a business Enzo very much wanted all for himself. As if he didn't have enough, what with the multiple businesses he owned outright and all the others he invested in. The business that had made him famous though, was his chain of high-end Beresi jewellery stores, all of which stocked bespoke, exquisitely made and ethically sourced jewellery enthusiastically embraced by the rich and famous. She would love to hear what his investors and customers thought about the ethics of him marrying someone for their inheritance.

'My advice would be not to add any fuel to my anger. All I want from you is some honesty...' She came close to choking. 'If you're even capable of it.'

# CHAPTER THREE

FEATURES SET SO hard they could be carved from the same marble as the statue Rebecca had destroyed, Enzo slowly inclined his handsome face. 'Where would you like me to start?'

*I want you to start by telling me what I ever did to you that you could take my heart and use it as your personal plaything, you cruel bastard*, she wanted to scream.

But she would not scream. She would not show emotions. Not any more. She would maintain this dispassionate front until she had all the answers she needed and then walk out of his life for good.

'At the beginning. When did you go into business with my grandfather?'

'Thirteen years ago.'

She blinked in surprise. Their partnership went much further back than she'd imagined. 'How did it come about?'

'Do you remember me telling you how my first jewellery shop was a learning curve for me?'

She thought of their second date when he'd self-deprecatingly laughed as he'd explained how his business had almost ended before it had begun.

'I was naive and expected instant success but to compete with the big boys, I needed a unique selling point.'

'Man-made diamonds,' she supplied in a whisper, the penny starting to drop as she remembered Enzo saying how he'd figured the growing movement for ethically sourced products had meant an opening for ethically sourced diamonds.

'*Sì,*' he agreed tautly. 'Man-made diamonds. Your grandfather was a visionary who'd seen long before me that there would be a market for them, and invested heavily in it. But he was ahead of his time. When I came along, he was in major financial difficulties.'

The dropping penny landed in Rebecca's brain with a loud clang. The diamonds used in the jewellery Enzo's stores sold came from a laboratory. The technique used made their purity, which Beresi was famous for, indistinguishable from naturally occurring ones.

'You invested in Claflin Diamonds.'

'Yes. I bought fifty per cent of it.'

Thinking hard, she narrowed her eyes. 'How could you afford that? You could only have been twenty then…unless you were lying when you told me you didn't hit the big time until you were twenty-five.'

'No lie,' he said steadily. 'The diamonds from the laboratory played a big part in my success. The biggest part. A prominent company offered to buy the whole business from him. If he'd taken their offer, all his debts would have been paid and he'd have had cash left over to live comfortably for the rest of his life. Instead of taking it, he took a leap of faith with me and sold me the shares at a cut price. The price was enough to get him off the hook with his creditors but that was it. I paid for my half with what was left of my father's inheritance and took a personal loan for the rest.'

Rebecca would not let the mention of Enzo's father play on her heartstrings. His father had died at the age of twenty-eight when Enzo was six from a brain aneurysm, leaving an insurance policy for his son to inherit when he turned eighteen. She distinctly remembered Enzo telling her he'd used that inheritance to pay for the lease and stock of his first store. He'd made it sound as if the entire inheritance had been swallowed up by that first store. Another lie.

'And now you want all of Claflin Diamonds for yourself.'

He gave no reaction to her contempt. 'Your grandfather founded it but it belonged to both of us equally. We both made it what it is today and reaped the rewards. Without that partnership, your grandfather would have been made bankrupt and there would be no Beresi. It was agreed that when he died—and your grandfather knew he was dying—that his shares would pass to me.'

That threw her off course. 'He knew he was dying?'

His shoulders rose heavily. '*Sì*. He was diagnosed with stage four pancreatic cancer last October. Believe me, it came as a shock to us both. In all the years we'd been partners, his health had always been excellent. Your grandfather was sixty-eight but until the cancer he had the energy of a man my own age.'

Rebecca couldn't explain why this made her heart pang. She'd never met the grandfather who'd disowned her mother for marrying a man he'd deemed beneath her. His first ever contact with her had come a few weeks after her parents' deaths, a letter of condolence in which he'd asked to meet her. She'd replied with a terse, 'No thank you.' Despite her refusal, he'd taken to sending her birthday and Christmas cards with cheques enclosed. She'd returned them all, including the cheques. Just to imagine cashing them made her feel sick.

Unsure why tears were welling behind her eyes, she forced the conversation back to what really mattered at this moment. 'Okay, so he promised you his share of the business but instead of doing that, he made it conditional that you had to marry me to get it.'

And that's why it had all been one big fat lie.

Under the terms of her grandfather's will, Enzo only received the shares if he married Rebecca. If he failed to marry her before she turned twenty-five, then the shares—half of Claflin Diamonds—automatically became hers.

Rebecca turned twenty-five in approximately five hours.

'That condition my grandfather put into his will was unconscionable,' she stated into the silence. 'I don't see how any judge would have allowed it to stand.'

Enzo drained his Scotch with a grimace. 'If I'd contested it, litigation could have dragged on for years. We're talking different jurisdictions too, and there was no guarantee I would win.'

She shrugged. 'You could have waited until my birthday and just bought the shares off me. It wasn't as if you had to wait for long and you must have known

I wouldn't want anything to do with the business. I'm a primary schoolteacher for cripes sake!' *Was* a primary schoolteacher, she corrected herself. She'd quit her job at the end of the summer term, which was also the end of the school year, nine days ago.

To think she'd believed Enzo had encouraged her to quit before the school year ended because he couldn't wait to make her his wife when all along he'd been working on a deadline to stop her grandfather's shares slipping out of his hands and into hers. That deadline had been her birthday.

For the first time since their conversation started, she spotted a flash of anger on the too-handsome features. 'Do you not think I went through every scenario and eventuality before settling on this path?'

'Let me throw this out there—it's a radical idea, I know—but did it ever occur to you to just be honest with me and explain the situation?'

'For about thirty seconds.'

'That long?' she mocked.

'I had no way of knowing how you would react. Without Claflin Diamonds there would be no Beresi. I was not prepared to risk losing control of it to someone who taught small children for a living and knew nothing of business. If it wasn't for my investment and the partnership we formed, there wouldn't be a business and your grandfather would have been buried in a cardboard box.'

'You went to his funeral? I didn't even know he was dead until this morning.' And she couldn't understand why his death made her feel *anything.* Ray Claflin was nothing but a malevolent name to her.

'Your grandfather arranged his own funeral before he died,' Enzo said tightly. 'He forbade me from telling you about his condition or notifying you of his death. I was the only mourner. He did not want anyone else to attend. By the end of his life he was a man haunted by many demons.'

'Whatever demons he had, I'm sure he deserved them.' Rebecca could not comprehend how a parent could disown their own child for the crime of falling in love.

Aware she was derailing herself from her interrogation, she looked back at Enzo, battling to keep her features stony. 'Why didn't you tell me about the inheritance when he died? You were his executor.'

Having been appointed executor in her parents' wills meant Rebecca knew more about the role than she could ever have wanted. She'd been meticulous about her duties, not because she was a meticulous person—she wasn't—but because it was a distraction from a grief that had made it hard to breathe.

She'd only learned to breathe properly again when a tall, dark, gorgeous Italian had swooped into her life.

Fighting hard to keep the tempest brewing inside her quelled, she added, 'You had a legal duty to tell me of my inheritance.'

The business shares were only a part of it. Rebecca inherited everything else from her grandfather outright. She had no idea what that everything else was worth, and nor did she care. She didn't want any of it... Apart from the Claflin Diamonds shares. Those she found she wanted very much.

'I had a duty to tell you within three months of probate,' he agreed. 'Probate was granted three weeks ago.'

'Drag the process out, did you?'

'Yes.'

'I bet you were tempted to destroy the will.'

He smiled grimly. 'It was a non-starter—without a legally valid will, the English laws of intestacy would have taken effect and as his closest living relative, you would have inherited everything anyway, including his share of the business. I had no proof he'd promised me those shares, only my word.'

'Which wasn't worth the paper it was written on,' she supplied.

'*Esattamente.*'

'But if you hadn't learned that destroying the will scuppered all your chances of getting your sticky mitts on the shares, you would have shredded it?'

'I told you, I looked into every eventuality and scenario.'

She smiled serenely. 'He stitched you up like a kipper.'

His forehead furrowed in confusion.

She leaned forwards, her smile widening as a lightness cleared her brain. 'Stitched you up like a kipper. It means he played you. He promised you his shares of the business but then put a condition on it with a set time limit that should have been impossible to fulfil.' Would have been if Enzo hadn't played her so well. 'Non-fulfilment of the condition meant the shares transferred into the hands of someone else—*moi*—and you lost. On top of that, as he'd put you in charge of fulfilling his wishes, your failure to comply meant you would have been in charge of your own failure.'

He acknowledged this truth with a small but sharp nod.

If Rebecca wasn't the pawn in this sick game between two rich men, she would have found her grandfather's underhand methods against Enzo hilarious. It was nothing less than he deserved, something her grandfather must have thought too, else why play such a trick on him? 'He must have had one warped sense of humour to play you like that.'

'I never saw it when he was alive.'

'Were you close to him?'

It was only because she was watching him so studiously for signs of lies that she caught the flicker of emotion on his face. 'Yes.'

'And he did the dirty on you? Ouch.' Yes. *Hilarious.* If her heart wasn't still packed with the weight of her own emotions, she'd be holding her sides with unrestrained glee.

Handsome features taut, he poured himself another drink.

Still smiling, Rebecca took a sip of her gin, briefly averting her eyes so she didn't have to watch the generous mouth that had kissed her with such passion close around the crystal tumbler and the strong, tanned neck she'd adored dragging her lips over throwing itself back to admit the alcohol down it or see his throat moving as the liquid slid down his oesophagus.

When it was safe to look back at him, she said, 'So your failure to marry me means that come midnight, half the business you played such a major part in making a success and is such a vital component of your main business belongs to me, and as probate's been granted and you're the executor, it's your job to hand the shares for it over to me.'

He rubbed his head wearily as he nodded another agreement. It was the executor's duty to deal with all the deceased's assets and either cash them in for the beneficiary—in this case, Rebecca—or transfer them directly into the beneficiary's name.

'*Eccellente,*' she said in her best Italian. Sitting upright, she flashed him her very widest smile. 'Now that I understand the situation even better, I shall wait here until midnight and have the pleasure of you handing those shares directly to me.'

Though his stare held hers without flickering, for the first time since her interrogation had started, Enzo didn't immediately respond.

'You'd better not be thinking about how you're going to get out of giving them to me,' she said sweetly. 'If I've learned one thing since meeting you it's that the press are like bloodhounds. I imagine they'll stay camped outside until one of us leaves and they get the picture they need, or until one of us—*moi*—goes out and tells them how the ethical philanthropist Enzo Beresi was only marrying the English teacher because he wanted her inheritance.'

That's what had ignited such press interest in Rebecca—her job. Okay, the world's media would have been all over any woman Enzo had become engaged to, but that one of Europe's richest and most eligible bachelors had fallen for a nobody primary schoolteacher had taken it to a whole other level. No wonder Enzo had thrown his money into protecting her from them, issuing writs left, right and centre ordering them to leave her alone. She'd believed he was protecting her but all along he'd been protecting himself from any journalist discovering the link to her grandfather. Yet another lie.

Long fingers she'd imagined stroking every inch of her body tightened around his crystal tumbler. When his light brown eyes locked on to hers, regret—no doubt because he'd lost—blazed from them. 'I'm sorrier than you can know.'

She waved an airy hand. 'Easy words to say.'

An edge crept into his voice. 'Have I given you any reason to think I'm lying since we started this conversation?'

'Enzo, every word you've said to me in the five months I've known you has been a lie. You're so good at it you'd make Pinocchio feel like an amateur.'

'I have never lied about my feelings for you.'

All the amusement at her grandfather's dirty trick that had been hurtling through her flattened in an instant. 'Say that one more time and I'll give my share of the business straight to a dog charity.' She would do it too. She could not bear the fake sincerity in his velvet voice. Could not bear how she still ached to believe it. Could not bear how her body was still so acutely aware of him. Could not bear to be reminded of how completely she'd fallen into his web of deceit.

'Midnight,' she added before he could speak. 'I want the shares in my name at midnight.'

His stare didn't waver. 'Impossible.'

'You're Enzo Beresi. Nothing is impossible.' This was the man who'd landed his helicopter on her school's playing field at the end of the school day just so he could whisk her to Monaco for the evening, the man who'd magicked the best seats in the house for the opening of a sell-out Broadway musical she'd mentioned in passing that she quite fancied watching at some point. Before the musical, he'd also conjured up a table in New York's most exclusive restaurant, one that boasted of being fully booked for the next three years. This was the man who, with one call on a Friday evening about the prototype of a new sports car he was interested in, had it delivered from Germany to his Florentine villa by the time he'd woken early the next morning.

'It cannot be done,' he refuted. 'I will need twenty-four hours. Longer. Tomorrow is Sunday.'

'Midnight.'

'I am telling you, Rebecca, I need twenty-four hours.'

The pang in her heart rippled painfully. 'I have already told you not to say my name.'

'Then how do I address you?' he demanded with another flash of anger. In all the months she'd known him, Enzo had always kept tight control of his moods, rarely displaying any sign of temper and never directed at her. The shell of charming perfection he'd always presented to her had well and truly slipped off him and she was glad of it. Glad because it meant he was truly feeling the loss of the game he'd been playing at her expense.

Whatever he was feeling wasn't an ounce of the agony he was putting her through.

'You can address me in the same way my pupils do—as Miss Foley.' She looked at her watch. Nearly eight p.m. She could hardly believe how quickly time was passing. 'Eight a.m. That's my final offer.'

'It can't be done by eight a.m. Give me until three.'

'Twelve.'

'One o'clock. I will have the shares transferred into your name by one o'clock tomorrow afternoon.'

She folded her arms tightly around her chest, hating that she was thrown back to the day they'd negotiated the date of their wedding and all the reasons she'd believed he wanted to marry her so quickly.

But she had never *truly* believed them, had she? That nagging voice of doubt had always warned her she was just too plain and ordinary for a man as worldly and glamorous as Enzo Beresi.

'Okay. One o'clock. But I wait here until it's done.' Not only because she didn't trust him but to make him suffer her company with the full knowledge that he'd lost and that she was going to go skipping into the sunset with the very thing he'd fought so hard and so dirty to keep from her hands.

The flicker on his features before he nodded was unmistakable.

'And if you're one minute late getting it done then...' She snapped her fingers and smiled. 'I go outside to the press and sing like a canary.'

* * *

An hour after Rebecca had spontaneously decided to torment Enzo by camping in his villa until the shares of her grandfather's business were legally hers, and serious regret had kicked in.

Immersed in her tiny little mini power trip, she'd forgotten the reasons why she'd been so desperate to flee.

As soon as they'd agreed on a time for Enzo to get the shares transferred into her name he'd disappeared to get things in motion. She'd been left staring at the walls of the room he'd proposed to her in ever since.

Before she'd moved in a week ago, when the school year had come to an end, Rebecca had visited this villa a grand total of six times. She couldn't remember her first real impression of the villa Enzo called home. She'd been too stunned at being flown to Florence in a private jet and then amazed at the scale and richness of his home for any real thoughts to penetrate. She'd known he was rich but hadn't comprehended *how* rich. The next evening, he'd proposed…

She yanked at her hair so hard that when she moved her hand away, blond strands had woven between her fingers. She would *not* think of his proposal, or how he'd had to ask her three times before she'd grasped what he was saying.

'Why?' she'd asked dumbly.

Why, why, why, why, why. The story of her entire relationship with him.

'Because I can't imagine my life without you in it,' he'd replied with a sincerity she'd believed.

Once they were engaged, she'd given up trying to

comprehend and instead let her imagination run riot. In her mind, children had popped out of her in a procession of love, this richly imposing villa with its abundance of glass and marble slowly transforming into a nursery filled with tattle-tales and hair pulling and scratching and biting and cuddles and giggles and mischief. They'd spent much time together in his London penthouse and Enzo had taken her for long weekends to his apartment overlooking Times Square in New York, but it was here in Florence that they would live and raise their family.

Unable to bear the memories and broken dreams any longer, she headed outside into the balmy evening.

*I can't imagine my life without you*, she mimicked under her breath as she stomped past the secluded swimming pool and the clay tennis court to the vast landscaped grounds at the rear of the villa. The cicadas had just stopped singing for the day, so the only sound was the gentle breeze rustling through the trees that formed the perimeter of Enzo's grounds and ensured absolute privacy.

At the far end, hidden from the villa, was a hanging double egg seat. Rebecca barely glanced at it as she parked her bottom on the curved marble bench close by. Three nights ago she'd sat on that egg seat with Enzo, her legs hooked over his thighs, trying her best to tempt him into making love to her as the seat gently swung them. It made her core throb to remember how she'd cupped his straining hardness through his trousers, rubbed her nose along his throat inhaling his delicious woody cologne, and provocatively whispered—

'There you are.'

Shoulders sagging, she closed her eyes and swallowed the lump in her throat. It took every ounce of resilience to evoke nonchalance into her voice. 'Here I am. Have you started the process?'

'Yes.' He sat at the other end of the bench, far enough away that there was no danger of their bodies accidentally touching. But not far enough to stop his alluring scent from dancing into her airways.

Awareness threading through every part of her, she crossed her legs tightly. 'Nothing else you need to do for it?'

'For now, everything is in hand.'

It had to be the night air magnifying the effect of him, heightening her awareness, making her yearn to close the distance between them and…

Unable to bear it, she jumped to her feet and made to leave. 'Good.'

Before she could escape him, he said, 'I have had the possessions you left at the hotel delivered here.'

Images of the sheer white negligée she'd planned to wear that night flittered into her mind's eye. She quickly blinked it away and said stiffly, 'Thank you.'

'They have also sent me CCTV footage of the woman who delivered the package to you.'

'I've told you already, I don't care.'

'It was my mother.'

# CHAPTER FOUR

REBECCA'S HEART THUMPED at this. Her mind jumped to the svelte raven-haired woman who'd welcomed her into her palatial home with a warm embrace that had touched her heart and eased her fears. She doubted anyone met their future in-laws without a smidgeon of panic and Silvana Beresi had gone out of her way to make Rebecca feel welcome...

Her thumping heart changed direction and plummeted as the implications of what Enzo had just told her suddenly made themselves clear.

She turned to face him. 'Your mother?'

His back was ramrod straight, palms pressed down firmly by his thighs, splayed fingers gripping the bench. He gave a brief, grim nod.

'Your *mother*?'

Another, terser nod.

'But...' She swallowed and shook her head. 'She helped choose the design for my wedding dress. She helped plan the menu. She chose the wines to pair with each course.' Rebecca was aware of an hysterical tinge coming into her voice but could do nothing to stop it. 'She lent me her grandmother's wedding tiara for my something borrowed! Why would she do all that and then sabotage everything at the last minute? It makes no sense. Why would she do all that if she didn't want me to marry you?'

'You misunderstand her motives,' he said emotionlessly. 'She had no objection to you marrying me. She objected to me marrying *you* under what she considered to be a falsehood.'

'*Why*? She must have known what would happen.' She slammed her hand to her chest in a futile attempt to control a heart that had lost the ability to thump rhythmically. If it had been anyone else but his mother she'd be cheering them to the rafters and planning the delivery of a crate of champagne as a thank you. But his mother? His own *mother*?

His nod that time was so sharp it could slice butter.

'She knew I wouldn't go through with the wedding?'

'She never does anything without considering every eventuality. In that respect, I am my mother's son.'

'But...' But Rebecca's overloaded mind had gone blank. Legs feeling like noodles, she dropped onto the egg chair and tried to make sense of her thoughts.

Enzo's deep, velvet voice laced with bitterness broke the silence. 'Telling her was a mistake on my part.'

'Then why did you?' she whispered.

His gaze searched hers through the violet sky. 'Guilt.'

Her laughter was unbidden and tart. 'Guilt? You? Now I've heard everything.'

He was on his feet and standing in front of her before she could even blink.

The emerging moonlight made the bronze of his skin more marble-like than ever, his beautiful bone structure carved slashes by the sculptor who'd created him… But the hand that clasped hers was warm flesh and the blaze in his eyes a reminder of the passion that lurked beneath that sculpted surface.

Leaning his face into hers, his taut features became darkly animated. 'Look into my eyes and tell me I am lying.'

The heat from Enzo's breath matched the look in his eyes, and for an impossibly long moment Rebecca found herself caught in the magnetism that had ensnared her all those months ago from the very first glance. Ensnared her completely. Her pulses jumping, the ache deep in her pelvis that had started when he'd entered her life flared with brilliant, needy colour but as her gaze drifted down to his mouth, a sharpness tightened in her chest and she snatched her hand away.

Turning her face away too, she said with as much strength as she could muster, 'I thought we'd already established that your Pinocchio skills are top-notch.'

A finger brushed her cheek bone. An involuntary shiver laced her spine, and she had to clench her hands into fists to stop them reaching to wrap around him, and tighten her core to stop herself leaning forwards to press her cheek against the comfort of his solid chest. So many evenings spent wrapped in his arms, her body fizzing with unfulfilled desire but the strong, rhythmic thuds of his heart against her ear making the heat of it bearable. In his arms, Rebecca had felt a sense of safety that had been missing since her parents' deaths. Enzo had unshackled the chains of her grief and given her the tools to see beyond the day to tomorrow. He'd given her an anchor to the world she hadn't known she'd become unmoored from.

And now she was rudderless again. The anchor had been nothing but an illusion.

He stepped away from her. From the corner of her eye she saw him sit on the lawn facing her.

When she finally dared to look at him, the expression on his face turned the tightness in her chest into a physical pain.

Long legs stretched out before him, he'd propped himself semi-upright with his hands flat on the ground behind him, his black T-shirt straining over his muscular torso. Gazing at her, he quietly said, 'If I could do it all again I would do it differently. There would be no lies.'

Her chest hurt too much for the retort she wanted to throw at him to form.

His lips twitched then twisted into a grim smile. 'I told my mother the truth the night before you moved here.'

'You mean the night before I quit my career and the only home I've known so I could move to a country whose language I don't speak.'

He inclined his head slowly. '*Sì*. I knew what you were giving up. The closer the day got, the more I felt it.'

'Felt what?' She wanted him to spell out exactly how his guilt had felt to him. Maybe he could spell it sufficiently well that she actually believed it.

'The…' He grasped for the right word. 'Magnitude?'

Enzo's T-shirt had risen up, exposing his naked navel. Thick dark hair arrowed down to the belt of his jeans. A rush of heated awareness flooding her, Rebecca hastily averted her eyes.

That was all she'd ever seen of his naked form before. Odd snatches. That was all he'd ever allowed.

'I'm the last person to ask how you felt.'

'I never...' He cut himself off and took a deep breath before saying, 'It had become this huge weight inside me. My guilt. It was too late to tell you the truth. I couldn't risk losing you.'

'Couldn't risk losing the shares, you mean,' she muttered, bringing her knees to her chest and closing her arms around them, and wishing with all her might that she wasn't aching for Enzo's arms to be around her.

His gaze didn't falter. 'No. I stopped caring about the shares when I fell in l—'

'Don't you dare,' she interrupted shakily, blinking back another surge of hot tears. 'Just don't. I've already told you. Any more talk about love or feelings and I will destroy the business by any means I can find.'

He contemplated her with an expression she couldn't dissect. 'I've hurt you very badly.'

She brushed away the one tear that had broken free. 'You've ripped my heart out.'

He winced, jaw clenching.

Afraid he'd use this as an excuse for more worthless apologies, she swallowed before adding, 'I don't want to talk about my feelings any more than I want to hear more lies about yours. You've played me like a cat with a mouse for the sake of the shares and I will not let you play me again. If you have even an ounce of feelings for me then give me your word—no more talk of them or I swear I will do my best to destroy *everything*.'

His stare penetrated her through the encroaching darkness. Eventually, he sighed. 'You have my word.'

Throat suddenly choked, Rebecca nodded her acknowledgement.

'But not because of your threats,' he added, his gaze still fixed intently on her. 'Even if I believed you would go ahead with it—and I do not underestimate that your pain and anger could lead you to do it—I give you my word because there is nothing I would not do to put right what I've done to you.'

The silence that followed this was profound, filled with an agonising tension that added weight to the pain in Rebecca's chest. Knowing the emotions she sensed emanating from Enzo were nothing but a figment of her imagination only made it harder to endure. They had as much value as his words.

Such fine words. Such cheap words. Words that cost nothing to say but everything to hear.

'So you confided the truth in your mother,' she prompted quietly, bringing the conversation back on track.

Enzo stretched his neck back before lifting his head again to look at her. He grimaced. 'A mistake.'

'Not from my perspective.'

He pulled a face. 'I should have remembered her contradictory morality. Alcohol loosens lips and that night I'd drunk more than I should.'

Unsure what he meant, Rebecca's eyebrows pinched together.

His eyes continued to penetrate. 'I have not been completely open with you about my mother or my relationship with her.'

'You do surprise me.'

A tiny flash of amusement twitched at the corners of his lips at her sarcasm. 'When I first pursued you, I wanted nothing to make you think I was less than perfect. Getting those shares was too important to me. I could not risk you having any doubts about me or the family you were marrying into.'

So his seeming perfection *had* been an act. Of course, she already knew this, but to hear it from his own mouth managed to make her feel both wretched and relieved. In many ways, Enzo's perfection had awed her more than his wealth and lifestyle but to think everything he'd done for her, all the little things from filling a hot water bottle to help soothe her period cramps to giving her a head massage to soothe away the stress after a particularly difficult meeting with a parent whose child had been caught repeatedly hitting another child who refused to play with him, had all been so calculated… Oh, but that made her heart shrivel.

Clearing her throat that had closed up again, she flippantly said, 'Is your mother some kind of criminal or something?'

'Was. But not in the convicted sense. Let me put it this way—the jewellery she traded did not always have the cleanest of provenances.'

His answer was so unexpected that Rebecca felt the strangest compulsion to laugh.

As his mother had retired into being a lady of leisure

before Enzo had tricked his way into her life, Rebecca knew little about Silvana's business other than that she'd been a hugely successful international trader of jewels and that growing up in that world had inspired Silvana's only child to make his own forays into the jewellery business. He'd freely admitted to her that his mother's advice on the trade and the nuggets he'd picked up over the years had been invaluable to him when opening his first store. Any mistakes made had been his own.

What he'd failed to mention was that buying into her grandfather's diamond business had been the biggest component in his success, a thought that quickly killed the bubbling laughter.

'Are we talking stolen jewels?' She watched his reaction carefully.

He raised a shoulder. 'Nothing identifiably stolen. To any external observer, she ran a clean business. She only traded items with origins that had the correct supporting paperwork or could not be identified—nothing that would get flagged up on a database of stolen items for example.'

'But you think she did trade them?'

'I know she traded them, just as I know she had certain jewels stolen to order.'

'How does that work? Surely they'd go on that database you just mentioned?'

'If you know what you are doing, it is not difficult to remove gems from their settings and melt gold.'

'You have proof she did this?'

'None. But I'm her son. I travelled the world with her. I learned the signs. I am not a believer of coincidence.'

She wanted to scratch her head. 'Right, so your mother's a retired criminal mastermind.'

'Yes.'

'That explains you then.'

His handsome features tightened. It should please her, his obvious dislike that she should make that comparison between mother and son.

'I understand why you might think that but I grew up in constant fear of my mother's criminality being discovered and her being dragged away by the police or Interpol. There was never a chance I would follow in her footsteps. I can account for the provenance of every item ever sold in all of my stores. I run a clean business. I employ a team who do due diligence on every business I look to invest in and on-the-spot checks to ensure the businesses are being run legally and ethically.'

'Then what changed? If you've never broken the law before or allowed unethical behaviour in your businesses, why try to steal my inheritance?'

'I didn't try to steal it, damn it.' He punched the lawn in frustration. 'I always intended for you to have the cash value of the shares.'

'Which is?'

'Claflin Diamonds is currently valued at one hundred million.'

Five months ago it was a figure that would likely have made her faint. 'What's the rest of my grandfather's estate worth?'

'Including property, twenty million.'

'So come midnight I'm going to be worth seventy million euros?'

'Pounds.'

She let that sink in. Seventy million pounds.

'Woo-hoo,' she said flatly. 'I'm going to be rich...' There was not a cat in hell's chance she would keep the money. It made her feel dirty just to imagine it. 'Although still a pauper compared to you.' Adding a few zeros to the end of the sum gave a ballpark figure of what Enzo was worth. 'Supposing I take at face value that you intended to give me the cash value of my half of the business, that still doesn't explain how you could go against the strong ethics you expect me and the world to believe you possess and do what you did to me.'

'At the time, I told myself it was the principle.'

'*You* have principles? Very funny.'

He closed his eyes and took a long breath. 'Reb... Miss Foley,' he corrected, speaking slowly. Wearily.

'What?' she asked when he didn't say anything further.

He shook his head and sighed. 'I was going to ask you to stop the sniping at me but I cannot blame you for being like this. It is nothing I don't deserve.'

'Oh, stop playing the martyr,' she muttered, squirming, unable to understand why she should feel guilty for her sniping when, if Enzo's mother hadn't ratted him out, they would at this very minute be newlyweds looking to escape their wedding reception so they could make love for the first time.

She wanted to open her mouth and scream. Right at this moment she should be delirious with happiness celebrating her marriage to the love of her life and the man of her dreams.

Dreams that had been made entirely of smoke.

She swallowed back the heavy wave of nausea rising up her throat and strove for strength in her voice. 'Going back to your mother… You were telling me about her criminal masterminding ways and contradictory morality.' Strangely enough, it took no stretch of the imagination to imagine Silvana as a criminal mastermind, not in the way it did to imagine Enzo as being like that.

'Let me give you an example. You have heard of the Hollywood producer Rico Roberts? He was accused of groping young actresses last year. There were voice recordings.'

'It rings a vague bell.'

'Six years ago, two million dollars' worth of jewellery was stolen from Rico's LA home while he and his wife were at a movie premiere.'

'Your mother?'

'She was in Florence at the time but they were stolen on her orders, I am certain of it. She had met Rico and his wife at a party some years before the break-in and took a dislike to them. Rumours that he was a sex pest had circulated for years but until the recent scandal, there was no proof and he was too big a player in the movie industry to bring down without concrete evidence. Those were the kinds of rich people my mother targeted. People she didn't have to feel guilt over.'

'A modern-day Robina Hood?'

The corners of his lips twitched again. 'Yes, but with the proceeds only filling her own coffers. If she had liked Rico and disbelieved the rumours then I am certain he and his wife would still be in full possession of their jewellery collection. I am certain that if she'd been presented with an opportunity to steal from someone she knew and liked, and given a cast-iron guarantee that she would get away with it, she would have refused. If she decides she likes someone then she will be their friend for life. And you, Miss Foley, she likes.'

'I'm flattered,' she said drolly and was rewarded with a widening of Enzo's mouth and a flash of his dimples.

'You should be. She's never liked any of my other lovers.'

The lightening of the atmosphere came crashing down. 'We were never lovers,' Rebecca said, trying hard to keep the hurt from her voice. 'I suppose that's one thing I should thank you for, that you never let it go that far. I don't think I could cope knowing you'd made love to me on a lie too.'

Her cheeks scalded to think of all the times she'd begged him to make love to her, her hunger for him the flame of a lit candle whose wick never tapered even when they were apart.

What, she wondered desperately, would it take to douse the flame? Because even now, with Enzo's lies exposed, the flame burned as brightly as it ever had, the sticky heat of arousal and awareness as thick in her as it had ever been.

Enzo had induced the flame. Deliberately. He'd fed it and nurtured it and stoked it.

She couldn't hate him more.

'Why do you think I never allowed it to happen between us?'

'Because you didn't have to.' Bitterness crept back into her tone. 'I guess you didn't want me enough. As soon as you established I was a virgin you used it as an excuse not to—'

He sprang from a recline to his haunches before she could finish her sentence.

'Yes,' he said savagely, hands pressed down on the padded egg chair either side of her hips, eyes boring deep into hers. 'I used it as an excuse because I had to. When I first set out to seduce you into marrying me, I told myself you were your grandfather's blood and likely to be as devious as him. You can have no idea the depth of betrayal I felt when I read his will. I didn't think of you as a person but as an obstacle, and an underserving obstacle at that—you'd never met him and had turned down his requests to meet. You returned his cards and cheques. You'd made it clear you wanted nothing to do with him or his money and still he left you everything, including the half of our shared business that he'd promised me; that he *owed* me. Believe me, I was prepared to hate you in the flesh as much as I hated the very idea of you and when I met you it was a relief to find you attractive enough to not have to fake desire for you along with everything else.'

Somehow, while he'd been making his biting but impassioned speech, Enzo's hands had taken hold of Rebecca's waist. Trying desperately not to fall into the hypnotic swirl of his eyes was as impossible as telling her flesh not to react to his grip on her, the ache at his touch too strong for her to find the sense needed to shove his hands off and push him away as she knew she should. She'd been a slave to his touch from their very first kiss.

His fingers tightened their grip, the tip of his nose almost touching hers. 'Do you remember our first date? By the end of it…' He sucked a sharp breath in through his teeth. '*Dio*, you can have no idea how sexy you are. The way your lips move when you eat…' His eyes flashed. 'But as soon as you told me you were a virgin it changed everything for me. It didn't matter how much I wanted you—I knew on a fundamental level that making love to you on a lie was unforgivable.'

Fighting with everything she had against the tumult of emotions Enzo's words and closeness had induced, Rebecca had to plead with herself not to fall into the trap he was laying, to keep her hands tightly fisted at her sides, to stop herself inhaling too deeply so his divine scent couldn't snake its way down to her lungs and tip her over the edge.

'What about our wedding night?' she whispered raggedly. 'Would you have gone ahead with it without telling me the truth?'

'Yes.'

'Even though it would have still been unforgivable, what with it still being based on the same lie?'

'Yes. Because by then you would have been my wife and tied to me, and I would never have let you go.'

And then his mouth found hers.

# CHAPTER FIVE

REBECCA'S FISTS WERE clenched so tightly in her vain attempt to keep her lips clamped and airways closed that her nails dug sharply into her palms.

There was nothing she could do to stop the violent trembling of her body or the thumping tattoo of her heart against her ribs. Those reactions were involuntary and completely beyond her control; physical reactions fighting with equal ferocity to the sane part of her brain pleading with her mouth to stay clamped and not give in to the desperate, burning ache for him.

*Don't give in*, she begged herself. *This means nothing to him. It was all a set-up from the very start.*

Her pleading words to herself penetrated the memory of the very start and threw her back to the night she'd come out into this garden to forget. The night Enzo proposed.

He'd taken her out to dinner on the river, an exclusive floating restaurant where they were served the most exquisite food she'd ever tasted. After a dessert of chocolate mousse on a chocolate crumb with flakes of gold leaf scattered over it, they'd taken their after-dinner liqueurs onto the top deck. The cloudless evening sky had been chilly. Noticing her shiver, Enzo had draped his suit jacket over her shoulders...how she had *thrilled* at the pleasure of being warmed by the remnants of his body heat. By the time they'd returned to the villa, Rebecca had been floating like the boat they'd dined on in a sea of happiness she'd never known before.

She'd smelt the roses from the moment she stepped through the front door.

Hundreds and hundreds of red roses encircled the main living room, set in so many crystal vases Florence must have declared a shortage. There, in the centre of the room, a plinth had been placed. On it, the largest vase of all. Wrapped around it had been a red ribbon onto which had been tied a small black velvet box.

Enzo had been the one to untie it. He'd held it in his hand and sank onto one knee before her.

Her heart had beat so hard and so fast she'd feared she would be sick.

He'd opened the lid. Inside it glittered the most beautiful oval diamond ring.

'Will you marry me?'

Three times he'd asked the question before what he was asking actually sank in, and even then she couldn't comprehend it or comprehend what was happening to her. Barely a month before, Rebecca's world had been grey with grief but then Enzo had come into her life and saturated it with colour and now he was asking her to marry him?

'Why?' It was the only word she could form in her brain or on her tongue. Why her when he could have anyone?

His eyes had glittered. 'Because I can't imagine my life without you in it.'

And still she'd gawped at him, hardly daring to believe this could be true and that she wasn't dreaming.

He'd risen to his feet slowly and taken her hand, and suddenly she'd detected something new in his eyes, something she could never in a hundred years explain but when he'd then quietly said, 'What do you say? Will you marry me, Rebecca?' her heart had exploded with joy.

'Yes.'

Such a contortion of emotions had flashed over his face that she'd been certain she'd only imagined the shadow that darkened it before the heartbreaking smile she'd fallen in love with widened his whole face and he pulled her into his arms for a kiss so deep and passionate that the pulses in her core throbbed throughout her entire body.

He'd broken the kiss to cup her face in his hands. 'I love you, Rebecca.' There had been a dazed quality to his voice that matched the dizziness she'd been feeling. 'I love you.'

To know it had all been fake, every last part of it, broke her heart all over again and gave her the impetus needed to turn her cheek and wrench her mouth from his with a plaintive, '*Stop!*'

The wonderful pressure of Enzo's mouth against hers disappeared leaving nothing but tingles on her lips. The grip on her waist loosened and then disappeared too but the heat from his body remained as he covered her fists, a gentle, tender pressure that made her want to cry harder than anything else had that whole day.

'My desire for you was never a lie,' he said fervently.

She shook her head violently. 'Stop *lying* to me. I told you, I don't want to hear this.'

'Why would I lie about this? What purpose would it serve?' He pressed her hand to his chest. 'I've already lost you. But you haven't lost me. Everything I—' He cut himself off and swore under his breath. Gritting his teeth, he squeezed her fisted hand tighter against his heart and said, 'Whatever you believe of me, never think I didn't want you. Resisting you is the hardest thing I have done in my life.'

How could she wish so hard to believe him when *everything* was predicated on a lie?

Another memory slammed into her, straddling Enzo on the loveseat of his New York penthouse, both fully clothed, their pelvises locked together, the rock solidness of his erection burning, tantalising and frustrating her in equal measure. She'd been desperate for him to make love to her. 'I've spent my whole life waiting to feel like this,' she'd whispered into his ear.

His kiss had been deep and hard, and then he'd fisted her hair in his hands and tugged her head back to gaze deep into her eyes. 'What I feel for you is like nothing I have felt before.'

'Then make love to me,' she'd pleaded.

He'd kissed her again, fervently. '*Cara*, there is nothing I want more than to carry you to my bed and make love to you but our wedding is so close now. Let every part of our day be special. We have the rest of our lives to satisfy our desires.'

She closed her eyes to the memories and shook her head even harder. 'Please, Enzo, just accept that you've lost. You're demeaning us both.'

'Do you really think so little of yourself?' he demanded.

'It's nothing to do with how I see myself but how I see you, and how I see you is as a ruthless liar prepared to do anything and say anything to get what he wants.'

Hands suddenly abandoned her fists and cupped her cheeks. Rebecca squeezed her closed eyes even tighter.

'If it is nothing to do with how you see yourself then why are you so willing to accept that everything including my desire was a lie?' he asked savagely, his breath hot on her face. '*Dio*, I do not believe there's a man alive who—' The abruptness with which he cut himself off this time was matched only by the swift release of her cheeks and the removal of his heat.

She opened her eyes as he rose to his feet.

Dragging his fingers through his hair, he shook his head before landing his gaze back on her. 'You never believed in me, did you?'

With the chill that had replaced the warmth of his body having stolen her breath, Rebecca could only gape at him.

His firm yet generous lips twitched before a short bark of laugher escaped them. 'Or is it better to say you never believed in yourself? I remember when I proposed, you kept asking, 'Why? Why me?' I didn't know you like I do now and I thought you were putting on an act, but you were being genuine, weren't you? You have such low esteem that your first thought when receiving a marriage proposal was to ask why—'

'Turns out I was right to ask that,' she interrupted shakily.

His brow drew into a disbelieving line. 'Would you have asked the question if you had confidence in yourself? You are beautiful and smart and funny but I think of all the times we went out and you were always worried you didn't look good enough or would show me up, and I think too of how frightened you were to meet my mother because you were afraid she would think you weren't good enough...'

Rebecca's heart was thrashing wildly against her ribs. 'Stop twisting things. This isn't about me, this is about you.'

Another bark of laughter and a widening of his mouth into a smile that contained more bitterness than warmth. 'Without you there is no me, don't you understand that? If your insecurities hadn't made you question yourself so much, you would already know it and not only understand but feel right *here*,' he punched a fist into his chest, 'that as big a bastard as I am and as terrible as my behaviour has been, not everything was a lie.'

How she wished it was possible to close her ears as easily as it was to close her eyes. She wished even harder that she could close off her emotions and the longing to believe him, but the hard shell she'd managed to erect around herself earlier had softened into mush.

What ordinary woman in her position wouldn't have

questioned why a wildly attractive billionaire who could have anyone he wanted would want to marry her? And what ordinary woman wouldn't worry about making a fool of the man she loved when out in the high society world he inhabited and which was so alien to her own that it could have been set on a different planet? She'd thought the hotel they'd met in had been posh? Within days of that meeting, Rebecca's definition of posh had been blown out of the water. Compared to the places Enzo had taken her to, that hotel had been a rundown dive. She, a primary schoolteacher who, apart from her university years, had lived her whole life in the same end-of-terrace house in the suburbs was suddenly thrown into a world of glamour and limousines, Michelin-starred restaurants and private member clubs. If she'd actually engaged her brain and thought back to that first meeting, she'd have realised that something about it was all wrong, that there was no way Enzo, whose London offices were in the capital's highest skyscraper, would conduct business in such an ordinary place.

But she'd been too caught up in the glamour and the awakening of feelings smothered for so long she'd forgotten they even existed in her. Feelings like happiness.

Being with Enzo had made her so happy.

The grimace that had been so much of a feature since they'd been holed up in the villa returned to his face at her silence. 'I'm going to get something to eat.'

She stared at him blankly at the sudden change of subject.

He took a visible, deep breath. 'It is getting very late.

I have not eaten all day. I don't imagine you have either. Do not starve yourself out of spite of me.'

Turning, he set off towards the villa, but had only taken five paces before he stopped and twisted back to face her. 'One other thing. If I really was prepared to do anything to get those shares, as you seem to think, I would have made love to you every single time you begged it of me.'

When Enzo's tall frame had disappeared into the shadows, Rebecca flopped back into the curved support of the egg seat, then drew her knees to her chest and wrapped her arms around herself. Her cheeks were still enflamed from his parting shot, her stomach so tight and cramped she didn't think she would ever desire food again.

If only her desire and feelings for him could be so easily switched off.

She'd been an idiot for thinking she could maintain her hard shell and survive the night here without hurting herself further. Having Enzo personally hand over the shares he'd coveted so badly wasn't worth what being with him did to her.

She'd lost count of the times she'd begged him to make love to her, and for him to throw that back at her was mortifying and cruel.

But there had been no cruelty in his matter-of-fact delivery.

If he was telling the truth then his refusal to make love to her had been as agonising for him as it had been for her.

The worst of it was that she did believe he was telling the truth on this. It had been the fevered sincerity that had blazed from his eyes; and she hugged herself harder, knowing she mustn't think like this. If she accepted this one part of their relationship as the truth then what else would her foolish heart beg her to accept? That he did love her? And what excuses would her foolish heart start making for him then? Would it make her think he'd been perfectly justified in lying about absolutely everything? Would it make her think he had a point about her never believing in herself? Would her foolish heart make her gaslight herself?

She rubbed her chin into her knee. She really should have followed her initial instincts and headed straight to the airport. She might be home by now and not sat in Enzo's garden…

Home? She almost laughed. She didn't have a home any more. Not one she could live in. She'd signed a tenancy agreement before she'd moved to Italy. A newlywed couple were now living in the only home she'd ever known and were legally entitled to stay there for a year.

A place to live was just one of the many things she would have to sort out when she returned to England. Finding herself a job was another. Her replacement had already been appointed, and her heart swelled painfully to realise all her now ex-colleagues had witnessed her jilt Enzo at the altar. He'd paid for them to fly over and paid for their accommodation. He'd paid the expenses of every friend and family member she'd included on the guest list.

Rebecca sprang off the egg seat and blinked furiously against yet another batch of hot tears. She didn't want to remember Enzo's incredible generosity, all brought about when she'd voiced doubts about marrying in Florence because the price might prohibit many of those she wanted to be there from attending. He was generous to a fault, and she didn't think it was an act. He had more money than he could ever hope to spend in a thousand lifetimes and donated a set percentage of his annual income to various children's and animal charities, a philanthropy that predated her entry into his life by many years.

Acknowledging this only made his treatment of her harder to understand. How could a man with such a generous heart be capable of such deviousness, and as she followed his footsteps and slipped back into the villa, her chest tightened and she found herself wishing almost as hard as she'd wished that the oncologist's diagnosis of her mother's cancer was wrong that Enzo had convincingly denied that everything between them had been staged. Wished he'd successfully given her a plausible explanation for everything.

But there had been no denial or plausible explanation. He'd pleaded guilty and she would not gaslight herself into believing anything else.

All her stuff from the hotel had been left by the front door with the rest of her belongings. Silence surrounded her. Wherever Enzo was in the villa, he wasn't close by.

Her phone was in the handbag she'd left at the hotel and she pulled it out, in two minds over whether to call for a taxi and leave immediately.

No, she decided. She didn't see how she could return to England and rebuild her life if she still had unanswered questions. There were some things it was impossible to move on from and if she hadn't lived through the death of both her parents within days of each other, she doubted she'd ever be able to recover from this.

One thing Rebecca had learned in those dark, bottomless days had been that unanswered questions could drive you crazy. Her father's death had been straightforward in the respect that he'd suffered a massive heart attack. There had been no ambiguity to it. Her mother's death, though, might have been prevented if their local doctor had taken her symptoms more seriously instead of fobbing her off with things like calcium deficiency and menopause. It was the *might* in the equation that had turned Rebecca into a red-eyed insomniac, because that was the part no one could definitively answer. If their doctor had arranged a full range of blood tests when she'd first gone to see him two years before her death about being constantly tired, if her mum hadn't accepted that her symptoms were consistent with the menopause and ignored that she was bruising easily… All the *ifs* that led to the *mights*, because there was no way of knowing if her mum would still be alive even if she'd been diagnosed sooner. She *might* have lived another five years. She *might* have made it to old bones.

It had taken a full year for Rebecca to accept the diagnosis question could never be answered. She wasn't prepared to tear herself apart with unanswered questions again. Not when her only means of answering them would be through the man she would never set eyes on again after she left this villa.

Rebecca found Enzo in the smaller dining room, the one that only comfortably sat twenty people rather than the one in which he could host a hundred.

He was sat at the far end of the marble table, features set tightly, almost slouched in his chair stabbing a fork into his plate, the light of the chandelier landing like drops of gold on his skin. The scents wafting from his plate sent a hunger pang rippling through her, and a different, stronger pang. It was the scent of his favourite food, a simple layered aubergine, tomato and mozzarella dish, the Enzo Beresi version of comfort food that was the polar opposite of the fancy food he usually ate when dining out.

Of course he was comfort eating. He'd lost; a blow that must be particularly hard to bear for a man who always won at everything.

As soon as he spotted her, his demeanour changed. He straightened. His chest rose, neck extending as he nodded his acknowledgement of her presence.

Leaning into the door's frame, it took effort for Rebecca to make her mouth and throat move. 'I'm going to get something to eat. Wait in here for me?'

His lips a thin line, he inclined his head.

It took more effort to control the next pang that ripped through her when she discovered the chef had prepared her own favourite comfort food of macaroni cheese for her. She didn't need to ask to know he'd made it for her on Enzo's instructions.

Removing it from under the grill, he served it bubbling and golden into a warmed pasta bowl for her and would no doubt have carried it to the dining room if she'd let him. Thanking him, she carried it on a tray back to the dining room and took a seat halfway down the long table. If she sat facing Enzo at the other end to him then she'd have to shout. This way she was close enough to converse but not close enough she risked having any part of her body make contact—accidental or otherwise—with his. Also, being side-on meant she didn't have to look at him unless she wanted to.

It hurt immeasurably that she did want to look. Staring at his gorgeous face was something she'd thought she would never tire of doing.

'Thank you for getting Sal to make this for me,' she said quietly.

'You're welcome.'

She hated the softness in his tone. Hated it and loved it in equal measure, and as she dug her spoon into the gooey mixture, it came to her that she hated and loved *him* in equal measure too.

# CHAPTER SIX

REBECCA'S MUM HAD always described love and hate as being two sides of the same coin. She'd known her mum was referring to Rebecca's grandfather when she said this, but having never hated anyone herself, it was a concept Rebecca had never fully understood.

She understood it now, sitting in this suddenly claustrophobic dining room. Such were the emotions crashing through her that if she'd been standing, the dizziness from it would have caused her to stumble. Her heart throbbed painfully, the beats sending needles of pain through her veins, infecting every cell in her body.

'Would you like a glass of wine?' he asked after she'd been sat there for a good minute without uttering a word.

She nodded without looking at him.

He rose from his seat. 'White?'

She gave another nod. If her grip on the spoon got any tighter the metal would bend.

A few moments later, he placed her glass on the table beside her.

She tensed and held her breath. She'd become conditioned to Enzo never being within a foot of her without touching her in some way, whether a brush of his hand against her back or the drop of a kiss into her hair, and she didn't know if her body was giving signs of relief or distress when he retook his seat without a whisper of physical contact.

When she dared reopen her airways, she breathed in the remnants of his woody cologne, and took a large gulp of her wine in an attempt to drown it. The attempt was a dismal failure. All the questions consuming her were drowned in the sharp but sweet crisp liquid too, her mind a blank and it took more co-ordination than she'd needed since she was a toddler to spoon a mouthful of the meal that usually brought her the greatest comfort between her lips. Whatever Enzo's chef did to make the simple infusion of pasta, milk and cheese into a culinary masterpiece was something she'd been happy to never understand; delirious devotion of its comforting amazingness had been enough. This time, there was no comfort to be had. She couldn't even taste it.

It didn't help that Enzo's gaze was locked on her. Its burn seeped deep inside her.

'You didn't finish telling me why your mother basically ratted you out to me,' she said when she feared spontaneous combustion from the heat his stare was inducing had become more than a distinct possibility.

From the corner of her eye she saw him take a drink of his red wine, heard him follow the silent swallow with a deep breath. 'No,' he agreed. 'I didn't.'

'I need you to explain what you meant by saying she didn't want you to marry me and not the other way around.'

'My mother does not like many people in this world

but, as I said, she likes you. If she could have chosen a daughter-in-law, it would have been you.'

She didn't know how to respond to that. Should she be flattered that a jewellery thief considered her the ideal daughter-in-law?

'She took to you for many of the same reasons I did,' he explained quietly. 'You are genuine. A good person. You wear your heart on your sleeve and speak your mind, which is very refreshing when you are used to being surrounded by calculators.'

Rebecca dipped her spoon back into her bowl. 'Calculators?'

'That is what we call those who want us only for what they can get and calculate every word they say in our company. An in joke I think you call it.'

She swirled the spoon slowly through the thickening sauce. 'That must make you a calculator too, seeing as you calculated every word you ever said to me.'

'I suppose it must,' he agreed. 'But not the words you think. Not once I learned there was no calculation at all in your nature and I—'

He broke himself away from saying what Rebecca instinctively knew would have been more forbidden words about feelings.

'Why would she sabotage our wedding though? It doesn't matter if she liked me or not—you're her son.'

'It was revenge for forcing her to dissolve her business.'

She whipped her head towards him before she could stop herself.

His gaze was already locked on her. Fingers tightly

gripped the stem of his wine glass. His handsome features were like granite and when he opened his mouth, his voice had the same stony quality. 'Five years ago I threatened to report her to the authorities. I had enough circumstantial evidence of the robberies she'd masterminded to make them investigate her.'

She blinked her shock at this unexpected twist.

Incredibly, his features hardened even further. 'Someone needed to stop her and that someone was me.'

It took a moment to unfreeze her vocal cords. 'Would you have done it?'

No hesitation. 'Without a doubt.'

'Shopped your own mother to the police?' she asked, disbelieving.

'Reb...' His eyes closed briefly, lips tightening. 'Miss Foley... My relationship with my mother is complicated.'

'It seemed perfectly normal from what I saw of it.' Well, relatively normal. Enzo and Silvana's world was so different to Rebecca's that it was impossible to judge their relationship by her own experiences. When Rebecca had returned home for weekends and holidays in her university years, her father had always collected her in the ancient family hatchback. For Enzo and Silvana, it was normal to visit each other via helicopter if traffic was particularly bad. Not that they drove themselves in any traffic, each having drivers on rotas to chauffeur them wherever they wanted to go. Then there was the nature of the visits. When back home, Rebecca and her parents had mucked in together with the cooking and cleaning as they'd always done. Enzo and Silvana each employed a fleet of domestic staff to prepare their meals and wipe away any dust before it dared land on their highly polished surfaces. There was also a heap of formality between Enzo and his mother as opposed to the affection and gentle teasing Rebecca and her parents had enjoyed, but in the formal settings of their respective homes, it had seemed natural.

'Appearances can be deceiving,' he said.

*You're the expert in that.* The words jumped to the tip of Rebecca's tongue but she pressed her lips together to stop the dig from escaping. It was the blaze from Enzo's eyes that did it. Fire and ice.

'Let me explain something to you.' Every word was delivered with bite. 'My mother never wanted to marry or have children. I was not planned. I was an accident. She handed me to my father when I was born because she did not want me.'

It wasn't just Rebecca's throat that froze at this. Every cell in her body turned to ice.

Not once in all their many talks had Enzo confided this to her. Not a hint of it.

'For the first six years of my life, my mother was nothing but an occasional visitor to our home. I barely knew her.'

'Then… How…?' She closed her mouth, unable to articulate a single one of the dozen questions swarming in her head.

'She did not want me or want to love me but, as she has told me many times since, she had no choice in the matter. She never wanted to have any involvement in my life but her love for me was stronger than her self-ishness, and let me tell you, she hated it. To her, love stifles freedom. When my father died that love compelled her to claim me and take me in.' He let out a grunt and added, 'The day after my father's funeral, she collected me and that was it. The world I knew was gone and I had to live with this woman who was almost a stranger to me.'

Her heart throbbed, lungs aching for breath.

'If I'd been given the choice I would have lived with my grandparents. They lived on the same street as us. I had always treated their home like my own. I loved them and they loved me. But I was six and not given a choice.'

Given a choice, Rebecca would have ripped her gaze away from him but her eyes refused to obey, soaking in the stony features, her fingers now gripping the spoon to stop them reaching across and stroking the hard edges away. This hardness was a side to Enzo she had never seen before and for reasons she would never understand affected her far more deeply than if he'd been relaying everything in a *pity me* voice.

She knew in her guts that everything he was telling her now was the unvarnished truth.

She'd known his father had died when he was six, known his parents weren't together when the aneurysm killed him, but had thought he'd always been raised by his mother.

Had she assumed that or had Enzo led her to believe it?

He'd deliberately let her make that assumption she

realised dimly, because to have told her the truth would have been to open the can of worms that would have revealed his mother's true nature. As he'd already admitted, he hadn't wanted Rebecca to have any doubts about marrying him. He'd wanted nothing to make her believe he was anything less than perfect.

This time, though, she couldn't summon the energy to be angry about the revealing of yet another manipulative lie, not when she felt so sick inside for the little boy he'd once been.

Swallowing back bile, she forced herself to ask, 'What kind of mother was she once you were living with her?'

'Terrible,' he said bluntly. 'She is the most selfish person I know and had no idea how to raise a child. I went from a typical Italian life with a big extended family to living in an apartment where I was forbidden from touching anything. She resented me for cramping her style and I resented her for taking me away from my family and for not being my father.'

'What was your father like?'

There was a slight softening in his eyes. 'He was a great man. He worked as a painter and decorator. He painted cars all over the walls of my room for me. I have nothing but good memories of him.'

Another pang rippled through her chest. Words of comfort itched to jump off her tongue but she clamped them tightly, knowing she mustn't say them, that it was no longer her place to say them. That she shouldn't even want to.

Even if she felt she could, the look in Enzo's eyes

told her comfort was neither wanted nor needed, that his past was something he'd already come to terms with and that he was only telling her the unvarnished truth because he owed it to her.

'Living with my mother...' He raised a shoulder. 'Neither of us liked the situation but there was no choice in it for either of us.' He shrugged again and drained his wine. 'She had no choice in loving me and I had no choice in loving her. Her love for me is the only reason we still have a relationship. She either likes people or she doesn't. If she likes you then she will do anything for you. Cross her and she will discard you as if you never existed. She is unable to discard me and that infuriates her. The threats I made to force her into becoming a law-abiding citizen would have seen anyone else cut from her life. I am quite sure she wishes she could cut me off but she can't, and she has spent five years seething with resentment. She saw the opportunity to strike at me and hurt me, and no doubt sated her conscience by telling herself she was doing it for your benefit.'

'Robina Hood has a conscience?'

Immediately she regretted her effort to lighten the oppressive atmosphere when a glimmer of humour passed between them.

She didn't want to be reminded of all the other glimmers that had passed between them because then it would lead to her remembering all the laughter and the sheer joy of just being with Enzo.

'I told you—her morality is complicated,' he said. 'If she had disliked you then I am certain she would have let you marry me and waited for a different opportunity to take her revenge.'

'Did she get some kind of kick out of being a criminal mastermind?' What other reason could there be for being so full of resentment?

'Undoubtedly.'

Rebecca stirred her spoon some more around her mostly uneaten meal and tried to square the Silvana Beresi she knew with the woman Enzo had just described, trying again to muster anger that in all the months they'd been together she'd bared her soul to him like she'd never done with anyone before while he'd blatantly omitted the most important aspects of his history to her.

He'd given her the skeleton of his life but failed, deliberately, to add flesh and blood to it.

But anger still refused to rise. Her heart continued to ache for the small boy he'd been, a child the same age as the children she taught. Those children were spontaneous in their affections and open with their emotions but not yet mature enough to hide whatever they were feeling. It was those who could hide it, she'd learned in the short time frame she'd been doing the job, that you needed to worry about. Would Enzo have been one of those children she'd watched closely, longing to hug them tightly and tell them everything would be all right?

Whatever kind of child Enzo had been, he was not that small boy any more. He'd grown into a man every bit as manipulative as the woman who'd given birth to him. He'd omitted the most important aspects of his life because he hadn't wanted to shatter the illusion of perfection and thus risk Rebecca having doubts about marrying him.

But she only knew this because he'd admitted it.

Now that everything was out in the open, he was giving her the honesty she demanded, and it made her heart hurt to think that if only he'd been honest with her from the start about her grandfather's will, maybe they...

There was no point in thinking like this. There was no *they*. Enzo didn't love her. He'd never loved her. Robina Hood had done her a huge favour.

Rebecca took a deep breath then pushed her chair back and got to her feet.

She sensed him watching her every move.

'It's late,' she said, turning her body away from him, too full of emotions she no longer understood to dare looking at him any more. 'I'm going to try and get some sleep.'

There was another painful clenching in her heart to remember that she should already be in bed. With her husband. Making love for the first time. Celebrating a love that had never existed.

His velvet voice drifted to her ears. 'Stay a little longer. I have something for you.'

She closed her eyes. 'The shares?'

'No. Something else.'

'There is nothing else that I want from you.' Other than for time to be reversed five months and to refuse a hot drink by the hotel fire with the most gorgeous man she'd ever set eyes on.

Too heartsick to breathe the same air as him a moment longer, Rebecca headed for the dining room door.

'Five minutes, *cara*. Stay with me until the clock strikes midnight.'

She stilled, closing her eyes again as fresh longing swept through her. 'You don't have a clock that strikes anything.'

'I was trying to be poetic.'

Despite herself, she smiled. Only a small smile but she was glad her back was to him and he couldn't see it. He shouldn't be able to amuse her still. She wished he didn't.

Footsteps sounded behind her. 'If we go now, we will be in the garage when midnight strikes.'

'Why the garage?'

'It's where your birthday surprise is.'

She shook her head violently. 'I don't want anything from you. Whatever you got for me, send it back.'

'That is not possible.'

The roots of her hair tingled at the warmth of his breath swirling through it. He was so close that every atom in her Enzo-starved body leapt towards his heat, and as she clenched her hands into fists to fight her yearning, she instinctively knew he was fighting the impulse to put his hands on the top of her arms and slide them down and then…

She started walking again, through to the main living room, fighting with everything she had not to look back. To look at him now, to find herself captured in the eyes that always pierced her soul, would drive her to madness.

'Okay, I'll have a look at your surprise.' She was thankful for the defiance in her voice. 'But don't expect me to be all gushing and grateful for whatever it is.' Undoubtedly a car. Enzo was a collector. His garage, filled with dozens of gleaming supercars that each cost more than her English home, had a larger footprint than her English home multiplied three times. Thankfully, Rebecca had no interest in cars. Her attachment to her father's old car that had led her into putting it into storage rather than selling it or, as she should really have been done, scrapping it, was purely emotional. Whatever car Enzo had bought her would have no emotional impact, and it surprised her that a man who'd proven himself so intuitive to her emotional needs—intuitive enough to manipulate her, she quickly reminded herself—would think otherwise.

Still not looking back, she crossed the vast room to the corridor and headed to the far end and through the door that opened into the stairwell and led down to the garage. Absolutely no way would she dare risk sharing the elevator with him.

Only the tread of Enzo's steps in her wake let her know he was behind her. That and the buzz in her veins and the pounding in her chest; the hyperawareness of his closeness she had once revelled in.

She quickened her pace down the stairs and stepped into the sprawling whitewashed underground lair that was as much a garage as a bed-sit was a mansion.

Folding her arms across her chest, Rebecca craned her neck in all directions. She would give her birthday car a cursory glance and then she would lock herself in the bedroom she'd never expected to sleep in again and take as cold a shower as she could stand and freeze all the dreadful heated feelings zipping through her veins and pounding in her heart.

In the third row to her left she caught the glimpse of a giant red bow. 'Is that it?'

'Yes. Come and see.'

It was only when she'd weaved through the second row and caught a glimpse of yellow that her heart lurched up into her mouth.

On legs that suddenly felt made of water, she virtually staggered to the vehicle she'd covered with a blanket only three weeks ago with the promise that she wasn't abandoning it and that when the time was right, she would take it out of storage and find someone to finish her father's restoration of it.

It took a long, long time for her to be able to speak and even then all she could muster was a choked, 'How?'

'I think you know the answer to that,' Enzo murmured before digging into his jeans pocket and pulling out a key. He held it out to her on his palm. 'Happy birthday, *cara*.'

She dragged her stare away from the car, and locked eyes with the man who'd made good on her father's dream.

The faded, battered vintage car that had so recently possessed so many dents it was impossible to count them all was now as smooth as the other cars in the showroom garage and gleamed with the same intensity, the ripped and stained upholstery now a richly textured leather… Nothing had been missed. Even the steering wheel and gear stick looked brand-new. And yet, it retained the original charm her father had fallen in love with. It was still the same car that had thrilled him so and which he'd been determined to wind the clock back on and restore to its former glory.

If her dad could see it now his face would be alight with that snaggle-toothed grin Rebecca missed so much.

The tears spilled out unbidden, and before she could stop herself, she ignored Enzo's outstretched hand to throw her arms around him and sob into his chest.

There was only the briefest hesitation before he wrapped his arms around her. One arm tight around her back, a hand cradling her head, his chin resting on her hair, he did nothing but hold her close, tenderly, wordlessly letting her purge the deluge of emotions she'd fought so hard to contain.

By the time her chest stopped heaving and the tears slowed to a trickle, his T-shirt was soaked.

She lifted her face. There was a tightness to Enzo's features, different to the hardness from the dining room, as if he'd had to clamp the muscles of his face to stop himself from speaking.

'Thank you,' she whispered. The restoration of her father's car might only have been made possible due to Enzo's limitless funds but he'd thought to make it happen. For her. Because he knew how much it meant to her.

He gave a taut smile. 'I didn't mean to make you cry.' And then he winced as if remembering that he'd already made her cry an ocean of tears that long, long day.

'You didn't.' She swallowed to clear her throat. 'I'm just really feeling it today. Missing them.'

His face contorted into another wince. The fingers cradling her head threaded through her hair, the thumb from his other hand brushing away the dampness beneath her eyes. 'That's my fault.'

She couldn't argue with that. But she wanted to. Wanted to excuse him. Forgive him. Move her face the few inches needed for their lips to fuse together and find the dizzying joy his deep, passionate kisses always filled her with. Let him break her heart again.

And from the pulsing in his eyes, Enzo was fighting the same temptation too.

Breaking out of his hold, she stepped back, straight into the side of one of his Porsches.

But she couldn't break the fusion of their eyes. Couldn't tear her gaze from his.

And neither could he tear his gaze from her.

Eyes still holding hers, he dropped to his knees. She didn't know he'd dropped the key until he picked it off the ground and pressed it into her hand. His touch sent shocks of electricity darting through her skin.

The lock of their eyes somehow even stronger, hot, dark desire swirling in his, Enzo closed her fingers around the key. She could hear the shortness of his breaths. It matched the shortness of hers. The only other sound was the roar of blood in her ears, a roar that deafened when fingers gripped her hip as he rose, and hot breath danced over her mouth before she closed her eyes.

# CHAPTER SEVEN

REBECCA NEVER NEEDED to muster any resistance because the kiss never happened. Enzo's lips barely brushed against hers before he shot back as if he'd actually been shot.

He blew out a long breath and gripped a hank of his hair. 'I apologise,' he said stiffly.

Rebecca covered her flaming cheeks, mortified that he'd been the one to stop their kiss before it had even started. She'd been too far gone to stop it. Too caught in his spell.

It destroyed her that despite everything, her need for him was as strong as it had ever been whereas his control was a tap he could turn on and off at will.

He must have read something of what she was thinking on her face because suddenly he closed the gap he'd just made between them. His hands cradled her face roughly, his breath once again hot on her face. 'Do not think like this, *cara*,' he said savagely, then caught her hand, dragging it down his hard chest and abdomen and pressing it between his legs. 'Feel that and tell me I don't want you.'

Her breath hitched, eyes widening at the thick hardness straining against the denim of his jeans. A low, heady thrill rushed through her making her already watery legs weaken at the knees.

'I want you more than I have ever wanted anyone and I would give anything…' His nostrils flared. *'Anything* to make you mine. But I will not manipulate your emotions to my advantage. I will not be that man again.'

And then he released her completely and walked away.

Rebecca, still backed against the Porsche, stared at his retreating form, in too deep a stupor to even move her feet let alone comprehend what he'd just said.

Moments later, he disappeared into the elevator.

Rebecca brushed her teeth as hard as she could to scrub the taste of her own desire from her mouth. She'd taken another shower to wash the fever from her skin but all her efforts to sanitise herself against Enzo were fruitless. Every time she closed her eyes she felt his hardness against her hand. Every time, the pulse between her legs throbbed in response.

The purge of her tears had catharized everything except her desire.

How could she still ache so badly for him? After everything he'd done? So he'd done one good thing with the restoration of her father's car? That didn't change anything else or excuse him.

But he had done it. For her.

Telling herself to get a grip, she rootled through her wash bag for her moisturiser but came up empty. With a vague recollection of leaving it in the bathroom of the hotel room, she slipped back into the bedroom hoping one of the hotel staff had noticed and popped it in her case.

Her hope was fulfilled but as she wrapped her fingers around the cold jar, the side of her hand brushed against silk and her stomach turned over.

Gathering all her courage, Rebecca pulled the white negligée from the case and shook it out.

Her eyes swam. Memories of the dreams that had sustained her for so long flooded her.

This was what she'd planned to wear for Enzo on their wedding night. This night. In their honeymoon penthouse suite. All the possessions within the case open before her should have been moved to the suite in anticipation.

She'd planned it all out in her head, from the shower she'd take using the beautiful, sensuous shower gel she'd bought especially for this night, to the tempting makeup she would paint her face with. She hadn't wanted her first time to be all about her virginity. She had wanted it to be for the both of them. She had dreamed of Enzo's touch on every inch of her skin and dreamed of touching every inch of him too. In her dreams, their wedding night would *be* from the realm of dreams. Enzo's refusal to make love before their nuptials had only fed this fantasy.

And he would have made love to her that night. He would never have risked an annulment.

Almost unthinking, Rebecca took her pyjamas off and replaced them with the negligée she'd bought with her final monthly salary payment. She'd wanted to pay for it with her own money; her gift to the man she worshipped.

She stood in front of the mirror just as she'd done when she'd first bought it and had imagined the desire in Enzo's eyes before he stripped it from her.

The flattering cut made her look curvier than she actually was even if it didn't enhance her small breasts. Its spaghetti straps joined with the main body of silk, which skimmed her cleavage in a plunging V. The hem barely skimmed her bottom. This was not an item intended to be slept in. This was an item to be shared and enjoyed.

Still staring hard at her makeup-free reflection, Rebecca cupped her breast and imagined it was Enzo's hand caressing it. Closing her eyes, she imagined him replacing his hand with his mouth, and when her other hand slipped between her legs and brushed herself, a swell of rage burst through her and she wrenched her hands away from her hypersensitive zones and threw herself onto the bed she was never supposed to have slept in again.

It wasn't just her dreams for their wedding night Enzo had fed but the sickness raging in her blood—and there was no doubt her desire for him had morphed into a sickness, or else how could she be feeling so sick with desire for him now? His promise that the wait would all be worth it had set up in her mind impossibly unrealistic expectations and built what should have been perfectly ordinary desire into a fever that would never now be realised.

Was all this a punishment for being some kind of heinous person in a previous life?

Would she be feeling such heightened emotions for

the man who'd broken her heart if she'd had previous experience of men? Would she be lying with her face buried in a pillow stifling screams if she'd already known another man's touch?

She couldn't kid herself that she wouldn't have fallen in lust with Enzo even if there had been men before him, but would she have been suckered in so completely? Would she be going through such agony now?

If only she'd found someone she felt strongly enough for to take the plunge and sleep with before her parents died then maybe she would have been better armed to spot the lie of his feelings and intentions from the beginning, but it had never happened. Her experience with men before Enzo had been practically nil. His good humour, charm, glamour and looks had dazzled her. Blinded her.

But she *had* continually asked questions, she argued with herself, angrily thumping the pillow for emphasis. Right from the start. Asked herself why a man like Enzo could fall for an ordinary woman like her.

She'd never questioned her own feelings though. Those she'd accepted from the beginning. She'd *welcomed* them, revelled in them because for the first time in so, so long, she was experiencing an emotion that wasn't grief.

Rebecca's natural shyness meant she'd always been most comfortable blended in a pack, the girls she hung around with her entire school life a middling gang who stuck together and went mostly unnoticed by their peers. When she got to university, she'd made new friends in her halls of residence. Unlike her old sedate school friends, these girls were wild—in comparison in any case—and dragged her out partying. She'd enjoyed it enormously but had been shocked with the ease some of her fellow students were happy to swap bodily fluids with people whose names they'd struggled to remember in the morning. She hadn't wanted her first sexual experience to be a drunken one-night stand. She'd wanted it to mean something. By her third year, her wild peers began to settle as the reality of the approaching big wide world loomed in their minds and made them knuckle down and actually do some work, but any hope Rebecca had of finding someone was forgotten when her mother's constant exhaustion was finally diagnosed as blood cancer. Two weeks later she was dead. Three days later, her shattered father suffered his fatal heart attack. In hardly the time it took to blink, Rebecca's world fell apart and she was plunged into a grief so complete it took her a full year to resume her studies.

The shell she'd hidden herself in had coated her until that cold, grey winter afternoon when Enzo had changed the tyre she now knew he'd punctured himself and bathed her world in colour.

He'd pulled her out of the fog of grief, brought her back to life and turned on the tap of her desire. But it had all been a lie and now she would never know what it felt like to give herself fully to a man and this awful fever would never be purged…

She pulled her face out of the pillow and shot upright, her heart thumping wildly.

This was all Enzo's fault. Everything. All those

damn promises about their wedding night. He'd built this fever up in her.

Before she could change her mind, she scrambled off the bed and stormed out of the room, the fury driving her to Enzo's bedroom as alive in her veins as the desire.

Knocking loudly on his door, she didn't wait for an answer before shoving it open.

The curtains were open, the silvery light from the moon and stars pouring through the three windows enough for her to see. At the far end, in what she was convinced was the biggest bed in the world but one she'd been forbidden from sleeping in until they were legally husband and wife, Enzo lifted his head.

'Rebecca?' There was no sleepiness in his voice.

'Miss Foley to you,' she corrected angrily, kicking the door shut with her heel and crossing the vast floor space to him.

'What's wrong?' he asked, sitting up. The bed sheets slipped down to his waist revealing his bare chest.

The pulse between her legs throbbed with the same rage as the fury in her veins. All these months she'd fantasised about the moment she saw him undressed for the first time and the muscularity of his chest and the light smattering of dark hair covering it was so much more than her imagination had conjured. It only fuelled her anger; that she should be seeing it now, like this and not in the dreamlike state she'd so anticipated. That the power he held over her was stronger than it had ever been increased it to fever pitch.

It was time to claim that power for her own. She had

let Enzo dictate everything for long enough. No more. Never again.

'I want the wedding night you promised me.'

He stared at her for a long moment before breathing deeply, leaning back against the headboard and closing his eyes.

'Don't close your eyes to me,' she snarled.

Jaw clenched, he fixed them on her face. 'You shouldn't be here.'

Ignoring him, she pulled at the straps of her bridal negligée. 'I bought this for you. For our wedding night. You were supposed to strip it off me with your teeth.'

His breathing became erratic. The throat she'd adored nuzzling moved convulsively. 'Go back to your room, Miss Foley.'

'I thought you wanted me,' she flared, climbing onto the bed. 'Or was that just another lie after all?'

He shook his head with ragged movements.

'Do you want me or not?' she demanded, straddling his lap. 'Is your desire for me a truth or a lie?'

His voice was thick. Pained. 'You know it's the truth.'

'Do I?' Grabbing the hem of her negligée, she whipped it over her head and threw it to one side. Something dark and angry had taken possession of her and she was glad of it, welcomed the fury firing through her veins. 'Then prove it.'

She would never have a wedding night. Not now. When Rebecca left this villa, that would be it for her. There was not a chance in hell that she would let another man get close enough to lay a finger on her.

Even if she ever felt she could risk it, she knew in

her heart it would be pointless. No man could make her feel an ounce of what Enzo made her feel, and she *hated* him for it. Hated that he'd destroyed any chance of her forging a truly loving relationship.

He'd ruined her. For everyone but himself.

Enzo's eyes had darkened, his face taut, chest rising sharply. Not taking her eyes from his, she rested her hands on his naked chest for the first time and rubbed her fingers over the dark hair lightly covering it.

He sucked in a breath and shuddered. Somehow his eyes darkened further. Became hooded.

The pulse between her legs was throbbing stronger than ever, mingling with the sickness for him and her furious desire.

Suddenly he straightened from his recline against the headboard, hooking an arm around her back to stop her from losing her balance. His other hand cradled the back of her head.

'Who are you punishing here?' he asked in a thick undertone, long fingers spearing her hair, his face so close their lips were only a feather away from touching. 'You or me?'

The tips of her breasts brushed against his chest. The sensation was almost more than she could bear.

She cupped his cheeks and deliberately dug the pads of her fingers into the stubbly skin. 'Both of us,' she whispered harshly.

The grip on her hair tightened. The brown eyes boring into hers with such intensity were molten swirls. And then he groaned. In the breath of a moment, his lips fused to hers in a kiss so hard and passionate the pain of it was almost as acute as the pleasure.

Rebecca melted into it. Parting her lips in time with his, she dragged her fingers to the back of his head and clasped it as tightly as he clasped hers, the lock of their mouths deepening furiously, tongues plundering, teeth clashing.

She could have screamed her relief. This was what she wanted. What she needed. The hedonistic pleasure of Enzo's touch driving out the pain and obliterating her thoughts. She didn't want to think. For this one night, she just wanted to lose herself in Enzo.

Whatever was infecting her was clearly contagious.

Her breasts crushed against his chest, a strong hand swept feverishly over her naked back, over her shoulders, exploring her contours, dragging down her spine to the curve of her bottom and then sweeping back up again. The silk bed sheets were still across his lap, beneath it the full strength of his arousal hard against her mound, and it filled her with a burning heat to know that soon, finally, the wanton hunger so alive in her veins for him would be sated.

Breaking the lock of their mouths, he gazed at her. '*Mio Dio*, you're beautiful,' he muttered hoarsely before smothering her in another deeply passionate kiss that she felt all the way to the tips of her fingers and toes.

He'd been holding back she realised dimly when he wrenched his mouth from hers and pulled her head back, exposing her throat for him to devour. The fever she'd tasted in his kisses all those times before and the desire in his eyes had been mere shadows of what he was giving her now.

A hand slid beneath her bottom and raised her onto her knees before resting on the base of her spine, holding her steady as his lips and tongue caressed down to her breasts. The sensation that shot through her when he took one whole in his mouth made her cry out and wrap her arms around his neck. Pressing her mouth into the top of his head, she moaned at the intensity of it all. When the sensuous assault continued with her other breast, she barely noticed Enzo rip away the barrier of the sheets and lean her back until she was laid on the bed.

Only when he abandoned her breasts to taste and explore the rest of her body did Rebecca learn how acute pleasure could really be, how it could arouse every cell until she became nothing but a receptacle writhing at an intimacy she'd spent months anticipating but which her imagination had utterly failed to do justice to. Frustrated desire had led her to explore her body alone many times since Enzo had come into her life but those briefly satisfying solo manipulations had in no way prepared her for the headiness of Enzo's face buried between her legs, his hands holding her waist tightly whilst he groaned in pleasure.

Any control she had over her own responses was lost when the thickening sensation building deep in her pelvis reached its pinnacle and exploded before she even realised it was going to happen. With a loud cry, her legs jerked involuntarily and her back arched as spasms of ecstasy ripped through her so powerful and consuming that only Enzo's hands gripping her waist stopped her from flying to the ceiling.

Slowly, the sensations lessened, all except the mad thrumming of her heart, and she became hazily aware of Enzo's mouth and tongue snaking their way back up her belly. She shivered as he licked her throat and then he was covering her entirely, his weighty erection jutting against the cradle of her thighs.

Opening her eyes, she gazed into his hooded stare and was hit by a tsunami of emotions.

The look in his eyes was everything she'd dreamed of seeing on her wedding night. Everything she was feeling, everything she was experiencing...

'I hate you,' she whispered raggedly when she was capable of drawing a breath.

His jaw clenched. 'I know.'

And then he kissed her with a savagery that stole her remaining breath.

Arms wrapped around his neck, she returned the kiss with equal fervour, all the love and all the hate she felt for him spilling out in an infusion of desire that pulsed deeply and was laced with an anticipation that made her heart beat even faster and harder.

This was it. The moment she'd spent so many long, lonely nights dreaming of.

He lifted his head.

The tips of their noses touching, his breathing uneven, he placed a hand on her thigh and gently spread it, then slid a hand beneath her bottom to raise it. All the while, the weight of his erection teased against her opening sending delicious, anticipatory heat flooding through her core.

Her whole body trembled.

She would swear his body trembled too.

He pressed his cheek against hers and then the thick, solid weight of his arousal slid into the place she ached the most for him to be, and her body opened like a flower.

With infinite care and tenderness, Enzo slowly, slowly filled her.

Rebecca's eyes were screwed shut. She was hardly breathing. Any pain was cocooned by the sensations flooding her. When their groins finally met, he placed his mouth to her cheek then brushed it over to her lips and kissed her with the same tenderness he'd taken possession of her.

'Hold on to me,' he murmured.

Closing her eyes even tighter, she tightened her hold around his neck and pressed her thighs closer against his.

Her heart raced so hard now it could be a humming-bird's wing.

With his hand still holding her bottom, he pulled out of her slowly, just a few inches, then drove slowly back to fuse their groins. And then he did it again, this time withdrawing a little further. When he drove back this time, the sensation made her gasp and her eyes fly open.

It was the concentration on his face that made her racing heart melt. He was holding back. Holding back because he didn't want to hurt her, and as she realised this, her lips found his and she wrapped her legs around him, suddenly needing them to be as close as it was humanly possible for two humans to be.

'Make love to me,' she whispered before clasping his head and deepening the kiss.

'*Mi amore,*' he groaned thickly into her mouth, his grip on her bottom tightening.

As the tempo of his lovemaking steadily increased, Rebecca was transported to a world of Enzo-induced bliss. Mouths locked together, she dragged her hands over his back, revelling in the smoothness of his hot skin, searching the contours and the bunching muscles, needing to touch him with a desperation she would never have believed possible, and all the while the pulses in her pelvis thickened as they'd done earlier, but this time with a completeness she hadn't even known had been missing, spreading through her burning veins, seeping down into her bones and up into her skin, drowning her in a sensation that crested to a peak and sent waves of the deepest, purest pleasure rippling through every part of her.

Arching her neck, she clung to him, crying out her ecstasy at the same moment Enzo called out her name and thrust into her so deeply and so completely that for one long, glorious moment, it felt like they were one and the same.

# CHAPTER EIGHT

WHEN THE RIPPLES of her climax subsided enough for Rebecca's head to clear, she squeezed her eyes shut and wished she could switch her brain off. Wished she could switch her senses off and not be inhaling Enzo's warm skin or have the taste of it pressed against her lips or have his slowly steadying breaths in her hair or feel the heavy thumps of his heart against her own. Wished she could bring herself to push him off her and stalk out of his room with the same brazen fury with which she'd entered it.

But the passionate fury that had driven her to his bed had evaporated and now she was left with the consequences of allowing the sickness that had infected her to override any sense she had.

She should have been less inhibited and joined in with the body fluid swapping her party-loving university friends had indulged in. She might have struggled to remember the names of the faces she woke beside but at least she wouldn't be holding on for dear life to stop hot tears from spilling at the monumental mistake she'd just made.

What she'd just experienced was more than in her wildest fantasies; not the things they'd done but the intensity of the feelings evoked in her. And, she suspected with a choked heart, evoked in Enzo.

But not the same ones. Whatever alchemy they'd just shared, for him it had been nothing but a chemical rush. When Rebecca left this villa, he would feel her absence only fleetingly. To miss someone, truly miss them, they had to have touched your soul. Enzo would not miss her. For him, this passion between them was nothing but a side effect of the game he'd been playing all these months.

The game had been played without Rebecca's knowledge, but it had been everything to her. He'd been everything to her.

He still was, and she had to swallow hard to stem the tears as the impossibility of her love punched through her with the strength of a heavyweight's blow.

Making love with him hadn't purged her of anything. It had made everything worse, and now she had to double the strength needed to walk away as the emotions raging in her choked heart felt fit to burst. Because only now did it hit her, fully hit her, that it wasn't just the tools to mend her shattered heart she needed to find but the tools to navigate her life without him.

The only positive she could find to cling to was that her insanity wouldn't result in a pregnancy, but even that positive lasted only a flicker as it set off another pang of loss. Rebecca had gone on the pill a few months ago. They'd both agreed the first year of their marriage would be just for the two of them and then they'd start trying for a baby.

There would be no baby now. Not for them. Never for her. Not now.

Enzo slowly turned his face and kissed the top of her ear. 'Say something,' he murmured.

Unable to speak, she pressed her mouth even tighter into his neck and shook her head.

Carefully, he shifted his weight off her, rolling onto his back, taking her with him so she was cuddled onto him, her cheek on his upper chest, his chin resting on the top of her head.

One arm tight around her, he caught her hand and threaded their fingers together. 'Did I hurt you?'

She couldn't stop herself from squeezing his fingers. 'No.' Her voice was barely audible.

There had been no pain. Only bliss. Any pain in the aftermath was entirely her own fault.

He pressed his mouth into the top of her head and kept it there.

She wished he could keep it there for ever.

So many wishes. None of which could come true.

The silence stretched until he quietly said, 'Tell me what you're thinking.'

Her answer came without any thought. 'That my parents' marriage gave me completely unrealistic expectations.'

'What makes you think that?'

Rebecca laughed morosely and finally made herself move, slipping her hand out of his hold and using his chest as a lever to sit herself up. Somehow they'd managed to end up on the other side of the bed to the pillows. She was certain there was a kind of symbolism in this but was too heartsick to think what it could be.

The silk bedsheets were all unravelled and she

pulled at them to cover herself, holding them across her breasts and shuffling so her back was to the pillows.

Now facing him, she met Enzo's stare and the longing that ripped through her to throw herself back on him and be held tightly to him, skin on skin, had her gripping the sheets with all her strength. 'Their marriage was happy.'

He hooked an arm behind his head as a prop, his magnificent, naked body stretching with the motion. It had been barely a minute since she'd moved away from him but already she felt bereft without the comfort of his touch, and, as hard as she tried, she couldn't stop herself from gazing at him.

'Is happiness in a marriage unrealistic?' he asked.

Less than a day ago she would have said no. What she'd felt in her heart and believed Enzo felt in his heart had convinced her a lifetime of happiness was theirs for the taking.

'The level of happiness they shared is.' She'd been a fool to think she could have it too. 'They were just so wrapped up in each other. Sometimes I felt like a third wheel.' Not sure where this admission had come from, she leaned forwards and gripped her calves. 'Did my grandfather tell you he tried to pay my dad off?'

'Yes.'

That made her eyebrows rise. Who would actually admit doing something like that? 'Was he ashamed of that?'

'No. He never stopped believing your father was bad for your mother.'

Anger flared at the grandfather she'd never met but

whom Enzo had known well enough for Ray Claflin to confide the most personal information to. Known and trusted.

'He was only bad for her if you don't believe women have free will,' she said with an attempt at tartness. 'Mum quit university because she couldn't bear to be parted from him. That was her choice but he blamed my father for it and he'd never even met him. He *refused* to meet him. He didn't know my father. He had no right to make that kind of judgement.'

'He came to accept that his attempts to drive them apart backfired and pushed them closer together.'

'I think that's pretty arrogant of him. If he'd given my father a chance instead of judging him as unworthy because he left school at sixteen and worked as a mechanic then he'd have seen my father adored my mum and would have done anything for her.'

Enzo didn't say anything, just looked at her, and another flare of anger burned to know he was remembering how she'd mentioned that her first visit to Florence to see him had been only her second trip abroad, the first being a school trip to France her parents had scrimped and saved to pay for. It always made her feel wretched to know they'd been so close to doing all the things they'd never been able to afford before. Their mortgage had nearly been paid off, Rebecca close to finishing her degree and becoming financially independent... They'd barely hit middle age. They'd assumed they had multiple decades left to explore the world.

'They might have struggled financially but I never

went without and I always had emotional security. I never had a single fear that they would divorce. They were devoted to each other and just so affectionate… always having to touch each other. It was like they needed reassurance the other was there.'

She closed her eyes. Hadn't that been one of the things she'd so adored about Enzo? His need to touch her? It had been as strong as her need to touch him. Had been one of the many things that had convinced her their marriage would be as strong and as happy as her parents' had been. And hadn't she quit her job to be with him just as her mum had quit her degree? All her life, she'd had a romantic, idealised vision of her parents' marriage…

'*Cara?*'

She blinked back into focus and looked at him. The concern in his stare made her heart clench. Looking away, she put her focus on her toes, painted a deep cherry red to match her nails. She'd never been one for bold colours before but there was something about being with Enzo that had made her feel bold. Seen…

'My expectations for our marriage were entirely unrealistic,' she whispered. 'All along I knew there was no way a man like you would look at a woman like me but you were so convincing. And then there was the fable I grew up with of my parents; of the rich girl from the right side of town falling for the poor boy on the wrong side of town, and it all worked in my mind to convince me that you and I were meant to be, but all along, what I was looking for was *their* marriage, to be the most important person in someone's life, to not…'

To not what? Rebecca hadn't meant to say any of that. Not consciously. The words had fallen off her tongue as she'd been thinking them, but now she'd hit a block and there was a heavy pulse beating in her brain. *To not what...?*

'To not be the one left behind?' he supplied quietly when her unspoken words remained unformed and unsaid.

Her heart punched her ribs and, completely thrown, her gaze shot back to him. 'Why would you say that?'

He sat up. His clear brown eyes shrewd, the outer part of his thigh pressed against hers, he took hold of her hand. 'Why did you feel like a third wheel?'

Rebecca had always thrilled at the muscularity of Enzo's masculine physique compared to the slender femininity of hers. With the moonlight pouring on them, she noticed properly for the first time the paleness of her skin set against his olive tone. A day ago, she would have marvelled at the contrast, *delighted* in it. Now, for reasons she could never begin to understand, it opened another fissure in her heart. 'It was just a saying.'

'You would not have said it if it didn't mean something. Did you feel that you were in the way?'

Cheeks burning, she shook her head vehemently. 'No. They loved me. I never doubted that.'

'But not as much as they loved each other?'

Her heart gave another punch, and she snatched her hand away. 'What a cruel thing to say.'

There was compassion laced in the steel of his stare. '*Cara*, I am trying to understand—'

'There is nothing to...' *understand,* she meant to

add, but something like panic had thickened her throat too much for any more words to form.

'There is everything to understand,' he said, perfectly reading the train of thought she barely understood herself. Leaning his face into hers, close enough that Rebecca could see the flecks of gold swirling in the pupils, he pitched his tone low but with the same formidability as in his stare. 'If you could see into my heart and head, you would know the insecurities that made you question why a man like me would want a woman like you were without foundation—'

He'd said exactly the right thing to make her fight the panic. With a bark of ironic laughter, she interrupted him. 'Enzo, have you forgotten that I know exactly why a man like you wanted a woman like me? You set everything up between us so you could get your greedy mitts on my grandfather's business shares.'

'That only accounts for how things started, and if I hadn't been so afraid of losing you I would have told you the truth a long time ago.' He put a finger to her lips to stop her interrupting him again. The flecks of gold had turned into flames. 'I *know* it is over for us. I know that in a matter of hours you are going to leave my life for good and that nothing I say will stop that. I will not go against my word and tell you how that makes me feel but if you didn't have the insecurities that made you feel you're not good enough for me, I wouldn't need to tell you. You would already know. You would still have left me at the altar and wanted to punish me but you would never have doubted *me*. Those insecurities came from somewhere.'

She snatched the finger pressed at her lips, but instead of shoving it aside, squeezed it. 'Nice try. If I was writing a school report, I would say you were imaginative but given to flights of fancy.'

His eyes narrowed. For a long moment he stared at her with the stillness of a statue.

With a cauldron of emotions bubbling and swirling so violently inside her, it took everything Rebecca had to maintain eye contact and keep her own features poker straight.

And then he gave a disbelieving smile and shook his head slightly. 'If you think I said that in the hope of changing your mind then you have just made my point for me. You, *cara*, are worth more to me than anything. I'd give you my own damn shares to make you believe that.'

Almost giddy with relief at the change of direction and being back on familiar territory, she smiled. If he wanted to play the game some more then fine. Better than him trying to dissect *her*. 'Go on then.'

His right eyebrow shot up. 'You want the whole business?'

'Not particularly. I wouldn't know what to do with it, but you're welcome to give it all to me and see if that makes me believe you magically developed feelings for me beyond lust.' This was better. Now she felt in control of herself. The pulse in her brain had quietened to a low beat, the panic lessened to a thrum.

A gleam came into his eyes, lighting his whole face with a lascivious magnetism that sent liquid pooling deep in her pelvis where the aftereffects of their love-making still gently buzzed.

Dropping his voice and leaning his face even closer to hers, he murmured sensuously, 'Ah, so you believe now that I wasn't faking my desire for you?'

The liquid contracted into a throb. Loosening her hold on his finger to spear their hands together, she had to swallow the moisture that had suddenly filled her mouth to speak. 'You proved that very well, thank you, and if you want to prove all the things you spouted about how your feelings and stuff were true by giving me all of Claflin Diamonds then feel free. Maybe I'll turn into a business mogul…or maybe I'll give the whole thing to the dog charity I mentioned earlier.'

The fingers threaded through hers tightened, the gleam in his eyes deepening. 'Marry me and I'll sign all of my business interests over to you and you can do your worst with the lot of it.'

Thick thrills of desire racing through her blood, Rebecca inched her face even closer. 'Throw in the New York apartment and the jet, and I'll think about it.'

His face tilted, his gaze drifting to her mouth. 'You can have it all. Everything.'

Arousal had built so thoroughly in her that she could hardly speak. 'Either you're desperate for those shares or you really do think I'm an idiot.'

'No, *cara*, just desperate to keep you in my life.' His lips caressed hers.

She was completely unable to stop a moan escaping. Staring into his eyes was like gazing into a dark pool of lust and she knew he was seeing the same from her own stare. Her words when they came were a breathless whisper. 'Think I'm going to have to add to your school report, "Enzo tries too hard."'

He pulled her hand down to his abdomen where his arousal stood to attention. '*This* is the only thing that's too hard.'

Her eyes widened and she instinctively wrapped her fingers around the long, thick velvet. Fresh moisture filled her mouth as it throbbed and strained at her touch.

He shuddered and clasped her hip. 'This is what you do to me,' he said hoarsely. 'You can't deny this. This is all you.' And then he parted her lips with his tongue and delved deep into her mouth.

There was no more conversation.

When Rebecca awoke, the room was still in darkness. Beside her, face turned to hers, his hand heavy on her stomach, lay Enzo. From the heaviness of his breathing, he was deep in sleep. Her own sleep had been brief, a snatch of slumber brought about by her body's exhaustion but which turned out to be no match for her overloaded brain. She didn't need to look at her watch to know she'd had no more than an hour of oblivion.

She tried to take her own heavy breath to stop the prickling of tears releasing but the compression in her chest was too much. She needed air. Needed to escape this bed before the thoughts in her head and the emotions churning in her took control again.

Still trying desperately to breathe, she crept out of bed, pulled her discarded negligée over her head and quietly left the room. In the corridor she wiped the tears away and put her hand to her thrashing heart, and managed to drag a tiny amount of air into her tight airways before staggering to the room she should have slept in.

The bed she would have slept in if she hadn't allowed her emotions to take control was still rumpled from where she'd thrown herself on it in a fit of frustrated pique. Her suitcase was still open, half the contents spilled messily around it.

Rubbing at another leaking tear, she pulled her robe out of the suitcase and slipped it on, tightening it around skin still tender and alive from Enzo's passionate lovemaking. Just to think about that made her legs weaken.

God help her, it had been the best night of her life.

And the worst.

Self-recriminations were pointless. She'd known what she was doing, going to his bed.

But she'd never dreamed how good it would be. Not that *good* carried a fraction of the meaning of what it had been like. The dizzying heights he'd taken her to, again and again. The sheer exhilarating headiness of it all. If she could switch her heart off she'd be tempted to move all her stuff to his room right now, straddle him awake and demand he be her sex slave for as long as it took to slake the passion between them. Just to imagine his response to this demand made her core throb with an arousal she could hardly believe hadn't been spent through the hours they'd passed with their limbs wrapped around each other.

But her heart could not be switched off. Each kiss,

each caress, each climax, it had all pushed her further over the line of being hopelessly in love, and it was a love that would never be reciprocated. It couldn't be. Not from him.

All these thoughts were pointless. She needed to pull herself together and stop wishing for things that could never be.

Padding quietly down to the kitchen, she didn't even consider pressing an intercom to wake the duty member of staff to fix a drink for her. Turning the switch by the door, she blinked away the effect of the bright lights assaulting her unadjusted eyes and headed straight to the cupboard that contained the coffee. She pressed the cupboard door open and her heart jumped.

Blinking again, she reached for the rectangular box neatly placed next to the large bag of coffee beans. It was no trick of the light, and in an instant she was transported back to the very beginning when she'd accompanied the gorgeous Italian who'd selflessly changed her flat tyre into the hotel. She'd been giddy at the thought of spending an hour in his company; a spring in her step and a zest in her veins she'd never felt before. It was when Enzo had steered her past the bar to a table that she'd spotted the clear jars filled with the distinctive triangular teabags of her favourite brand in a neat row beside the barista machine. Her thoughts of having a hot chocolate had been immediately abandoned. At least five times the price of her usual tea, this was the brand she treated herself to a packet of each year for her birthday, something she had a dim recollection of telling Enzo when they gave their order.

She'd been utterly thrilled to see it on the bar's shelf, and as she'd sat there sipping it, eyes glued to Enzo's face, she had wondered if her day could get any better.

He'd remembered, she realised, her head swimming. He must have done. She'd never even mentioned tea since that day—well, who in their right mind discussed *tea*?—but she knew it hadn't been in the cupboard three days ago, the last time she'd fixed herself a drink here.

Enzo had bought it for her as a birthday surprise.

# CHAPTER NINE

STILL DAZED AT the teabag find, Rebecca carried her mug up to the roof terrace, a sprawling area with a swimming pool and seating dotted around its perimeter. The last time she'd come up here it had been in the dead of night with Enzo, when romantic solar-powered lights had guided their way. That early morning, a glimmer of orange lined the horizon. The sun was waking up.

Inhaling the sweetly scented air of the climbing flowers around the perimeter wall, she peered out of the section that overlooked the front of Enzo's grounds. Looking hard, she could make out the shadows of the reporters still camped on the other side of the electric gate and her heart sank. Barely half a day ago she'd been fully prepared to give them all the ammunition they needed to destroy Enzo. But that was before. Before she'd found paradise in his arms.

She could no more destroy him than she could kick a puppy.

To stay though, would be to destroy herself.

Enzo's villa was located on the top of a hill with some of the best views money could buy. Curled up on a white sofa on the other side of the terrace, she watched the sun rise over a sleeping Florence.

The morning after he'd proposed, Enzo had woken her early and insisted she join him in this exact spot to enjoy this exact view. He'd watched her reaction, his dimples prominent.

He'd wanted to share it with her. He'd wanted her to love the sunrise as much as he did.

Suddenly unable to bear the memories the beautiful sunrise was evoking, Rebecca pulled her phone out of her robe pocket and, in desperate need of distraction, finally turned it on.

She'd guessed there would be numerous messages left on it but had massively underestimated. Messages from names she'd hardly thought of in years were interspersed with family, friends and recent colleagues. All the messages were a variant of the same theme.

What's happened?

Are you okay?

Please let me know you're okay.

Call me.

Let me know you're safe.

Taking a deep breath first, she got busy replying, prioritising her aunt and cousins.

I'm fine, I promise. Will explain everything when I see you.

Would she really? Could she really do that? Explain that the great love of her life and the romantic story it had been based upon had all been a lie? Put Enzo at risk of someone sensing a way to make themselves some money and tip a reporter off?

She almost laughed. She was worried about putting him at risk? Seriously, someone needed to give her a martyr's badge or something. She wasn't going to lie for him. He'd made his bed. He didn't need her protection. Besides, he could afford some swanky lawyers to suppress any rumours, she was sure. That's what rich people did when it came to stopping the exposure of stories with narratives they didn't like, wasn't it?

But there was nothing he could do to stop them reporting Rebecca's jilting of him at the altar, and before she could talk herself out of it, she keyed in the name of the UK's biggest selling tabloid.

Its homepage filled her screen. *Jewellery Magnate Jilted!* screamed the headline. Two photos lay beneath it. One was a distant, blurry image of Rebecca climbing onto the back of her saviour's Vespa. The other was a close-up of Enzo on the cathedral steps, his gaze fixed into the distance. Searching. Searching for *her*. His handsome features—and, God, didn't the camera just adore him—were tight, giving nothing away. But his eyes… They were wild. If she looked closely enough she could imagine she saw distress in them.

Unable to endure the image a second longer, Rebecca swiped the page away and sucked in a huge gulp of air.

What had she done?

Hold on a minute, what had *she* done? Was she really

that desperate for a martyr's badge that she'd forgotten this was all on Enzo? If he'd told her the truth about her grandfather's will from the beginning then none of this would have happened and she'd never have gone to the cathedral in such an emotional state. And if she accepted that he'd been too angry at her grandfather's trick to want to discuss it with her—and he was right in that he hadn't known her back then—then why hadn't he paid his swanky lawyers to talk to her? Wasn't that what lawyers were paid to do? Overcome obstacles? But it had been the will itself that was the biggest obstacle so why not try to overturn it? His excuses on this score were only plausible when you weren't talking about a multibillionaire. Enzo could afford the finest legal team money could buy. She would have been no match for him.

Movement behind her cut her thoughts off in their tracks.

Twisting her head, her insides contracted as Enzo's messy dark brown hair appeared at the top of the stairs. The rest of him appeared in stages until he was stalking the terrace towards her wearing nothing but a pair of black swim shorts.

All the mornings they'd spent together and this was the first time she'd seen him not fully clothed. The first and the last.

Rebecca swallowed and smiled a greeting at the man she knew it would take every ounce of her strength to walk away from.

He gazed at her, nostrils pulling in at the deepness of his breath. And then his dimples flashed. 'Enjoying the view, Miss Foley?'

She let her gaze drift down to his chest, her heart swelling, pulses stirring. 'Very much.'

Eyes glittering, he sat himself on the chair beside hers, stretched his long legs out and looked out at the colourful city of his birth under the cloudless sky. 'All your grandfather's liquid assets have been transferred to you. The house is yours. The shares will be yours within hours. When the banks open tomorrow you will be rich enough to buy yourself a view anywhere you want.'

The anger that usually flared at the mention of the shares refused to rise. Whether it was the realisation that this, here, now, was the beginning of the end for them or because she could still see the tabloid head-line and feel the tendrils of guilt at the scandal that had erupted about them, or because of the buzz in her veins to be sat next to a semi-naked Enzo; whatever the rea-son, the tempest in her chest had receded.

She didn't want to argue any more.

Rebecca lifted her face to the lightening sky and tried not to wish that this was the sky she woke to for the rest of her life. 'I'm not keeping any of it. Don't ask about the shares—I need time to think about what I'll do with them and I can't think straight when I'm sit-ting next to you, but I know I won't keep the rest of it.'

The Claflin Diamond shares were a quandary to be resolved when she was alone but whatever she did with them, she knew now that she would never use them as a weapon against Enzo. Even if he did deserve it.

He was quiet for a long time. 'I understand why you would want to reject it but do not make any hasty de-cisions.'

'He never told my mum my grandmother died. Did you know that? She only learned her own mother had died by chance—a friend of hers read the obituary. Can you imagine what that did to her?' Broke her mother's heart is what it did to her. 'How can I keep the money when it comes from someone who caused such pain?'

There was another long pause of silence. 'All I will say is that you're feeling raw. Do not make the same mistake as me and let betrayal and grief take you in a direction you come to regret. I know you found my world overwhelming at times but I also witnessed your happiness at seeing new countries and in all the new experiences we shared. Do you really want to go back to a world limited by suburbia?'

'It wasn't limited,' she disagreed.

'That is not what I observed from your reactions to my world. *Cara*, your parents felt it too. They had plans to travel. You told me. They were waiting for you to finish your degree and to pay off their mortgage.'

'Travelling was their dream, not mine.'

'That money will free you,' he told her bluntly.

'I already live mortgage-free.' The rent Rebecca currently received for her house would pay for her to rent somewhere until the tenancy ran out and she could move back in.

Such sad irony though, that her parents had to die to be free of all their debts, their insurance paying the remainder of their mortgage off, and as she thought this, she realised that, as when they'd talked about the shares, yesterday's pain had receded. She had a strong suspicion it wouldn't last but for now it was bearable. She would take that.

In the distance, breaking the early morning silence, a horn tooted. The sound reminded her of the way her Vespa boy saviour had tooted at pedestrians in lieu of running them over when she'd run from the cathedral.

She turned her face to Enzo and smiled. 'You stole a Vespa.'

His lips pulled into a grin. '*Sì*. I took the keys from the hand of a delivery boy.' He twisted in his chair and leaned into her to rub a finger over the rim of her ear. 'You have made a criminal of me.'

She arched a brow, shivering at the pleasure of his light tough. 'Made a criminal of you? Are we really going to go there?'

He shook his head and threaded his fingers through her hair. 'I have already made contact with him and transferred the value of the Vespa with extra for the inconvenience.' Something sparked in his stare and for a moment he gazed intently at her before his dimples reappeared. 'Shall we go for a ride?'

'A ride?' she echoed.

'The Vespa is now mine. Let's take it for a ride. Enjoy the morning before the sun gets too hot for your delicate English skin to cope with.'

His teasing made her mouth smile and her heart twist. There had always been so much teasing between them. In seven hours or so, there would be no more. They would never tease each other again.

'What about the press?'

His dimples deepened and he lowered his face to

whisper in her ear, hand slipping through the gap in her robe to grip her hip. 'There is a secret route off my land.'

His touch and breath on her skin provoked another, deeper shiver of pleasure, and Rebecca did the only thing that made sense and closed the small distance between them so her breasts were flush with his chest, and turned her face so their mouths brushed together. 'You've never mentioned it,' she murmured, arousal turning her veins to hot, thick treacle.

Teeth tugged gently at her bottom lip in complete contrast to the delicious pain of his fingers digging harder into her hips before splaying down to her bottom and diving beneath the silk negligée to clasp a bare buttock.

'That's because a car cannot travel it.' His voice was hoarse. Ragged. His other hand stole around to the small of her back then drifted lower to hold her other buttock. 'A Vespa can.'

One moment she was on her chair, the next lifted off it and straddling Enzo's lap. His erection jutted hard through his shorts. She writhed against him and groped for the button of his shorts.

How was it possible to still feel such dizzying *need* for him after the night they'd just shared and with hardly any sleep?

A moment later, his erection was freed. The moment after that Rebecca stopped thinking at all.

Florence was on the cusp of waking up when Rebecca and Enzo escaped the villa. Those of its people not enjoying a Sunday morning lie-in would be opening their eyes to another beautiful summer's day. Rebecca doubted that anyone would appreciate it in the way she was determined to.

Only seven a.m. With only one hour of sleep, she should be shattered but there was a glow to her skin and in her heart that overrode any exhaustion, and as they zipped through the lemon trees of Enzo's estate, her hands rested lightly on his hips and she lifted her face to the slowly rising sun, determined to make the most of these last six hours with him. It wasn't as if she could do any more harm to herself. She couldn't love him any more than she did. Leaving him couldn't hurt any more than it was going to do. The price to be paid would be the same if she spent the next six hours locked in a room away from him.

After a couple of minutes spent following the narrow trail, they reached a small gate in the perimeter wall. Enzo punched the code to open it and then they were riding on a dust track that soon connected to the main road the press was camped along. In moments, the press pack was far behind them, unaware their targets had evaded them.

The roads they travelled were mostly empty of traffic but the deeper they rode into the city, the more human life began to emerge, street cleaners sweeping away the night's litter, young parents with babies and toddlers in prams and strollers, dog walkers; all interspersed with the odd vampiric figure staggering back to their bed after a night of hard partying. Unlike the Vespa boys of the day before, Enzo rode at a sensible pace. Rebecca didn't doubt that if she hadn't been riding as his passenger, he'd be extracting every inch of speed he could out of it.

The scent of fresh coffee filled her nostrils and she wished she could remove the helmet and press her cheek into his back and close her eyes and fill her lungs with both Enzo's scent and the scent she would always associate with this beautiful city. Tempting though it was, he would go berserk if she removed it. They'd only the one helmet between them and he'd insisted she wear it, going as far as to put it on her himself and securing the strap. Oh, well, it wasn't as if he couldn't afford the fine that would be slapped on him if they got pulled over for Enzo's own failure to wear one.

After crossing the river, they entered a part of the city she'd never visited before. Soon they turned the corner near a vast piazza and entered a narrow street lined with all manner of grocery shops that, if it were not Sunday, would have cheeses, hams, fruits and vegetables displayed under the colourful awnings.

Enzo pulled over by—yippee!—an open coffee shop with outdoor seating. After parking the Vespa next to two others, he helped Rebecca dismount then, with a smile, unclipped her helmet and pulled it off her head. Immediately she fluffed her hair up, making him grin at this little display of vanity and ruffle her hair, which in turn made her slap his hand.

'Pack it in,' she scolded, straightening her buttoned olive-green dress which fell to just above her knees.

His eyes sparkled. 'Make me.'

She gave him her best schoolteacher face, making

his grin widen so much she could practically see all his straight white teeth.

He was still grinning once he'd taken his seat, his dimples flashing when a member of the waiting staff, eyes still puffy with sleep, came out to take their order. With a strange, almost manic energy fizzing inside her, Rebecca couldn't stop smiling either. She didn't think she'd ever felt the rays of the early morning sun so strongly before or experienced such awareness of her surroundings, as if all her senses had been injected with caffeine, making everything sharper, from the scent of Enzo's cologne to the smart khaki shorts and black T-shirt his beautiful body was wrapped in. The pigeons scavenging crumbs and the few people milling about were sharply in focus too, although she doubted any of them would think for a moment that the couple sitting al fresco at this ungodly time for a Sunday were at the top of the European press's most wanted list. And if they were recognised...well, they'd get back on the Vespa and Enzo would whisk them away.

Not until their breakfast had been brought out to them and the pastries demolished did Enzo put his phone down from reading a message he'd received, don his shades—the sun really was gaining strength and today promised to be a scorcher—nod at the five-storey faded yellow building that ran the length of the street on the other side of the road facing them, and idly say, 'That's where I lived with my father.'

Startled at this unexpected revelation, she tried to read his stare beneath the darkness of his shades before giving up and turning her attention to his early childhood home. 'Which apartment?'

'Directly opposite. Third floor above the pizzeria.'

She counted up to the Juliette balcony with potted plants showing between the rails.

'It was a greengrocer when I was a child,' he told her. 'The owner would give me an apple every morning when I walked to my grandparents'.'

The grandparents she'd never met.

'Which one was theirs?'

'First floor above the florist.' She found the balcony, one of many on the building with laundry drying on it. 'They had a communal garden I played in. It was only small but it had a slide and a swing that I would fight with the other children to play on.'

Rebecca closed her eyes and slowly filled her lungs, trying to hold on to the fizzing energy, trying to eradicate images of a small Enzo hurtling himself down a slide. Twenty-four hours ago she'd still been unaware that Enzo had spent the first six years of his life living with his father.

In a few short hours it would be exactly a day since his mother had thrown the grenade that had imploded her world. 'Why are you showing this to me?'

'Because I wanted you to see where I really come from before you leave. And because I owe it to my father. I should never have diminished his role in my life or the role my grandparents played in those early days. Another regret for me to live with.' He gave a quick, wry smile then sighed and looked back at his childhood home. 'I can still hear his voice and hear him telling me off for trying to climb onto the balcony railing and I can still smell the turpentine he used to clean his brushes, but his face disappeared a long time ago. I can spend an hour looking at a photograph trying to fix him back into my mind and then the next day he's gone again, and now I have to live with knowing I pushed him further away in my mind for my own ends. My grandparents too.' He grimaced. 'They asked many times to meet you before the wedding. I made all the excuses to them.'

'Couldn't risk them telling me the truth about your early years?'

'Yes.' This time she could see through the darkness of his shades to his eyes and the self-recrimination blazing from them. 'I saw little of them after I moved in with my mother but for the first six years of my life they were a huge fixture of my life. My grandmother collected me every day from school. She always cooked my favourite food for me—you think Sal makes a good *melanzane alla parmigiana* but no one makes it as good as her.'

It took a beat for Rebecca to realise he was talking about the aubergine and mozzarella dish he so loved.

'Like your family, my father and my grandparents struggled for money but I never went hungry or cold. What I remember most about the first six years of my life is being safe and happy.'

There was nothing Rebecca could say to this. As when discussing his mother's initial abandonment of him, everything Enzo was telling her was delivered matter-of-factly. Sympathy and platitudes were neither expected nor required.

He wouldn't want to hear it but it hurt her heart to think he'd only known safety and happiness for his first six years.

She had to respect that he could hold his hands out and admit to the wrongs he'd committed.

Finishing her cappuccino, she couldn't help but wonder how a man so clear-headed and principled—she could hardly believe she was thinking of Enzo and *principled* in the same sentence, but that's why she usually limited her caffeine intake—could go to the lengths Enzo had done. He didn't *need* Claflin Diamonds. With his fortune, he could have created a dozen brand-new fully staffed laboratories in every country on earth and still had change to spare.

Before she could find the question to probe, his lips quirked and he reached over and wiped her top lip.

'Cappuccino moustache,' he explained with a grin, then popped the finger used to wipe the froth away into his mouth.

Rebecca couldn't begin to explain why this one little gesture felt more intimate than all the things they'd done in bed together or why it made her chest ache so badly.

'Always the gentleman,' she said lightly.

'Always.' He held his hand out to her. 'Come, Miss Foley, I have one more place to show you.'

'Your mother's apartment when she first took you in?' she guessed.

He leaned across the table and kissed her. 'Didn't I say how smart you were?'

# CHAPTER TEN

TRAFFIC WAS DECIDEDLY heavier on the second leg of what had become a tour of Enzo's childhood, but still much lighter than during the working week and on Shopping Saturday. Although keeping to the safe speed he'd adopted on the first leg, Enzo nipped in and out of the traffic like a pro, and when he came to a stop outside an apartment building in a decidedly swankier district than the one he'd lived in until his father's death, this one screaming wealth in the same way his father's district had screamed family, the first thing Rebecca asked when he'd removed her helmet was, 'Have you had a Vespa before?'

His dimples popped and his teeth flashed. 'A Vespa was the first thing I bought when I turned eighteen.'

'You were a Vespa boy?'

'Much to my mother's disapproval.'

'Is that why you bought it?'

'Her disapproval was a plus but not the reason.'

'Girls?'

He tapped her nose and laughed. 'You really are *incredibly* smart, Miss Foley.' Then, taking her hand, he led her to the oak front door, which opened as if by magic without even being touched.

The interior was even swankier than the exterior, a pristine white and gold reception with a distinct trace of chlorine in the air, staffed by a severe-looking raven-haired woman who must have magicked the door open. She gave a familiar smile of greeting to Enzo before launching into a spiel of Italian that was delivered too fast for Rebecca to even attempt making sense of. Enzo conversed back at equal speed and then the next thing she knew, he was guiding her to an elevator.

'We're going to the apartment?' she asked, stepping inside it.

He pushed the button. 'My mother still owns it. I would have shown you inside my father's but he rented it and I didn't think the current tenants would be happy being woken on a Sunday morning by a stranger asking to show his...' He cut himself off mid-sentence as the doors closed, his features morphing into something she couldn't decipher before he shook his head and laughed harshly. 'Do you know, I don't have any idea how I am supposed to refer to you now.'

Rebecca's gaze fell to her bare wedding ring finger and, suddenly frightened at how much she missed the weight of her engagement ring on it and alarmed that she was letting Enzo hold her hand, unthreaded her fingers from his and hugged her arms around herself.

'It doesn't matter how you refer to me,' she said in a lighter tone than she could have hoped to manage. 'I'll be gone in four hours. I won't know.' Mercifully, she didn't have to see his expression at this statement for the elevator doors slid back open and she stepped into a small room that contained two doors.

Enzo pressed his thumb to the box beside the door on the left. The light on the box turned green and he opened the door.

Suddenly nervous, her feet refused to move across the threshold. 'She's not in, is she?'

'We wouldn't be here if she was,' he answered shortly.

'You've been in contact with her?' He must have been if he knew his mother's current whereabouts.

'Only to tell her to stay the hell out of my life.'

'Not planning to forgive her anytime soon?'

'I will never forgive her.'

'Never is a long time.'

His clear brown eyes suddenly swooped on hers. 'Can you ever forgive *me*?'

Her heart burst into a frantic canter. 'That's different.'

'Is it? Do you think I am kidding myself that these aren't the last hours I'll ever get to spend with you? My relationship with my mother is as beyond repair as my relationship with you is. I don't expect your forgiveness, *cara*. All I hope for is that you leave Florence knowing in your heart that what I did to you was never about you, and that it is something I will regret to my dying day. But I cannot forgive her. My mother betrayed me for vengeance and betrayed me in the worst possible way.'

She swallowed. 'Because she knew you'd be publicly humiliated?'

A contortion of emotions showed in his tightened features before he flashed a smile that didn't meet his eyes. 'Come, Miss Foley, let me give you the tour.'

It was the first time since she'd demanded honesty from him that he'd evaded answering a question. Some instinct warned her not to probe.

Taking a subtle deep breath, Rebecca followed him into the apartment then found herself blinking in reaction to the sudden brightness surrounding her.

'Has it changed much since you lived here?' she asked.

'Not much.' His voice had regained the lightness from earlier but she detected an edge behind it. 'The colour scheme is the same as it has always been.'

Colour scheme? Is that what he called it?

Silvana's apartment was essentially a condensed version of her villa. Everything was white, from the soft furnishings to the marble flooring to the frames of the few paintings hanging on the white walls. Even the paintings themselves were daubed in muted hues. The only real colour came from the sun filtering through the window. Enzo's villa had the same pristine quality to it but it also had an abundance of colour and warmth. Once Rebecca had got over her shock at its palatial size and quality, she'd felt comfortable enough in it to snuggle on any of the myriad of sofas with her feet tucked under her bottom.

She didn't imagine anyone would ever feel at ease enough to sit in this sterile place: she imagined visitors just hovered. She could not begin to imagine how a small boy used to running and playing coped with being plunged into a sterility a hospital would be proud of, and as images came to mind of Enzo as that small boy, she quickly shoved them away.

She didn't want to think about his childhood. She

didn't want another heartfelt conversation. Too many of his revelations had hurt her heart and all it served was to make her vulnerable when she needed to be strong in the face of what was shortly coming for her.

All she wanted now was to recapture the fizz and energy that had been alive in her veins and the light-hearted mood they'd shared since Enzo joined her on the roof terrace and, for these last few hours together, to forget the past, forget the future and live for a present she would never have again.

Grabbing his hand, she tugged at it and smiled brightly. 'Come on, you, give me the grand tour you promised me.'

It took a moment for his dimples to appear. 'Miss Foley, your wish is my command.'

She would not think about how he'd picked up on her need for lightness without her having to say anything. Or think that maybe he needed the lightness too.

With Enzo now playing the role of tour guide, Rebecca was led into a pure white kitchen that had to be a nightmarish magnet for sticky fingers, a dining room that no one in their right mind would dare drop so much as a crumb in and then the tidiest office in the entire world. So this was where Silvana had masterminded her criminal empire...

At the other end of the apartment were the bedrooms.

'The guest room,' Enzo announced, opening the first door to which Rebecca's only thought was, *God help any guest who suffered a nosebleed in the night...* before he opened the next door. 'Robina Hood's room.'

She snickered before poking her head into a much

larger room dominated by a white bed carved in the shape of swan, and then Enzo opened the last door with a flourish and Rebecca found her eyes adjusting to a space so dark he switched the light on so they could see properly.

The walls were painted a deep grey, the bedding on the king-sized bed a deep blue that matched the carpets and curtains, the wardrobes, desk and dresser black. She didn't have to ask to know he'd chosen the colour scheme and that part of it had been with annoying his mother in mind. Well-thumbed books, mostly biographies of sports stars, lined the shelves and on the wall to the left of the bed hung a faded poster of a scantily clad, pouting supermodel.

She turned to him and fixed him with her best unimpressed face.

He stalked over to her with an unapologetic shrug. 'I put that up when I was seventeen.'

'That's the kind of woman you go for?' She turned her back to him and looked again at the long-legged glossy beauty with eyes that purred seduction and experienced a sudden urge to tear it from the wall and rip it into tiny pieces.

'It was when I was a Vespa boy.'

How pathetic that she could feel jealousy towards an airbrushed woman on a teenage boy's poster. 'You must have been thrilled when you made it to the big time and could date those women.'

He slid his arms around her waist and pressed himself against her back. 'It was *very* thrilling, Miss Foley,' he murmured, resting his chin on the top of her head.

'Beautiful women like the ones I once fantasised about threw themselves at me. For a long time I thought I'd died and gone to heaven.'

'I'll bet.' She had no control over the tartness in her voice, but thrills of her own were zinging through her veins and she leaned back into his strength and closed her eyes to the poster her fingers still itched to destroy.

One of Enzo's hands splayed over her stomach and up her ribs to cup a breast that was much smaller than even the skinny supermodel's, the other flattening against her belly, holding her securely as he ground himself against her. His erection jammed hard into the small of her back. She raised herself onto her toes and pushed back against it with a moan that deepened when he squeezed her breast with just the right amount of pressure to send the zing she'd been trying so hard to find back into her veins, but deeper, needier…

'Yes, Miss Foley, I thought I'd found heaven.' He dipped his head and nipped at her ear. 'But when the thrill wears off and you find yourself sharing your breakfast with a beautiful woman you feel nothing for and who you know feels nothing for you, you quickly learn heaven is nothing but an illusion.'

The sensation of Enzo's lips and breath against her sensitive skin was so electrifying that when he twisted her so they no longer faced the poster but a full-length mirror, she hardly noticed until she opened her eyes and saw their reflection.

His chin resting again on the top of her head, he met her stare in the mirror's reflection and undid the top two buttons of her dress. 'I had no wish to peer inside their heads,' he whispered, undoing the next button and slipping his hand through the material's opening, then sliding it under the lace of her bra to cover her naked breast.

Hot, liquid desire shot through her, melting her core and turning her legs to jelly.

Mouth now hot in her hair, eyes still locked on hers, fingers still unbuttoning her in more ways than one, his voice thickened. 'They never distracted me from my work.' He gently pinched her puckered nipple and ground himself tighter against her. 'I never watched the time crawl to when I would next see them.'

Her dress entirely undone, he dragged his mouth against her cheek and dipped his fingers beneath the lace of her knickers. 'I never felt so mad with desire that I feared the touch of their bare skin would make me lose my mind.'

He slid a finger over her swollen nub, making her jolt at the depth of the pleasure, and she slammed her hand over his to keep it there and held on tightly to stop her jellied legs from collapsing.

And then she caught the dark gleam reflecting in his hungry eyes, the intensity of it making her thundering heart skip a beat…but there was barely time to acknowledge it for Enzo turned her around and then his hot, greedy mouth was plundering hers.

Rebecca's last real thought before she dissolved into sensation was that time was running out and that this would be the last time she would ever be in his arms. The last time she would ever feel like this…

In moments, her dress and underwear were puddles

on the floor, Enzo's clothes thrown with them, and they were in a naked tangle of limbs on the bed, devouring and writhing together like two starving people finding a meal in each other.

She would never know how kisses could be hard and furious and yet tender all at the same time, or how fingers could bite into flesh causing both pleasure and pain.

But that's what loving Enzo was, pleasure and pain, and the desperation thrumming so tightly with the hunger in her veins was the knowledge that soon the pleasure would be nothing but a memory. Enzo would be nothing but a memory. All this would be gone...

Holding his skull tightly, she kissed him even harder, as if the duelling of their tongues could stop the thoughts in her head, and when he wrenched his mouth away and moved down her body to pleasure her with his tongue, she screwed her eyes shut and did everything she could to banish her own consciousness.

Sensations were saturating her but no matter how hard she tried to close her mind and simply revel in the headiness of it all, the switch in her brain wouldn't turn off.

Reaching down to clasp the sides of his head, she tried to close her thighs to him. 'I need you inside of me,' she whispered urgently. Needed him inside her. Part of her.

He muttered something, Italian words she couldn't decipher, and then crawled back up her and kissed her hard enough to bruise her lips. She locked her arms around his neck and wrapped her thighs around him.

With a ragged groan, he drove deep inside her.

She cried out loudly at the glorious sensation and raised her bottom to deepen the penetration.

Scraping her fingers through his hair, their mouths fused back together…every part of them was fused…and Enzo was pounding into her, hard, frenzied, an urgent maniacal possession capturing them both, teeth and nails biting into flesh, pleasure and pain, pleasure and pain…

As desperately as Rebecca wished that she could make this last time last for ever, she could more easily hold back the tide than control the climax building inside of her, and then she was crying out again, clinging to him as waves of pleasure exploded, carrying her on an undulating crest she tried frantically to ride for as long as was humanly possible.

As if he'd been waiting for her release, Enzo's eyes opened and bore into hers, the flame from them touching her as deeply as the pleasure engulfing her before he gave a strangled groan and shudders vibrated through the whole of his body and he collapsed with his cheek tight against hers and the weight of his body covering her.

The crest she'd been riding rippled to the shore.

Neither of them moved so much as a muscle. Not for the longest time. Neither of them spoke. The only sound in the room was the matching unsteadiness of their breaths and the thrum of Rebecca's heartbeat pounding in her head. And a clock. Somewhere in this room, a clock was marking the passing seconds.

She could feel the staccato beat of Enzo's heart, she realised dimly. It was pressed against her own. Feel the last twitches of his orgasm inside her matching the last, dying spasms of her own. The dampness of his skin matched hers too.

Tears burned the back of her retinas. All she could hear now was the ticking clock, and as it grew louder in her ears, she thought how easy it would be to stay and have this completeness for the rest of her life.

But it wouldn't be for the rest of her life, would it? She would spend the time they had together always knowing the truth, always waiting for him to casually bring up the issue of the shares, always waiting for the day he'd had his fill of her and no longer cared what went on in her head.

Oh, God, did that mean she believed he actually cared what went on in her head now?

Was she losing her *mind*? How could she possibly find anything like happiness, never mind completeness, with a man she could never trust? And this completeness…it was just sex! Perfect, beautiful, loving, desperate sex.

She was losing her mind. She had to be.

Somehow the ticking of the clock grew even louder.

How much longer did they have now? Three hours? Two?

Unable to bear her tortured thoughts any longer, she swallowed a sob and groped for something to say to break this awful, stretching silence, words that wouldn't betray the tumult of emotions battering her. 'Is there a reason Robina kept your room like a time capsule?'

The silence stretched even longer before he finally answered. 'Not that I know of.' Shifting his weight off her, not by much, just enough so she could breathe more easily, he threaded his fingers through hers and brought her hand to his mouth, rubbing his lips over her knuckles.

Another sob tried to break free and she fought as hard as she'd ever fought in her life to keep it contained.

'Did she think you would move back in?' She remembered Enzo telling her he'd moved into the apartment above his first jewellery store the moment the lease for it became available when he was nineteen.

His nose nuzzled into her cheek. 'I have long given up trying to guess what goes through my mother's head.'

'Maybe she kept it like this in case you ever changed your mind.'

'Unlikely.'

'As a reminder then, of the son you'd been before you moved out and became a man.'

He lifted his head. Gaze tight on hers, his brow furrowed. 'Why are you trying to humanise her?'

'Because she's your mother and her being a vindictive Robina Hood doesn't change that.' A short burst of laughter at what she was saying flew from her lips. What did it matter to her if Enzo cut his mother from his life completely? They were as bad as each other, something she needed to reinforce in her mind with concrete. And her heart.

A whole day had now passed since she'd received Silvana's package and despite Rebecca's best efforts, Enzo had managed to re-humanise himself fully in her eyes. Now, with the desperation of their lovemaking still alive in her veins, she was in the most dreadful danger; in danger of forgiving what he'd done to her and forgetting what he was capable of.

'What pushed you over the edge and made you threaten her?' she asked, trying her hardest to fight the panic now clawing back at her. 'It's not a very Italian thing to do is it, ratting out your own flesh and blood.'

He gave a grunt-like laugh and finally withdrew from her. 'If she'd forced my hand, I would have had to hand my citizenship in.'

Terrified at how bereft she felt with that last connection between them gone, Rebecca scrambled to sit up. 'Exactly.' She grabbed a pillow and placed it to her chest before drawing her knees up and wrapping her arms around her legs. 'And you waited until you were twenty-eight, so something must have spurred you on.'

The eyes that had narrowed while watching her cover her nudity held her stare for what felt like an age before he sat up too. 'Because I couldn't live with the fear any more.'

Wishing he'd said his reasons had been because of a threat to his business, Rebecca pressed her thighs to the pillow against her chest even more firmly and tightened her arms' hold around them, knowing even as she did it that this was a variation of what she'd done in the aftermath of their first lovemaking, a futile attempt at using her body to protect her heart, which would only make sense if her heart could still be protected from him.

But it couldn't, and she understood exactly what he meant about living with the fear because it was the same reason she still needed to walk away from him, otherwise she would be doomed to living with that fear too, for as long as it took for Enzo to walk away from *her*.

'How much longer could her luck have held?' he asked tautly. 'If she wouldn't quit, not even for my sake, then I had no choice but to force her—her reputation is as important to her as mine is to me. A police investigation into her business, even a fruitless one, would have destroyed that reputation and she knew it. I wish I could say I did it for noble reasons and that I believed even the scummy people she targeted didn't deserve to have their jewellery collections stolen from them but that would be a lie, and I have promised not to lie to you. I made my threat because it would have killed me to see my mother thrown into a prison cell.'

Rebecca pictured Silvana; tall, beautiful, whip-smart, brimming with energy. Locking her into a prison cell would be like locking a Bengali tiger into a tiny cage.

Despite herself, she pictured a young Enzo too, grieving the loss of his father and the loss of everything that was familiar, slowly growing up with the fear gripping his chest increasing as his mother's criminality and the implications of what would happen if she were caught became clearer to him.

He wasn't that child any more. She had to remember that. Had to. *Had* to.

# CHAPTER ELEVEN

'Is it a coincidence that you made your threat when you were the same age as your father when he died?' The question formed before Rebecca's brain had even thought of it.

Enzo's eyes narrowed. A groove lined his forehead. The corners of his lips twitched before he finally answered. 'And you believe you don't know me?' He shook his head and gave a disbelieving laugh. 'It was no coincidence. Turning twenty-eight was a big deal for me. As a child, it seemed *old* but the closer I got to it…' Grimacing, he dragged his fingers through his dark hair, mussing it up even more than it already was from their lovemaking. 'I spent much of the year doing all the reckless, dangerous things a single man with too much money can do.'

Ice prickled her spine and chest, goose bumps rising on her arms. If she weren't holding her legs so tightly she would rub them for warmth. 'What kinds of things?'

'I climbed Everest. Went white-water rafting down Nepal's Karnali River. Completed six skydives. Jumped off the Kawarau Bridge. Pickled my liver too many times to be considered clever or advisable.' His eyes closed before locking back on to hers. 'I had this feeling inside me that if this was to be my last year on this earth then I needed to live it and experience every shot of adrenaline it had to offer, and while I was on this voyage of destructive discovery, I came to the conclusion that I could not meet my maker without knowing my mother was safe from her own destructive genes. If I was to survive to see twenty-nine I could no longer live in fear of her liberty being taken from her.' Another twitch of his lips. 'Even if she did deserve it.'

*Even if she did deserve it…*

A paraphrasing of the same words Rebecca had told herself earlier on the terrace when she'd realised she would never be able to use the Claflin Diamond shares as a weapon against him.

'So you gave her the ultimatum,' she said slowly. A pulse was beating loudly in her head, nausea roiling in her stomach.

'I did. And she never forgave me. I expected that. I expected she would seek her vengeance. I crossed a line.' His eyes flashed. 'What I did not expect was that in her vengeance she would not only cross the line but firebomb it.'

'Sure about that are you?' She lifted her chin to look him square in the eye. 'Because from what you've told me about her, you should have expected it.'

Enzo's shock at the change in her tone was apparent in the way his head reared back before he stilled and his pupils darkened with anger. 'My mother's reputation is everything to her. My humiliation is her humiliation.'

'I'm not disputing that—she must have factored that in when she decided to drop her firebomb and decided it was a price worth paying, but even so, it's a bit neat and easy for you to point the finger of blame at Robina rather than take responsibility for your own actions.'

His stare had become like granite. 'I do take responsibility. Full responsibility. I have done from the start.'

'Then accept that *you* sabotaged our wedding.' Laughter that tinged on the hysterical burst out of her. She couldn't help it, had no control over it. '*You* sabotaged our wedding and put your business in danger, Enzo, not Robina. You told your mother when you knew she was biding her time to take her revenge. Maybe you *do* have a conscience. Maybe that's what drove you into telling her—deep down you wanted her to do your dirty work for you and save you the bother of having to make the confession yourself.'

As the taunts continued flying out of her mouth. Rebecca realised she was trying to provoke a fight. She wanted him to defend himself and shout at her, to call her cruel, disparaging names, give her something to latch onto to hate him for and stop the awful, desperate longing inside her to stay.

'To be honest, I don't really care,' she continued. 'I don't care why you confessed to her or her reasons in exposing you to me, I'm just grateful that she *did* expose you as the liar you are and stopped me from making the biggest mistake of my life. The two of you are as bad as each other. Seriously, Enzo, don't cut her off. You deserve one another.'

So intent had Rebecca been on saving herself from herself that she barely registered Enzo's eyes had become devoid of all life and his features a blank canvas devoid of emotion, not until she found herself enveloped in the loudest silence of her life with the air between them so taut that she felt the slightest pinch would see it snap.

The silence stretched.

She tried to draw in a breath but her airways had closed.

Then his nostrils flared.

With a short bow of his head, he climbed off the bed in one fluid movement and reached for his shorts.

'Get dressed,' he said curtly. 'We're going back to the villa.'

The ride back to the villa was as different from the ride into the city as night was to day. Where earlier they'd ridden with a fizzing air of joy, the mood now had a distinctly different, darker hue. Enzo hadn't spoken a single word since telling Rebecca to get dressed.

She'd dressed in the bathroom. She'd put her clothes back on calmly but when she'd tidied her hair in front of the mirror, there had been a tremor in her hands.

When she'd returned to the bedroom, Enzo had gone. She'd found him in the sterile kitchen looking out of the window, drinking a glass of water. His shoulder muscles had bunched before he'd turned to face her. She'd raised her chin, holding her breath at what she'd find in his eyes but finding…nothing. Suddenly frightened at what he was hiding behind his shuttered stare, she'd quickly ripped her gaze from him and looked out of the kitchen window. That's when she'd seen what he'd been staring out at. She couldn't believe she hadn't noticed it earlier.

The kitchen window overlooked the cathedral where Rebecca had left him standing at the altar. The cathedral she'd humiliated him to the whole world in. And now, as he took the road that led to his villa, the press pack emerged in the distance just before Enzo turned onto the narrow dust track, and a stab of guilt cut through her.

*He'd* brought this on himself, she reminded herself. Enzo. Not her. She had nothing to feel guilty about. She'd been nothing but a pawn, not only in the game between him and her grandfather but between Enzo and his mother.

But she wished now that the pain of her emotions hadn't got the better of her and she'd chosen a less public way of calling the wedding off.

She hadn't done it to punish him. Truth was, she'd been in no fit state to think at all. If she had been then she would have...

What? Given him a chance to explain?

Explain *what*? His side? There was no side, only the truth, and her grandfather's will had revealed the truth. Enzo had never loved her. He was the worst of all liars. He'd used her for his own ends.

*You could have given him a chance.*

She closed her eyes. This was all pointless. She couldn't change the past any more than Enzo could.

Knowing this didn't stop her hand from flying to her throat when Enzo brought the Vespa to a stop beside the garage's rear entrance and she looked at her watch.

Eleven fifty.

Her vision swam. Where had the time gone?

Closing her eyes to clear them, she took a deep breath and unstrapped the helmet.

Enzo made no move to take it off her. He simply stood with his hands rammed in his pockets, his jaw set, gaze fixed in the distance. His hair was sticking up in all directions.

Apologies for the home truths she'd flung at him formed on her tongue. Somehow, she bit back them back. She'd only spoken the truth. This stoniness, though, was coming close to unbearable.

Blurring him from her eyes, she pulled the helmet off then climbed off the Vespa. This was what she wanted after all. Distance between them. The ability to walk away on legs that didn't stumble beneath her.

The pulsing in her head and roiling nausea in her stomach flared up again as she followed him inside the villa.

'I'm going to get my things together,' she said quietly when they'd crossed the reception room.

He jerked a nod and uttered his first words since telling her to get dressed. 'I will get Frank to bring your cases down.'

'No need. They're not heavy.' Hating his remoteness, and hating that she hated it, she tried to inject some humour. 'Well, they *are* heavy, but I've lugged them up and down the stairs so many times recently that I'm in danger of developing muscles.'

His dimples didn't even pretend to appear at this. 'Where will you go?'

'Home.'

His jaw clenched. 'England?'

'It's my home.'

His eyes closed, face almost seeming to suck in on itself before he bowed his head and stepped away from her. 'I will get the paperwork for the shares ready for you.'

'The transfer's already been done?' There was still an hour until the deadline she'd imposed. In the back of her mind she'd imagined him dragging it all out until the last possible minute.

He turned back to look at her. 'I received the notification of completion when we were eating our breakfast.'

'This morning?'

There was no apology in his stare. 'Consider my failure to tell you another mark against my name.'

If Rebecca put all her stuff by the front door one more time she thought an indent might just appear in the terracotta flooring. Through the window at the side of the door she saw the large black car had reappeared, parked in the same spot as yesterday, ready to whisk her away.

As she padded barefoot across the reception room she blinked away the image of shattered marble that flashed in her eyes and then, as she entered the main living area and found Enzo at the bar pouring himself a Scotch, a wave of déjà vu hit her.

Full circle.

'Gin and tonic?' he asked, keeping his back to her.

'No thank you. I'll just take the shares and get going.' No more excuses. They'd dragged it out—*she'd* dragged it out—long enough.

If he hadn't had her passport in his safe, she could

have followed her instincts and fled immediately to England from the cathedral.

But if she'd done that, she would never have experienced the heaven of making love with Enzo.

Whether she would live to regret that joy, only time would tell. Right now, she didn't want to think about it. She just wanted to go while she still had control of herself, without making a scene.

He turned, and held up a gin glass practically filled to the brim. 'I've already made it. You might as well drink it. The shares and business documents are on the sideboard. There are things about them I need to discuss with you.'

She spotted the envelope they were contained in. 'We've had plenty of time to discuss them.' She didn't add that he could have told her over breakfast that the deed had been done and that they were hers and discussed whatever he thought needed talking about then.

'It wasn't the right time before.'

Not responding, she pulled the documents out of the envelope and gave them a quick scan. He'd stuck by his word and transferred them. For that alone, she would give him some credit.

'You are welcome to get a lawyer to check it all over for you but I assure you, everything is in order. They have already been digitally transferred into your name. You are officially my business partner.'

That took her aback. She'd never considered it like that. Not in those terms.

As if reading her mind, he gave a wry smile and raised his full tumbler of Scotch. First taking a large drink of it, he then placed her gin on the glass table next to the squishy sofa she favoured and sat himself stiffly on an armchair she'd never seen him use before. 'I did consider transferring the whole of Claflin Diamonds to you but it would have been meaningless. You would just have seen it as another performance.'

Yes, she thought. She would have seen it like that.

He nodded at her drink. 'Please. Sit. Drink. What I have to tell you should not take long. I have booked a flight for you to England that leaves in three hours. The ticket's been sent to your email. You will still leave here by one and have plenty of time to reach the airport in good time for it.'

'Oh. Well…thank you.' Knowing it would be churlish to refuse after he'd gone out of his way to book her onto a flight, something she hadn't thought of doing for herself, Rebecca perched on the sofa with both feet firmly on the floor, and had a quick sip of her perfectly made gin.

Why hadn't she thought to book herself onto a flight? The notion hadn't crossed her mind, not even when she'd considered fleeing in the middle of the night.

'Are you hungry?' he asked.

'No.' The cramped feeling in her stomach had returned.

'Neither am I.' He took another, even bigger drink of his Scotch then cradled the tumbler in both hands and gazed moodily into the amber liquid.

'The shares, Enzo?'

His lips tightened and his shoulders rose. A swirl of emotions played over his face before his features rearranged themselves into something unreadable and he met her stare. 'Do you remember me telling you that your grandfather turned down a much better offer for the business so he could partner with me?'

'Is this relevant?'

'Yes. Are you not curious as to why he chose the riskier option of partnering with a young man whose only jewellery store was making a loss? Our deal paid his debts off but if we'd failed, he would have been left with nothing.'

She pinched the bridge of her nose. 'Honestly? I don't care. Probably he admired your burning ambition, but you didn't fail so why does this matter?'

'I had not proved myself in any way for that ambition to be anything other than a dream. I've come to believe the reason your grandfather took that risk was because he thought he saw in me a way to make amends to his conscience for what he did to your mother.'

Rebecca shot to her feet so abruptly she knocked the table and sent gin and tonic sloshing over the rim of her glass. 'You said you wanted to discuss the shares and the business, not give me a history lesson.'

'It is one and the same thing.'

'Then I don't want to hear it.' She stomped to the box of tissues on the side and grabbed a handful of them.

'I know you don't but as you intend to walk out of my life for good at any minute, I ask that you do me the courtesy of listening to what I have to say.'

Lifting the glass, she flattened the tissues over the spilt liquid. 'I don't want to hear justifications for his behaviour.'

'There is no justification for that. He should never have forced your mother into making that choice and should never have cut her off because of it. It was his inability to admit to his mistakes that stopped him making amends to her.'

Abandoning her efforts to clean the spill, Rebecca angrily wiped her hand on the side of her dress and walked quickly to the door. 'Forget it. I don't want to hear *any* of this.'

'I know you don't, but you have to.'

'No.'

Before she could reach the door, Enzo had passed her to block the exit.

Folding his arms over his chest, he stared emotionlessly down at her.

Rather than argue, she turned to leave by the wide French door that opened onto the garden.

'It is locked. If you want the key, it's in my back pocket. The dining room door is also locked.'

She spun back round.

He was still blocking the door, body and expression immovable.

Another wave of déjà vu. Another full circle reached.

'You will hear what I have to say, Rebecca,' he said quietly but with an implacability that sent shivers lacing her spine.

'Don't *call* me that,' she whispered, taking a step back.

'Rebecca. Rebecca Emily Foley. A beautiful name for a beautiful woman. Rebecca, I have respected your wishes as to what I can and cannot say and how I refer to you—'

'That wasn't respecting my wishes, it was because you knew I'd destroy the business if you didn't.'

Eyes flashing dangerously, his voice rose for the first time. 'When will you understand that I no longer care about the business? I agreed to your terms because I hoped the time I managed to negotiate with you would be enough for you to realise the truth for yourself, but you won't open your eyes to see and now I have nothing left to lose. Destroy Claflin Diamonds if you want. Destroy my entire business. I don't care. Go outside and tell the waiting press and the world what I did to you. I don't care. The minute you walk out of here my life as it is is over, but I will not let you walk away without hearing the full truth, so if you want to be gone by one o'clock I suggest you sit down, open your ears and let me speak.'

White noise swam through Rebecca's head. Her heart was thumping madly, the beats adding to the cacophony in her brain, making it hard to think coherently.

She had three choices. One: fight her way past him. Two: launch herself through the patio doors. Three: sit down and let him have his say. Only the second option held any appeal. It was by far the least painful of the options with the only wounds likely to be her body being torn to shreds from the glass she'd jump through. To fight her way past Enzo meant having to touch him. Smell him. All the things that played havoc with her senses and confuddled her brain. To sit down and listen meant…

Nothing, she realised. He couldn't *make* her listen.

If she concentrated hard enough, she could block his words out.

Storming back to her seat, she drank the entirety of what hadn't spilt of her gin and plonked herself down, crossing her legs and folding her arms tightly. 'Go on then. Get it over with.'

His chest rose slowly before he gave a sharp nod and retook his own seat. His gaze locked on her. Let him look, she thought. Enzo staring into her eyes didn't mean her ears would listen.

'Your grandfather was a self-made man. He started with nothing. He despised your father, not because of the age he left school or the job he did but for his lack of ambition. Your grandfather equated ambition with success. He saw in me a kindred spirit, a young man he could help mould in the way your mother refused to be moulded. I am certain that is part of the reason why he went so far as to cut your mother off—she refused to be your grandfather's carbon copy in female form.'

Currently trying to picture herself standing on a beach somewhere hot and imagining the feel of warm salt water lapping at her feet, Rebecca suddenly realised she was thinking of her idealised version of Mauritius and quickly tried to imagine herself somewhere else.

Mauritius was where they were supposed to fly that evening for their honeymoon.

'He always expected her to come crawling back. He never dreamed she would be taken so young.' He grimaced. 'People don't. We expect those we love to become like Methuselah before they die. We do not expect to lose our children. Her early death set his demons off. He never stopped loving her. And he always loved you.'

She snorted quietly. Disparagingly.

'He did love you, Rebecca.'

'He didn't know me.'

'He kept your graduation photo on his desk.'

Her head jerked at this and, against her will, her eyes focused on his. 'How on earth did he get that?'

He shrugged. 'He had his ways and means. He kept tabs on your mother over the years. Your graduation photo replaced an older one from when you were a little girl blowing out the candles of your birthday cake. I can't remember how old you were in it. Ten, maybe. Your graduation made him proud. Not having a relationship with you was his greatest dying regret and why I think he did what he did with his will.'

Her snort at this was much louder. 'He screwed you over because he regretted not having a relationship with me? Yep, that makes a whole heap of sense.'

'By the time he died, your grandfather loved two people. You and me. He loved you because you were his flesh and blood. He loved me because what started as a business relationship where he was the master and I the apprentice became a mutually respectful friendship. There was a great deal of affection between us. Even when Beresi took off and my wealth mushroomed and I no longer needed him as my mentor, our friendship endured. I have become certain that writing that clause in his will was his way of forcing you and me together.'

# CHAPTER TWELVE

THE DOLPHIN POD Rebecca had been trying to envisage herself swimming with evaporated into a mist. She stared incredulously at Enzo. 'Did you drink the whole bottle of Scotch while I was getting my stuff together?'

He held the now half-full glass aloft. 'I should have. It would make all this easier to deal with.'

'I'm not stopping you.'

'I will wait until you leave before I do that. For now, it is good to be clear-headed, and I do not want you thinking this is all coming from the mouth of a drunk.' He laughed grimly. 'I am certain now that it is what your grandfather wanted to happen. You and me. He would often show me your photo and say what a beautiful young woman you'd turned into and that it would be a lucky man who married you. I used to think he was just being a proud grandfather but now…' He swallowed some more of his Scotch. 'You and I were the only two people he loved and the two people with him when he died.'

Rebecca, having had to quit trying to imagine herself somewhere else, felt her heart somersault into her stomach.

'After his diagnosis, your photo was moved from

his desk to his bedside table. Always he would look at it.' Then he added matter-of-factly, 'After his death, I learned to hate your face.'

She recoiled, inwardly and outwardly.

His eyes rang with self-loathing. 'Yes, Rebecca, I admit I hated you. I was the closest thing Ray had to family. His wife and daughter were dead and his grand-daughter wanted nothing to do with him. It was me he named his next of kin with the hospital. It was me who arranged for him to have twenty-four-hour care in his home and who moved into his guest room so I could make sure they didn't cut corners with his care. I did all that because I loved him like he was my blood and then I read his will and learned that he had, as you put it, stitched me up like a kipper, and betrayed me for the granddaughter who'd rejected him and who he'd only seen in photographs.' That awful grim smile curled on his face. 'He set things up so we would be forced to meet. Whether he predicted my reaction to the clause I cannot say. I discounted the other routes I could have taken to overturn his will or come to an agreement with you because in my fury with him, my heart was filled with vengeance... I am afraid that is my inherited blood from my mother coming out in me...and the target for my vengeance was you, Rebecca Emily Foley.

'I had people watch your every move. I kept close to you. I was waiting for a plausible opportunity to hook you in. I knew it would be easy to seduce you because my money and the looks I have been blessed with mean women are easy for me. There is not a woman alive who I have wanted who has not wanted me in return.'

He spoke as if revealing a not particularly important fact. 'And then my opportunity came along and finally I came face to face with my nemesis.'

He broke away to take another drink, closing his eyes as he drained the last of his Scotch.

'I built you up in my head as a Medusa figure but meeting you in the flesh...' He took another long breath through his nose. 'You were so *nice*.' He laughed disbelievingly. 'Believe me, I was not used to nice. I was used to calculators. But you were nice and witty, and your *smile*... *Dio*, your smile. But I was set on my path and I was still too full of anger and hurt to see that I should step off it but every day my conscience was getting louder. I remember the first time we kissed—*Dio*, I can still feel it—and you would not believe how it made me feel. I could not believe it myself. It felt like you'd drugged me, and then the night you told me you were a virgin...' He stretched his hand over his forehead and rubbed it. 'I think I was already in love with you then.'

'No!' The word had shot out of Rebecca's mouth before she was even aware of the terror grabbing hold of her or aware that she'd jumped back to her feet.

'Yes.' Enzo's stare was bleak but unwavering. 'You need to hear this as much as I need to say it. No more hiding, Rebecca. It is too late for that. I told you last night, your virginity changed everything for me. My conscience would not let me take you to bed, but still there was a war going on in my head and if I had realised what was happening to me instead of continually justifying my actions to myself, I would have confessed everything to you. I wish to hell I had confessed it all then.'

'Not as much as I wish you had,' she whispered, holding her stomach tightly.

'*Cara*, I will *never* forgive myself for what I did to you. I let my hurt and fury drive me to vengeance against a woman who had done *nothing* to deserve it apart from exist. I was fully prepared to detest you, but meeting you and hating you was impossible. You brought something out in me that I didn't understand, and I didn't understand it because I'd never felt it before. I had never walked a pavement with anyone before you and needed to walk along the kerb so I would be the one that was hit if a car swerved off the road, and I wish like hell that I'd understood what the hell was happening to me before I proposed to you.' He gripped his hair, the knuckles of his fingers white. 'You made me wait so long for your answer that I thought my heart had stopped beating and then when you finally said yes... I have never had a rush of blood to my head like it. That was the moment that it hit me that I loved you and I have been living in dread of losing you ever since.'

Rebecca's legs finally gave way beneath her and she sank back onto the sofa. 'Why are you doing this to me? Haven't you hurt me enough?'

'If I could take back all the pain that I've caused you and inject it into my bloodstream then I would. I wanted to tell you the truth. I knew that to marry you on a lie was unforgivable and I tried many times in the months before our wedding to find the words and throw myself on your mercy but the fear in my heart...' He punched his chest. 'I've never known fear like it; worse than the fear I had of my mother being imprisoned. It left me so damn *cold* to imagine my life without you because for the first time in so very long I'd found true happiness, but the longer I left it, the colder I felt.'

He dragged his fingers down his face. 'I have thought of what you said about me sabotaging our wedding and I think you could be right.' The ghost of a smile flickered on his face. 'Your grandfather taught me irony and I have to say it is ironic that if he were still alive, it is him I would have turned to.' He gave a bitter laugh and shrugged. 'I don't know. I wasn't thinking straight when I confessed to my mother and two bottles of red wine did not help, but the closer the wedding got the harder it was for me to live with what I was doing to you and everything you were giving up for me. I never intended to tell her anything, not consciously, and while I know I have no one to blame but myself for all this, I will never forgive her either, because she took her vengeance knowing she would destroy the one thing that mattered the most in the whole world to me—you. Your love.'

Reeling at everything he'd just confessed, aching to believe him, aching even harder to forgive him, Rebecca hauled herself back to her wobbly legs and staggered to the bar.

'You cannot imagine what it has been like for me having you in my life,' he said quietly as she groped blindly for two glasses. Blindly because her eyes were swimming. But she didn't have to be able to see to sense Enzo rising to his feet and closing some of the distance between them. 'Before you, I enjoyed my life and the advantages my wealth gave me but always there was something missing. I never understood what it was until I met you. That something was you.'

Having just poured them both a hefty slug of whatever had come out of the closest bottle to hand, Rebecca pushed one drink along the bar for Enzo and took a large mouthful of her own. Vodka. Strong enough to make her eyes water and burn her chest. Strong enough to clear her mind of the haze she'd fallen into listening to him.

'Do you know, Enzo, words are really easy to say,' she said, keeping her back to him. 'I want to believe you. I would give *anything* to believe you. But I can't.' She downed the rest of the clear liquid, slammed the glass on the marble bar and spun around to face him.

He was leaning back against the floor-to-ceiling window. His arms were folded, his chest rising and falling in rapid, ragged motions.

'I'm sorry but you're not a teenager,' she told him quietly. 'You're a thirty-three-year-old man, worth billions, and all from your own hard work. It is beyond credulity for me to believe you were too frightened of losing me to tell me the truth if guilt has been eating you for months in the way you claim.'

His eyes bore into hers; lasers trying to drill into her mind before he unpeeled himself from the window and took the five steps to the bar. He closed his fingers around the vodka she'd poured him. 'What day is it?' he asked.

Taken off guard at the question, she had to grope for it. 'Sunday?'

'*Sì*. Sunday.' He raised the glass and peered into it in the same way he'd studied his Scotch. 'A day when business is closed.' He turned sharply to her. 'Have you not questioned how I was able to transfer the shares into your name and add your name to the business in such a short time frame and over a weekend?'

'Because you're Enzo Beresi and always get your own way about everything.'

His lips curled. 'I do not walk on water. They were completed so quickly because I had already set everything in motion. My plan was to give you all the documents the morning after our wedding over breakfast and confess everything because my one hope was that us being married meant you would feel obliged to try and forgive me.' He raised his face to the ceiling and muttered something under his breath before looking back at her. 'But you wouldn't have forgiven me, would you?'

Blinking rapidly to fight the burn of tears stabbing again at her eyes, she swallowed. 'I guess we'll never know.'

He shook his head slowly and brought the vodka to his lips before changing his mind and lowering it back to the bar. 'No. You wouldn't have forgiven me. I understand that now. And I understand now why I could never bring myself to tell you.' He brought the vodka back to his mouth but still didn't drink. 'I never realised why the thought of telling you made my chest cold when you are the best person I have ever known.

You have a warmth to you, Rebecca, and believe me, in my world that is rare. *Dio*, you won Robina over in ten minutes—that is normally the time it takes her to decide that she hates someone. I saw all the good-bye cards you got from your school. The children and their parents, your colleagues…they all loved you. A woman like you…' He rubbed the glass over his chin. 'But now I understand it. It became clear to me last night. I kept the truth from you because I knew in my heart that you were waiting for a reason to end things with me. Discovering your grandfather's will was the excuse you were looking for. If it hadn't been that, you would have found something else.' And with that he finally downed the vodka in one huge swallow, smacking his lips together and then wiping his mouth with the back of his hand.

Utterly gobsmacked, it took a moment for Rebecca's vocal cords to work. 'Honestly, I can't believe what I'm hearing. I wasn't looking for an excuse for anything, and I can't believe you're blaming me for *your* lies. I gave up everything to be with you. I would *never* have left you.'

Weariness seemed to make him compress into himself. 'I am not blaming you for anything, *cara*. This whole situation is on me. I created it and I will have to live with the consequences for the rest of my life.' Then he straightened and looked at his watch. 'It is nearly one o'clock. You should go. My driver is waiting for you. Tell him not to run over any of the press—they will have their cameras trained on the car. He is an excellent driver and I would hate to lose him to a prison cell.' He stretched an arm, coming within millimetres of brushing against her, and wrapped his hand around the bottle of vodka.

Pulling the bottle to him, Enzo cast her another glance with eyes that had lost all animation. 'Please, Rebecca. It is time for you to leave and for me to pickle my liver. Excuse me for not seeing you out but I have never been into masochism.'

He unscrewed the lid but before he could pour the liquid into the glass, Rebecca surprised them both by snatching the bottle from him. 'You can pickle yourself in a minute, but first I want you to tell me why you thought I was looking for a reason to leave you because, honestly, that's the most ridiculous thing I've ever heard in my life. I was *nuts* about you.'

'Excellent use of past tense there,' he muttered.

'What do you expect?' she cried. 'You have destroyed my trust. I would give anything to put this behind me and put my trust back in you but I can't.'

'And I cannot blame you for that but I think the word you mean is *won't*.' Taking back hold of the bottle, he prised her fingers from it, poured himself another generous measure and brought it to his mouth. 'Seriously, Rebecca, go. I've said all I need to say. Leave me to drink.'

Impulse and rising fury had her pushing his hand before he could drink. The glass tipped, spilling vodka over his T-shirt. 'Don't tell me what I meant—I meant *can't*, now tell me where you got the idea that I was just looking for a reason to leave you.'

His jaw clenched. He ran his hand over the spilled

liquid soaking into his clothes and, without saying a word, poured himself a replacement and drank it in one swallow.

When he turned his face back to her, his eyes were flashing dangerously. '*Can't* is an excuse. *Won't* is honest. You have always doubted my feelings for you.'

'For damn good reason!'

He leaned down so they were eyeball to eyeball. 'I love you. I have always loved you. I will always love you. I would walk on broken glass if it meant you would give me another chance but you won't because you're too damned scared. It is what I tried to talk to you about last night but you shut me down. You never believed in my love, not deep down, because your own insecurities make you doubt yourself too much.'

'Poppycock.'

'Is it?' A pulse throbbed in his temple. 'You felt like the third wheel in your parents' marriage.'

'Not that again. For the last time, I never meant to say that.'

'I know. But you did and that's what made sense of everything to me.' He stared at her for a long, long time before his shoulders dropped and compassion filled his velvet timbre. 'Your father had a fatal heart attack days after your mother died.'

It felt like she'd been scalded without any warning. 'What's that got to do with anything?'

'Everything. In his grief, he left you behind and left you alone.'

The burn he'd scalded her with drained out of her along with all Rebecca's blood. 'And I thought you couldn't stoop any lower than you already have...' she whispered hoarsely. 'My father was overweight. He was in agony over Mum's death. His heart couldn't take the strain.'

'I do not doubt it and I do not doubt that he loved you so do not for a second think I am saying that or implying it. Your father didn't choose his heart attack any more than my father chose to have an aneurysm but it happened. My father loved me and your parents loved you. It is your perception of your place in your family that I am talking about. You lived under the shadow of your parents' love for each other—you described it yourself as a fable and I can understand why; they were a modern day Romeo and Juliet but with a happier ending. From everything you have told me, they were as happy and loved each other as much at their deaths as when they first married, but somewhere along the way you came to believe that they loved each other more than they loved you and that it was because of this love that they left you behind.'

She backed away from him on legs that had become like jelly. 'I've thought a lot of not very nice things about you these last twenty-odd hours but I never thought you could be this cruel.'

Turning his back to her, he said, 'I made a promise never to lie to you again, but you wanted this conversation, *cara*, not me. I'd already said all I wanted to say. I just wanted to be left alone to drown myself in alcohol because every extra minute you are here cuts the wound deeper.' To make his point, he poured himself another vodka.

Rebecca took another step away from him. 'Then I shall go.'

'Good. Don't forget the package. My English lawyer's details are in it. When you decide what you want to do with the shares, contact him about it. He will act as a go-between for us. I would be grateful if you do not contact me. I think it best for both our sakes that we have a clean break.'

'I think that's best too.' How had she thought it would be cleaner this way? What had she been thinking?

After everything they'd been through, leaving like this was hell on earth.

As she picked up the package, she saw him lift his head and knew he'd tipped more vodka into his mouth. Knew, too, that Enzo would make good on his promise of pickling his liver. He'd lost.

But she'd lost too.

Her fingers closed on the door handle she could hardly see for the tears blinding her.

'Rebecca.'

His back was still turned to her but his face was turned in profile.

She swallowed a sob. 'Yes?'

His voice was so low she had to concentrate with everything she had to hear him. 'I cannot tell you if your perceptions about your parents were wrong but I know they loved you, very much. When your grandfather kept tabs on your mother he would have photos taken. I saw some of them once, not long after we went into business together. You must have been twelve or thirteen. You and your parents were on a picnic in some woods. I do not know what the occasion was but I remember feeling envy at the way your mother was captured looking at you. It was an expression my mother has never given me.'

She opened the door.

'One more thing.'

She stilled to listen to his last ever words to her.

'Your expectations of marriage were not unrealistic. Married or not, you will always be the most important person in my life.'

# CHAPTER THIRTEEN

SOMEHOW REBECCA MADE it to the front door without stumbling. Her legs were still holding her up. All her possessions except for her handbag and sandals had been taken from where she'd left them. She guessed Frank had taken them out to the waiting car.

Rubbing at her leaking eyes, she slipped the sandals on. Should have left her ankle boots. Now she'd have to root through her stuff for them before the flight so her feet didn't get cold. She hated having cold feet.

The last thing she did before leaving the villa was dig her sunglasses out of her handbag and put them on. She was glad she'd remembered to do that when she stepped outside. The sun, strong since she'd watched it come to life, was now scorching, the villa's grounds bathed in yellow from its rays.

Too intent on putting one foot in front of the other without her legs giving up on her before she reached the car, the dozens and dozens of cameras flashing on the other side of the electric fence hardly registered, nor the loud shouts being hurled at her.

The driver got out and opened the back door.

Inside, she fastened her seat belt.

The car slowly rolled forwards. A short wait and

then it drove through the electric gates. Camera lenses were pressed against the windows, flashes going off, but the tinted glass dulled the effect.

She clenched her teeth together and refused to look anywhere but forwards.

And then the cameras were gone and the car was gaining speed and Rebecca was, finally, on her way home.

Pressing her cheek against the door, she closed her eyes. A tear trickled under her sunglasses and down her chin. She wiped it away. Another fell. Soon her sunglasses were so wet that she took them off and absently placed them beside her.

The more the miles slipped by and the further she was taken from Enzo, the more acute the pulsing agony in her heart.

She saw a sign for the airport. Which airline had he booked her with? Knowing Enzo, the plushest airline. Knowing Enzo, she'd be travelling in the highest class the airline had to offer.

In five hours from now, they were supposed to be taking his private jet to Mauritius for their honeymoon. Enzo had suggested it because it was a paradise he'd never visited before. He'd wanted them to experience it for the first time together. Rebecca would have been happy to go anywhere so long as it was with him.

She pressed her knuckles to her forehead and tried as hard as she'd ever tried at anything to banish him from her thoughts.

What would happen to the suitcases she'd packed for their honeymoon the other day? Frank had taken them so they could be loaded into the car...

Were they in the boot of *this* car? Would she get to the airport and the driver unload them?

No sooner had this thought came into her head than an image of Enzo standing in the doorway of her bedroom followed, laughing at the sheer amount of clothes bulging out of the open cases.

'You don't need to pack any clothes, *cara*,' he'd murmured seductively, stepping to her to wrap his arms around her waist. 'Our honeymoon will be spent in bed.'

Her heart racing frantically, Rebecca breathed in as deeply as she could and glimpsed another road sign for the airport.

*Why* hadn't she booked her own flight back to England? Or thought to get Frank to book it for her?

It was when she saw the third airport sign that a pain cramped in her chest, so acute that she doubled over with a howl.

Struggling to breathe, she crossed her shaking hands over her heart. Her knees were knocking together, every part of her trembling. She'd thought the pain from losing her parents had been enough to kill her, but this...

This was a different kind of grief, and it came to her in a vivid, painful flash what the difference was. Her parents had been taken from her. She was taking herself from Enzo.

Taking herself away from the man who'd blown away the cherry blossom that had landed in her hair when he'd taken her to Japan during her school's half-term break. The man who'd stroked her hair for hours when she'd been curled up next to him on the sofa suffering menstrual cramps. The man whose smile could have powered the earth when he'd watched her face during her first sunrise on his terrace. The man who'd secretly had her father's old, battered vintage car restored *for her*.

Another realisation punched her. Rebecca's mind had refused to let her think about booking a flight back to England because, at a subconscious level, a part of her brain was working in tandem with her heart. England wasn't her home any more. Enzo was.

Maybe he was too much like his mother when it came to his need for vengeance but at least he could admit to his mistakes and had tried to put them right. That had to count. And couldn't she be accused of being like the grandfather she detested for his treatment of her mother? Hadn't he refused to put right his relationship with his only child even when his actions proved how much he'd missed having her in his life? What had stopped him from reaching out to her? Pride? Sheer stubbornness? Or as Enzo had said, a refusal to admit to his mistakes? She would never know because it was all too late. The dead didn't speak.

Is that what she wanted for herself? To live the rest of her life with regret? To reach old bones haunted by demons of the past?

Rebecca was barely aware of undoing her seat belt and flinging herself forward to bang on the dividing window. 'Take me back!' she cried, then remembered the intercom and slammed her hand on the button. 'Take me back! Please, take me back!' Terrified the driver wouldn't understand her she scrambled for the words in Italian but the only ones she could find were, '*Portami a casa!*'

*Take me home.*

The driver must have caught the hysteria in her voice for he brought the car to a stop with a screech. In seconds, to a blast of furious horns, he'd performed a U-turn and then they were flying back in the opposite direction on the roads they'd just travelled. No matter how fast he drove though, it wasn't fast enough for Rebecca. Her agitation got too much when they were back at the electric gate and waiting for them to open. Flinging the car door open, she jumped out. Catching the press off guard, she elbowed her way through them, squeezed her way through the small gap that had appeared in the gate, and then ran over the gravel driveway to the front door.

She shoved the door open and raced inside. 'Enzo!' When he didn't immediately answer, she ran into the living room, shouting his name again. 'Enzo!'

The room was empty but the French doors were ajar.

Tears pouring like a waterfall down her face, she sprinted across the room and dived out into the garden. Craning her neck in all directions, she sucked in all the air she could and then screamed his name. '*Enzo!*'

Far in the distance, past the swimming pool and tennis court, a shadow appeared.

Rebecca didn't hesitate. Arms and legs pumping, running faster than she'd ever run in her life, her heart pounding with exertion, tears almost blinding her, she hurtled herself to the statue-like figure and then, before she could even think of what she was doing, leapt at him.

If not for Enzo's innate strength she would have sent them both sprawling. Instead, he caught her, and when her arms flew around his neck and her legs wrapped around his waist, strong hands gripped her tightly to him. Sobbing incoherently, she only realised he'd carried her to the egg seat when he'd sat them both on it.

Straddled over his lap, she disentangled her arms, unburrowed her face from his neck and gazed into bloodshot eyes that were staring at her with complete disbelief.

'Either I did drink too much or this really is you,' he muttered shakily.

'I'm sorry,' she whispered. 'So sorry.'

His lips pulled together and, a sheen appearing in his eyes, he shook his head. 'Don't. You're here. That is enough.'

She caught his hand with both of her own and pressed it against her chest, right in the place her swollen heart was thumping. 'I love you.'

His chest rose. His throat moved as he swallowed. 'And I love you. More than anything.'

'I know.'

His eyes narrowed searchingly. 'Do you?'

Still keeping his hand tight against her chest with one hand, she brushed his cheek with the other. The usually smooth skin prickled with thick, dark stubble.

'You've proved it in so many ways...' Her throat caught as she remembered the teabags she'd found in the cupboard that morning. So many little things. They meant more than all the big things put together. 'What you did was… Well, you know what it was.'

Pain spasmed over his haggard face. 'Unconscionable.'

She squeezed his hand. 'Yes. And I want to blame you for making the last five months one big lie but that's not fair. Some of the blame is on me too.'

His head jerked vehemently. 'None of this is on you. None of it. It is all me.'

'Don't be so egotistical.'

Now his head jerked with surprise.

The pain that had come close to crippling her was abating at the rate of knots, her lungs opening to allow her to breathe. Smiling, she rubbed the back of her fingers over his stubble. 'We were both frightened, Enzo. You called it right when you blamed my insecurities for making me doubt your love but there were other factors at play too. I had doubts from the beginning. Some of that was insecurity but some of it was because you were just *too* perfect. This gorgeous, charming, generous, rich man was pursing me and he was perfect. Honestly, you were so perfect Zeus would have admitted you on Mount Olympus.'

His forehead crinkled and he croaked a laugh. 'Have you not read what those gods got up to?'

She sniggered. Oh, Zeus, but laughter felt good. Wonderful. 'You were perfect and that frightened me because it was a perfection I could never live up to.'

'You are perfect for me.'

She pressed a finger to his lips. 'Shh. Let me speak.

Let me get this out and then you can tell me how perfect I am for you.'

His dimples appeared and her heart almost smashed its way out of her. She hadn't realised how desperately she'd been longing to see his dimples again.

'You hid your early years from me because you didn't want me to think you anything less than perfect but I opened up to you about everything, and learning what you'd hidden hurt me until I realised I hadn't bared my soul to you. Not as much as I thought I had. I held things back too, not deliberately, but because I hardly understood them. You did.'

'You mean your parents?'

She nodded. 'I wish you could've met them.'

'I wish I could have met them too.'

She squeezed his fingers. 'They would have adored you. My dad would probably have fallen into a faint if he'd seen your car collection. They really were happy together. I would see my aunts and uncles, and my friends' parents and none of them acted like my parents did, you know, things like squeezing each other's bums when walking past each other and dancing in the kitchen together when a song they both liked came on the radio. That kind of thing.' She sighed. 'I know they loved me. They did. We were a close-knit family but...' She swallowed away the feeling of disloyalty rising up her throat and whispered. 'Sometimes I wanted them to dance with me too.'

He smoothed a lock of her hair. 'I doubt they meant to exclude you.'

'I don't think they even realised they were doing it,

but I suppose that feeling of being second best has been in me for so long that I didn't even realise it was there, and that is what I'm trying to explain to you, that there is no way I would have even tried to explain my feelings about it to you, not even two days ago, because deep down I was terrified it would make you look differently at me. You were so ruddy perfect that I kept waiting for the day you realised you were settling for second best and that you could do better than me.'

His nostrils flared with anger, head shaking violently. 'Never.'

'If I'd known about your early years and what an evil witch your mother is, it would have humanised you, because, Enzo, you weren't human. You were the perfect specimen of man, in looks, temperament and good deeds. Even the way you proposed to me, it was just *perfect*, and then there was your superhuman control when I would be begging you to make love to me. Well guess what? I'm glad you have feet of clay. I'm glad that you're as capable of feeling anger and having irrational thoughts and stupid ideas as the rest of us mortals. Most of all, I'm glad that you're mine.'

He pulled his hand out of her hold to cup her cheeks and bring the tip of his nose to hers. 'I will always be yours, Rebecca. Always.'

'I know you will,' she whispered. 'And I will always be yours.'

Their lips fused. Dizzying heat and incredulous wonder filled her. 'Marry me,' she said into his mouth.

Enzo pulled back just enough to stare into her eyes,

that searching expression stark in his. His fingers threaded through her hair. 'You are sure?'

'I've never been more sure of anything. Let's marry as soon as it can be arranged. Just you and me.'

Slowly, the same wonder filling Rebecca appeared as a shine in his eyes. And then his dimples flashed. And his mouth crushed hers.

The sun had long gone to bed before they went back into the villa.

# EPILOGUE

'DO YOU, ENZO ALESSANDRO BERESI, take Rebecca Emily Foley to be your wife? To have and to hold from this day forward, for better, for worse, for richer, for poorer, in sickness and in health until death do you part?'

Enzo's clear brown eyes didn't leave Rebecca's face. 'I do.'

Their interlocked fingers squeezed.

'And do you, Rebecca Emily Foley, take Enzo Alessandro Beresi to be your husband? To have and to hold from this day forward, for better, for worse, in—?'

Unable to follow the Italian words for excitement, Rebecca's promise zoomed off her tongue, interrupting the priest in his full flow. 'I do!'

Even the priest laughed. If there had been a congregation watching them, they no doubt would have laughed too, but the only four people invited to witness their marriage were Rebecca's aunt and uncle and Enzo's paternal grandparents. No one else was wanted or needed.

The tiny chapel in the tiny Tuscan village that they were marrying in was a world away from the famous cathedral Rebecca had jilted Enzo at the altar of, and she adored the intimate simplicity of it. Adored that it stripped back all the façade and made it only about the pledging of their lives together. Because that was all that mattered. Their love and commitment to each other. Even their clothing had been stripped of all the pomp and ceremony of their original wedding day, Rebecca's white dress a flowing, bohemian creation, her hair loose, her posy a bunch of sunflowers, Enzo's wedding suit much less formal too, although as snazzy and dapper as the clothes he always wore.

Feeling the weight of the gold ring slide over her finger made Rebecca's heart swell, and when she slid Enzo's ring onto his much larger finger, the expression dancing from his eyes turned the swelling into a balloon bursting to escape the confines of her ribs.

*I love you*, he mouthed.

The happiness infusing her just too much to contain, she flung her arms around Enzo's neck and kissed him. With more laughter echoing around them, he kissed her back with such enthusiasm her feet were lifted from the ground.

Once all the official stuff was done and they were husband and wife legally and under the sight of God, they left the chapel to find a crowd of local well-wishers had gathered. In the distance, a lone paparazzo was beetling his way up the hill towards them. Considering the lengths Enzo had gone to ensure this wedding was as secret as humanly possible, Rebecca had to admire the pap's tenacity. At her insistence, Rebecca and Enzo had released a short statement which blamed a severe dose of nerves on Rebecca's failure to go ahead with the original wedding—she would tell a thousand lies if it saved Enzo from further humiliation—and ended with their intention to notify people of the rearranged wedding date as soon as possible. All that had been ten days ago, and, despite the press continuing to follow and report on their every move, they were now properly married and other than this one lone paparazzo, they'd got away with the intimacy and privacy they'd craved.

Flinging her arms back around Enzo's neck, she gave the pap his shot. After all, he'd earned it.

Five years later

Three-year-old Lily was the first to spot her grandmother's arrival. Practically throwing herself out of the garden playhouse that was almost the same size as the home Rebecca had grown up in, she tore across the lawn to throw herself into her grandmother's arms, squealing, 'Nonna!'

Rebecca and Enzo exchanged their usual bemused 'is this really happening?' looks and watched as the immaculately made-up Robina happily allowed her granddaughter to drag her off to play. She'd arrived for the wedding anniversary party five hours early to look after Lily while Rebecca and Enzo supervised the preparations. Why she'd thought it a good idea to wear a tight-fitting white couture dress for a playdate with a tiny child was anyone's guess, but that was Robina for you.

The rapprochement with her had come about in the days after Lily's birth when Rebecca's sadness that her parents would never meet their first grandchild had tinged the piercing joy of her precious baby. Her daughter only had one surviving grandparent and it had suddenly felt incredibly cruel that she was destined to never meet her. She wouldn't say Lily's birth had softened Enzo when it came to his mother, but he'd agreed to try to put the past behind them and let her back into their lives.

In a move that no one had seen coming, least of all Robina, Lily had taken to her *nonna* right from the start, as content in her arms as she was in her parents'. Bestowing Robina with her very first smile that wasn't wind had resulted in the selfish, narcissistic, morally corrupt retired jewellery thief falling head over heels in love with her granddaughter in return. Watching the couture-dressed and immaculately coiffured Italian woman crawl around on the floor chasing a toddler was something that never grew old, and though Rebecca knew Enzo still struggled to forgive and would never be able to forget, even he accepted that his daughter had enacted a fundamental change in his mother.

With Lily taken care of and their hardworking staff and the army of unobtrusive caterers they'd hired steadily turning the grounds and swimming pool area into an enchanted fairy-tale setting, Rebecca was more than happy to slope off with Enzo for a quick bout of gentle lovemaking; eight months pregnant with their second precious child, it had to be gentle.

She could scarcely believe five years had passed since they'd made their vows. They'd been the happiest years of her life, and they never failed to mark the occasion. Usually they kept their celebrations private but this year had decided to finally throw the big party they'd never got round to having after their secret nuptials.

Later that evening, with the party in full swing and Lily half asleep on Robina's lap, she was glad they'd done it, delighted too that so many of her family and friends had flown over from the UK for it and that none of them were the slightest bit daunted at the company they found themselves partying with. She couldn't stop herself giggling to watch a member of the old Greek royal family flirt manically with one of her cousins: the aristocrat and the hairdresser, ha!

'What are you laughing at?' a deep, velvet voice whispered behind her ear.

She tilted her head and grinned, but before she could explain, the DJ put on a song that made her heart skip a beat—it was 'their' song.

Enzo held his hand out to her.

Threading her fingers through his, Rebecca gladly let him help her to her feet then heaved her hugely pregnant body onto the specially created dance floor and wrapped her arms around the neck of the man who'd never given her cause to regret marrying him.

'I love you,' she murmured, rising onto her toes to brush a kiss to his lips.

'*Mi amore*,' he breathed into her mouth, filling her with the delicious sensation that time seemed to be in no trouble to lessen.

From the corner of her eye she saw Lily's eyes were wide open, her thumb in her mouth, staring at them with a wistful look.

Unwinding an arm from Enzo's neck, she beck-

oned their daughter to them. Lily didn't need beck-
oning twice. Jumping off Robina's lap, she raced onto
the dance floor and linked hands with her mummy and
daddy. The three of them danced together until Lily's
little feet could dance no more.

\* \* \* \* \*

# BACK TO CLAIM
# HIS CROWN

NATALIE ANDERSON

MILLS & BOON

For Kat—here's to 50 before 60—we got this!!!

# CHAPTER ONE

'IT NEEDS SEVERAL more stitches, Princess.'

Zara Durant gritted her teeth and remained dutifully still while the severe tailor secured her dress with surgical precision. She'd been standing for over two hours already but today everything needed to be perfect. If her bodice slipped and exposed her to a cathedral full of people, that would *not* be perfect—so it wasn't too hard to summon patience while multiple hair and make-up artists hovered, occasionally swooping close to enact other minor adjustments. She'd unintentionally lost a little weight in the run-up. Her mother had been delighted this morning when she'd finally arrived in Monrayne and seen Zara for the first time in weeks. The brusque seamstress not so much.

Monrayne was the smallest but wealthiest nation on the Scandinavian peninsula, famed for its pristine alpine environment, gleaming palaces and glittering modernity. Zara had been stunned when she'd driven through the city for the first time just over a week ago. It was a snow globe perfect scene with its tall spires, ancient architecture and sparkling snow-capped surroundings.

Right now, as the emergency alterations were made to Zara's dress, her too-proud mother, the Queen of Dolrovia, was taking her seat in Monrayne's magnificent stone cathedral. Zara watched her mother's sweeping entrance on the television screen that had been set up in her suite. Millions were watching the live stream, including her invalid father, King Harold, in his bedroom back in Dolrovia. Their much smaller, much less wealthy country bordered the Baltic Sea and her father had been deposed just over a decade ago. The revolution had been peaceful but complete—their titles were now purely honorific and almost the only thing that remained of their history. The only property they'd been allowed to keep was the crumbling castle deep in the lowland plains. The other properties, plus the art, jewels and antiques, had moved to public ownership. But, despite rejecting their Royal family, her country—indeed the whole world—was fascinated by Zara's wedding today.

Clearly loving every moment, her mother imperiously acknowledged the hundreds of dignitaries, politicians, royals and celebrities who'd gathered in their finest couture to witness the Royal wedding of the decade—revelling in the resurgence of the kind of attention that had faded for their particular family a number of years ago.

Becoming powerless, penniless officially 'ex' Royals hadn't been easy for Zara's elderly parents, despite the fact the situation had been decades in the making. They believed it was because they lacked a male heir—nothing to do with their own denial of reality, their own continued excesses, their own failure to adapt to the modern world. They'd never imagined that their very late lamb—an unplanned, unnecessary, unwanted extra girl who'd rarely been allowed past the castle gate—would secure such an advantageous marriage contract. That there was interest in their dusty lineage once more was something they would make the most of.

So many citizens in Dolrovia were suddenly interested in the youngest princess, who hadn't been seen in so long most had forgotten she even existed. She'd been stuck there in the countryside, caring for disinterested parents, while her much older sisters lived in the city. If Zara failed to show at the ceremony now there wouldn't just be outrage but complete condemnation—and that was only from her parents.

It still didn't seem real, but the fact was *she* was the bride in this spectacle. Furthermore, she'd not just agreed to this madness, she'd actively pursued the position. She was marrying the Crown Prince of Monrayne—the head of a Royal family most definitely still brimming with money, prestige and real power.

Not that *she* wanted these things. She wanted greater personal freedom, and that was far more precious. And it was that which she'd been promised. When born to a life like hers, one had to seize opportunities and strike bargains.

Now Zara stared at the stranger in the mirror. The hours taken to create this fairy-tale facade had been worth it. Her make-up was flawless. The diamond-encrusted hand-made lace covered her back and arms, hiding the unsightly pink mottling that smothered her skin when she was nervous. It also gave her a modest, innocent air, one they apparently considered crucial. She considered it archaic. But she gritted her teeth, determined to forget the mortifying questioning from the Crown Prince's advisors and the utterly humiliating examination she'd subsequently endured before being deemed an acceptable bride.

'I'm finished.' The seamstress spoke in English, the second language that both nations shared and that Zara spoke fluently.

Moments later, Zara slowly followed one of the liveried footmen, allowing the attendants a final hyper-critical inspection as she passed. Despite their wafting air of disapproval, she was grateful for their frosty insistence upon perfection.

Monrayne's palace was far larger and more opulent than her castle on the verge of collapse and it was ridiculously easy to get lost in. The portraits which had once hung in the main atrium, but had since been sequestered in the furthest wing in which she'd been confined for this last week, had been way-finders for her. The first depicted the late Queen Kristyn and

King Lucas on their wedding day. The second was of their only child, Prince Lucian. As always, Zara's glance lingered on the young man. His arresting gaze always caught her attention—those pale blue eyes, that winning smile, the heart-stopping handsomeness for ever young. The portrait had been painted when he was only sixteen—two years before his tragic disappearance in a diving accident a decade ago.

Zara had barely been thirteen but she remembered the global outpouring of grief and shock when it had happened. The frantic searches in the Mediterranean had gone on for weeks but his body had never been recovered. He'd been immensely popular, the dreamy Prince Charming of billions of girls all over the world. The elite boarding school he'd attended had been oversubscribed fifty times over as every wealthy family on the continent and beyond had tried to get their daughters alongside him in class. His mother, Queen Kristyn—already widowed—hadn't recovered from the loss and had died within days of the young man's death.

And now Zara was about to marry Lucian's cousin Anders, who'd become the new Crown Prince of Monrayne on Lucian's passing. He would be crowned King in just a few days when he came of Monraynian regal age on his twenty-fifth birthday. Their wedding today was merely the first of an elaborate series of celebrations, each bigger than the last.

The wedding. The birthday. The coronation.

She'd not been Prince Anders's first pick. His uncle, Garth—currently Regent of Monrayne—had discreetly visited her parents' castle. Her sisters had dropped everything and made one of their rare visits home to welcome him 'properly'. His query had taken them by surprise. That he was quietly searching for a suitable bride for the Crown Prince had sounded like something from the last century. Mia, the eldest, had politely explained that she was already in a serious relationship, while Ana had also declined, noting that at thirty-three she felt too old for Anders.

That was when Zara had stepped from the corner to volunteer. She'd stunned everyone. But while she might be ten years younger than Ana, she was old enough to make up her own mind. She was capable of far more than either her parents or her siblings knew.

Garth—who'd unsurprisingly forgotten her existence, given her cloistered life—had assessed her with calculating eyes and, to everyone's astonishment, had immediately agreed.

He'd admitted later than he'd not realised she would be there. To the world she was still the late arrived child, the much younger sister of the two beautiful princesses who'd embraced Dolrovia's democratic revolution while their parents had been forced to retreat from public life and curb all excesses.

Of course, there'd been caveats before complete agreement of the marriage contract. There'd been requirements to complete, including that absolute awkwardness…but then there'd been acceptance and surprising speed. It was less than two months since that initial meeting.

The terms were simple. She couldn't overshadow her future husband—no problem, given she disliked publicity and didn't court self-promotion. She was more than happy to stand supportively in the background. Because in private there could be more freedom than she currently had. She would be able to support charitable causes close to her heart and she might actually earn some respect from her family—but an element of freedom from them at the same time. Because she wasn't precious to them, in fact the opposite. Expected to be dutiful while being ignored and ill-educated at the same time, this was the only acceptable escape from the castle-bound life they'd prescribed for her.

Yet as she entered the eight-horse-drawn crystal carriage that would now take her to the cathedral, doubt almost devastated her. She breathed deeply, telling herself her nerves were only because she was the focal point for millions of people. She wasn't used to the spotlight. But today would be the worst. It would only get easier. She would remain in the background after this moment because the King had primacy. She'd be the safe option Garth had said they wanted.

Ten minutes later the carriage stopped outside the cathedral. She swallowed back nausea. She felt very alone. But then she'd been alone almost all her life.

Neither of her sisters were her bridal attendants. Mia and Ana had left home when Zara had been young. They rarely visited and when they did it was only to emphasise Zara's 'duty' to her parents and how perfectly her life suited her. So when Garth had decided that a bridal party of delightful children would be the thing, Zara had readily agreed. She didn't mind that she didn't know the children nor got to choose anyone else. She had few personal friends. So now she carefully held the stunning bouquet, maintained the smile the stylists had made her practice for hours and followed the assortment of sweet-looking offspring of favoured courtiers in petite silk dresses and sailor suits. Everything looked perfect. Even her. It was quite the miracle.

*Breathe. Walk. Slowly. Carefully. Evenly. Calmly.*

It didn't matter that she barely knew Anders. This was a political arrangement, not personal. There was plenty of time to get to know him. Yes, she was a little forlorn that he'd been too busy to see her this week. That there'd been no time for the two of them to be alone *at all* in their engagement. The many photos of them spread across the Internet had been the result of a single day's shoot which had involved another massive array of make-up artists and stylists.

He didn't turn to watch her walk towards him now. It was probably protocol. She ought to know, but she'd been so nervous at the rehearsals she hadn't really heard the detailed explanations why all these things were done in such convoluted ways. Yet, despite their fondness for tradition, the courtiers had been unashamedly delighted that she had no escort to walk her up the aisle as her elderly father was too infirm. Apparently, it would give everyone an unrestricted view of her elaborate dress. Diamond-studded, it was a gleaming work of art and masked the fact that Zara was no true beauty but merely a smaller, less vivid rendering of her stunning elder sisters.

She counted through the music and took each careful slow step over the centuries-old stones beneath her feet. But just as she finally passed the halfway mark she heard another sound repeating behind her. It took a moment to realise it was other footsteps on the flagstones. Heavier ones, moving a touch faster than her own—catching up to her, in fact. She faltered. The bride was supposed to be the last to arrive. Should she pause and allow whoever it was to get themselves seated?

As she hesitated the organ stopped. Then the trumpets. She hadn't actually made it all the way up the aisle, yet now the cathedral was abruptly silent.

Except for those heavy footsteps. They kept going.

She was a full ten feet short of where she was supposed to stop. But there didn't seem a lot of point to keep going when the music had stopped as well. She looked towards Garth, the chief architect of this entire pageant and her advisor in all of this. To her astonishment, as she watched he changed colour—first turning pale before his skin was suddenly awash with red. It was only deep emotion that caused an uncontrollable reaction like that.

Garth didn't meet her enquiring gaze but stared hard behind her, his expression aghast. Anders, her groom, finally turned. He didn't so much as glance at her but also immediately fixated on the person coming up the aisle behind her. His jaw dropped but the rest of him stayed still, apparently transfixed.

She was being upstaged on her wedding day, even when

wearing the world's most ludicrously expensive wedding dress with its diamond-encrusted lace. It was so typical that she couldn't get through this like a *proper* princess would. Not only was her title merely a superficial nod to placate her elderly parents, she didn't have the education or the experience, nor the looks nor even the polish she needed to really pull this off.

There were hundreds of people inside the cathedral. Hundreds of *thousands* lining the streets outside. Yet it was eerily silent except for those footsteps. She straightened her shoulders and made herself turn.

It was a man. A mountain of a man. Tall and unbelievably broad-shouldered, his muscular frame dominated her vision. He simply consumed the space of the aisle. As she turned, he stopped walking—now only three feet away—and stared right back at her.

He was clad in full ceremonial attire—*regal* attire. Black trousers…starched white jacket. The scarlet sash across his shoulder emphasised the menacing breadth of him. His hair was cropped close in military fashion, making his facial structure prominent—high cheekbones, square jaw and a nose that looked like it might have been broken more than once. He had an incongruously full mouth but it was currently tightly held, while a jagged, puckered scar cut through his left eyebrow and into his eyelid. She suspected he was lucky to still see from that eye. He was motionless now but he emanated repressed energy—*anger*.

Her heart frantically shoved burning blood through her body. She felt entirely alight—as if she'd somehow spontaneously combusted yet was still standing. He said nothing. He didn't seem to so much as breathe. But he stared back at her. The rest of the world blurred until she saw only him in the vast cathedral. It was as if they were utterly alone and then she felt the strangest compulsion to step towards him—to reach out, pulled by the emotion barely banked within him. She didn't. She was too lost in the palest, iciest eyes she'd ever seen.

In fact she'd seen eyes that colour only once before. In a portrait hanging in the corridor of the palace she'd just come from.

In a portrait of a dead man.

# CHAPTER TWO

IT HAD BEEN ten very long years but Lucian Monrayne had picked his moment to perfection. Every Royal—major and minor—on the continent was present. Every prime minister. Every president. There were generals and dukes, authors and actors, models and musicians. The crème de la crème of societies both modern and traditional mingled today to witness a spectacle Lucian personally found repulsive. But best of all were the cameras. There were so *many* cameras covering every possible angle, which was exactly what he needed.

He'd visualised this moment over and over, yet for all the mental preparation he hadn't factored the impact the cathedral itself would have on him—the deep ache of familiarity, the slicing regret as he took each step further inside. The times he'd spent in here as a boy flashed in his head—memories he had no time or emotional capacity for now. He couldn't allow such self-indulgent distraction. This moment was vital and he needed to be alert. Yet being here was like taking a spear to the heart—it struck deep and released something long suppressed. After an eternity adrift he was *home*. And it almost unravelled him.

So he stared at her instead. The woman. He'd stopped the second she'd turned. Not what he'd intended, but he suddenly couldn't take another step.

She was a few feet from him, a short figure in an enormous jewel-encrusted gown that had to be heavy for her slight frame to wear. Her white-blonde hair was swept back from her face, while the whole of her was enveloped in a gossamer veil. Beneath it he saw her elfin face—pointed chin, smooth skin, full rose-coloured lips and big eyes a far deeper blue than his own. Blue eyes that seemed to search right into him as if seeking out his soul.

She'd been the impetus in this. The cause of an opportunity he didn't think he'd have and that he couldn't ignore. If he had any humanity he would feel sorry for her. But his humanity had gone. All that remained was the survivor he'd been forced to become. A warrior. A strategist. He was a disciplined shell burnished by shame. So there was no soul for her to see.

But he would ruthlessly reclaim his rights, not because he deserved them, but because others deserved them even *less*. And yes, he would have some small revenge. He would finally do his duty. He would protect his kingdom and his people properly—give them the time he'd taken away. Guilt scoured him but determination steeled him.

And yet still in this most crucial of moments all he could do was stare at the woman in white. Time hung, the vision of her overwhelming him. She gleamed like a beacon of serenity, calming the chaos churning inside. He was instinctively drawn to her light—he who'd hid in the shadows for so very long.

The silence seemed endless. No one in the room breathed. Not her. Not him. Not any of the hundreds around them. So the sound—when it finally came—roared.

'Lucian! Lucian! *Lucian!*'

His name crashed into the cathedral in waves, each increasingly louder and more passionate. They were the cries of the commoners beyond the palace walls. The ones watching the large screens that had been specially erected for today's extravaganza. The chant rapidly became deafening and reminded him why he was here. Because it was the name he'd not been called by in the same decade. He was the prince feared drowned long ago. Breathing. Returned at last.

Lucian finally forced his focus to the ruddy-faced fury standing to the right of her. Garth. Then to the rear of her. To the cruel. To the coward. His cousin and would-be assassin. Anders. Currently frozen in fury.

Lucian lifted his hand. There was the barest delay from the telecast but almost instantly the crowds outside hushed—attentive, agog.

'I suppose you didn't think you'd ever see me again, did you, cousin?' he muttered huskily, opting for English, the language common to most present.

He ignored the collective intake of breath of over a thousand people. He would have found it theatrically comical if he weren't so bitter. But bitter he was.

The last time he'd looked Anders in the eye was as he'd sunk beneath the water. He'd never forgotten the malevolent glint in his younger cousin's gaze and his almost gleeful intake of breath as the blood poured, blinding Lucian. He'd wanted to dismiss it as a nightmare—a figment of a confused, concussed brain, his memory filling the blanks with some warped version of events. But the vision was clear. He'd dived and hit his head—that *had* been an accident. But his young cousin had not attempted to rescue him. Anders had lifted the boat hook not to help Lucian out, but to strike another blow.

'You're an impostor.' Garth stepped forward.

Of course it was Garth who answered. Garth the puppet master. The one who'd wanted control from the start. Not Royal by blood, but whose nephew was. The man who'd been de facto ruling Monrayne, his corruption deepening through the decade. He'd siphoned riches for himself while trying to control—*hide*—the increasing cruelty of his nephew. Hence this distasteful charade today.

'Prince Lucian has been dead for a decade,' Garth added. 'Where have you been all this time—getting plastic surgery to try to pull off this elaborate ruse? It won't work.'

'I decided against plastic surgery,' Lucian said calmly. 'I have no desire to hide *any* of the wounds I've suffered.'

Gasps rippled through the cathedral. Anders looked greenish now. Wide-eyed, he remained half hiding behind his bride. Of course.

She hadn't moved either. That perfect princess still glittered in the light. The one he couldn't help looking at.

He'd endured that decade of banishment, waiting for this—the most public moment to reveal himself. To have his revenge on the man-child who'd tried to take everything from him and who'd succeeded in some ways Lucian still couldn't bear to acknowledge. He couldn't be distracted and fail now. So he welcomed the cold anger that rose in the wake of memories too hideous to allow. Anger was the best emotion of all.

'Allow me to show you.' Lucian steadily unbuttoned his jacket.

It hadn't been made by the tailors of Monrayne palace but those of King Niko of Piri-nu—no less valid, frankly more soft against his hardened skin. Finally unfastened, he let the jacket slide down his arms. With a soft swish it slipped to the floor. There was another collective intake of breath.

He'd deliberately worn nothing beneath it—a perfectly normal choice for the temperatures on the Pacific Island kingdom where he'd lived out this time, but here in Monrayne the cold bit. He refused to let it penetrate.

He also wore no bulletproof vest. In theory, someone could step up behind him and make an attempt, but his hearing was attuned. Plus he'd brought one guard with him, who was watching his six right now. If a sniper wanted to take him they'd go for a headshot anyway. But they wouldn't want blood spattered on the bride's beautiful dress. Not in front of an audience of millions. He'd counted on that.

So he stood in the centre of the cathedral. Bare-chested. His not-so-ceremonial sword at his side.

But, after all this time, it wasn't his enemy he watched. It was her. She still hadn't moved but her gaze dipped. He saw her curiosity. But something else bloomed as her gaze raked over the skin that he'd barely shown anyone, let alone the entire world all at once. For a flash he felt vulnerable. He was never this exposed. Her attention lingered on his tattoo. Then moved to the scar he'd had for most of his life. The scar the whole of Monrayne knew he had.

As her focus slowly slid even lower his entire body tensed. He was battered and scarred but he needed strength now and as he stared at her he felt it surging within him. All that should matter was *beyond* her. Yet he couldn't take his eyes off the ethereally beautiful bride. Her lashes lifted and for a second he thought he saw heat in her eyes. Surely not. Not a woman about to wed another man.

But then she nodded, almost imperceptibly, and it gave him the impetus he needed.

'You'll see the scar from the ice-skating accident I had when I was three.' He lifted his voice for all to hear—all anger and authority and using more words than he sometimes spoke in a day. 'And, as you can see, I've acquired a few more since.'

Everyone knew about the ice-skating accident. The permanent scar on his ribs had been documented in embarrassing paparazzi photos of him as a youth.

'Does anyone here desire to draw my blood *again*?' he asked coolly.

It was a direct, deliberate challenge. An unsubtle hint that the accident hadn't really been an *accident*. He'd become aware that there'd been rumours and speculation in the kingdom for years, and of course his body had never been found. But he *had* been declared dead and his cousin Anders pronounced heir. But Anders's guardian and uncle, Garth, had become the Regent, despite not being in the royal bloodline, because Monrayne liked its kings mature. Garth hadn't dared meddle with the ancient laws of succession. Besides which, it had suited him to retain power for as long as possible. But twenty-five was mere days away for Anders now.

'Naturally I will provide a sample for a DNA test. We will live stream that draw and put a tracker on the sample. We will keep the world's eyes on it while it is tested.' Lucian finally looked at Garth again. 'Won't we, Garth?'

There would be no mix-up or loss of his sample. Garth now understood this was no bluff and he didn't like it. He paled but inclined his head in mute agreement.

'I understand how much of a shock this is.' Lucian allowed his gaze to slide to the groom. 'Especially for my young cousin Anders.'

Anders hadn't moved a muscle. They were dressed in identical ceremonial attire. But Anders had no right to wear the sash of the Crown Prince. Not then. Not now. Not *ever*. He might be next in line to the throne but Lucian would do everything required to prevent that from happening.

It was the woman who broke the tableaux. He watched as she glided closer in that sparkling dress. Her gaze was locked on him and once more he found he couldn't tear his own away. It was wrong. Peripherals were important. The soldier within—mercenary really—knew prioritising her was foolish. But once more the world around them disappeared. She stopped a foot away. Her full focus on him this close was like an unbearably soft caress on his bare skin. And to his aston-

ishment—and even more astonishing *pleasure*—she grace-
fully dropped into a deep curtsey.

'King Lucian.' She pitched her voice perfectly so the cathedral acoustics picked up her words. There wouldn't be a
person present who wouldn't have heard her acknowledgement of his identity.

He didn't know her name. He should have, of course. He'd
worked hard to restore his mental acuity and hadn't slipped
in years. So this was vexing. He gritted his teeth and quickly
covered the lapse.

'Princess.' He inclined his head.

He knew there were allies here. Those who did not wish to
see Anders take the Crown. Those who knew something of
the truth of the man. Lucian had done his research. But there
were things he could learn only by being here on the ground
and he had not expected Anders's bride to be the first to acknowledge him.

After a moment an army general left his position at the
end of the second row and marched towards him. Lucian's
intelligence had kept him apprised of the factions within the
court and this older soldier had long been a servant of Monrayne. A sheen of emotion glistened in the older man's eyes.
He didn't bow. He knelt in front of Lucian. His bones almost
creaked with the effort.

'King Lucian,' he echoed huskily. 'Long live the King.'

Because Lucian was more than twenty-five. He was twenty-
nine. Thus he was automatically King, whether he'd been officially crowned or not. He should've been the King for years
already. But he'd been presumed dead. And he'd been hiding,
biding his time for this rarest of opportunities.

Everyone in the cathedral was already standing but now
his citizens bowed from the waist. The rulers of other nations
nodded in acknowledgement at least.

'King Lucian.' The chant rang through the cathedral. 'Long live King Lucian!' Over and over and over again.

A swell of bitter rejection rose inside. He was not worthy to be King. But Anders was a worse alternative. So he would do what he had to do. He allowed it for a few moments, to let it fully sink in to Anders. To Garth. That he was back. And he let the anger resurge. Yet, even so, he couldn't take his gaze from the pretty woman, pale in that resplendent dress. Now the icy anger *burned*. Because anyone who knew Anders well—and Garth knew him—would know the man's tendencies and inclinations. And yet here was this ethereal, petite princess looking too perfect to even be real, about to be sacrificed to him. Did *she* know Anders—the truth of him? Or did she not care about those he'd hurt? Did she think herself safe somehow? Not even Lucian had been safe. That cold anger seeped out, driving him to test them both.

'Please don't let me interrupt the wedding a moment longer.' He bowed slightly towards the bride. 'I apologise for the hold-up in proceedings.'

The flicker of reproach in her gaze stabbed. He tensed, more alert than he'd been all week. The greatest threat to anyone present—to both this woman and to *himself*—was right now. But he was ready.

'*What?*' Anders finally stepped into Lucian's full line of sight. The man was visibly shaking and his expression was one Lucian had seen many times in his youth. Petulant anger. Where Lucian harnessed his, allowing adrenalin to make him more alert, Anders succumbed to rage and irrationality. And he was still that wilful, greedy child now, furious at being denied what he wanted. He'd been spoilt—Lucian knew it, because Lucian had been spoilt too. And it took only a spark to set Anders's rage alight—to goad him beyond control. It was exactly what Lucian had expected—what he'd *wanted*—to happen. In front of the world.

'Please continue with your wedding, Anders,' Lucian said coolly.

'If you think I'm going to marry this frigid bitch now, you're crazy!' Anders snapped.

It wasn't a collective intake of breath this time, the entire congregation gasped in shock. Then there was a smattering of boos while a few people called out Anders's name in reproach. But the cretin stormed out of the cathedral. Not stopping to bow to Lucian as protocol dictated he should. Lucian didn't turn. He didn't savour the moment as he'd imagined he would so many times. He just watched the woman's face whiten and felt terrible.

'Get down. Give me that!'

The orders Anders gave to some hapless soldier outside the cathedral echoed within it. Then a cracking sound as a horse was whipped. More shouts.

She blanched.

No one would be able to deny what they'd just witnessed. Anders was cruel. Unfit to be King. He always had been. His jilted bride remained a single step away from Lucian, absorbing the murmurs and condemnation of the crowds. For the briefest moment she closed her eyes and the knife of remorse twisted inside him.

'I apologise for my cousin,' he said. 'He always lacked manners.'

'And yours are any better?' She barely moved her lips as she spoke in a response so soft that not even those amazing acoustics nor the myriad microphones would pick it up. It was a miracle Lucian heard it. But he did.

Was she angry with him? His gaze narrowed. Naive little fool. Surely she knew the rules of public life? There was a glimmer of pride in the way she kept her head high. The smattering he knew about her came back to him. She was the youngest princess of a much smaller realm across the Baltic that had removed all power from the royalty. She hadn't ever been on the social circuit, though she had two older sisters who were. Rumour had it her parents were desperately clinging to their regal nomenclature and still in denial about the disintegration of their aristocracy despite it being years since they were deposed. She'd met Anders only a couple of months ago. She might not appreciate it right now but Lucian had just done her a massive favour.

'May I have your permission to leave, Your Highness?' Chagrin glowed in her eyes but there was more than a glimmer of defiance too.

'Go with the bishop,' he muttered and nodded beyond the altar. 'That will give you more privacy.'

She turned her back on him and walked to the nave—her head high, those jewels still glittering. Lucian's gut twisted as he grimly watched her go. The bishop swiftly guided her to the small side door. In that sanctuary she could escape all the cameras. He would never see her again and that could only be for the good.

He waited until that side door closed before taking the last few steps to the altar himself. Then he turned to face the cathedral full of people. As he bowed before them he drew on that old, cold anger. It restored his determination and discipline. He would devote his life to becoming the King they deserved—to being better than the man he was. There would be no distraction, no decadence.

While providing heirs would be an imperative part of his future, he would not marry for a decade at least. He owed his country. Giving it his undivided attention for the duration that he'd been absent would ensure Monrayne was settled and secure. Even then his marriage would be a formal exercise, based on duty. He'd prioritised his private life in the past and he would regret it always. There was no room for personal indulgence, Monrayne would be his primary concern for ever, and of course the first item on his *to-do* list was to change the succession—Anders could not remain Crown Prince a moment longer than necessary.

He met Garth's rigid gaze. The fury that had accompanied him for what felt like all eternity coursed through his veins more strongly than ever.

'I am King Lucian of Monrayne,' he said clearly. 'And I am here to serve for as long as I live.'

# CHAPTER THREE

ZARA CLOSED HER eyes and tried once more to unfasten her wretched wedding dress. She'd managed to rip the veil from the intricate hairstyle but the rest—the bobby pins, the earrings and the millions of tiny buttons down her back were all too much. Contortionist she was not.

*Hours* had passed since those horrific moments in the cathedral in front of millions, in which her fiancé had brutally rejected her. Hours since Prince—*King*—Lucian Monrayne had returned from the dead.

The very distracted bishop had shown her to a tunnel and promptly abandoned her. To her amazement, the tunnel had emerged within the palace walls. After a couple of wrong turns she'd passed that portrait and finally found the suite she'd been staying in. Since then she'd been transfixed by the constant televised coverage. All those efficient palace assistants had vanished—presumably too fascinated by the return of the long-lost King to bother with an unwanted bride. She truly didn't blame them.

But while she'd appreciated the chance to be alone, she'd not expected it to be this long. Why hadn't her mother and sisters come to check on her—to take her home, even if it were to be in disgrace and mortification? She'd been rejected by her fiancé, dismissed from the King's presence and instantly forgotten by everyone. No one had knocked on the door in eons.

But then the world had plenty to occupy its collective mind. King Lucian's declaration at the front of the cathedral only moments after she'd left had been everything. It had been on repeat for hours and caught her attention every time it replayed—*he* caught her attention. Completely. In the cathedral when she'd stood before him the rest of the world had disappeared. All she'd been aware of was him—those ice-blue eyes, the scarred, angry, visceral strength of him. He was so cold. He'd been utterly expressionless as he'd personified the grenade which had decimated not just the day but obliterated the expected succession with a short couple of sentences.

Most of the foreign dignitaries had abruptly left. There was an endless series of private jets flying overhead, stoking an air of danger and political uncertainty. The world was agog with curiosity as to where Anders had fled. But the crowds outside the palace had continued to swell. Any citizens who'd not bothered to line the streets for Anders's wedding were now out in force for the return of Lucian. There was continuous chanting, cheers and revelry. It seemed the public were pleased.

The King had issued a statement asking everyone to go home and rest. That there would be formal televised announcements over the coming days, together with a full explanation of what had happened all those years ago and where he'd been for all of this time.

It didn't seem as if Garth had been altogether pleased to see Lucian, despite his acknowledgment of him. Zara's doubts about Anders intensified. She had the horrible feeling some of those more outlandish conspiracy theories about Lucian's disappearance all those years ago might not have been so outlandish after all.

So she really just wanted to get out of her dress now. Then out of here *entirely*. Though quite how she was going to do either, she didn't know. Even if she had been able to twist herself to undo the tiny buttons she couldn't because of the stupidly long nails the beauticians had insisted she wear to make the rings look nice. Nor could she cut the minuscule hand-stitching that seamstress had spent hours putting in. She was ready to scream with the frustration of it.

Thankfully, just then the door finally opened. But Zara's relief and appreciation died as she saw who strode in. Lucian himself.

The door slammed behind him and he'd taken only one step before he spotted her in the corner and abruptly halted. She watched him swiftly visually sweep the rest of the room before his gaze paused on the yards of silk tulle in a heap on the floor. His hands curled into fists.

The sight of him shocked her all over again, despite the fact he'd been emblazoned across the television screen for hours. He wasn't wearing his jacket but, to her immense relief, he'd put a top on. The black tee shirt ought to look incongruous with the formal trousers, yet somehow he pulled it off. It hugged his enormous muscles. He didn't look anything like a pampered Royal, more like an elite soldier. Or mercenary.

That was when her mind decided to replay the image of him standing bare-chested and statue-still in that cathedral. The light had shone down on him like some celestial intervention—highlighting the tattoo; the childhood scar on his ribcage; the tanned frame; his ridged abdomen; the dusting of hair on his chest that arrowed at his waistband. Ripped and raw, his was the hewn body of a fighter and every inch of it was imprinted on her mind—not budging even when she tried to blink it away.

She'd not seen her fiancé in such a state of undress. She'd not seen *any* man in such a state. Yes, she'd been that sheltered. She'd not even been allowed to bathe at public beaches. Not to protect her, not because she was that 'precious', but to help hide her family's drastically depleted resources. Her parents' pride wouldn't allow them to let her be seen in anything less than designer and, as they could afford none, then she couldn't be out.

Her older sisters had backed them up, adamantly insisting she remain in the countryside. She'd been stuck there so long she'd *almost* accepted it...until now.

'What are you doing in here?' He interrupted her thoughts with that arctic tone. 'Are you alone?'

Of course she was alone. She'd effectively been alone her entire life.

'What do you want?' His eyes narrowed. 'Why are you here?'

His accusatory tone made her hackles rise.

'This was the room I was assigned,' she said. 'I've been staying here for the last week.'

He didn't move, yet somehow he seemed even bigger. 'Once upon a time it was my room.'

She stared at him in horror. The man hadn't been home in who knew how long, for reasons also unknown, and she was in his room. Had she been sleeping in his *bed*?

'I wasn't aware of that. I apologise.'

She'd just been deposited here and left to her own devices and now she was utterly mortified. Again. But King Lucian showed no embarrassment. No emotion at all. He stepped closer, his gaze neutral. She almost shivered but she didn't want to betray her fear.

Except it wasn't fear making her shiver.

'I forgot you were...' He trailed off.

*Right.*

'Of course,' she muttered awkwardly. 'It's been a very busy time for you.'

Everyone had forgotten her. Especially him. Except the media chose that exact moment to remember her—airing the replay of Anders's rejection of her in the cathedral in that instant—

*Frigid bitch.*

She picked up the remote and turned the coverage off, but the insult echoed in the room. Somehow, she'd lived through that utter humiliation in front of millions, yet being alone with this particular man brought her anger forth now. He'd destroyed the day so clinically.

'If you could get someone to find me another room, I'll gather my things and go right away.' She turned towards the bedroom.

She heard his swiftly indrawn breath and next instant his hand landed heavily on her shoulder.

'What have you done?' he snarled huskily. 'You've hurt yourself.'

She froze at his touch. He must have moved *incredibly* swiftly.

'I haven't,' she choked.

'Your back is—'

'I can't get out of this dress,' she snapped. She was already so mortified there was no point striving for any dignity now. 'I was a little thinner and they had to stitch me into it last-minute—' She broke off and twisted to face him.

His hand dropped but he was uncomfortably close now and he didn't back off. Nor did she. But there was fire in his eyes—a different kind of anger to the one she'd seen before.

'So you were trying to rip your way out of it and scratched yourself to pieces in the process?'

She hadn't scratched herself—or not as badly as he was suggesting.

'Where's your maid?' He glared at her.

She didn't actually have one. All those assistants had been supplied by the palace.

His expression tightened. 'What about your sisters? Your mother?'

'I don't know where any of my family is,' she mumbled.

He looked at her so intently she had the feeling he was holding something back from her.

'You should have been out of this get-up hours ago,' he said harshly.

'I agree.' She closed her eyes, refusing to cry. She'd been struggling alone for hours and suddenly she was hot and furious. The damned wedding dress made her skin crawl. She reached up behind her again to try to tug the back of the tightly stitched lace bodice apart.

'Stop hurting yourself.' He moved quickly, his hands encircling her wrists.

It brought him too close to her. No one had ever invaded her personal space like this. Her breathing quickened as he held her hands above her head. She felt a vulnerability that was absolute. He was so much stronger than her. But she also felt a sweeping yearning that was—

'You're badly marked,' he said huskily.

'I'm not,' she denied despairingly. She had zero pride left, zero strength to battle control on two fronts. So she just told him the truth. 'I get a rash when I'm upset or anxious, nervous, whatever. It looks worse than it is.' She drew a shaky breath. 'Hopefully, I haven't actually drawn blood. They'll kill me if I have—the dress is supposed to go on display later…'

There was a moment of awkward silence but she couldn't stop gazing up into his eyes. She could study that scar this close. It was a jagged, ugly mark that clearly hadn't been stitched by a skilled surgeon. It gave him a dangerous look. But his grip on her wrists was gentle. He smelled of caramel—a rich, sweet softness she'd not expected. She sensed he was holding himself rigid while within her all kinds of reactions

were detonated. Weird ones. But ones she didn't quite want to
end yet, which had to be why she remained so stupidly still.

'I will assist you,' he said gruffly, releasing her.

She shot him a startled look. 'You don't want to summon
a maid and leave me to it?'

That serious expression didn't lighten. 'I am uncertain of
which palace staff—if any—I can trust. I would prefer not
to allow anyone else into this suite just yet.' His voice was a
rusty monotone.

He was the most suspicious person on the planet. But then
perhaps he had reason to be. She'd seen the footage of Anders's expression when he'd registered it was Lucian standing
before him. And Garth's. Raw shock had widened their eyes
before undisguised horror burnished them. Ultimately ugly
fury had contorted Ander's entire stature. Lucian's return had
been his living nightmare.

So she nodded. Truthfully, she didn't want anyone else to
see her even more abandoned. This man had seen her worst
moment and he was more than enough.

'Well, if you wouldn't mind just cutting the back of the
dress where it's been stitched? Then I'll get out of here and…'

She trailed off. She had no idea where she was going to go
or what she was going to do.

Impossibly, he was watching her even more closely now.
'And…?'

She swallowed. 'I'm not sure.'

'No?'

She couldn't help hearing his cold tone as judgement. 'Gosh,
it's not like I've been jilted at the altar and humiliated in front
of an audience of millions or anything. I can't think why I
would need some time to get my head together.'

Anger flickered across his face. It pleased her, oddly, to
have forced a change in his plank-of-wood impression.

'You may stay the night here while you work out your plan for tomorrow,' he said stiffly.

'How very kind of you,' she said sharply. 'But if I could just borrow a phone, I'll call my mother.'

'You have no phone?'

'Clearly not.'

His pale gaze flicked around the room again.

'There isn't one in here either,' she added.

His attention returned to her, yet she felt as if he'd been aware of her every movement, every quickening breath all along.

And now he was even more stone-like. 'Unfortunately, your mother has already left.'

'What?' Her legs felt wobbly.

'Your sisters took her. They left in a jet two hours ago. Hitched a ride with the prime minister, I believe.'

'*What?*' How could he tell her this with such ambivalence? Her confusion grew. 'But you just asked me where they all were! Why did you do that if you already knew?'

His mouth tightened. Then he released a sharp breath. 'I wanted to see if you knew. If you'd chosen to remain deliberately.' His gaze travelled down her dress and his mouth tightened. 'Perhaps you didn't. But perhaps your mother wanted you to be stuck here.'

'Why would she want *that*?' Zara stared at him uncomprehendingly until her sluggish brain crawled to the most embarrassing conclusion. 'You don't think she wanted me to throw myself on your mercy?' She stared, aghast, at the obvious cynicism sharpening his gaze and spoke again before thinking. 'To throw myself at *you*?'

The thing was, it was exactly what her mother *would* want. She'd just have no faith that Zara would ever be capable of it. Rightly so, because Zara wasn't. She was appalled and ached unbearably at her family's rejection. The negative assumption of the man standing before her merely compounded the misery. She was *stupidly* hurt.

'A distasteful idea, I see.' A self-mocking smile flashed on his lips too briefly.

It was her mother's abandonment that was distasteful. Not, unfortunately, *him*.

'Do you think I am more dangerous to you than Anders?' he asked.

Yes. A million times *yes*.

Anders had never left her breathless. Or confused. Or questioning everything. Feeling oddly dizzy, she rubbed her forehead, trying to think and failing to ease the tension headache that had been building in intensity for hours. The diamond drop earrings on loan from the Monrayne vault were heavy. She wasn't used to wearing jewels like them. How had she ever thought she could carry off this performance? Because it was just a performance. A charade she'd tried to get through in order to make a better life. And yes, she couldn't get herself out of costume. She was stuck. Shamed. Unwanted and abandoned in a palace she couldn't escape.

Story of her life.

'You need assistance with those too, I see,' he muttered sardonically.

He leaned in, not giving her any space to escape. She was too surprised to step back anyway. She felt that warmth of him again—so at odds with his cool demeanour.

'Hold still,' he growled.

With slow care he removed one earring. Then the other. She held her breath the whole time. It seemed incongruous that this very large, lethally strong man who was clearly suppressing raging fury could be so gentle. Her heart thudded. He wasn't the charming-looking young prince of a decade ago. He was angrily ice-cold and ruthless and could easily hurt her. Yet she wasn't afraid. Because there'd been that moment in the cathedral where everyone had disappeared and she'd seen only him and he'd looked right back at her and maybe it was all in her head but she was sure something had passed between them. A recognition of emotion. Of understanding.

It happened again now. For a long moment she was lost in the depths of his eyes—like a crevasse in which she endlessly plummeted—until she blinked and inwardly cringed at her own flight of fancy. It would be so mortifying if he guessed what she was thinking.

'Better?' He sounded almost tender—but as if he cared?

She was mistaking quiet query for tenderness. And her, 'Thank you,' came out sharper than she intended.

He weighed the earrings in the palm of his hand and then set them on the low table near them. 'Why do you have your nails so long when you can't seem to do anything with them that length?'

'I don't usually. I bite them. These are fake.' Her whole look today was fake. 'My natural nails are so unsightly they had to be covered up.'

'Rendering you incapable at the same time?'

Because she wasn't used to them. She gritted her teeth. Did he have to point out the obvious quite so brutally? Did he have *no* heart—no compassion for her situation?

No. Compassion wasn't something this man would feel. He was too full of vengeance.

Yet she couldn't step away from him. Couldn't seem to do anything other than absorb his presence. Vital energy emanated from him with such intensity she couldn't understand *how* he had remained hidden for so long.

Suddenly her dress felt too tight. It ought to be her wedding night and here she was, being helped by the man who'd destroyed her day. Whose arrival had led to her absolute humiliation. And yet—she finally admitted to herself—she was more physically aware of him than she'd been of any other man in her life. She needed to get away from him and out of here. ASAP.

'Are you ever going to help me out of this dress?' she muttered impatiently.

'Are you ever going to turn around?'

# CHAPTER FOUR

ZARA'S PULSE RACED and she frowned at him. 'Are you going to use your sword?'

'No.'

Was he going to shred her dress with his bare hands?

To her fascination—and horror—he swiftly retrieved a small dagger that was strapped to his ankle. 'I'm going to use this.'

The blade glinted. It was no ceremonial weapon. He'd concealed that he carried it. It was for real.

She shivered. 'You have that with you at all times?'

'This and more.' He looked at her directly. 'But I also know how to kill with my bare hands.'

She wasn't surprised and she knew he was trying to shock her. She *refused* to be intimidated.

'Yes, but my new nails might give you a run for your money.'

There was the slightest tightening at the corner of his mouth. 'If you were to push your thumbs into the eye sockets of an assailant then perhaps those nails could actually be useful.'

She swallowed. He wasn't smiling. He was perfectly serious.

'You should know how to take care of yourself,' he added.

The anger she'd kept at bay all afternoon seeped through her final defences. 'You don't think I already do?'

'No,' he said. 'You can't even seem to get yourself undressed.'

*Seem?* Did he *doubt* her struggles with this? Did he truly imagine that she'd been deliberately waiting for him to show up and strip her?

*Perhaps your mother wanted you to be stuck here.*

Didn't he believe that she'd been here with no idea that he'd walk in on her? Did he really think *she'd* tried to engineer this somehow?

The thing was, if Lucian had been the fiancé on offer in the first place, her sister Ana would have said yes in a heartbeat— even though he too was still younger than her. Because Lucian Monrayne hadn't just been gorgeous as a teenager, he'd been charming and intelligent and an all-round superstar.

Now fully grown, he was lethally attractive-looking. But he wasn't *charming* any more. He was hardened. Zara guessed he'd survived who knew what and, as a result, a sense of danger emanated from him. Yet he still stoked a different response within her. One that couldn't be more inappropriate. Angry about it, she pushed back, unable to restrain her curiosity.

'Why did you reveal yourself today?' she asked baldly.

He regarded her steadily and she knew he was deciding what—if anything—to reveal. He was irritatingly measured in his responses. Every word was considered and used sparingly.

'I required a public occasion for my return.'

He'd wanted a big show? Was that all?

'The coronation would have been even more public,' she pointed out.

'I didn't want to leave it that late,' he said with slow precision. 'I needed to ensure safety. For everyone. I needed time to ensure the coronation—'

'Was your own?' she interrupted as fierce emotion swamped her. 'And I was just collateral damage?'

His expression hardened. 'I wanted to stop the wedding,' he said. 'I wanted to rescue you from—'

'Did I *ask* you to rescue me?' she snapped.

His mouth thinned. 'You are disappointed.'

'*Disappointed?*' She should laugh.

He had no idea of what he'd done to her future. Suddenly all her anger was directed at *him*. 'You don't get to come here and leave me in a worse position than where I began.'

'Is that what I have done?'

'Of course it is. I've just been publicly humiliated by—'

'The man who was supposed to be in love with you. Not by *me*,' he pointed out coolly, but twin flames glowed in his eyes. 'You really wanted to marry him?'

'Well, I was standing in the church in a big white gown—'

'Because you're in love with him?'

She stilled, lost for words. Mortified, she remembered again how Anders had labelled her so cruelly. The reason for all her underlying, instinctive anxiety was finally clear. She'd known in her gut something wasn't right. But she'd been too desperate—too delusional about her future—to pay attention.

'It was a political arrangement,' she said, trying to salvage her dignity. 'Mutually beneficial for both our nations.'

'Your *nations*?' he echoed sarcastically. 'Did you anticipate any *personal* benefits?'

She was an idiot for pursuing the idea in the first place. She'd thought she'd done something strategically clever. She'd even thought she'd managed to please her parents.

'I anticipated that I would have more personal freedom than what I've been accustomed to.'

She'd wanted respect too. She suspected now that she wouldn't have got either.

'Freedom?' he scoffed. 'And you were expected to provide an heir? Perhaps a spare as well?'

'Of course.'

'So, even though it was primarily a political arrangement, you were prepared to lie back and think of those other benefits?'

'I hadn't decided on the degree of intimacy I was willing to allow him.' She gritted her teeth. 'After all, there are methods other than the traditional for getting pregnant.'

He blinked and drew in a sharp breath. 'Indeed there are. Yet I can't imagine Anders agreeing to something so clinical. He's far more animal in his approach.' The words were ground from him. 'So you hadn't already slept with him.'

Her jaw dropped but, before she could snap back at him, he stepped closer.

'Had you kissed him?' Huskily, he asked more intrusive, more inappropriate questions. 'Have you kissed *anyone*, Princess?'

She held her ground, but only just. 'I don't see what business that is of yours. Or what relevance it has to *anything*.'

'Because now here you are, with your untouched lips and untouched body, trying to get yourself into a barely dressed state for me to discover. Was that the new plan? To make yourself even more irresistible to me?'

*Even more irresistible?*

She gaped. The man was mad.

But he suddenly froze, his jaw angular. She just knew he would bite those words back if he could. The outrageousness of his accusation was incinerated by the heat she felt at that giveaway. But she wasn't going to let him *apologise* for admitting it. She was too busy trying to ignore her own inappropriate internal combustion.

Her pulse scurried. 'You're obviously overtired and stressed,' she said. 'That's the only explanation for your insanely rude assumptions. I never for a second imagined you were about to walk into this room and it's the height of arrogance to think that I would want…would want…'

'Me to touch you in any way?' he finished for her, his cool recovered. 'Yet isn't that just what you've asked me to do? Because apparently you need my help to get out of that dress. So turn around and I'll cut it off you.'

The *last* thing she wanted was his assistance now. And equally she knew it was the last thing *he* wanted to do now too. Which in all made her defiantly toss her head as she did as he'd commanded so savagely and turned her back on him.

There was a moment of stillness, yet her temperature soared as she felt the frisson of sexual promise that he surely hadn't meant. Then she felt his breath on the back of her neck. She closed her eyes, gritting her teeth so she wouldn't shudder in response. He carefully—far too slowly—worked the thin blade.

Her muscles screamed with the effort to stay still—not to lean back into him or to run away. Both urges were overwhelmingly intense. She'd never had a more intimate moment with any man. He was undressing her—or at least trying to. The flare of heat kept rising. She ached to be free of the confines of the horribly constricting dress. Her breasts felt crushed, her taut nipples ached. It was appalling. She needed his *help*. That was all. She didn't want anything *more*. Yet the drive deep within her was breathtakingly strong. And she just knew that he wasn't at all the cold-blooded warrior he appeared.

'Is it done?' she asked impatiently, embarrassed by her breathlessness. She couldn't stand to be this close much longer.

She heard a muttered imprecation beneath his breath, his control audibly weakening too.

'It's very tightly stitched,' he gritted.

'You can rip it to shreds for all I care.' She *desperately* needed to get away from him.

The second she felt it loosen she stepped forward for breathing space and—

'Wait—'

She heard a sharp shredding sound as she turned. A sudden coolness hit her skin. It was a blink before she realised the bodice had slipped to her waist.

He went rigid. 'Cover yourself.'

Her humiliation was overridden by a flare of fury unlike any other and, instead of doing as he ordered, she let her hands drop. It was in absolute defiance of everyone who'd told her what to do all day—what to do all her *life*. She was so sick of doing as she was told, trying to please, trying to be perfect, and failing. Her reason was obliterated in the heat of this last horror.

'*You* stood bare-chested in front of an entire *cathedral* of people, not to mention the millions watching on camera,' she spat. 'It means nothing. What does it matter if I'm bare-chested now?'

He'd already whipped the tee shirt over his head and now held it out to her. 'Put this on. Immediately. Or I'll put it on you myself.'

His gaze didn't waver from her eyes—not dropping to look at her half naked body again. He—unlike she—had too much self-control. She snatched the tee, turning away to put it on. It swamped her and was scented with that soft hint of sweet caramel and suddenly she was shaking. She held the skirts to her hips, shame and humiliation returning in a sweep. Yet she didn't entirely regret the flare. It had felt good to release just some of the fury.

But *he* flared now. 'You wore that dress for someone *else*.'

'I wore it for *myself*,' she said angrily. 'I was very deliberate in the style I agreed to. I wanted modesty to protect myself from their judgement, not to emphasise any impression of *innocence*.'

'In what possible way would they judge you negatively?'

She snatched a breath. 'Because I'm nothing like the perfect image presented today,' she muttered with a wobbly smile. 'Not just bitten nails. No one usually even sees me. But today

I knew everyone would. So I went for the full makeover. I'm covered almost head to toe in diamonds and silk and lace to distract from what's beneath.'

'Why would you desire to distract anyone from what's beneath? I've just seen—' He bit his lip and didn't finish the sentence.

She wanted him to finish it. She wanted so many wild, impossible things. Most of all—right now—his touch. She wanted to lose herself in the overwhelming masculinity, the strength, the sensual drive emanating from him. She wanted him to sweep her away. It was absolutely insane.

He stepped away, only to suddenly swing back. 'You were the first to acknowledge that I was who I said I was. We have not met. What made you so sure?'

'Your eyes.' She answered automatically.

He said nothing.

'The colour,' she added in a mumble. 'The shape.'

'Despite the scar?'

'Of course.' She couldn't look away from him. She was almost overcome by the desire to trace the gap in his eyebrow with the tip of her finger. 'Did you get it—?'

'When I nearly died? Yes.'

'Was it…?'

'Anders who tried to finish me off? Yes. Not only had you not slept with him, you barely knew him. You may not like to hear it, but I *did* rescue you from far more than you realise.'

She glared at him, hoisting her dress again with her hands on her hips. 'Really?'

Her movement made him glance down. Now he stared at her hand and his voice was very soft. 'You are probably equally unaware that the ring you wear once belonged to my mother.'

Her anger evaporated. She wanted to die. Right now. She couldn't breathe as she tried to get it off her finger while still trying to hold her skirt up, but it was a desperate disaster. 'Please take it back. Please. I don't want it.'

'If you'll stop panicking and stand still for half a second, I'll do just that,' he snapped.

They both stilled. He was breathing as hard as she now. Both of them a whisper away from loss of control. But that intimacy resurged as he carefully worked the ornate ring from her finger. His scent enfolded her, his heat, his shocking gentleness, and her emotions were on the biggest rollercoaster—she was *not* going to cry in front of this man.

At last he held the ring and she stepped back. The precious stones glinted in the light.

His expression became that stark mask again. 'I came here to stop Anders's marriage because I know what lies beneath his facade. You're not collateral damage and you may now return to your home.'

'I *may*.' She echoed his patronising permission. 'What if I don't wish to return home?'

Why would she ever want to return there now?

His expression shut down. 'I have no desire nor need for a wife at present.'

She gaped. 'Do you *seriously* still think I'm here to offer myself to you? That I would go from one groom to another in a single afternoon?'

But the awful thing was, she *was* attracted to him. It was very sudden. Very strong. And she was trying so, *so* hard not to stare at his magnificent chest.

There was a slight twist of his lips, *almost* a smile. 'Well, what am I to think when I find you attempting to undress yourself in my bedroom…?'

'You're to think that I was being honest when I told you this room was assigned to me. That I've been staying in here all week.'

All week while she'd been alone—ignored by her prospective groom and her family.

'But you're not sure who—if anyone—is honest, are you?'

His expression shut down again. 'You no longer need to sacrifice yourself for family or country.'

'I chose to accept the engagement to Anders,' she said proudly. 'It was *my* decision. It wasn't forced upon me by my greedy family, if that's what you're thinking. I didn't need you to rescue me. I was here on my own terms with my eyes wide open.'

'Is that right?' he said with soft sarcasm. 'Because you knew your fiancé so well. You knew all about his particular preferences.'

She swallowed, unsure of what he meant but understanding at least that it was something ugly.

'And would an arranged, passionless marriage really have fulfilled you?' he added with a glint in his eye. 'Didn't you want more?'

Zara hadn't wanted to admit that Anders's crude insult had hit so hard mostly because she'd feared it might be true. At least regarding him.

'There are other things that lead to fulfilment,' she said obstinately. 'A physical relationship is not always necessary.'

'What if you'd fallen in love with someone else?'

'How was I going to meet someone to fall in love with? My lifestyle doesn't lend itself to finding lovers easily.'

She'd been cloistered in the castle in the country all through her childhood, slowly taking on more and more care of her ageing parents while being told over and over by her sisters how much life there suited her—that she was lucky because she was too shy and too awkward to enjoy working in the city.

'Well, now you are free to do as you wish,' he said stiffly.

'*Free?*' she said bitterly. 'You do not understand the perilousness of my position.' It was appalling. 'My lack of *preciousness*. I am a third-born princess who—'

'Do you really think your only value is your virginity on your wedding night?' he interrupted harshly. 'What century do you think this is?'

'Well, by everyone's calculations it seems I have little else to offer.'

'I too am a virgin, yet I find I still have plenty else to offer,' he growled.

'You—' She broke off, utterly shocked and unable to believe what she'd just heard. Yet in the next breath she did. 'You don't feel that need?'

There was a moment of mortifying silence in which she then couldn't believe she'd asked that.

Lucian Monrayne struck her as a man who'd take what he needed whenever he needed it. And somehow—with his size, his imperiousness—he seemed like he'd need a lot. Her mouth dried.

'Do you?' he eventually countered coolly.

Her heart skidded. Until today she'd have said she didn't. Anders's barb had struck home and she was certain Lucian was thinking of those cruelly thrown words too.

She squared her shoulders and lifted her chin. 'No. I don't.'

His scarred eyebrow lifted and she felt her face flush. But surely this *frisson* inside her right now was an aberration— shock or something.

'Whether or not I do is irrelevant because I have too much work to do. I suggest you find *your* work,' he advised bluntly. 'Then get on with it.'

'I don't need you to *mansplain* my options to me.' She was angry and insulted and *fascinated*. 'Perhaps I never had the opportunity to be *educated* for any real work in the way that you did,' she said. 'There was no exclusive boarding school for Royals for *me*.'

Lucian had been sent to one, she knew. So had her sisters. They'd all had an elite education abroad, just perfect for young Royals. But Zara had been unexpectedly conceived more than a decade after Ana's birth and by the time she was old enough for that school her parents had been banished to the castle.

'There was only house arrest for me. My parents wanted to hide their financial mismanagement and were too proud for me to be seen going to an ordinary school in ordinary clothes.'

'They kept you at home?'

Mia and Ana had been in their twenties by then. Even though they were powerless princesses, they were well-educated, well-connected and adaptable and still became social darlings. Neither had the time to deal with their parents. That was Zara's role.

'I was fortunate enough to have a governess.' She shot him a look.

'A governess?' His eyebrow lifted crookedly. 'For all this time?'

'I've been caring for my parents and helping run the castle since finishing what education I was offered.'

Even as she'd got older her sisters had leaned upon her to stay there. She was needed at home and 'so good' at managing her parents' demands. And she was too 'shy', too 'awkward' to want to go to university or to work in the city. But that was only because she'd never had the practice, the chance to get used to it or grow in confidence.

For so long she'd believed them—part of her still did. She'd been cast as the shy youngest, 'happy' to live in seclusion. In truth, she'd effectively been stranded in the countryside, caring for parents who couldn't have cared less whether she was there or not. In the end her resentment at having her life suppressed by the assumptions and expectations of her family had grown.

She stiffened at the thought of it all now. 'So when Garth came to visit—'

'*Garth* approached you?' Lucian interrupted.

'My sister Ana. She said she was too old for Anders.'

'So you stepped in?'

'Yes.'

'Had you even *met* Anders at that point?' His frown deepened as she shook her head. 'What was so awful that you needed to escape?'

She paused. How could she explain it to *him,* given all he'd been through? Her discomforts paled in comparison in terms of trauma and isolation. Yes, she'd been stuck in her ramshackle castle, yes, she'd been emotionally neglected, but at least she'd been physically safe, whereas Lucian had been in the wilderness for a decade. Declared dead. *Wanted* dead.

'I thought it was an opportunity for a better life,' she explained weakly. 'But it seems he was only interested in my enthusiasm to give him my innocence and even that in itself had to be *proven*—'

'Before he'd take you as his bride?' Lucian finished harshly. 'Yes, that sounds very like Anders. Given his depraved proclivities, I don't think he was going to accept your idea of some alternative method of impregnation.' Lucian said. 'I think you should consider yourself lucky that Anders walked out of the wedding.'

'I should consider myself lucky that I was publicly humiliated all over again, after already enduring that medical exam?' she asked bitterly.

'He would have humiliated you in far worse ways than that, had the marriage gone ahead,' he said unfeelingly. 'So isn't it fortunate I turned up when I did?'

She stared at him, exasperated. But his scent and warmth and proximity confused her all over again and she suddenly had the most absurd urge to fall in and let him embrace her— as if he'd ever do that. This man had returned for his Crown and had no compunction about doing whatever was necessary to restore his rights. He was also wildly arrogant about it.

So she lifted her chin and made herself take a step backwards. 'I apologise for my apparent lack of gratitude,' she said. 'It's been a very confusing day.'

'I also apologise,' he replied roughly. 'You're in a vulnerable position. Get some sleep. It won't seem so bad in the morning.'

She gritted her teeth yet again. She *really* didn't want his patronising reassurance. That was when she saw the glimmer of a smile in his eyes.

'You disagree, Princess?'

Honestly, she completely disagreed. She'd been publicly jilted. Her family had left without her. She'd been accused of trying to entice the new King—by the new King himself, who was infuriatingly attractive.

He was also determinedly self-sufficient. She paused. The man was obviously an absolute survivor. Which was what she now needed to be. So maybe she could learn a few things from him.

As if he would allow that. He had so much else to be getting on with. And now she felt absurdly melancholic. In all likelihood, she would never see him again.

'I can't sleep in here,' she grumbled. 'It's your suite.'

'It has not been mine for so very long that one more night will make little difference.' He turned and walked away from her. 'I'll ensure someone attends to you first thing and gets you wherever you would like to go. Goodbye, Princess.'

# CHAPTER FIVE

LUCIAN STEPPED INTO the corridor, released a tightly held breath and tried to summon self-control. He'd had only a few moments to himself before another meeting and hadn't expected to spend them stripping someone else's bride and trading lack of sexual histories with her. It had been *madness*. But he'd been unable to resist. In truth, that was the longest private conversation he'd had with another person in ages and, to his amazement, he'd enjoyed it. The little princess who'd usurped his bedroom was surprisingly forthright and feisty and now he needed a moment because his response to her had become *intense*.

Initially he'd thought he might learn something useful from her. While it seemed unlikely she was a confidante of Anders, given his ungallant outburst in the cathedral, his cousin could pull off a bluff better than anyone. So Lucian had held back the information about her mother and then watched closely for her reaction when he'd finally informed her. She'd been utterly transparent—humiliated, hurt and hopelessly honest.

She *hadn't* been waiting to greet him in that stunning redundant wedding gown. And the bluntness with which she'd admitted her 'flaws'—that her appearance was as fake as her nails; that she'd undergone a makeover to pretend to be a perfect princess; that she'd actually thought everyone was looking at her *dress* and not the delectable form beneath it or the beautiful depths of her eyes, all confirmed his gut impression that she was utterly naive. If he had a heart he'd consider it endearing. Instead, it infuriated him. How could Garth have ever considered her to be an appropriate match for Anders?

Furthermore, it infuriated him that she was still here. Because *his* reaction to her was infuriating. It had been from the first.

In the cathedral, in that moment when he'd finally been about to confront Anders face to face, he'd been blinded by her beauty. But now he'd discovered that beneath that cloudy veil and glittering jewels was no perfect princess at all. She was so much better—imperfectly *genuine*—and he'd been compelled to get closer still. It was shocking. But he reasoned that his awareness of her was just a base reaction because of his entirely stressed-out state. He was operating on pure adrenalin and *all* his senses were hyperalert. So this intensely physical response was merely an outlet for some of the pressure of this whole situation. It wasn't *real*. If he ever saw her again in the future he'd likely feel little. Because ordinarily he felt little for anyone.

His emotional bonds had been destroyed in the aftermath of his 'accident'. His cousin's betrayal was bad enough but his mother's death so soon after had devastated him completely and he'd resolved to remain focused on his duty first and for ever.

Because it was his fault that she'd died alone and heartbroken. His fault that he and Anders had been on that boat in the first place. Because he'd been a selfish, petulant teen who'd wanted time to himself, a holiday, leaving his mother alone when she'd needed him most.

His loyalty to his friend, King Niko of Piri-nu, was the last true bond that remained from his past. They'd met at school— one of those elite institutions that apparently Zara hadn't been allowed to attend. They'd been proud alpha princes, battling each other for academic and sporting supremacy and becoming best friends in the attempt. It had been Niko who'd saved his life after the accident when, injured and in hiding, Lucian had sent him coded word. But while Lucian would feel indebted to Niko for ever, he'd repaid him all he could in time and service. Now Monrayne needed all his attention.

He huffed out another breath to push away the ache that princess had left him with. Then he hunted down a servant and demanded they provide the princess with a phone and food first thing and then make whatever travel arrangements she wanted.

At last he returned to the courtiers who'd gathered in the throne room. The assorted dignitaries attending the wedding had rapidly left Monrayne. He wasn't offended. Given there was a chance of upheaval and civil unrest following his wholly astonishing return, he too would've advised anyone who wasn't a citizen to leave. Just in case. Which was why it was shocking to him that Princess Zara had been so abandoned by her family. And if she'd not been properly educated or able to enter society then no wonder she'd wanted to escape her home so completely.

But he knew it was safe enough for her to stay the night for there would be no constitutional crisis here. While the media was still in a frenzy, the swelling crowds at the gate were calm—holding candles and alternating between chanting his name and singing the national anthem. Their continued celebrations took him aback, as did the fact they were calling his return a miracle. Lucian just felt all the more guilty. He should have returned sooner. But he'd owed Niko and he'd needed to wait for the right time.

Anders's disappearance now was yet more proof of his nature. But he would be detained the second he emerged from whatever rock he was hiding beneath. He was too greedy to survive long without the luxury and excess he was used to. He was also too arrogant to believe he was in any real danger. But the fact was Lucian was the least of his threats, for without his protection officers Anders would be more vulnerable to the wrath of the criminal figures he'd tangled with in recent years.

Lucian's immediate duty had to be to stabilise his country. He didn't fear for his own safety now he was here and recognised. It wouldn't take long to secure the new succession plan so there was no chance of Anders taking the Crown, even if the worst were to happen. He dealt with Garth swiftly. Both sycophantic and defensive, the man actually offered his services. Lucian made him surrender his diplomatic passport and papers and then had him escorted to his apartment, where he would remain under guard. Tempting as it was to toss him straight into the palace dungeons, he didn't. There would be a trial for fraud. Until then, house arrest. Lucian would do things by the book.

It was only a few hours from dawn when he finally called a halt to the meetings. He slowly walked through the tunnel, returning to the cathedral—this time going down the stone steps and using the heavy iron key to unlock the family crypt.

His father had died so long ago Lucian barely remembered him, but he'd loved his mother. He pressed his hand against the cold stone that marked her resting place and bowed his head as remorse devastated him. Anders had caused so much hurt to a woman who had already lost so much. To a woman who'd offered him only welcome. But Anders had only been able to do that because of Lucian. The accident had been Lucian's own fault.

He'd been selfish. He'd known she was unwell but he'd pushed to go on his precious 'holiday' anyway. He'd left her alone when she was vulnerable. And she'd died believing him to be dead. At that moment he almost had been. He'd been fighting for his life in a battle with pneumonia on the other side of the world in Piri-nu. If he'd only done as she'd first asked, if he'd simply done his duty, then he wouldn't have been on that boat with Anders and his mother wouldn't have died so much sooner than she ever should have.

So now, as he bowed his head, he offered his apologies silently. But he could never forgive himself for it. He could only vow to do better. He would give his country the decade of service he'd denied it—his undivided, complete attention. He would become the monarch his country deserved and honour his mother's legacy at last.

Eventually he returned to his old wing and took a room that had once been reserved for his servant. But he couldn't sleep. Memories tormented him. Such betrayal. Such bitterness.

But suddenly *new* memories stole in—ones infinitely preferable to the usual nightmares. He closed his eyes and breathed deep—hearing Princess Zara's soft gasp as he'd stood too close to her; feeling her slender wrists and the warmth of her sensitive, silken skin with its patchwork of pink and scarlet; the curve of her breasts had made his mouth water. He hadn't touched anyone in a long time and her skin was tantalisingly soft. His body ached *hard*.

But Lucian couldn't let desire consume him. He had too much to do. He threw back the bedclothes and strode to the shower.

Hours later he stalked into the small dining room. He needed food and he needed a moment away from the suited, wide-eyed courtiers, police representatives and politicians. But he froze in the doorway, struggling to suppress his reaction as he registered who was seated at the polished table. The rush of revitalising energy was undeniable. It was as if she were a portable power pack. One that all but electrocuted his brain.

He grimly shook the paralysis off and stepped forward. Her face grew impossibly paler before flushing in a swathe of scarlet blotches. Once more she clearly hadn't expected his arrival.

'I didn't realise you were still here,' he muttered before

thinking. 'And I certainly didn't expect to find you in my private dining room.'

He'd told that servant to attend to her properly. Perhaps her plane out of here was delayed?

'I didn't realise this is your private dining room,' she hissed indignantly. 'This is just where they put me to feed me.'

Yet she hadn't done all that much eating, had she?

He sat opposite her and took in the vast untouched array of breads, salads and sliced meats separating them. He didn't feel like eating any of it either. He'd not given a public speech in a long time and there were going to be millions watching him this afternoon. Analysing every word. Words he still hadn't written.

He poured himself a strong coffee and sat back to study her. To his utterly inappropriate pleasure, she stared right back at him. In the resulting silence he realised he was absurdly amused. He ought to be working—he faced endless meetings, apologies, information to absorb, questions, diplomatic visits and decisions…not to mention that speech ahead of him in less than an hour. He needed this time to collect his thoughts. Instead, he succumbed to the urge to let her disturb his few moments of respite—making them a delight.

Those ridiculous talons had gone and, sure enough, her natural nails were bitten to the quick, unpolished and frankly painful-looking. She wore a high-necked jumper as if trying to hide the skin that gave her emotions away, but he could still see the blotchy colour at the neckline. The perfect princess in the cathedral had definitely been aided by make-up, diamonds and lace coverings. Good for her. Yet now she looked too young, too defenceless, and suddenly that cold anger resurged from deep within. For a man filled with regret, he had none about destroying her wedding ceremony. Not a single one. Anders would have been cruel. He would have destroyed *her*.

'Can we get some fresh fruit, please?' he finally glanced

away and requested from the warily hovering servant. 'Un-peeled and uncut.'

He wanted to bring the sparkle back to her eyes and banish the flicker of hopelessness that dulled them.

'Did you get *any* sleep?' she asked in a low voice once the servant had left the room.

Was that her way of telling him he looked as terrible as he felt?

'Did you?'

'The crowds kept calling for you all through the night.' That colour washed her skin again. 'And you've been busy.' She gestured to the headlines on a tablet she had in front of her instead of food. 'Garth's been arrested for financial misman-agement. Anders appears to have banished himself.'

Lucian stiffened. 'I'll be happier when he's found and faces justice.'

'You're looking for him?'

'Of course.' He hadn't brought a large team with him, but he had people looking now. It wouldn't be long before An-ders surfaced.

'You wanted to take him down in the most public way possi-ble,' Zara said. 'You say that was for safety, but you can't deny there wasn't an element of revenge in there. You wanted to see the look in his eyes as he realised exactly who you were, and you wanted the rest of the world to see it too. You wanted to provide incontrovertible proof of his true nature to the world.'

He spread his hands. 'Does that make me a monster?'

She shook her head. 'No. It was the choice you made.'

'What other choice was there?'

'To come back sooner?' She regarded him carefully. 'Why did you stay away so *long*?'

The question burned. He would have to explain exactly this to his nation shortly.

'You sound angry about it.'

'If you'd come back sooner this mess with Anders wouldn't have happened. I wouldn't be in this position. I wouldn't have had to—'

'It's quite amazing how you can turn all of this into my fault,' he said thoughtfully. 'Are you saying you wouldn't have considered marrying Anders if he weren't going to be King?'

She stiffened. 'You make me sound calculating. It wasn't like that. I wasn't being entirely selfish.'

He didn't actually think she was. In fact, he felt a tug of understanding. Things were invariably more complicated than they appeared—like his reasons for being gone so long. Zara didn't know he hadn't been well for a long time. That he'd gone through not one but two near-death experiences—the accident itself and then pneumonia only days later. Nor did she know he still wasn't *good* enough to take the Crown—he was only here because he was a better option than Anders. But he was hardly about to tell her all of that.

'My physical recovery after the accident took some time,' he explained briefly. 'I made it to Piri-nu and convalesced there. But my mother died before learning I was safe. The situation in Monrayne then became complicated.'

He'd not had health or strength or money. He'd been utterly powerless to take on Garth at eighteen. But he was never going to be in that position again. He would ensure Monrayne's stability and his own strength.

'Ten years is a *long* time,' she said.

'I had to wait until the time was right.'

'Is all this horrible stuff about Anders true?' She gestured to the news articles on the screen. 'Or is it a smear—part of the campaign to restore faith in you? Have your people been leaking stories all night?'

He read a few of the more salacious headlines upside down.

'The media reports have nothing to do with me.' He glanced up and that hardness inside eased a little at the concern in her eyes. 'And what you read there is all true. It's not even half of it,' he added. 'Anders routinely gorged on drugs, drink and enjoyed exerting power over unwilling women.'

Her face flushed. 'How could I not have known that?'

'Because until last night Garth had control of the media.'

Her eyes widened. 'And now you do?'

'No. Now there is a *free* press. I'll not allow that corruption to continue. I'll not be a dictator.'

'Why did no one warn me? Surely people must have known something—or suspected? Why would Garth let me…?'

That had been another source of his anger.

'Perhaps he thought that Anders wouldn't dare harm you, given your status. Or his own greed blinded him to the depths Anders had sunk. I think he was arrogant enough to believe he could control him.'

She stared at him in horror. 'I get that you needed to gather your strength. But surely that didn't take a decade.'

'I needed to accumulate all kinds of resources for my return. Niko had done too much for me already. I couldn't ask for more assistance.'

'King Niko of Piri-nu?' She regarded him thoughtfully. 'It says online that you worked in his security team.'

'He saved my life,' he said harshly. 'I owed him.'

'So you repaid him with loyalty and time?'

He nodded. 'I also needed the opportunity. I couldn't fail and I couldn't leave *any* room for doubt. I needed the eyes of the world upon Monrayne in that moment I returned. There could be no risk of violence. No one else could be hurt.'

'At least not physically,' she muttered.

He paused. 'Right.'

She stared down at the headlines again. 'I never would have resented my *rescue* if I had known about this.'

'Is that your way of saying "thank you" at last?'

She glanced back up and there was a sad smile in her eyes.

'I'm not afraid to say the words, but only when they're warranted.'

'Are they not now?' He inclined his head. 'Are you still angry with me for interrupting the wedding? He would have enjoyed forcibly removing that dress from you, Zara. He'd have done it with far more violence than I did, and he'd have done far worse once he had.' His tension built until he sighed in frustration. 'You should go back to your family.'

Her expression grew pinched. 'My family didn't wait for me. They won't be interested in how I'm *feeling*. They'll want me to hide in that castle like a pariah princess for the rest of my life. I'll be scorned and shamed.' She shook her head. 'I'm not exactly raring for that to happen.'

He could help her disappear. Get her a new name, a new identity. But he knew how lonely that life was and his gut told him that wasn't right for her.

'So you don't wish to return home.' He glanced at another of the headlines on the screen. 'At least sympathy is on your side.'

'*Sympathy*.' She grimaced. 'Well, isn't that just all I've *ever* wanted?'

Zara watched Lucian pull his dagger and begin peeling an apple from the bowl of fruit the servant had brought in.

Pity wasn't something this cold, clinical man would indulge in. Nor was pleasure, apparently. His claim of virginity still shocked her, yet it also made sense. She suspected self-discipline mattered to him. Proving his self-control. He'd apparently been so patient—biding his time as he'd focused on only one thing—was it revenge?

He'd spoken of his time in banishment, of his mother's death and of his physical recovery with zero emotion. But there'd been loyalty to Niko, the King of Piri-nu. She'd heard of that beautiful Pacific Island nation of course. She suspected Niko meant more to him than merely being the King he owed. He was Lucian's friend—which meant he must be less of a block of ice sometimes.

Now he sat there peeling more of the wretched fruit with skilled, swift precision. He was silent, predatory, *lethal*. Yet she wasn't afraid of him. Her current adrenalin boost wasn't based on anxiety.

The realisation that her family had been all too willing to accept her sacrifice churned her innards. Surely her sisters *must* have heard whispers about Anders, given they were so socially connected back in Dolrovia? But even if they hadn't— even if they were as oblivious as she'd been, shouldn't they have stayed after that horror in the cathedral to ensure she was safe? She was beyond hurt that they'd simply abandoned her. But her mother was probably still deluding herself that they were some grand, important family and thus had needed to escape quickly. She would now be watching Lucian with eagle eyes.

'My mother is probably hoping you'll honourably save my mortification by marrying me yourself,' she mused morosely.

'No,' he responded instantly and uncompromisingly. 'That wouldn't be honourable. Besides which, I won't marry for years.'

Yeah? Well, she wasn't going to marry *at all* now. She'd thought it would be the solution to her problems once and she couldn't have been more wrong. Lesson learned. But she was momentarily diverted. 'You have no desire to secure the succession of *your* lineage?' She suddenly smiled. 'Oh, no. No desire at all, I forgot.'

'I have as little desire in me as you do, Sweet Princess.' He sliced the apple clean through and offered her a piece. 'Don't worry, I've begun the process to ensure Anders cannot take the Crown. Some other distant cousin will inherit if I die before having heirs of my own. But I won't be marrying anyone for a decade at least. I need to focus fully on Monrayne and I would never risk bringing children into this tumultuous time.'

He was so very serious and controlled, it annoyed her.

Taking the apple slice, she cocked her head. Periodic cheering could still be heard in the streets. 'Doesn't sound that tumultuous to me. They're out there celebrating.'

He lifted his head coolly. 'So you think—'

'That your marriage and subsequent children would only bring *more* security to Monrayne.' She couldn't resist provoking him a little. 'So perhaps, for your people, you ought to do that sooner rather than later.'

'Absolutely not,' he said softly. 'Not—'

'For as long as possible?' she finished softly.

'Exactly.' Implacable and definite, he clearly had a plan and was sticking to it.

His cold, measured certainty was both compelling and aggravating. What if he met someone amazing and fell instantly in love—would he still not marry for a 'decade at least'?

He returned to the task of peeling and slicing the apple. He offered every other slice to her. It was oddly intimate, though she was quite sure that he didn't intend it that way. But the gesture gave her the excuse to keep watching him.

She hadn't thought it possible for him to be better-looking but, even with the ravages of a clearly sleepless night and the weight of a nation on his broad, broad shoulders, he was gorgeous. Yes, it hadn't been those noisy crowds outside that had kept *her* awake all night.

'Where are you going to go?' he eventually asked.

Unlike him, she didn't have an eight-point plan perfectly formulated—*yet*.

'Where do you suggest?' she asked a little bitterly. 'A friend? There's none of those. My family, who abandoned me in their haste to ensure their own safety? Never. And with what money shall I make my escape? Where was I supposed to go when I left the cathedral, trapped in an enormous dress that I couldn't escape? So—' she counted the failings off on her fingers '—no funds, no friends, no family, no car, no clothes, no… I've got nothing.' She shrugged. 'Maybe my marriage might not have been ideal, but at least I had some kind of plan—'

'With a psychopath.'

'Maybe I would have had palace support,' she muttered valiantly. 'I would have had time to figure something else out once I'd realised.'

'You have no idea of the danger you were in.'

'Maybe not then, but I do realise that I'm *still* in danger of a sort *now*. I can't go back to my life as it was. It doesn't exist any more anyway. I'll always be the frigid, jilted non-princess now. I need time to figure it out, otherwise I'll end up trapped again and being told what I can and can't do.'

He glanced up from the apple. 'So what's your solution?'

She held her breath in a last attempt to bring inner calm, but then just blurted it out. 'People are selfish. Most people, in fact. Even you. So *I'm* going to be selfish. You're not getting rid of me. I'm staying here.'

He stopped peeling the apple entirely. 'Pardon?'

'I'm staying. Here. Just for a little while longer.' She pressed her lips together.

'And if I say no?'

'You wouldn't want to be seen as ruthless and uncaring,' she said. 'Because if you said no, then I would have no choice but to walk out the front gates in my shredded wedding dress and tell the world that the King of Monrayne abandoned me in my hour of need. Shamed again.'

His ice-blue eyes remained trained on her. 'Are you blackmailing me?'

'I guess that could be one interpretation.'

'You realise I could truss you up and have you on a flight

out of here in less than ten minutes? And I could do that with one hand tied behind my back—'

'And no doubt blindfolded as well,' she added drolly. 'But you won't.'

'No?'

'No. You don't want anyone hurt. You want your country safe. You need to be well regarded for that to happen.'

He looked at her a second longer and then his attention dropped to the half-decimated apple. 'I suppose I could inform your family that you've gone to a private sanctuary. Buy you some time to sort your life out.'

'A private sanctuary?'

Was he going to send her away? Oddly, that wasn't what she wanted at all.

But, of course, he had far bigger things to be concerned with than some lowly princess who had no riches, no real kingdom and no real purpose. Of course he didn't want her to remain under his actual roof.

'Do you mean like a spa or something?' She tried to summon enthusiasm and appreciation. 'A luxury health retreat?'

'No. That would just be the cover for you staying here. Despite the fact that if I so much as sneeze it will be reported on, you can likely hide best right here behind the palace walls.'

Stupidly relieved, she popped another piece of apple into her mouth to hide her smile.

'Just for a day or so,' he added, still watching her closely. 'Please yourself, Princess. Rely on no one. *Count* on no one.'

'Is that your mantra?' She regarded him curiously. She didn't believe that she couldn't count on *him*. He'd helped her multiple times already and, honestly, she was considering asking him for even more. She didn't particularly want to—but what she'd said was true. She had nothing. Would he consider giving her a loan, perhaps? So she could upskill and get an actual job. She'd pay him back with any interest he wanted. But having just secured his permission to stay a couple more days, she decided now wasn't the time to push for more. Especially when he seemed determined to keep his distance.

'You can have full freedom within the palace.' He ignored her question. 'I'll be busy so our paths are unlikely to cross. If there's more you need, ask Victor, the new servant.'

He didn't want to be bothered by her. Of course, why would he when he had an entire kingdom to restore? Yet she couldn't help feeling slightly piqued.

'May I? Thank you so much.'

He paused peeling yet another apple and focused his attention on her again. 'You want more from me?'

Some vestige of emotion? An iota of humanity—of heat? What she *really* wanted was…*not appropriate*. She froze as she realised that truth, staring at him while desperately fighting off the sudden yearning inside. The silence thickened. His ice-blue eyes were suddenly hot and awareness of his mounting tension rippled through her.

She put down her apple slice. 'I appreciate your patience in putting up with me. I know I can be…'

To her astonishment, a smile suddenly flickered on his face. She was so surprised she couldn't finish her sentence.

'What do others say you can be, Zara?' he prompted softly.

A disappointment. An annoyance. A drain on resources. But this was a man who'd survived an assassination attempt. She couldn't complain to him more than she already had in the last few minutes. That would be too pathetic.

'It doesn't matter.' She shook her head. 'I promise I'll be good. Quiet. You won't even know I'm here.'

He studied her even more intently and she felt that sensual awareness bloom anew.

'I won't know?' He regarded her consideringly. 'Do you equate being good with being quiet?' he asked slowly. 'Because that's not appropriate in all situations.'

Tension simmered as she stared at him. Was that *innuendo* from the virtuous King? He was too measured, too considered for it *not* to be deliberate. But—

'I would be very disappointed if you were silent, Princess.'

Her mouth dried. 'Sometimes survival is dependent upon silence.'

'True,' he agreed. 'But, equally, sometimes it's dependent upon screaming.'

He meant for help. He didn't mean in some sexual way. Only that wasn't how her brain was interpreting it. She stared at him.

'I guess the trick is knowing when to employ which option.'

# CHAPTER SIX

ZARA DIDN'T SEE the King for three days. Well, not in the flesh. She saw plenty of him on screen. She watched his speech. Watched the footage of him emerging from meetings with politicians and the elite. Watched the endless repeats of those moments in the cathedral. His progress was swift and dramatic. The plans for the coronation were delayed until the dust had settled as he focused on steering the nation through the change smoothly, but indeed it was a swift, bloodless restoration. King Lucian of Monrayne—with his undisputed lineage—reclaimed the throne utterly unopposed.

The crowds kept cheering. Zara watched constant deliveries of letters, cards and gifts. Political pundits and social media opinion writers commented on the vast change from smiling, personable young man to remote, solemn king. They were saddened by his lack of smiles and the obvious physical trauma he'd endured, despite his incredibly strong physique now.

The murky truth of that fateful day was analysed over and over. The official report had always been that Lucian and Anders had been on a summer holiday in the Mediterranean. They'd gone out on a small vessel to go diving. Lucian had gone overboard and hit his head. Anders had been in shock and struggled to raise the alarm. The boat with Anders wasn't found for hours and Lucian's body never recovered in the intense searches in subsequent weeks. Lucian's mother had rapidly declined in the immediate aftermath and died only days later. It seemed her cancer had been kept secret from the public. It had all been a dreadful tragedy.

But now there were other whisperings about what might really have occurred on that boat, especially as Anders had fled the second Lucian had reappeared.

The press repeatedly showed an athletics team photo in which a teenage Lucian stood shoulder to shoulder with a young King Niko of Piri-nu—Prince back then. Right before that accident the two men had spent several years at boarding school together. And that was why Lucian had somehow made it to Piri-nu.

There were hints that his physical recovery had taken a long time. He'd remained on Piri-nu incognito as King Niko's head of security. He'd rarely been captured on film but they'd found a few photos with him in the background—those aviator sunglasses, that muscular body. He was much tougher-looking than the charming teen he'd been in that earlier portrait.

But Lucian's fight for public approval was well and truly won, even though he'd been away for so long. In part it was because of the underlying concerns that people had about Anders. More and more horrible stories had emerged about the man.

The coverage on Zara was mixed. 'Sources' from the castle at home had asserted that Princess Zara was perfectly well and taking time for herself. Some commentators cast her as naive. Others as cold. Others still questioned how she could not have known about her fiancé's unsavoury reputation. But most were too consumed with raking through Lucian's missing years and with assessing him now.

As the days slipped by she stayed in the private wing, chatting to the same two servants who'd appeared the day after the wedding-that-wasn't. One was a man from Piri-nu who she suspected was also a soldier. The other was the man Victor, who Lucian had mentioned. He was older and had come out of retirement to serve Lucian. He was particularly attentive and had kindly asked for all her preferences. It was the first time anyone had done so and she hadn't quite known how to answer.

After that first night she'd slept deeply—still in the room that had once been his. She hadn't yet contacted her family, but she probably should soon. She should also probably move soon.

But here, for the first time, she had no need to please anyone. In this small wing she was absolutely free to be herself and figure her future out. Even if she was going to need a little more help to make it to the next stage, it was still better.

In the early evening on her fourth night of such freedom she sat in the small dining room reading more rubbish headlines on the tablet they'd provided for her while Victor placed a vast array of silver dishes on the table. There was no way she was going to be able to eat everything he was putting out for her.

That was when Lucian walked in. She ignored the thud of her heart and tried not to stare. She failed. He still looked tired. He looked leaner too—that square jaw sharper. While she'd got rest, he was seemingly still in the trenches.

'You're still here, I see.' He took off the aviator sunglasses that he so often wore and sat opposite her.

'Nowhere else I'd rather be.' She smiled at him breezily. 'The rest of the world feels sorry for me, whereas you don't actually care, and honestly that's better.'

'What makes you think I don't care?' He shot her an oblique look. 'Surely if I didn't care I would have thrown you out of the palace while you were still stuck in your wedding dress. And why do you read the rubbish if it bothers you?'

'I wasn't. I was checking the classifieds for jobs.'

'Anything appealing?'

'Sadly, there's not a lot of demand for ill-educated virgins who don't know how to turn a washing machine on.'

'And who are incapable of unbuttoning their own dresses,' he added helpfully.

'I was stitched into it, as well you know.'

'Yes. I remember.' He grinned.

She blinked at him. Then blushed.

'Is something wrong?' he asked after a moment of screaming silence.

That wariness returned and she didn't want that—so she was forced to be honest.

'You smiled.' She served herself from the dishes so she wouldn't have to look at him as she admitted that.

'And my smile rendered you speechless?'

'Only momentarily, and only because it's quite rare.' She took a large bite of food to stop herself saying anything more stupid, but the ensuing silence was even worse.

Especially as he now sat so still, apparently contemplating the vast selection of food instead of using it as a displacement activity like she was.

'They're calling it the bloodless restoration—' she tried to chat positively '—that your accession has been amazingly swift and stable.'

He nodded but that gorgeous smile still didn't return. If anything, he looked more wary.

'You're not happy about that?' she asked.

The people were still shouting his name, yet he couldn't seem to accept the adoration and accolades. Nor could he seem to decide what to eat.

'Things can change quickly,' he said before nodding to her tablet again. 'So if there are no advertised jobs that are suitable, what are your options?'

'I could work for you. Taste your food, perhaps? Make sure it isn't poisoned.'

His eyes widened. 'Pardon?'

She suddenly realised how terrible the suggestion might sound, given his past.

'It's just…' She blushed. 'You seem reluctant to eat. But I can assure you it's good. Delicious, actually.'

'I know.' He pointed towards the lamb dish. 'This was my mother's favourite. I've not eaten it in a long while.'

She stared at him in consternation. 'I'm sorry. I had no idea. Victor asked what I'd like and I wasn't sure so I asked him to prepare whatever was the usual back when you were younger...'

He still didn't answer. Still didn't move.

'I have to admit I didn't expect it to be five courses.' She offered an apologetic smile. 'I guess you were a hungry teen.'

He finally huffed a little laugh.

'I haven't felt this hungry in weeks,' she added, distracting herself from her own stupid ramblings by simply rambling more. 'I think I was anxious about the wedding.'

'Not starving yourself to fit into that dress?'

'Gosh, no. I just felt sick most of the time.'

'Not pregnant?'

'Not possible. Virgin, remember?'

His scarred eyebrow lifted. 'Stranger things have happened.'

She shot him an amazed look. 'Like once, in the Bible.'

He laughed properly this time. She stared at him, perplexed because she had the feeling he was thinking of something very specific and she couldn't fathom what. But it didn't matter because he was slowly warming up and it was a stunning revelation.

'You act like this cool customer but you're actually full drama, you know that?' She inclined her head. 'That entrance in the cathedral couldn't have been more dramatic. Especially the bare-chested bit.'

He speared her with his ice-blue gaze. 'You liked that bit?'

Now her blush engulfed every inch of her skin. 'They keep replaying it on the television, so I don't think I'm the only one who enjoyed that.'

'Seeing my scars?'

'There aren't that many scars. It was more your muscles that I found fascinating.'

He stared at her, his jaw dropping.

'I've decided that not only am I going to be selfish, I'm going to be *honest*,' she said, even as she fought her way through another atrocious blush. 'Speak freely. Let it be known what my thoughts are. No more trying to stay silent and perform prettily like a perfect princess.'

He pressed his lips together, but she saw them twitch.

'So, yes, you've got an amazing body,' she declared defiantly—her mouth running away with her again before her brain thought better. 'You didn't just recover your physical fitness. You maxed out. You're like *built*.'

'If this is yet another attempt to seduce me—'

'For the final time, I do *not* want to marry you,' she replied hotly. 'Or anyone, actually. I'm done with that.' The more honest she was, the easier it became. 'But I like looking at you. Feel free to strut about in not very much as often as you like.'

'You seem to think I'm here to serve your every request.' He laughed again. 'Thank you for giving me permission to do as I like in my own palace. Sadly for you, however, it is too cold.'

She giggled and lifted her fork in acknowledgement that he'd just won that round.

'This is really delicious,' she said. 'I can see why it was your mother's favourite.'

Unable to stop herself, she prattled on, half hoping she might make him smile some more. But while she yapped, he ate—lots—and that pleased her more than anything. He relaxed so much he even sprawled back in the seat.

'We don't dine together at home,' she informed him. 'I read. Dinner is often just a sandwich. So all this…' She gestured to the laden dishes. 'Amazing. Only now I've gorged myself to the point of discomfort. I believe it's known as emotional eating. Feeding the void inside.'

'Void?' he echoed drily.

'The lack of love from my family. The lack of purpose in my life.' Mock dolefully, she helped herself to another slice of the rich caramel apple tart just because she could. 'This gives me sweet courage. I'm not afraid of you. Or your silence.'

'And yet it seems you can't stand silence yourself. You have a need to fill it. Incessantly.'

'You mean I'm annoying?'

'No. I mean you're talkative.' His lips twitched again.

'I'll have you know it's hard work maintaining a conversation all by oneself,' she said with spirit. 'You're the one who joined me for dinner. If you wanted to eat in silence you should have taken a tray to your room.'

He sipped his wine and leaned back even more, that elusive smile playing at the corners of his mouth. 'You're saying I'm an impolite host?'

'I'm saying you're impenetrable. Fortress King Lucian.' For a moment she thought she'd gone too far. 'You're probably tired though, to be fair. Got a lot on your mind.'

'Oh, no, only a little on my mind,' he countered drily. 'So please, if you wish to converse, let us converse. What would you like to discuss?'

She met his gaze, all but dying of curiosity about so many *intimate* things. Utterly inappropriate things—like why was he as sexually inexperienced as she?

'Can you not think of anything?' he pressed when she didn't immediately reply. 'When you've been such a chatterbox until now?'

Still she could only think of intimate things. Hot things. And now her face was even hotter.

'Are you bored and lonely?' His smile was positively evil. 'Perhaps it's time for you to move on to your next phase in life. *Away* from the palace.'

'I *can* be quiet,' she declared, hardly about to concede defeat. She still had nowhere to go and nothing to get there with. 'I just need a good book.'

He blinked then a wide smile spread over his face. 'Then for heaven's sake let us find you one.' He pushed back from the table. 'Come on.'

'Now? Where?' She had to skip every few steps to keep up with him as he strode through the wing. 'What are we doing?' she puffed. 'A HIIT workout to burn off the caramel apple calories?'

He shot her an amused glance but checked the length of his strides. Finally, he opened a door and gave his customary security search look inside before standing back for her to enter.

'Oh, wow.' Zara gaped.

'You've not been in here already?' he asked.

'Of course not. I'd need a GPS system to find this and I'm not going to wander about as if I own the place.'

'But I said you have the freedom of the palace.'

'Yes, but—'

'Have you been to the indoor pool? The games room? Any of the other drawing rooms?' He looked displeased. 'Or have you just been sitting in your room marinating in the embarrassment of being jilted in front of millions?'

She gasped.

'Or perhaps watching the replays of me half-naked in the cathedral?'

He added that last so expressionlessly it was a full second before his words sank in.

'Did you just crack a joke?' Astounded, she shot him wide side-eye. 'Are you *teasing* me?'

His smile flashed. 'You do it to me all the time.'

She couldn't help laughing. 'Yes, but *that* was too far.'

'Well, you're hardly subtle sometimes.' He shrugged and walked into the library.

It didn't look as if anyone had been in here in ages. There

were mountains of boxes all over the place that seemed to have been sent from publishers. They hadn't even been opened. But Zara was still catching her breath from his good humour explosion.

He studied the labels, his expression turning sombre. 'My mother had a standing order from several publishers. She liked to read the latest releases. Every quarter she would cull the collection and donate the books to various places. It looks like the books have still arrived, only to mount up over all these years. It desperately needs sorting.' He glanced at her. 'Would you do it?'

'Are you asking me to sift through all these books and decide which to keep and which to donate?'

'Yes.'

'But what would be the criteria for choosing which stay and which go?'

'Your personal preference,' he said negligently. 'I'll read anything.'

'Obviously that won't be a problem for me.'

'I didn't think it would.' He smiled again.

She hesitated, realising the truth. 'Are you just finding something for me to do for a few days? Busy work that isn't really important?'

It was awful to be so pathetic that she needed a pity project.

'Books are very important,' he said gently. 'They can save people from all sorts of things.'

So, yes, he was simply finding her some work, but she also knew he wasn't entirely teasing. He meant that last. Her curiosity mushroomed.

'Did a book save you?'

'Audio books certainly helped me rebuild my concentration and helped distract me through tough times. I'd like others to enjoy the books that we don't need here. They shouldn't be in boxes not being read by anyone.'

It was the smallest personal detail and she wanted to know much more. But he stepped back to the doorway and she instinctively moved with him.

'I truly would appreciate your assistance in dealing with this,' he said.

'I didn't think you liked to accept assistance from anyone.'

'In this instance I'm willing to make an exception.'

On the surface he seemed as cool as ever but something in his eyes compelled her closer. He stood so still—half in shadow, half out of the doorway, his back to the hinge. She realised he was ready to escape if he needed to. He was constantly alert to his surroundings yet he was also attentive to her and she just couldn't drag her gaze from him.

'Then thank you,' she muttered. 'I'd like to help.'

She could do this—quite well, she thought. And she wanted to, for herself and for him. But now neither of them moved and she realised he was staring at her mouth and she could almost *feel* it…

'Actually, there is one more thing you can do for me,' he said slowly.

'Yes?'

'Have dinner with me each night while you're here.'

She almost fell over.

'I won't disturb you with my incessant chatter?'

'Disturb?' His unscarred eyebrow quirked up. 'No. You're a good distraction.'

So she was his light relief? Her senses sharpened. She'd achieved what she'd set out to do. Only now she wanted more.

'And I realise I need to brush up on my *manners*,' he added.

'By practising on me?' Something deep inside melted and tightened at the same time. She'd told him off for his manners in the cathedral. It had been a tiny moment but he clearly remembered it. He clearly was needling her about it now, under the guise of fake politeness. His ice-blue eyes were almost dancing and she couldn't possibly refuse him.

'Of course I would be delighted to dine with you each evening,' she replied primly. 'I'm so glad to have found a small way in which I can repay your generosity. I promise I'll do my very best to distract you, Your Highness.'

'Your very best?' He seemed to consider it and find it lacking. 'What if I wanted you to do your very *worst*?'

That frisson between them shimmered.

'That wouldn't be good manners, though, would it?' she breathed.

'I thought you were done trying to be a perfect princess.'

# CHAPTER SEVEN

LUCIAN'S INSISTENCE THAT she dine with him each night was a rare moment of frippery that he shouldn't have indulged in. Since when did he want companionship at meal times or any other? But he was curious about her—she was a puzzle he didn't need yet couldn't seem to put down.

Dressed in the same long black skirt and black turtleneck, she'd become an elusive shadow about the place. He'd heard her chattering to Victor from down the corridor earlier today and had felt oddly as if he were missing out on something. And as she'd demanded sanctuary from him, he reasoned dinner wasn't too much of a price for her to pay. Plus it was a complete change of pace in his otherwise incessant schedule of high-level meetings and decision-making. It was meaningless and unimportant. And he did want to spare her from being hounded by the press and whatever else she was avoiding while she sorted herself out. A couple of days more would do no harm.

Yet she shot him such a contrary look when he walked into the dining room the next night that he had to bite the inside of his cheek to stop his smile. His feelings on seeing her were equally mixed. He could just hide it better.

'Distract me, Princess.' He took the chair opposite hers. The one that afforded him a view of the door and windows. Though aside from the usual initial room scan he focused on neither. He gazed directly at her.

'Are we not here to brush up on your manners?' she enquired.

'Not tonight.'

He'd been staving off a dull headache all day, having to exert too much patience and concentration. But just looking at her restored some energy. That black outfit hid what he knew were sweet curves. Her blonde hair was in a low ponytail and she wore no make-up so her cheeks flushed. Every time she smiled her eyes sparkled. Every time she challenged him she seemed to glow. He just wanted a few moments by her fire. Yes, he was weak, but it was only dinner. Just the smallest respite.

She cocked her head. 'Shall I tell you about the miseries of my life for your entertainment?'

He sank more comfortably into his seat and drawled, 'Go on then.'

'You were witness to number one, of course.'

'I've been relegated to witness now? Not chief instigator of the wedding jilting?'

She shot him another sharp look. 'No, that was all Anders.'

'What's number two?' he prompted.

Her lips pursed. 'Are you going to respond in kind?'

'You're here as *my* entertainment. Not the other way round.'

'So I'm now your court jester.'

'If you like.' He succumbed to a devilish urge. 'I feel like you'd prefer that option to courtesan...'

'I think I'd make a marvellous courtesan if it weren't for my frigidity.'

He shrugged. 'You could always fake it.'

'True.' She suddenly sparkled and leaned a little closer. 'After all. You wouldn't know any better either.'

He slowly smiled. 'Intrigued by that fact, aren't you?'

'Surprised,' she corrected. 'There must have been the opportunity...'

'I've been very busy.' But she was right. There'd been opportunity both before the accident and after in Piri-nu all these years. But he'd not taken up the chances entirely before and he'd been determined to be duty-focused since.

'For all that time?' She shook her head. 'All work and no play...'

Made him better at his job. And he needed to be better still. But for this one moment he couldn't resist. 'Why are we talking about me?'

She pulled a face. 'You enjoy teasing me.'

Yes. He'd discovered a keen pleasure in teasing Princess Zara. She was ridiculously talkative. She didn't seem to consider what might pop out of her mouth—as if this environment were completely safe. It wasn't entirely. His inner predator itched to devour her, but he ruthlessly suppressed that part. But he let himself enjoy her artless chatter as she sampled the array of dishes the palace cooks prepared. He enjoyed watching her eat and, better still, watching her laugh. It could only be a brief interlude before going back to work. Yet he lingered over dinner. So did she.

On his way to dinner the next night his private phone rang. As only one person had the number, he answered it immediately. 'Niko?'

'You've caused quite the furore my friend.'

'Apologies if it has meant more problems or media intrusion than usual for you.'

'Oh, I can handle all that. The question is, can you?' Niko paused. 'It's been a while since you've fronted the crowds. Is there anything I can do to help?'

'I have it in hand for now, though it might be good if you visited soon to help reassure the rest of the world that we've not descended into lawless anarchy.'

'Name the date and I'll be there,' Niko immediately promised. 'What's happened to the bride? She seems to have vanished.'

Lucian hesitated. His loyalty to Niko was strong but he'd made a promise to Zara this time. 'I believe she's taking refuge while the interest rages on.'

'And Anders?'

'Won't survive long in the wild. We'll pick him up soon.' Several women had come forward, prepared to press charges against him. Anders would face justice the moment he surfaced. Lucian was confident that wouldn't be long now. 'Garth is chastened and the prosecutors are putting together the case.'

'Good,' Niko said grimly. 'Stay in touch.'

'Of course.'

Zara was already in the dining room. Preoccupied with Niko's questions, he took his seat silently and barely noticed the numerous dishes. A few minutes passed before he realised she was sitting perfectly still and staring at him.

'What?' he asked.

'Are you going to take your sunglasses off? Maybe say hello?'

He'd forgotten he was still wearing them. He took them off and shot her a deliberately broad smile. 'Better?'

She blushed and helped herself to something from a silver dish.

'The sun on the water in Piri-nu is very bright, just as it is on the snow in our mountains here. My eyes are very pale,' he found himself explaining.

She nodded. 'Was your sight damaged in the accident?'

'Fortunately not. But there wasn't good medical care in the immediate aftermath and I declined plastic surgery subsequently. I don't want to pretend that it never happened.' He ran his fingertip across the raised scar as he saw her frown. 'You think I'm wrong about that?'

'No, I don't think we can forget the events that have shaped us. At the same time, there's something to be said for healing the best you can so you can move forward and not live a life that's too impaired by something that could actually be sorted if you wanted it to be.'

She was right up to a point, but this was different. He needed to see this in the mirror every morning—to focus.

'Physical reminders matter.'

'Maybe. I guess everyone has scars, whether they're visible or not.' She looked at him. 'My skin reveals secrets without my consent. I can go all blotchy just by thinking something stupid. It's a real skill.'

'You're sensitive, that's not a bad thing.' She was human—vulnerable. 'Does anything help?'

'Avoidance of any sort of mortifying situation.'

She shouldn't be avoiding anything. She'd been hidden in a castle in her own country and she was choosing to hide again now. She should have far greater freedom.

Instead, she had another enormous dinner, tucked away in a corner of the palace, secretly keeping him company.

'This is just delicious,' she declared happily as she had yet another slice of caramel apple tart. It amused him that she liked it almost as much as he did. 'Why do I still feel like I haven't eaten in weeks?'

He had no idea, only that for him it was the same.

'I struggle to remember this isn't the last time I'll ever have this. But that I'm home. For good,' he growled. 'It's ridiculous.'

She smiled at him a little sadly. 'It'll sink in eventually, I guess.'

He didn't want her pity, he wanted distraction. That was all. 'Talk to me, Princess.'

She sighed. 'I'm not sure I have the energy for the monologue tonight.'

'It's been a challenging day?'

'Actually, I've made great progress on all your books.' Shy

pride briefly illuminated her eyes before dimming. 'But I've been going round in circles about the future.'

His stomach tightened. Had she decided what she wanted to do? Was she leaving already?

'Oh?'

Zara desperately needed a more detailed plan. Instead, she was the failure her sisters had predicted she'd be when they'd patronisingly encouraged her to remain in the country and care for their parents because that was what she was 'good at'—the implication being that there wasn't anything else she could handle.

But they hadn't realised she'd done more than simply bring them trays of tea and cake. She'd ended up running the castle, being the one to deal with the contractors and suppliers in the never-ending quest to stop it falling down. So surely she could figure out her future, it couldn't be anywhere near as complex as repairing the collapsed north wing had been.

'Maybe being stuck in the library all day isn't ideal,' he said. 'Some physical activity might help your mood.'

She felt that frisson scrape her nerves. 'Does it help yours?' she asked softly.

'Often and absolutely,' he answered with a glint in his eyes. 'Not just my mood but my entire wellbeing.'

'Gosh,' she marvelled. 'So what physical activity is your favourite?'

He almost smiled. He knew, didn't he, that she was end-lessly curious about him, that she was even more intrigued by that elusive smile and the brief flashes of the charming young prince he'd once been. But he didn't pick up on the less than subtle sensual turn their conversation was taking.

'I like building things,' he said, leaning back and watching her expression with an amused one of his own. 'I worked on a building for Niko for a long time.'

Yes, she'd read that in his time on Piri-nu he'd lived for the best part of two years on King Niko's private island. 'Was this the holiday home?'

'It was badly damaged in a cyclone. Took a lot of time to rebuild, actually.' He nodded. 'It was a way of maintaining my physical fitness.'

Yes, Lucian had rebuilt himself. And then the house. And now his monarchy.

'Sadly, you don't seem to have a house for me to literally rebuild, so what alternative physical activity would you suggest?' she enquired a little too innocently.

His mouth twitched. 'Given you're concerned about the sensitivity of your skin, perhaps something indoors might be best.'

'Indoors, you think?'

He inhaled deeply. 'Tell me about the situation in Dolrovia.'

She smiled as he changed topic. 'Do you want the diplomatic, docile Princess's response or my actual opinion?'

He did smile then. 'You choose.'

'We're a small nation, dependent on good trade ties with those nearest and there isn't a need for its old Royal family any more. There hasn't been for a long time. But my father can't accept the reality that the duty he was born for doesn't exist any more. They've become something of an embarrassment with their belief in their grandeur. Especially for my more modern older sisters.'

'And for you?' he said. 'You're unusually reticent about your reasons for wanting to escape, Zara.'

'Honestly, it doesn't seem right to moan about my life, given what you've endured. I'm going to sound pathetic.'

'Shall I tell you what I know already? I know your parents were older when they had you. You were very much a 'late lamb' who—'

'Was a disappointment because I wasn't a boy.'

'So you weren't an indulged baby?'

'There was nothing to indulge me with.'

'Not even attention?' He watched her curiously.

Definitely not that. Zara sighed—if he really wanted to know, she would tell him. She was the distraction, after all.

'Despite our family finances heading into decline, my parents kept spending as if every cent earned in Dolrovia was theirs by divine right. Maximum consumption. The public weren't crazy about it and parliament hit them with their first ever tax bill. My older sisters were already educated and had built their lives. Mia works in an art gallery and is engaged, while Ana's a successful academic at the university—both of which are considered acceptable roles. They like their life in the city and it doesn't matter that our titles will die with us. Neither of them wants to deal with our stuck-in-the-last-century parents. But I was young when they were deposed and my parents couldn't afford the fees to send me to the same elite school. My parents wouldn't let me go to the local one because that would look even more *shameful* and common.'

'Hence the nineteenth-century governess business.'

'Exactly.' She shot him a small smile. 'That was just one way they tried to hide the true state of our affairs. So, while theoretically I'm still a princess, there's no power, no perks, no privileges. My duty is to my parents and that's okay, but they allow me no self-determination. They seemed to think I'd always be there and to the rest of the world I've just been kind of…forgotten about.'

'What do you do all day in this prison?'

'I try to accommodate the demands of an old king who still can't grasp he has no power.' She paused and lifted her chin. 'I actually have taken on a lot of the admin of running the castle, and some of that is okay, but the problem is there's no choice and no chance for anything different. That's what I'm angry about. I don't expect things to be handed to me. I *want* to work but my parents view paid work as beneath

Royal life. My sister Ana gets away with her career only because she's literally a genius and so has actually brought us a sort of prestige, and Mia is so stunning she's really the 'art' in the gallery. I can't even do charitable work because apparently that would require me to have a designer wardrobe that they can't afford. Not to mention the fact that I lack the right social skills because I get too awkward and babble and the nerves have to be covered up.' But she'd never been given the experience to overcome them. She'd done what she could in the castle—taking over the official correspondence as well. Her parents weren't even aware she did all that—a small fact always made her smile, somewhat sadly.

'The total control isn't protective, it's not because they care about *me,* but more how our circumstances *look.* I'm not as pretty as Mia, not as smart as Ana, and neither of *them* are interested in helping me because it's convenient that I remain in the country bearing the burden of our parents' demands and they can just live their lives...' She sighed. 'While I was younger I guess that made sense. But they barely know me now, yet they've always said over and over that they know how happy I am in the country, how I would hate to have to work in the city, that I don't understand what having to work in the real world is like...'

She looked at his deepening frown. 'And maybe I don't understand all that, but only because I've never been given the chance to try and they don't stop to listen. I need to get on with my own life and not be dependent upon the little that's left. It's not like here, where the Royal family still carries such importance.'

'So that's why you sought importance with Anders?'

She shook her head. It wasn't about importance as such. 'I just don't want to waste my life and I don't want to be lonely. And I have been.' She shrugged. 'I wanted to be what my family needed me to be. I wanted to please them. I thought the engagement would do that...'

'And it did?'

'First time my mother actually gushed over me.' She wrinkled her nose. 'But you know I don't feel the need to please them any more.'

'Fair enough,' he said and drew in a deep breath. 'So now what?'

Frankly, her plan was pretty nebulous and definitely required some assistance. Something she was instinctively still wary of asking him for.

'I'm slowly working that out...'

His hard expression eased. 'I suppose I can handle your presence a little while longer.'

'I'm sorry. I've been pretty useless 'til now.'

'I disagree, I've seen those boxes of books you've sorted already. I think you're clever and curious. I definitely think you're courageous. And I think you care about a lot of things. You'll get there.'

The decisions she'd made so far hadn't exactly been brilliant but his confidence in her was kind. Except she didn't really want his *kindness* now either.

'Well,' She looked at the table, embarrassed by her own docility for all these years. 'The best decision I've made today was asking for the caramel apple tart again, right?'

The next night Lucian frowned when he got to the dining room. The dinner dishes were in place but Zara was nowhere to be seen. He listened but couldn't hear her footsteps or chatter. Two minutes later he paused in the open doorway of the library and checked it over. Boxes of books were now neatly stacked, labelled and sorted. Yeah, not useless at all, Zara had cleared the large table and was now sitting at it in her long-sleeved black turtleneck and that long black skirt, with her long blonde hair tumbling down her back. Her face was still pale but vitality sparkled in her blue eyes as she concentrated on whatever she was writing. He couldn't resist walking in, closing the door behind him.

'You are late and I am hungry. You know you don't have to spend every waking moment sorting this, it doesn't matter if you don't ever finish it before—' He broke off. He didn't like to think of her leaving.

'I've actually thought of something else I could do for you,' she said quietly.

His body leapt to attention.

'I wondered if I could help with the palace correspondence.'

Not *quite* where his mind had gone, but she had such nervousness in her blue eyes, he needed to pay attention to her. She was sweetly earnest.

'Have you seen all the mail filling up the purple stateroom?' she added.

Uh, no. He hadn't been in that stateroom in years. She stood and picked up a box from behind her and lifted it onto the table. It wasn't full of books but cards, letters, posters, paintings even. Lucian's chest tightened. He'd been stalling on engaging directly with the public. He'd needed to focus on the politicians first.

'I've been watching the constant deliveries into the courtyard from the library window. I asked them to bring me a selection.' She looked awkward. 'I hope you don't mind.'

'Mind you reading correspondence meant for me?' He tried to tease but his voice was suddenly rusty.

'I thought I might be able to help you answer some.'

He stared, surprised she'd even want to.

'I do sort of know how palaces are run,' she muttered quickly. 'Especially when there are limitations on staff, and your staff are really busy right now.'

He glanced down at the table and saw she'd written screeds in strong, clear script.

'I draft my father's letters,' she added. 'So I've written some responses to the sorts of letters you've been getting. A skeleton response is easy to tweak and personalise for each. They should get a reply, given they've taken the time to write to you.'

She was right. He quickly skimmed what she'd written. It was good.

'Isn't your father missing you doing this for him now?'

Colour washed over her skin and an intriguingly cheeky smile lit up her face. 'He doesn't know I do it. When I was younger the communications team was in the room next to my schoolroom. It was the most fun room in the place. My governess realised I liked reading and writing and figured I could be left in there while she went and flirted with one of locals in the village. As we lost more and more staff, I took on more and more—not just correspondence with the public, but the contractors and general management of the castle.'

Judging from what she'd written here, she was good at it.

'So you *do* work,' he said. 'It's just that it's unpaid and unrecognised. Wouldn't your father appreciate this if he knew?'

She shook her head. 'I'm scared he would stop me.'

Well, the last thing Lucian wanted was to stop her doing something she wanted, but at the same time *he* wasn't going to take advantage of her. 'If you do this, I'll pay you.'

She frowned.

'You will not be a slave for me, Zara.'

'Well, I don't want you to be my *boss*.' She looked grumpy. 'You're helping me, I'm helping you. That's all. I'm giving you some of my time to repay your hospitality, just like how you helped repay Niko with your time and skills.' Her eyes sparkled. 'Have you read *any* of these letters?'

'Obviously I've not yet had time.'

But he didn't really *want* to. He'd been resisting this more intimate, direct contact with his people. He knew he needed to see them and speak directly to them but he couldn't quite face it yet. His mother had been a wonderful Queen. Selfless and loyal, she'd been deeply loved by everyone. Lucian wanted to honour her legacy and live up to the example she'd set. But he wasn't there yet. It was going to take him time to get anywhere near her level—that undivided attention for the next decade.

Zara lifted a page from a neat pile. 'Read this one.'

Reluctantly, he took the paper she held out for him. It was handwritten and he frowned in an effort to decipher the spidery writing. It was from an elderly resident of Monrayne who remembered not just his mother and father, but his grandfather too. It included everything he'd feared. It gushed with pleasure at his return, detailing hope and pride in his reign—remembrances of the greatness of his mother and her father. He could never live up to the ideal this man wanted.

Because he was a fraud. He hadn't been anywhere near a good enough son to his mother. He'd not listened closely enough, he'd mulishly wanted his own time, he'd let her down so completely—futility flooded him, pushing him back into that angry corner where memories made mincemeat of his soul.

Someone touched his arm. He instantly spun, instinctively grabbing the assailant and neutralising the threat.

'Lucian?'

His pulse thundered. Zara was a breath from him. Her blue eyes flared wide. Her wrist was in his hand.

'I didn't mean to startle you,' she said.

He'd been so lost in his own quagmire of bitterness he'd not been aware how close she'd got. Yet he didn't release her. Instead, he drew her closer still.

'I said your name like three times,' she added a touch defensively.

He breathed out harshly. He was *always* fully attentive to

his surroundings. To any possible threat. But somehow she'd literally sneaked under his guard.

'You're probably used to a different name,' she said, breaking the searing silence.

Zara was the only name in his head right now. It was Zara's fault. Zara who distracted him in so *many* ways.

'Pax…?'

So she'd been paying attention to the information the media had been ruthlessly excavating about him. *Pax* was the name he'd used in all his time away—when there'd been no title, no expectation, only anonymity. Where—in theory—he could do what he wanted. *Selfishly.* Which was his true self after all—like the teen who'd taken off on holiday instead of taking on work for his mother. And he'd reverted to type—the urge within him now was nothing but selfish. The hunger that had driven him to this room slipped its disguise. It wasn't *dinner* he wanted to have with her.

'Don't call me that,' he growled, tightening his grip on her.

She'd been his nemesis's fiancée. A fact he absolutely and irrationally *loathed,* even though he knew it had been nothing for her other than a means of escape. She hadn't known she'd have been going from frying pan to fire. But now she'd landed in an infinitely hotter, more dangerous hell. With him.

'I apologise, Your Highness.'

But she didn't look sorry. Her eyes glinted with something more fiery. His title was the *last* thing he wanted to be reminded of.

'Don't call me that either,' he snapped.

'Then what?'

Forbidden desire roared—not just deafening him but swamping his reason. The only thing he could do was silence her taunting mouth with his own. He smashed his lips onto hers. Instantly the provocation increased threefold. Because she melted against him, her softness entirely his to enjoy. He swept inside her sweet mouth—tasting the heat of her, revelling in the touch he'd been aching to feel for ever. The hunger that hadn't been assuaged in days was now ravenous and there was no getting close enough, no number of kisses that could possibly satisfy him. But that didn't stop him trying. He released her wrist and wrapped his arms around her. Clamping her to him, he plundered her soft lips and hot mouth with increasing greed.

Zara gripped his shirt, desperate to keep him close as desire was unleashed. She burned with an unfettered need to reach him. She rose on tiptoe, deepening the kisses, seeking to push closer still. His growl of hunger, of pleasure, of desire made her entire body tremble.

Only just as swiftly as it had ignited, it ended. With another guttural growl he sharply pulled away. She would have stumbled had he not kept that firm grip on her waist. But, instead of holding her close, he kept her literally at his arm's length now and she couldn't catch her breath.

'Don't tell me you're speechless?' He finally spoke. 'Now I know how to get some peace around here.'

'Was that just a way to shut me up?' Zara panted, hurt.

Because she wanted it to be more. She wanted it to happen again. But, as she watched, wariness returned to his expression. Worse, she swore she read *regret*. His walls were rebuilding before her eyes.

'Zara—'

'You must think I'm a terrible person.' She cut him off before he could say anything to make her feel worse.

He looked appalled. 'Why would I think that?'

Scalding-hot embarrassment crawled over every inch of her. She could prattle on about meaningless things easily enough, but talking about anything deeply personal or important was much harder. But, despite her awkward shyness, she had to explain because she refused to let him minimise what had just happened. That kiss hadn't been trivial for her.

'Because only a few days ago I was going to marry someone else and now I just want to kiss you.'

'You never wanted to kiss Anders?'

'I tried not to think about it.'

'The first time you kissed him was going to be at the wedding?'

'That was going to be the first time I kissed anyone.'

There was a long pulsing pause. She saw the heat reignite within him—his pale irises obliterated by the dark pupils.

'I don't give a damn about Anders,' he growled. 'I will not allow him to steal a minute more of my life or my mind. If you want to kiss me then you just go ahead and kiss me. You're not trapped in your castle now, Zara. You can do whatever you want.'

The heat overwhelming her was now fuelled by desire. He was testing the truth of her assertion and she wouldn't shy away from his challenge. She stepped closer as he remained frozen in place beside the large table.

He was so very still. But she had his permission. And she would use it. She had to rise right onto her tiptoes again—and even then it was a stretch—so with a trembling hand she grabbed his shirt again and tugged. For a split-second he remained like a statue. But then another groan escaped him and he bent and she pressed her mouth to his. His movement then was swift and complete. She was crushed in his arms before he spun them both and somehow she was on her back on that table and he was pinning her there as he kissed her and it was heaven.

'Zara...' He paused for just a moment and met her eyes. When he smiled he stole her breath. Which meant she had no chance of survival in this moment. Suddenly she was greedy. She tugged his shirt again, pulling him back.

'You want more?' he asked thickly.

'I want it all,' she confessed. She'd never had it—not anything like *this*.

Because this wasn't just kissing, this was touch, this was heat and light and such tormenting pleasure. The need, the delight quickened and deepened. He stroked her so cleverly, his fingers teasing her taut nipples through her top, sliding beneath the waistband of her skirt, rendering her weak and willing and hot.

She shuddered at the sheer eroticism of his touch as his fingers delved lower still. 'I thought you said you were a virgin,' she gasped.

'I am,' he muttered, pressing hot kisses up her neck before teasing her mouth again. 'But I'm not completely inexperienced. I know how to please a woman.'

Oh. He did. He really did. Zara arched, grateful that she was on the table and didn't have to take her own weight. But she was desperate for *his*. She wanted his massive, hard body pressing utterly and absolutely *into* her. But she couldn't speak now—unwilling to ever break this kiss. She spread her legs wider, letting him slide his fingers against her even more intimately, her sighs quickening as he did. She never wanted this to end. Yet the sweeping rise of her arousal was unstoppable. She moaned again and again—breathless and hot and feeling as if every cell within her was shimmering.

'Take pleasure from me, Zara,' he growled roughly.

Honestly, he gave her no choice. He kissed her ruthlessly and his fingers teased right where she was so sensitive, so wet, so deeply aching. She bucked against him, her body shuddering as he stroked her to the brink and beyond—her next sigh cut short by a harsh scream of pleasure. Spasms shook her and he pressed close, anchoring her through the ecstasy.

When she finally opened her eyes she was too dazed to interpret the depths in his, but she felt the gentleness with which he readjusted her clothes and released her from that intimate hold. She'd never experienced anything like it and she was still too stunned to speak. But he wasn't.

'Zara, I'm so sorry. That shouldn't have happened,' he said huskily. 'I showed an unforgivable lack of self-control.'

# CHAPTER EIGHT

LUCIAN HAD NO idea *how* he'd walked away. Only that it had been imperative he had before he'd lost all control and taken exactly what he wanted with no thought to the consequences. He'd not slept. He'd worked through—determined to focus on his work. These were long days and the level of concentration required in the meetings was intense. What she'd shown him last night—one letter of thousands—should have helped him stay on track. Instead, he'd been overwhelmed by a temptation unlike any other. For years he'd avoided emotional entanglements, not wanting to risk exposure or identification, and because he'd been determined to maintain his single-minded focus on rebuilding his health and resources in readiness for his revenge and restoration. But these last two had come so shockingly swiftly now.

Was this bone-deep need for her simply the result of such long self-denial? An outlet for the stress of the situation? A new fixation to fill the void? The answer mattered little because the total loss of control just couldn't happen again. For *her* sake more than his. He couldn't trifle with her. She didn't deserve to be messed around by another Monrayne Royal. She'd been publicly crushed and her future was uncertain. That was enough. And he needed to put his country first for a long, long time—the decade he'd promised. He had no room for anything more with anyone. So he needed to stop this now.

All day he resisted the urge to seek her out. To say sorry

again. To kiss her again. But he walked more quickly than usual to the dining room that next night. Then he saw the determinedly proud tilt to her chin.

'*Manners*,' she said pointedly the moment he took the seat opposite hers. 'Let's discuss them.'

'Manners in what setting?' he answered with more calm than he was feeling.

'The bedroom.' Her cheeks were scarlet and the pink blotches extended down to her neck.

She really wanted to go there right away? Of course she did. This sweet princess could be astoundingly brave. And blunt. Well, so could he.

'I don't recall us making it to a bedroom, Zara.' His muscles rippled with the recollection of her on that table, her soft body pressed beneath his as he'd cupped her hot, slick core.

'Sexual relations then, you know what I mean.'

'Did I not please you?' he asked quietly.

She swallowed. 'The problem is more that *I* didn't please you.' Her voice was low and husky.

His entire body tensed as he was engulfed by a sexual ache so strong he had to grit his teeth.

'It pleased me to please you.'

There was another moment where he just knew she was summoning her strength too.

'Was that really enough for you?' she asked.

He couldn't answer.

'You didn't have to do anything at all if you didn't really want to,' she said resentfully.

His hold began to slip. Her guilelessness and her dauntlessness were both unique and irresistible. 'I was the one who started it, remember?'

'And then challenged me to take more if I wanted.'

Yes. He'd selfishly sought her attentions—greedily aching to know she desired him the way he did her, and then he'd lost himself, desperate to discover her and yes, to please her. But he lost control with no one, and she threatened that rule so completely with her all-in softness and heat. Hell, she'd only had to look at him and she'd made his resolve evaporate. When he desperately needed to be better for his country, this self-indulgence was unacceptable.

'And then you just left,' she added.

She was right and that had been unacceptable of him too. He cursed himself inwardly. He needed to be mindful not just of his duty to his country, but of his duty of care towards her.

'It was better to walk away than to do something that couldn't be taken back,' he said tightly.

'Was that what was about to happen?'

His gut twisted. 'Zara...'

Her vitality and *honesty* challenged him. She had such courage. Maybe he needed more of the same. His hunger for her wasn't going to disappear. But maybe they could restrain it—allow a manageable, acceptable level of release. Maybe that was the only way through here. Because they *couldn't* go all in. That wasn't right for either of them. But if they compromised just a little they could at least *ease* the ache enough to survive it.

Zara furiously stared at him, trying to work him out. He'd given her such pleasure, only then apparently regretted it so intensely that he'd walked out on her. She wanted to know *why*. Why, when he'd kissed her, when he'd made her come apart in complete pleasure...why had he left so quickly?

Because for her it had been a revelation and she wanted more of it. *With* him.

'Would you walk away without taking pleasure from me again?' she asked.

She wanted to be intimate with him, but not if he wasn't going to allow her to give him that pleasure too.

His tension mounted. 'You can trust that I will not take your virginity.'

She did trust him. With all of her body. 'So you'll only go so far, is that what you're saying?'

He closed his eyes briefly. 'Yes.'

Her blood hummed. He would touch her but not take all of her. And he wouldn't give her all of him either.

'Don't you trust me?' she asked softly.

His eyes flashed open and he stared at her directly. 'I don't trust anyone. Ever.'

'You trust Niko,' she pointed out. 'He's never let you down.'

'Niko can take care of himself. I don't have to worry about him.'

'You don't have to worry about me either.' Her anger spiked.

'More importantly—' he ignored her interruption '—I won't take advantage of you.'

'I don't need you to *patronise* me.' She lifted her head proudly. 'I'm not going to be here for long, Lucian. I'm going to leave. Why can't we enjoy what's between us? It wouldn't be taking advantage. It would only be for a little—'

'Zara—'

'You're not going to break my heart—' she brazenly asked outright for what she wanted '—it's just sex.'

He shook his head but his eyes glowed. 'It wouldn't be right for us to go that far, Zara.'

'Why not?'

'You've just been jilted at the altar. Is this the best time to make that decision? And you know that if anyone found out, it would make things even more complicated for us both. Not in a good way.'

Annoyed because she could see his point but hurt by yet another rejection, she snapped back, piqued, 'Fine, maybe I'll just *please myself*, as you once so wisely suggested.'

'Really?' He suddenly shot her a tight, feral smile. 'I

think you might find that that's not the same now. It won't be enough.'

'We'll see, I guess.' She shrugged even as her insides seemed to melt.

'All right,' he said silkily. 'Why don't you prove it to me?'

She stilled. 'Now?'

'Why not?' he challenged provocatively. 'Go on, Zara. You do you.'

The atmosphere crackled. It was as if she were thrown right back into that sensual crucible he'd created for her in his arms last night.

'Is that what gets you going—*watching*?' But she felt her skin flush. What he was daring was outrageous, yet she was dangerously hot. 'Can't you let yourself be touched?'

She heard his sharp intake of breath. In the next second he pushed away from the table, stalked around to her seat and pulled her out of it. The second after that she was clutching his shoulders as he bent her back and kissed her straight back to the searing edge of ecstasy. His hands were *almost* everywhere—his clever, tormenting, sweeping hands that stopped just short of where she burned most for him.

'See?' he growled fiercely. 'It's not enough. You need *my* touch. You ache for it.'

It had seemed like such a good idea to challenge him directly but now, as she writhed against him in shocking desperation, she felt utterly undone by her own desire.

'And I will touch you, Zara. I will kiss you. I can give you the satisfaction you crave,' he muttered hotly against her throat. 'But *only* up to a point. You won't suffer *harm* from me. You've suffered enough of that with Anders.'

'He never touched me,' she growled back. 'And you taking my virginity *wouldn't* harm me.'

'I will *not* hurt you, Zara,' he gritted hoarsely.

'That wouldn't happen!'

But he stilled.

Anger swamped her at the impasse. She'd been so alone, so forgotten, and she'd tried to sacrifice so much. With him—in this—she suddenly wanted *everything.* Not the few crumbs he cared to toss her way. And she could *feel* his arousal against her right now. Why was he so determined to deny them both this release?

'I'm tired of people pretending I don't exist,' she said in frustration. 'Of ignoring my desires. My wishes have value.'

'And I will do everything *else* you wish,' he argued.

She ached as he stood so close she could feel his uneven breathing, but she didn't want to feel this emptiness. She didn't want to settle for less any more. She made herself push him back, *hard.*

'Then I want *nothing* of that from you.'

He stepped back. 'What?'

'I say no. To everything.'

Astonishment flashed in his eyes. 'All or nothing? Is that your position?'

'Yes. We either go all the way or we don't go anywhere.' She just knew she was scarlet in the face as she said that.

He stared at her and the most fascinating smile tugged at the corners of his mouth. 'I think I can make you change your mind.'

Now she was so angry she almost stomped her foot. 'You don't take me seriously?'

His gaze hardened and, impossibly, the atmosphere thickened with the fire of challenge. 'I take you extremely seriously. And I will be extremely serious in my efforts to win a compromise from you.'

Win? The arrogance angered her but the *playfulness* simply stunned her. Who *was* this man?

'Because you just have to win?' she asked huskily. 'I didn't think you would play such games.'

'Perhaps I surprise us both,' he agreed. 'But surely you must concede that *some* is better than none.'

'I thought you were all about protecting me from harm and being honourable.'

'I am.' He cupped her face. '*Neither* of us is in a position to handle a full-blown affair. I have too much work. You have too much uncertainty.'

*Neither* of us. That little admission soothed something deep inside, reminding her that he too was at sea. He too faced all kinds of upheavals and challenges right now.

'But perhaps we can handle a little indulgence. The slightest, smallest tryst. Just to smooth the edge off it.'

Tryst? He was trying to contain this—he wouldn't even call it an affair.

'Control is important to you,' she said slowly.

'You want control over your life too. Correct? Face it, Zara. Both of us have too much else going on to deal with anything too intense.'

She felt a little hit inside. Because he was right. But while he was offering to tease and flirt and give her unspeakable pleasure, though it was the most tempting offer of her life, she *couldn't* agree to it. She couldn't let that be enough.

'Then I think it's best that we not deal with it at all.'

'Ignore it?' He shook his head. 'That won't work.'

'Sure it will,' she said resolutely. 'That's what you excel at, Lucian.'

'What?'

'You think I can't handle you—that's why you're so honourably suggesting we keep this under "control". But I think the truth is that *you* can't handle *me*. You literally ran away from me last night.'

'Because—'

'You haven't let yourself have any fun in *years*,' she said hotly. '*I* haven't had the chance to have fun before, but *you* have. You've made it your *choice* not to indulge.'

He stared at her. Silenced. But she saw the flare in his eyes and knew she was onto something.

'What's holding you back, Lucian?' Did he not want to be vulnerable with anyone—or did he feel as if he shouldn't have pleasure for some reason?

He didn't answer. And that was an answer in itself. It came back to trust.

She leaned closer to him. 'Until you're able to talk to me, there's nothing. Until you can allow yourself to indulge in pleasure—in *all* intimacy—then there'll be none. At least not with me.' She squared her shoulders. 'Now, let me sit down. I refuse to let this delicious dinner get cold.'

There was a long moment when she really wasn't sure what he was going to do. There was a wildness in his eyes and she felt like he was either going to storm out and slam the door, or tumble her to the floor and take her here and now.

He did neither. He stepped back and took his seat at the table. But that glittering emotion in his eyes heightened every one of her senses.

Too late she remembered that Lucian Monrayne had already proven himself a patient man. And one who always ensured he got payback.

Lucian had once prided himself on patience. He'd thought he could play a long game. In this case, he was utterly wrong. He paced through the palace, burning with frustration. Wanting her to say yes to anything he asked. Like a dictator. Like a selfish, lustful jerk. What was so awful about the proposal to be together yet remain within controllable, easily definable boundaries?

'I'm going on a tour of the country,' he told her the next

night at dinner. 'I need to be seen everywhere and by everyone. It is important for security and confidence in my return.'

'How long are you going for?'

Her crestfallen expression demolished him even more.

'Why? Will you miss me?' he asked.

'I doubt I'll notice your absence, I'm far too busy.'

'Is that so?' he said drily. 'I'm only taking day trips. I'll return to the palace every night so you're still stuck with my company for dinner.'

She looked at him for a long moment. 'You're ready to spend time with your people now?'

He stiffened because no, he wasn't really. 'I need to.'

'You're a good listener, Lucian. They love you already. Listen and smile and they'll love you even more.'

He looked into her wide eyes and appreciated that she really meant that. She was too sweet.

Only she suddenly frowned. 'You won't tell anyone I'm still here?'

'It amazes me that you doubt this, Zara. Please be assured I *can* keep a secret.'

She smiled suddenly and he couldn't resist nudging her chin up and stealing a kiss. It was hardly theft though, was it—when she softened in response, when she opened to him like a flower. When she lifted her hands and touched him until he growled in pleasure. He lifted away and gazed into her dazed eyes. But then they gleamed with something else.

'Dare you to tell me one of yours,' she teased.

Yet it wasn't a tease. This was a battle. They wanted each other, yes, but he knew she was vulnerable. More than she wanted to admit. Taking her luscious offer now would be doing her a disservice. She was alone, feeling abandoned by her family and perhaps simply seeking comfort from him. He couldn't take total advantage. She deserved more than that.

He liked her more with every moment he spent with her.

There'd been too many of those moments already, when Monrayne needed his full attention. He'd made that vow to serve his country. It was weak to be side-tracked so soon. It simply served to remind him he still wasn't worthy of his Crown—he was still putting personal pleasure ahead of duty.

Yet she was determined to crack him open emotionally. And while he tried to keep her at arm's length, he ended up pulling her close and silencing her with his mouth after all. He couldn't resist sparring with her—even if it were sometimes just silly double-entendres designed to make that dusky bloom appear like magic on her silky skin. She was extra delicious when she blushed.

At the end of the evening his usual cold shower no longer cut it. He went to the gym for a workout. Then to the pool. Then to the ice bath at the end of it.

He'd just immersed himself—cursing inwardly—when Zara appeared like the elusive shadow she was—haunting him even more than ever and making him forget every good intention he'd just managed to resurrect.

'What are you doing?' She halted.

She had a swimsuit in her hands. It seemed she'd taken his advice for some physical exercise seriously.

'What does it look like?' he gritted.

'Torture.' She stared in horror. 'Your extremities will fall off. Which would be a shame. You have nice...' she glanced at him archly '...fingers.'

'You're worried about my fingers?'

She studied her own fingers for a second before shooting him another coy look from beneath her lashes. 'Amongst other things, yes.'

He chuckled. 'Ice baths bring mental clarity,' he explained. 'I need to think.'

'Oh? Have you forgotten how?'

'Around you, it seems I have.'

She gaped for a split-second, then smiled. 'I will take that as a compliment.'

He reached for a towel, hiding his reaction to her before standing up. To his immense pleasure, she didn't step away—she couldn't. Apparently she was transfixed by his bare chest. Yeah, sometimes a man had to play dirty—with whatever cards he held.

'You're cold,' she muttered distractedly as he stepped nearer.

'Then help me warm up,' he breathed. 'Kiss me, Zara.'

She did. His skin heated the second it touched hers. But after the merest moment she shivered and pushed back on him. Reluctantly he stepped back, meeting her beautiful, baleful blue eyes.

'You don't play fair,' she muttered.

No. He didn't. He never really had.

Zara sat in the library, quietly trying to ignore the fact that frustration was killing her. Lucian been away from the palace all day—welcomed with thousands cheering in the streets. She felt absurdly jealous of them. She wanted that time with him—because there could only be a little left. She had to leave soon.

So she wanted to change *his* mind because there were already onerous limits upon them. She understood his rationale and yes, to anyone on the outside, the two of them tumbling into a hot-blooded affair would be insane, given her uncertain future and the public pressures he faced. But the intensity with which she wanted him was like nothing she'd ever felt and, frankly, she feared she'd never feel it again. No other man had ever been as attractive to her and, sure, she'd not met many but no man in the world was like Lucian.

And she wanted to feel as if she finally had her own life in her own hands. That she could actually get this *one* thing she actually, really wanted. That she could be independent and strong in making choices for herself before she left here for good.

She had more of an idea now. She didn't want to ask Lucian for financial help, given things had got complicated between them personally. It was embarrassing but she was going to have to reach out elsewhere. She couldn't stay in Monrayne, nor could she return to Dolrovia. So she was going to draft a letter to a distant cousin of her father to ask for a small loan and hope she'd agree. Then she'd go to England. It would be far enough away and big enough to give her a little anonymity. She'd take on an unskilled job, study in the evenings and repay the loan as soon as she could. People did that all the world over. She could too. And there were plenty of enormous old houses that needed management—that was what she was good at and, honestly, she'd liked her old castle far more than her family at times. A bubble of enthusiasm lifted her low spirits. She could definitely do that.

'Hello, Zara.' He tipped her face back and kissed her thoroughly.

She was so surprised she couldn't speak. She hadn't even heard him walk into the room.

He laughed as he pulled away. 'My manners are improving, yes?'

'You call those manners?' The man was taking liberties. 'I'm not your therapy dog who you can pet for comfort and then just ignore whenever you feel like it.'

'Ignore?' His eyebrows shot up. 'What's happened to put you in such a snit?'

'A snit?'

'Yes. A mood. Has something happened?'

'Since when do you care?'

'Wow. Okay. Won't ask again. Will just go away quietly and consume dinner alone.'

She glared at him. The last thing she wanted was for him to retreat into silence.

'Stupid article—' she opted for the least of her concerns '—from my stupid country. I am a disappointment to the entire nation now, not just my family.'

He gestured dismissively at the tablet on the table. 'Why do you *still* read them?'

'As if you don't?'

'I only do because I need to be aware of the mood, whether there are any rumblings. It's an intelligence-gathering exercise. You're out of this now, you don't need to bother.'

'But I'm the one they're judging.'

'They can't judge you when they don't even know you.'

'Doesn't stop them trying though, does it.' She sighed. 'I went from being the princess everyone had forgotten about to a supposedly perfect bride, which we all know is an impossibility. To the poor unwanted princess who's a coward.'

'You're not a coward, you're very brave. Not to mention beautiful.'

She had no time for flattery from him. 'Yet you resist me so easily.'

'On the contrary, it is you who resists me.' He shot her a look. 'I would be on my knees between your legs right now if you gave the nod.'

Her face flamed at the image he'd just put in her head. 'I can't. Not while you don't trust me enough to believe me when I say I know what I want and I can handle it.'

He regarded her in silence and that made her resentment burn hotter. She was sleepless. But he looked exhausted. He was pushing himself too hard.

'I mean it,' she said, knowing she was provoking him and doing it anyway. 'You should see a therapist for your trust issues.'

His mouth twisted. 'You think I can trust a therapist?'

'It is a conundrum,' she acknowledged. 'But you're going to need to trust someone some time or everything you're doing is pointless.'

He stiffened. 'It's not pointless to protect my people.'

'They survived without you before. They would again. No one is indispensable.'

'You're saying I'm unnecessary?'

'I think your *personal* sacrifices are unnecessary. You've given up too much of yourself and too much of your life already.'

'And you've not wanted to make sacrifices for your country or your family?' He regarded her sardonically.

But there was more to this. More she couldn't let go.

'I think I was far more selfish than you, actually.' She narrowed her eyes as he paled at her words. 'I think you don't want to trust anyone because you don't want to be hurt.'

'You don't think my lack of trust has anything to do with the fact that my cousin…'

'Your cousin what?' she recklessly pressed. 'What really happened that day, Lucian?'

Lucian clamped his jaw shut and stared at her. The exhaustion from touring was getting to him, as was the frustration of being around her and being unable to touch her in the way he craved more and more. He'd been so looking forward to seeing her he'd just *had* to kiss her. And now—

Now she'd stilled.

And he *had* worked his issues through with a therapist, as it happened. He'd taken that chance while in Piri-nu in an effort to work out if he could truly trust what he'd seen that day. But now he was furious, and Zara was looking at him with her big blue eyes and he knew she wanted more than the scant details that he'd given to the press. She wanted to know *why*. But there was so much more to it than that one morning.

'Anders came to live with us when he was seven,' he said roughly. 'My mother had already lost my father and then her sister and her husband died in a plane crash. As Anders was their only child, of course she opened up the palace to him. My mother was generous.' He took in a breath, remembering his mother's hurt and hating it. 'Garth came too. He's Anders's uncle. He always seemed reliable and willing to assist. My mother trusted him. I'd just gone to boarding school abroad so I saw Anders only in the holidays. Frankly, I wasn't as patient as I could have been. I thought he was always a bit spoiled. Of course I was equally spoiled, but I was just too arrogant to see it.'

'So you weren't close?'

'Not as close as we could have been.' If Lucian had made more effort, maybe things might have turned out differently—that was on him too. 'My mother wanted me to mentor him but I wasn't that good at it. I wasn't…'

'But you took him on that holiday with you,' Zara prompted. 'You took him diving.'

Only because he'd been made to.

'We'd left the big yacht moored and gone in a small boat to explore some of Greece's smaller uninhabited islands. Anders was on the boat when I did a bad dive and hit my head on a rock. I resurfaced but I remember the blood streaming in my eyes. I remember it hurt. I remember I called to him.'

Zara watched him steadily. 'What did he do?'

'He was only fourteen, Zara,' he said huskily. 'Maybe he was frozen with fear.' He'd wanted to believe that. He didn't want to believe he'd truly seen such malevolence in someone so young. That chill filled his body. 'I thought he was holding the boat hook out for me to grab. But he didn't hold it still for me to reach for it. Instead, he hit down with it.'

'Hit *you*?'

'Right on the wound. At first I thought he'd lost control of the hook. But he hit again and then I just dived. I swam underwater to get around a rocky outcrop so I could get away from him. My plan was to get to a beach, find someone somehow and phone for help. But on the other side of those rocks I got caught in a current and got carried out for miles.'

He paused and took a breath. He refused to think of this often. Now he remembered why. He'd been cold. And alone.

Zara put her hand on his wrist. To his amazement, he didn't flinch. Instead, he covered her hand with his and kept it there.

'How did you survive in the sea?' she asked.

'I was lucky enough to grab a bit of driftwood. I was hauled out of the water almost twenty hours later by a fisherman in a small boat. Miles from where I'd started. I was just lucky that the water hadn't been any colder.'

But it had been dark and he'd been terrified for too long.

'I think he thought I was an illegal migrant and he was certainly illegally fishing so we were both happy not to call the authorities. He stitched my split head back together. My eyes were swollen so much when I looked in a mirror that I didn't recognise myself. I was confused but conscious that I was in trouble. I stayed on that boat a couple of days but I knew I needed to get somewhere safe.'

'Piri-nu.'

'Niko, right.'

'How did you get all that way?'

'With difficulty. I managed to get a message to him using a satellite phone and stupid schoolboy code we'd developed at school. Niko sent transportation.'

But by the time he'd made it to Piri-nu infection and exhaustion had set in.

'I collapsed just after I made it there,' he admitted harshly. 'The only thing I managed to tell him was to stay silent about finding me. And he did. But it took me more than a fortnight to battle the pneumonia and while I was unconscious my mother rapidly deteriorated. Niko didn't know about that—the palace kept it quiet. She died before I came through.'

'Lucian…'

He couldn't stand to hear her softness.

'Niko had lost his own mother a few years earlier so he understood the impact of what he had to tell me. He was devastated that he'd not been able to get me home or to get a message to her before she went. But her passing was so sudden. As if any of it were his fault.'

'I'm so sorry, Lucian.'

He shook his head. It had all been his own damned fault. 'It took a lot to get my strength back. By then Garth had taken over as Regent for Anders. I knew I wasn't…*fit*.' Not physically, not mentally or morally. 'It would still be years before my possible coronation and at first I thought Garth might be best for Monrayne in the interim. I decided to get well and keep watch from afar and see.'

He couldn't look at her as he admitted how he'd let his country down. He couldn't tell her that he'd been paralysed with guilt about his mother's death. About his own part in her isolation at the end. He didn't deserve Zara's sympathy but right now he didn't want to lose the comfort of her hand under his.

'I kept tabs on all avenues for information and unfortunately in recent years the whisperings began. There were rumblings about corruption with Garth. But worse was one story about Anders abusing a woman. Then another. I knew things he'd done as a boy. His cruelty to a stray puppy. His temper tantrums. And when I read his account of the accident he'd lied. He said I went overboard in the afternoon. I didn't. It was the morning. And he just waited for hours and hours before raising the alarm.' He gazed into Zara's white face. 'I couldn't let you marry him.'

'I know,' she whispered. 'Not me. Not anyone. And you couldn't let him become King.'

Her acknowledgement didn't soothe—it scoured deep inside. It was his fault that accident had happened at all. It had been his selfish desire to be on *holiday* and not in Monrayne, helping his unwell mother. He wasn't fit to be King when he'd been self-indulgent and inattentive. But he would be a better King than Anders and he would work to be even better still. He could only do that with rigorous, single-minded focus.

Zara was right. He didn't trust people now. But the person he trusted least was himself. Which was exactly why he couldn't give her everything she wanted from him.

Because he wasn't really worthy of his Crown and he wasn't worthy of her either.

# CHAPTER NINE

LUCIAN UNEXPECTEDLY APPEARED in the library in the middle of the next day, carrying a laptop.

'Your sister has been in contact.' His gaze was unreadable. 'Apparently they haven't heard from you and now she's accusing me of holding you hostage or something outrageous.'

'Has she confused you with Anders?' Zara tried to laugh.

He leaned close and took her chin in his hand, making her look up at him. For such a big, strong man his touch was so tender, his voice soft. 'She wants to know where you are and how you are. The question is: do *you* want her to know these things?'

'It's taken them more than a week to remember my existence.' She'd deliberately not reached out to them. She'd wanted to see how long it would be until they tried to contact her. And yes, that was a little petty, perhaps, but she'd been deeply hurt.

'I'll scare her off if you want me to.'

She smiled but shook her head. She couldn't hide from her family for ever. Lucian had said she was courageous and right this second she believed him. After all, she'd stood up to him multiple times and he was the biggest, most intimidating person she'd ever met.

'Of course I'll take the call,' she said softly. 'Let's do it now.'

It took only moments for him to set up the link. Then he turned and shot her a bracing look. 'Don't let her get you down, Zara. Don't let her hurt you.'

'Even though she already has?' she challenged him. 'I'm *desperately* hurt, Lucian. Not by Anders, but by them. Absolutely. So why shouldn't I be honest? Why shouldn't I let her know how they've made me feel?'

He frowned as he stepped away.

'Will you stay in here?' she asked quickly.

He stopped, his eyebrow quirked. 'You would like that?'

She wasn't completely brave. She would like his support some more.

'To ensure your own reputation is protected, don't you think you should?'

He immediately took the seat diagonal from hers. 'The only thing I'm interested in protecting right now is you.'

Just like that, he stole her heart completely.

'Where are you?' her sister Ana asked as soon as Zara took her off mute.

'Still in Monrayne, as you obviously suspected.'

Ana's eyes rounded. 'Is he keeping you captive there?'

'Oh, no. If anything, it's the opposite,' Zara said. 'I forced him to let me stay.'

'I don't think anyone can make King Lucian do anything he doesn't want to,' Ana said.

Zara stiffened at the patronising tone. 'Did you know about Anders?'

Had her family been willing to allow her to marry a monster just for the money and prestige? Why had they abandoned her when she'd already been jilted? Their excuse that there might be unrest and therefore they might've been endangered was simply pitiful. Surely they could have cared about *her* safety—not just their own?

'Of course not,' Ana said impatiently.

Were they afraid that the truth now emerging about Anders somehow tarnished them too? Or that Lucian would somehow step in?

'You need to hurry up and come home,' Ana said. 'You know you're better off here. Mum and Dad miss you.'

They missed her so much they'd not bothered to get in touch. The fact was, her family simply didn't care enough about her. She'd tried to work out an escape route that would please them at the same time. She'd hoped to finally be of value to them *somehow*. But she obviously wasn't. At least now she knew for sure.

'I'm not coming back,' Zara said firmly. 'I'm renouncing my title.'

'What?' Ana almost screeched.

But Zara's attention flicked to the side. She caught Lucian's expression before it became stony again, but she knew she'd startled him.

'I don't want to be a princess any more,' she said more confidently. 'I'm going to be an ordinary citizen and live somewhere else entirely.'

'But—'

'I don't want to live in Dolrovia. I'll be back to visit, of course. Quite soon.' Her parents were old and her father an invalid and, despite everything, she still loved them. She always would. But she was going to live her own life. 'You don't have to worry about me. I just want a quiet existence. I'm going to keep my head down. I'll be fine.'

'Are you going to do that in Monrayne?'

She hesitated and this time she didn't look for Lucian's reaction.

'No. This is a stepping stone until the media storm blows over.'

It felt amazingly good to say it. She literally felt lighter. No more princess. It was a powerfully liberating thought.

'What about us—the family, your country? Your duty to them both?'

'You don't actually need me. I've tried to do everything

they wanted or what I thought they wanted and it didn't work out. Now I want to do something just for me.'

Ana sounded shocked. 'What about *money*?'

'I'll earn it,' she answered. 'Plenty of people do, you know.' And honestly it would be easier without the 'Princess' title. 'For now I'm going to have a holiday here, hiding away from the total humiliation. I'll be in touch again once I'm settled overseas.'

Zara avoided looking at Lucian long as she lowered the laptop screen. She still felt liberated but there was a moment of sadness. It was her family she was walking away from. But she needed the separation—at least while she recalibrated her own role within it and while she created a full life for herself.

'No more Princess?' Lucian said calmly.

'No.' She smiled. 'You know it's only an honorific anyway. Frankly, it's been more hindrance than help.'

'Do you know where you're going to go?'

She swallowed. 'I think England. There's lots of old historic homes that need administrators...'

'You want to do that?'

'I think I could, yes. I actually like the antiques and the art that tend to come with old country piles and I like the skill in the craft and the ancient architecture and making sure it survives.'

'Okay.' He nodded. 'But you think this is a *holiday* for you?'

She gave him a wan smile. 'I'm trying to make the best of a bad situation.'

He moved closer, his gaze almost tender. 'Then maybe we should make it even better.'

Her heart skipped. But he didn't pull her into his arms.

'Perhaps you should see some of *Monrayne's* ancient architecture before you go,' he said.

She shook her head, struggling to mask her disappointment. 'I don't want to be seen in public yet. Definitely not here.'

'Why, Zara—' he raised his scarred eyebrow at her '—are you not aware that I am a master of disguise?'

She giggled. 'Sunglasses aren't going to cut it in this case, Lucian.'

Lucian wished he was wearing his sunglasses right now. The luminescence of her hurt his eyes and maintaining an emotionless expression in the face of what he'd just heard was impossible.

She was leaving. Renouncing her title. Refusing her royal status. Ms All-or-Nothing was in action. And though he shouldn't be shocked by her decision, though he respected it, that old anger returned. Only it wasn't cold, it was hot, pure *frustration*. He knew she couldn't stay yet he didn't want her to leave. And how was she going to get to England? Who would she apply to for work—did she want a letter of introduction or support? Was she going to ask him to help her? He would in a heartbeat, of course.

But it was going to hurt like hell to do so.

So he turned his attention to something else—snatching at a weak idea while he settled the roiling emotion inside.

'You haven't seen some of the most beautiful parts of Monrayne. Some of our most stunning buildings. We'll get Victor to arrange it. You must at least go to the thermal springs.'

She flushed. 'Are you going to come with me?'

The invitation in her eyes bit deep. 'I can't, Zara.'

'You don't want to take a little respite? You've not stopped since your return. Not had a weekend—not even a single day.'

'No.' He ground out the refusal. 'The press would be onto you in a flash if I was with you.'

'Oh.' Her face fell. 'Yes, of course.'

But she'd wanted him with her and that made the temptation even harder to resist.

'You can bathe in the waters. Have a massage.' He almost choked at the thought. 'Eat what you want, do what you want.'

'A spa day at last,' she mock marvelled. 'What have I done to deserve such a reward?'

He gave in and pulled her close. 'Careful, Princess. Or I will demand payment.'

Her gaze turned smoky. 'What would you have me do?'

The willingness in her eyes almost undid him completely.

'You would like that, wouldn't you?' he said huskily.

He felt her trembling and knew the desire was as fierce for her as it was for him. But he resisted teasing her. He didn't even kiss her. At last he gave in to her insistence that there must be nothing between them. Because he was a breath away from taking the alternate deal—taking *everything* she offered.

'It can't happen,' he muttered, closing his eyes in sheer frustration, reminding himself more than he was telling her. 'You deserve so much better, Zara.'

She deserved someone who could give her all his attention.

But he had to be fully focused on his country. He'd promised himself he would on his mother's memory. He released her and walked away before she could argue. He'd go dwell in an ice-cold shower. For ever.

Early the next morning he was en route to a town a couple of hours' north of the capital. Zara's car was heading in a similar direction but would stop sooner. She was so pale. Some fresh air, sunlight—even winter sunlight—would benefit her. He wished he could join her as she bathed in those private, natural thermal springs. But this restorative experience was just for her. At least she would have it.

His day dragged and he was annoyed with himself for wondering about her when these people had waited so long to see him. So when he finally returned to the palace he hurriedly strode to their private wing. She should be back already. But the library was empty. So was the dining room.

'Where is Zara?'

Victor looked at him warily. 'There was an accident on the off ramp. The car was—'

Lucian stilled completely. The only word he retained in his head was *accident*. The last flicker of brain capacity tried to listen more, tried to… But his heart suddenly hammered, too hard, too fast, too loud. His throat tightened. A monster had its claws around his neck. He couldn't breathe.

Terror silenced him. Deafened him. All but immobilised him.

'Sir—?'

He stumbled as he forced his feet to move. *Alone*. He needed to be alone. To breathe.

She should have been back already. She should be telling him about the steaming waters. Instead, her rooms were empty. And he couldn't *consider* the word accident. He couldn't let himself think anything along those lines.

He needed to get to her. He needed to know she was okay. He needed that *now*. But, almost blind, it was all he could do to walk through the palace, feeling a sickening threat like no other until he came to the most central, most secure of rooms. Secure as a bank vault, it was dimly lit and had reinforced walls. Silence. Space. Safety.

He would wait there, uselessly holding his aching head.

He closed the door behind him then stared, aghast, at the empty gold throne that seemed to mock him. He was so weak. He couldn't think. He couldn't move. How could he ever be King when he reacted like this to just a word?

# CHAPTER TEN

ZARA WENT STRAIGHT to the dining room, her stomach rumbling. She hoped Lucian hadn't finished already, she wanted to tell him all about her day. But he wasn't there. Silver domes still covered the many dishes and Victor looked tense as he stood to attention.

'Has Lucian eaten?' she asked him.

The servant shook his head.

'Has he not come home yet?'

'He got back some time ago,' Victor said, almost hesitantly. 'He's been in the throne room since his return.'

Zara nodded. 'Is he in a meeting?'

'I believe he's alone, ma'am.'

Zara was unwilling to ask the servant anything personal about the King, but there was something meaningful in the way the man was now hovering beside her with an unusually worried expression.

'Perhaps I'll see if he's ready to dine,' Zara muttered.

Her heart skittered as she walked to the throne room. She knew it was in the very centre of the palace, a relic of the original castle that had been built here and added to over the centuries. It wasn't massive but the stone walls were thick and the steel door heavy and hard to open. A couple of side lights cast a minimal glow, yet even so the throne on the dais glittered. But it stood empty. The surrounding velvet drapery looked heavy and lush.

She peered in the dimness. Then she saw a movement in the shadows—his back was against the wall in the furthest corner of the room. She stepped in and let the heavy door seal shut behind her before speaking softly. 'Lucian?'

She heard his sudden sharp inhalation—an alarmingly rough gasp for air.

'Has something happened?' She hurried towards him.

She stared as she neared because his mouth moved but no sound emerged. But it was obvious what he'd tried to say—*Zara*.

'Lucian?'

He sighed—a huge release of tension.

'Go.' This time his voice was audible. A low, ragged growl. And the distress in his eyes was very real.

She swallowed. 'No.'

He flinched and his breathing became choppier.

She took a steadying breath of her own. Here, in this heart of the palace, there were no windows and only that one door. She instinctively understood that that was why he'd come here. He'd needed safety. She just didn't know why.

'I won't talk to you. I won't touch you. But I will *not* leave you alone. Not when you're obviously upset.' She bit her lip. She was desperate to reach for him but she didn't.

Storm clouds swirled in his eyes—she wasn't sure he could even see her properly. Sweat slicked his brow. His hands curled into even tighter fists. His chest rapidly rose and fell as he stared at her. She waited where she'd stopped, just a few feet from him. As he stared at her his breathing slowly eased.

'Zara.'

His voice was still rough and she couldn't tell if he was using her name as a curse or a prayer.

But she didn't answer. She'd said she wouldn't talk and she wouldn't break his trust. Not ever.

'I need you to tell me you're okay,' he muttered.

'Of course I'm—'

'There was an accident,' he interrupted harshly.

He knew that?

'It was nothing,' she said quickly. 'We got rear-ended on the way back. But it was barely a knock. I'm fine, so are both drivers.'

His breath hissed. 'Come closer,' he growled. 'Let me see.'

She moved before he changed his mind, stopping a mere breath from him.

His hands still shook as he framed her face—tilting it one side to the other so he could see better in what little light there was. And she saw better too—the concern in his eyes, the tension in his face. She realised the truth and it rent her heart.

'You were worried about me,' she whispered.

He stared into her eyes and his breathing roughened again.

'Lucian,' she added even more softly. 'It's okay. I'm fine.'

But his hands gently searched. Carefully he probed her neck, her shoulders, down her arms—feeling for himself that she was unharmed. Even more gently, he then swept the sides of her ribs, her waist…

*Her* breathing began to quicken. He was merely checking she was unharmed but she was becoming aroused. She'd missed him today. She was going to miss him for ever soon. And she just wanted—

'I need to see you,' he growled.

His hands were on her collarbone and he looked directly into her eyes. That was when she saw the fire now building in his. The fire that matched her own. She nodded and the next second he ripped the front of her dress apart.

'I cannot resist you,' he groaned as his gaze dipped to her chest.

'Why do you want to?'

'I don't know any more. I don't know anything any more. I just need you. I need to feel you.'

He cupped her bra. Her breasts felt heavy and she simply melted—pressing right against him. Because he was like a furnace and she was cast deep into his fiery passion. His hands slid around her ribs. He unfastened the strap and took her bra off completely before returning his attention to her now bared breasts. Skin on skin. She gasped at the gentle sweep of his thumbs across her nipples and shivered at the smile that then curved his mouth.

'Zara…'

He lowered her to the floor and joined her there. Her dress was in a puddle about them, while unbuttoning his shirt was almost impossible because he was so intent on kissing every inch of her. He removed her panties and slid the remnants of her dress up to her waist and kissed every inch he exposed in the process.

The intimacy was searing. He kissed her so wickedly that she groaned. But she wasn't ashamed at how hot she was already. She felt the thickness of his arousal pressing against her and knew it was the same for him. There was this between them. There had been from the beginning. When she'd been supposed to be marrying another man she'd turned in that cathedral and seen him and it had been like a bolt of lightning. So hey, she wasn't perfect either. But he'd held back for all these nights.

She reached for him. 'Are you sure?' she whispered.

'I want this. With *you*,' he growled, rising to lie between her legs.

He was heavy and she trembled with the delight of having him press against her so fully, so intimately.

She framed his face with her hand, feeling the heat of his skin. 'You were upset. I'm sorry you were so worried.'

'I haven't had a panic attack like that in a very long time.'

'You're very tired. You have so much going on. Maybe it isn't right to make this choice now…' She bit her lip but she had to make sure *he* was sure. 'I couldn't stand it if you were to regret this.'

'Regret is my constant companion,' he muttered hoarsely. 'I've regretted not doing this every night since we met. I wanted you the minute I saw you in that cathedral. I've only wanted you more with every day since.'

Stunned, she stared up at him.

'I'm tired of fighting how much I want you.' He pressed his pelvis against her to prove his point. 'I'm tired of not giving in to what I *really* want.'

And that was this. With her. She felt it in his straining muscles, in the care with which he kissed her and caressed her, she felt it in the huge erection digging against her now. And she could never resist because she wanted him too. To be so very much wanted was everything.

'Lucian,' she whispered.

She wriggled her hands between them and unfastened his trousers. He closed his eyes as she wrapped her fingers around his girth. She stroked him tentatively at first, then with increasing grip and pleasure as she watched his unfettered reaction.

'I'm really selfish, Zara,' he muttered through gritted teeth. 'I want *everything*.'

'Then take it.'

He gripped her wrist, stopping her strokes and lifting her hand away. He dropped his hips onto hers and she felt the hard head of him pressing against her slick seam. Then he thrust. Hard.

They both groaned—guttural and raw—as he breached her body at last. She met his gaze. They swapped a breath. Then swapped a smile. And both of them slid into a mingled sigh as he thrust again, even deeper. He was right there, absolutely inside her. It was so intimate. It was everything.

'Zara…' His passionate whisper echoed so deeply within her.

She swept her hands over his broad shoulders. In his huge

pupils she saw wonder—despite that storm of emotion before. Yet another storm brewed now. Emotion of an altogether different kind. Hunger and need and the determination to satisfy and be satisfied. Nothing less than everything would sate either of them.

'Don't hold back.' She instinctively arched, encouraging him to ride her.

'I won't,' he muttered.

And then he proved it—covering her mouth with his as he moved. He was so strong. So intent. And it was so good. Every atom within her quivered. It was all she could do to kiss him back, to hold him close, to wrap her arms and legs around him and cling as he surged into her.

'Zara—'

'*Yes. Yes!*' She let go and let desire swamp her entirely.

He growled and pumped furiously, utterly lost in her embrace. She revelled in the fever glazing his eyes and the need bunching his muscles. She was as incomprehensible, as uncontrolled as she arched to meet him with every muscle, loving the ferocity of their dance until they slammed into that end point, shuddering through tumultuous wave after wave of orgasm.

Long minutes later they were a loosened tangle of limbs, torn clothing and sweat but still intimately, deeply entwined. Zara never wanted to move again. But slowly their breathlessness ebbed and her wariness prickled.

'I'm too heavy,' he muttered with a small smile. But still several long moments passed before he finally summoned the strength to lift away to sit beside her with his back against the wall. Maybe he needed to be able to see the door, but his alert gaze was utterly focused on her. That smile turned rueful.

'We will marry immediately,' he said huskily.

'We will not,' she whispered sadly. That wasn't what either of them wanted. Especially him.

'You might be pregnant,' he pointed out. 'We just had un-protected sex.'

'I won't be pregnant,' she muttered obstinately.

'Sometimes it only takes the once.'

She looked at him. 'I'm on the pill.'

'What?' His eyes dilated and she felt him tense. 'That's impossible. Weren't you supposed to provide Anders with an heir?'

'Yeah, well, I wanted to wait a few months to see what married life was like first. I didn't want to get pregnant instantly like some brood mare. And most of all I wanted to control my cycle so I wasn't struggling up the aisle with cramps and a bloated belly. Call me vain, I don't care. There were so many cameras in there.'

He stared at her. 'Then we won't have a public ceremony. Ours can be private.'

'*We* will not have *any* kind of ceremony.' She shook her head. '*You* will give them a whole public performance with the perfect princess bride eventually. In a decade, right? But not with me. I'm never facing that scrutiny again, not after—' She broke off bitterly. 'Not even for you.'

She felt the crush inside at what her words had given away—*not even for you*. And, besides, it wasn't true. She would put on another stupidly sparkly dress and stand in front of millions all over again if he really wanted her to…but the point was he didn't really want that. He'd thought he had to ask in case he'd just got her pregnant. But he didn't want to get married for a decade. He'd made that more than clear. She suspected he didn't really want to ever marry anyone at all.

'But if you *are* pregnant—'

'We'd have to be extremely unlucky.' But her heart twisted. In her world it wouldn't be unlucky at all. Except while he wanted her, he wasn't in *love* with her. And she couldn't be in love with him, right?

'Stranger things have happened.'

She shook her head. 'No, Lucian.'

He glanced down at her. 'Your dress is ruined. I'm sorry.'

'I don't give a damn about my dress. And don't you dare apologise for ruining anything *else*. That was the most sublime experience of my life and you're not wrecking it with your regrets.' She threw her arm over her face so she didn't have to see him and he couldn't see her. 'Take them and leave.'

She heard him draw in a deep steadying breath. 'Zara—'

'You are *not* ruining the last of my afterglow.'

'Fine.'

To her surprise, he half laughed.

'I will not ruin the last of your afterglow,' he said. 'I'm very glad you have an afterglow.'

She kept her face covered, still unwilling to see his face as she asked, 'Do you?'

'I'm pretty sure those astronauts up in the international space station can see my afterglow.'

She lowered her arm and looked at his gorgeous smile and her tension melted all over again. 'Through the stone walls and everything?'

'Absolutely. I don't have any regrets about this, Zara. Not *ever*.' He gazed at her and his chest rose and fell that bit quicker again. 'You're amazing. That was amazing.'

Lucian watched her skin flush more enchantingly than ever. She swallowed hard and turned her gaze up towards the beautiful ceiling of the throne room.

'It's a beautiful palace,' she said eventually.

'Yes.'

'You missed it?'

'More than I realised.' He ached to be worthy of it. And, for this fleeting moment, worthy of her. In this one impossible moment he wanted everything.

She'd just seen him—held him—at his most animal. When instinct had overridden reason and the desire of the flesh had won. They'd assuaged that relentless ache and he could never regret it. Mind blown. Body broken. Yet he felt energised in an altogether new way. It was wonderful.

If she was lying about being on birth control—and he truly didn't think she was—then she might get pregnant. And, heaven help him, in this moment he didn't care. He, who'd vowed not to have children for years, would demand she marry him. She wouldn't be able to say no, and part of him would be *pleased*. Here was the horrible truth. He was greedy. A selfish monster who would not let her go. Who took what he wanted—uncaring of the impact of his actions on anyone else. He was as spoiled as his poisonous cousin and arrogant with it. Because he knew that was not what she wanted.

She wanted to renounce her title. She didn't want pomp and pageantry—she didn't want to live the kind of life he would have as King. She knew too well it came with peril. She'd only entertained the idea of marrying Anders because she'd thought it was her only way of escaping her home. But she had another option now. So he couldn't coerce her into something different.

He couldn't bear to think of those moments when he'd thought she'd been hurt. He couldn't relive it. Couldn't stand to analyse why it had almost destroyed him. Maybe it was just that he was overtired. But he couldn't resist running his hand down her arm, needing to touch her while he could.

She turned her head towards him. 'I can't believe you've never done that before,' she said softly. 'I can't believe *I've* never done that before.' She smiled a little sadly. 'We've been missing out.'

'We have.' His whole body ached to have her again.

An impish look lit her eyes. 'So when *did* you learn how to please a woman?'

He chuckled. 'I might have fooled around back when I was a senior at school.'

'Before you disappeared.'

'Yes. But I'd not quite got to have the full experience.'

She caressed his jaw and a smug look entered her eyes. 'I'm glad.'

He leaned into the soft touch—a balm he knew he couldn't indulge in for long. 'You're right to say no to marrying me,' he muttered. 'I'm not good enough for you, Zara.'

'Why do you say that?'

He kept silent for a few more moments, but in the end he was so tired and felt so accepted by her that the miserable truth simply came out.

'I meant it when I told you I was selfish. I truly am and that's what drives me to do better now. My mother was dying of cancer and I chose to go away on holiday instead of spending time with her. Instead of easing her burden I made it much worse.'

Zara's beautiful eyes widened. 'Lucian—'

'Listen.' Now he'd started he needed her to understand everything. He needed her to want to walk away from him because he wasn't entirely sure he could let her go now. 'My father died in a car accident when I was four. My mother buried her heart with him. She devoted her life to her country and to me. She was loving and generous. That's why she opened up the palace to Anders and Garth.'

'She was kind.'

'And loyal like no one else. She would have done anything for us. I had the opposite upbringing to you, Zara—I had full prince privileges. Almost everything I wanted, I got. I'd been away at boarding school—clueless about the burden of the Crown and wrapped up in my own late teen life. I was looking forward to starting my degree. I thought I had the world at my feet.

I hadn't seen that much of her, but I did notice she was thinner and she seemed more tired. I thought she was just older. I didn't consider the details as closely as I should have. It was a surprise to me when she asked me to defer going to university for a year and shadow her working in the stateroom. I realise now that perhaps she knew her time was limited and she wanted to train me while she could. But I wasn't gracious in my acceptance of her request. My trade-off was to have one last holiday. I insisted on it like the spoilt little prince I was.'

'Had she told you she was unwell?'

He sucked in a painful breath. 'Only right before I left. Because she asked me to take Anders with me. You can imagine I wasn't enthused. That's when she said she wasn't well—a small tumour, she said. I was shocked and didn't ask the right questions. I made some noises about not going, but she said she wanted to see both Anders and me have a nice break together before we got to work. So we went.' He frowned. 'It was ovarian cancer. They found it late, but there could have been more time. There should have been. But when I went missing the stress destroyed her. It was so fast, Zara. It monstered her.'

He couldn't bear to think of his mother lying so unwell and so alone. He should have been there to support her.

'She'd already lost so much. It's unfathomable to me how Anders could put her through more when she'd given him so much. But I'd been just as cruel. I'd been careless and self-centred. And the truth is I'm still not who I need to be. I'm not a worthy heir to her Crown. And I'm not the man for you.'

'You don't think you're being a little hard on yourself?' Zara said quietly. 'What teenager hasn't been the centre of their own universe? What young adult hasn't wanted to go on holiday at the beach?'

'If I hadn't made that choice then the accident wouldn't have happened. My mother wouldn't have died sooner than she should have and even more heartbroken, as she did.'

'You're not blaming yourself for your own attempted murder, are you? Or for the death of your mother from cancer? You're powerful, Lucian, but not *that* powerful.'

'I lacked critical judgement. My choice set in motion a cascade of events, and it hastened her death. She suffered greatly and it was utterly avoidable.'

'And that was Anders's fault, not yours.'

Zara was heartbroken for him. 'It sounds to me like she wanted you to go have that last summer of fun.' She paused. 'But now you don't allow yourself that. Is this why you live a life of personal denial? Because you think you don't deserve it?'

'Because I need to put my duty *first*,' he corrected. 'I need to remain focused on Monrayne. That's my vow—the decade I was away is the decade the country gets. Fully focused. By then I'll be better at it. Because I know that when I get distracted by personal wants or impulses, my choices aren't always wise. Look at me now...'

Yes, this wasn't wise.

'None of us make wise choices all of the time. We're not perfect, remember? Don't you think you deserve to have it all at some time in the future?' she asked. 'I want that for me. You should want that for you too.'

He shook his head. 'I can't fail my country. Or my mother's memory.'

'You're worried you can't live up to her. You already do, Lucian. You're a good King. You're a good listener.'

'You're wrong. I didn't listen closely enough to her. And I didn't see how bad Anders was becoming.'

'Because you were young too. And his betrayal was a shocking, terrible thing. Realising that someone you thought you knew was nothing like you imagined, that they're capable of cruelty... It makes you doubt everything. *Especially* yourself.'

She felt disillusioned by her own family. She'd been willing to do what was asked of her. She'd supported them. Yet they'd not stayed to support her. And that hurt. Desperately. Lucian had been left alone too. He had lost his family. His country. His sense of purpose. His belief in his ability to do and be what his job required. So he'd not come back for a while, and she didn't blame him.

'You didn't come back for revenge. You came back for *redemption*,' she realised. 'But you're already a worthy King, Lucian. You might have made youthful mistakes but you're more than good enough as you are. You can do your job and have an actual life. You shouldn't carry this burden and you don't have to sacrifice anything else. You should have everything. In fact you'll be a better King if you do.'

He was silent. She realised he disagreed. He was punishing himself for perceived failures from so long ago and he wouldn't change his mind on what he believed he needed to do. His decade of duty. He would stick to his plan.

She had to do the same. She had to reach for what she'd long wanted, and that was her independence. Getting further entangled with Lucian would only risk that.

'I'm not sorry we did this, but I think we both know we can't do it again,' she whispered.

He looked at her sombrely. 'Zara—'

She silenced him with a shake of her head. 'You need to focus on your duty and I need to find my freedom.'

Instinct told her that if she stayed much longer her heart would be trapped here for good. He had such a complete effect on her.

'So once we leave this room?'

'It ends. We both have things that need our full attention.'

'You don't want this to become an affair now? You said yourself you're not going to be here long.'

She reached for the courage he'd told her she had and whispered the uncomfortable truth. 'I'm scared I'll end up wanting more. And that can't happen.' Even though she had the horrible feeling it might already have. 'It's just really bad timing, Lucian.'

He stared at her with such intensity her too-vulnerable heart melted. She had to stop this conversation now. She couldn't expose herself any more than she just had.

'But we haven't left this room *yet*,' she muttered in one last surrender. 'And I've not yet seen you fully naked...'

He suddenly swooped.

'Lucian—'

'Indulge me,' he said huskily. Lifting her into his arms, he carried her to the throne. 'I don't want to crush you. I want to see you too.'

He set her on her feet and quickly stripped them both of the last clothes tangled between them. Then he sat back on the throne and lifted her again so she straddled his lap. That meant she got an up close and wonderful view of his chest. As he did of hers. And that meant there was then a battle of playful kisses and nips and tweaks and tongues until in the end there was only wild movement and absolute abandonment. Again.

And then—even when they were exhausted and sweaty—again. It was a slow, aching indulgence and so tender her eyes watered. She had to close them to hide the tears from him. But he knew anyway because she couldn't seem to hide anything from him. He simply cradled her close and neither spoke a word.

It was a long, *long* time later before she pulled the remnants of her dress back on. She paused at the door and glanced to where he remained sprawled alone in that massive chair, needing to admit one last truth of her own.

'I'll always be glad I did this with you first, Lucian.'

# CHAPTER ELEVEN

THE ANGER WAS BACK. She was pleased she'd done that with him first, was she? The predator within him wanted to be her *first* and *only* and *always*. But he couldn't be. He knew with his brain that Zara was right in calling a halt to any affair before it had really begun. His blood, however, was dead certain she was wrong.

She'd been so brave—leaving her home, prepared to make a deal in the hope of a better life; resilient in the face of public rejection and the worse private rejection of her family; courageous in standing up to him and saying what she needed. She was tough. He wished she would take a little more solace—steal a little more pleasure—with him. Yes, in these weak moments he changed his mind completely. He ached for more time alone with her. Fortunately for him, she was strong—determined to maintain her new boundaries. Because she *was* leaving and what they shared was perhaps too intense.

She was right about other things too. He *had* denied himself pleasure all this time. And didn't it serve him right that the one woman he now wanted was unavailable to him? Because, of course, he would respect her decision. This was a woman who needed agency. To take control of her own life. She wanted her independence. But Princess All-or-Nothing had twisted that on him again in the most frustrating way.

Yet thank goodness she had, because he had that lifetime of work ahead of him. But, in truth, his return to claim the

Crown had gone better than he'd ever imagined it would. He was extremely busy but there was no crisis in the country. He just had to stay calm and stick to the plan. Keep going. Step by step. And that meant not seducing Zara again. That meant regaining his self-control entirely.

Monrayne now needed global recognition of its stability and he knew exactly how to prove that. The next day he visited another town and then lost track of time in planning after his return. Which meant he was very late for dinner by the time he realised the hour. Naturally she'd long left the dining room so he went searching and found her in the library, sorting through the never-ending letters now that she'd finished with the books.

'You dined without me,' he said mock-balefully.

'Did you expect me to wait when you were so very late?' she countered archly.

'Of course not. I wouldn't dream of making you go hungry, Princess.' He was unable to resist a little verbal tease. He didn't think it possible for them to end that altogether.

She shot him a look. 'And I haven't.' Her smile widened to the point that a dimple appeared in her cheek. 'I even have some supper.' She gestured with her hand and he saw a laden tray on the table behind her. 'Would you like to share?' she asked blandly.

Their favourite displacement activity again? He promptly sat down.

Zara nudged the tray nearer. 'I'm sure you must be hungry. You don't eat when you're on show.'

He mustered a faint smile. 'I genuinely don't feel hungry when I'm out there.'

'I know.' She nodded in complete acceptance. 'You're concentrating hard on everything else. Knowing everyone's names, keeping tabs on what they're all doing and saying.'

He nodded. That was exactly it.

'So have something to eat now.' She picked up a piece of cheese and bit into it with a cheeky smile. 'Before I eat it all.'

'Temptress,' he jeered softly.

'I do try.'

He leaned unnecessarily close to her as he reached to select a small slice of tart. 'I wish you really would.'

The look she shot him then was sharper. He chuckled as he chewed. The bone-deep weariness morphed into an aching cross between contentment and yearning. He was *relaxed*, with another person present—frankly, a miracle. But it was *because* of the other person present. Only he wanted more from her still.

'I'm going to hold a ball.' He told her his plans to keep himself on track. 'To show the world that the situation here in Monrayne has settled and that I'm here to stay. It seems a shame to waste the fireworks that were planned for Anders's celebrations.'

'Your coronation ball?'

He tensed. 'Not the coronation. Not yet. Just a ball.'

'Is there reason to delay it?' Zara asked.

'Is there reason to rush it?' he countered.

'You still don't feel worthy?'

He drew a breath because she was so very acute and he never should have told her all that he had. 'I am King already, Zara, that pageant is purely ceremonial. Right now, I need to focus on doing the job and part of doing the job is showing the world that Monrayne is politically stable.'

'Monrayne is humming. I've seen it on the news—the place is filled with chatter and vibrancy. They're all clamouring to get closer and see you. It must be nice to know they're so happy you're back.'

He sighed. He knew he had to be seen and seen to be confident. 'It's important the world sees serenity, stability, security. That foreigners aren't afraid to visit. It's important for tourism and investment.'

'Will the guests you need come?'

'Niko will definitely be here.' Lucian smiled. Once the confirmation that Niko would attend was made public more acceptances would come quickly. Niko was popular at parties. 'I'd like you to attend as well.'

She froze. 'You're not serious.'

'You can't hide for ever,' he said softly. 'You need to show your face.'

'That's ironic, coming from you.'

'Quite. You have the benefit of learning from my mistakes. Nothing good comes from not facing your fears, Zara. You can't live the rest of your life hiding from what's happened.'

'Why not? I could just slip away to England, never to be seen on that public princess circuit again.'

'Aside from the wedding-that-wasn't, have you *ever* been on the public princess circuit?'

She stared at him reproachfully.

'No. You haven't,' he answered for her.

She should have had so much more. She should have had everything. *He* had. He'd had all the luxury experience of being born royal. He'd also had that time away in Piri-nu, out of the spotlight, where he'd had a physical freedom unlike any he'd experienced before and probably would never have again.

But Zara was a princess who'd never been enabled to enjoy any of the perks. She'd been short-changed. She'd had the restrictions without the rewards. She'd been more than hidden, she'd been ignored and isolated. So she should have a few moments of the fun that could be had. Because it wasn't all bad—far from it. It was an honour and privilege to meet the people he got to meet. And she'd never got to understand just what a natural she could be. As someone who could talk to literally anyone—who could set the most uncomfortable man in the world at ease—given the chance, he believed she could excel. Because she was a genuine sweetheart. He wanted her to understand that too.

'You can do this, Zara. You know it's just a party with fancier food than usual.'

'Stop trying to amuse me into acquiescence.'

'Shall I go with issuing a command instead?'

She swallowed. 'Why is it so important to you that I attend?'

He hesitated. 'Honestly, it would be helpful to me if you would come and keep King Niko's wife Maia company. She's very new to royal life. She hasn't been to plenty of palace receptions and could do with some support in an environment like this.'

'You really think I'm the right person for that task?'

'I think you're kind. And you're really good at filling strained silences.' He smiled at her. 'I think you understand how uncomfortable you can feel when you're not used to it.'

'Solidarity in awkwardness?' she asked. 'Will you invite anyone else from my family?'

'Not if you don't want me to. I think you can represent your family beautifully.'

'It can be my first ball and last official duty ever as a princess. But I don't want to be seen *with* you,' she said in a low voice. 'I don't want...'

Regret welled within him. 'I know. There will be no speculation about anything between us. You'll have returned from your sanctuary, that's all.'

There was no "them".

'People are going to stare at me,' she muttered.

'Maybe.' He adopted a teasing drawl. 'They'll stare at me more, though. So I'll stay on the other side of the room and distract them for you.'

At last she smiled. 'How very chivalrous of you.'

'I'll even go without my sunglasses so they can all unsubtly stare at my scar.'

Her smile grew. 'I don't think anything can surpass the bare chest in the cathedral moment.'

'You think I should wear something revealing?' He chuckled. 'Perhaps, just for you, I will.'

'Full drama, Lucian. I have to hand it to you.'

'So you'll go?'

'If you really want me to.'

'I do.' More than that, he wanted her to *enjoy* it. It mattered so much to him. That she wanted to turn her back on this life didn't sit right when she didn't really know what it could be like. 'You'll need support to get ready. I'll arrange a maid.'

He'd show her that she truly was a princess.

'I don't need a maid—' she laughed '—I've *never* had one.' She lifted her chin. 'I can manage on my own perfectly well. I can even put my own toothpaste on my own toothbrush.'

'All the essentials of life,' he teased.

'Quite. I might not be able to survive on the streets just yet, but I'm going to be fine on my own.'

He really didn't want to think about her leaving. Not yet. Even though he knew it would happen sooner rather than later. Even though he knew he was going to help her get away in the end. She hadn't asked him yet, but he knew he would fly her out of here when she did.

'Have you something you can wear to the ball?'

'Well…' She lit up. 'I do have this really big white dress that's only been worn once.'

'*Not* that.' He laughed. But he didn't want her wearing anything associated with Anders. None of those perfectly princess-appropriate dresses that Garth's minions had ordered either. 'I'll arrange something.'

'Given they're all going to be looking and judging me, that would be amazing and thank you. But please just rent something, you don't need to buy anything.' She wrinkled her nose. 'I definitely don't want another total makeover.'

'No? Hadn't we better get a beautician in for these horror nails?' He couldn't resist taking her hand.

'Not those scary assistants again,' she groaned.

'Someone else, I promise.'

'I'm not having them that ridiculous length again. And at least I'm not going to have to flash around some massive ring.'

'Such a relief not to have that burden,' he agreed gravely and lifted her fingers to his mouth. 'You'll need some jewels though.'

He'd missed her softness. Her scent.

'I think my family vault has been depleted,' she muttered jerkily.

'This time you may borrow from me.' Something tightened in his gut at the thought of draping a chain of diamonds across her sensitive skin.

'Oh, no.' She shook her head. 'It would not be wise to wear *anything* associated with the Monrayne Royal family, given I've just been jilted by the Crown Prince,' she said caustically. 'Even if he is now a fugitive.'

'He's no longer Crown Prince.'

'That change in the law went through?'

'There was no objection to its speed either.' But Lucian wasn't satisfied on that score yet. He wanted Anders found and to face justice for the hurt he'd caused those women and who knew what other cruelties.

He drew a breath, focusing on what he could do here and now. And the one thing that he wanted that he could actually make happen was for Zara to attend the ball. 'So we'll find you something else to wear.'

'I don't need anything else.'

He rolled his eyes, annoyed with her rejection on many levels. 'You know that's not how these things work. You'll look all the more pitiful if you're in a plain ill-fitting number with no bling.' He paused and appealed to the pride he knew she had. 'You need a revenge dress.'

She looked at him for a second and then laughed with such amusement that he couldn't help but join her.

'Wow,' she breathed. 'Well, you are the King of Revenge Dressing, what with the bare-chested cathedral moment.'

'And we're back to that.' His amusement—his attraction—soared.

'It isn't something I'm ever going to forget. Honestly, it was the highlight of that horrific day. The one thing that saved it.'

He faux flexed in response to the compliment. 'Aside from the small fact that you didn't end up marrying an absolute jerk.'

She sighed.

'And I remember other moments from later in that day that weren't so awful,' he added. 'Plus I know how to make you change your mind about certain things,' he said softly. 'All I have to do is take off my shirt.'

'Well now, that wouldn't be fair,' she whispered.

'Life isn't fair, Princess. You and I both know that already.'

'Which is why we respect each other's space.'

He read the conflicting emotions in her beautiful eyes. Slowly, reluctantly he released her hand. He noticed she slipped it beneath the table into her lap, a trembling fist.

He gritted his teeth as his delight evaporated. But he refused to regret all that had happened between them. Never those moments in the throne room, when that explosion of emotion had culminated in the most shattering experience of his life.

But if she came to this ball she would be back in society—possibly for the last time as a princess. And if she renounced her title, if she left and lived in England, she would meet other people. Other men. A *better* man than him, no doubt.

He glanced down and saw his own hands were curled into fists now. He made himself inhale. Exhale. Relax even, as he faced hard facts. She *couldn't* stay hidden here indefinitely. She had to go. She had to live her life as she wanted.

From the moment she entered that ballroom anything between them would be over.

# CHAPTER TWELVE

ZARA DIDN'T WANT to be cast adrift in the ballroom alone, but it was a necessary moment for her to live through. Just to prove to herself that she could. To prove it to Lucian too. Though, in fairness, she knew he already believed in her. That he considered her brave gave her the lift she needed to take the final step inside.

It also helped that he'd imported a team from an eye-wateringly expensive Parisian fashion house to help her get ready. They'd signed a non-disclosure agreement and arrived armed with an assortment of couture, jewels and make-up. There'd been no need to be stitched into her gown this time. Nor was it a loud, overly ornate showstopper that she drowned inside.

It was a deep blue simple column that clung to some curves then fell in a silky sweep to the floor. The bodice rose right to the base of her throat, it was long-sleeved, high-backed. In fact it would be considered extremely demure if it weren't for the tiny buttons that ran from that high neckline to her narrow waist. The buttons were set beneath each other a few inches apart, while each half of the fabric they held was set the merest millimetre apart—so from her neck to her navel, all the way down her sternum, there were glimpses of skin exposed and no hiding the fact she wore no bra. Though one had to stand close to see *that*. The only jewels she wore were the sapphire earrings that had arrived in her rooms that afternoon. They were astonishingly light, unlike the heavy diamond drops from her failed wedding day.

The ripple that ran through the crowd as her entrance was announced was impossible to ignore. Unfortunately, most of the guests were already in place in the ballroom but it had taken longer for her hair to be done than she'd anticipated. Every last one turned to stare. She felt the familiar prickling sensation over her skin but kept her chin lifted. She wasn't going to hide the impact of her emotions on her body. She wasn't going to let herself down. And she was also here for Lucian. Serene and secure, like Monrayne itself.

She knew that tonight was essentially a dress rehearsal for his formal coronation in a few months and she wanted to do everything she could to help it be a success. He needed this—he needed belief in himself. Her presence was a symbol of healing—that he'd not done harm to her by interrupting her wedding.

The days before the ball had slid by too quickly. And throughout every one she'd regretted requesting that they not repeat the intimacy they'd shared in the throne room. But neither of them was in a position to have any kind of relationship. She was trying to be wise. But it was so very hard to be sensible when they'd still dined together each night. Still discussed the day. Still laughed. And perhaps that was the mistake. Because that was the connection they had—it wasn't only that earth-shattering sex. And even though she still saw him then, more and more she missed him terribly and she slept less and less.

After navigating the steep stairs and enduring everyone's eyes, she scanned the room. He stood with his back to the wall, ensuring he could visually check the ballroom in a single sweep. But right now his gaze was fixed on her. Even from this distance she felt his heat singeing her heart.

She made herself turn. Made herself do what she'd said she would.

'It's an honour to meet you, King Niko.' She curtseyed to the man who knew more about Lucian than anyone, nervous to make a good impression on him.

'Princess Zara.' He bowed and then turned. 'May I introduce my wife, Maia.'

The tenderness with which he drew the pretty woman forward tore Zara's heart a little. They chatted for a time—simple talk of differences in climate before a more honest smile about palace regulations. Other people came up to speak with them—though mostly with Niko. But eventually the more curious addressed Zara directly.

'You've had a very challenging time.' One loud woman openly stared at her.

'Indeed. But I feel very relieved,' Zara said softly. 'It seems I had a lucky escape.'

It was mortifying to have been so naive and ignorant of her fiancé's nature. To have been so gullible and then rejected so publicly, so brutally.

'Royal alliances can be complicated.' Niko stepped in smoothly. 'It will settle down, I'm sure.'

King Niko very clearly only had eyes for Maia but he turned to Zara intently, shielding her from the other people present. 'Though I do find it fascinating that you've remained here through this challenging time.'

What had Lucian told him? Zara licked her lips nervously.

'King Lucian has been very kind to me,' she said diplomatically.

'*Kind?*' Niko said in a low voice only Zara could hear. 'The Lucian I know isn't *kind*. He's austere in every element of his life. Fiercely and ruthlessly focused on his work.'

'Indeed, it is difficult to get him to talk of much else. But he *is* very kind.' She stoutly defended him to the one man she'd thought *would* know and appreciate Lucian's depths.

She couldn't help glancing across the ballroom towards the

tall figure. She knew it was safe enough to do so. *Everyone* was watching him, all as fascinated as she. It wasn't just curiosity but the fact he was compelling. Not to mention unbearably handsome. But his ice-blue gaze was upon her right now and she stilled, feeling the heat rising within her. All she had to do was look at him and she was lost.

She quickly turned back.

Niko had leaned away to murmur something to Maia before they both smiled, but he then stepped back to her. 'Will you dance, Princess Zara?'

'Oh.' Her nervousness spiked. She hadn't thought she would dance at all. She'd half hoped to escape the ball early. She'd planned to show her face, hold her head high, stay just long enough to settle Maia in and then quietly leave once everyone had got over the surprise of seeing her present. Dancing would put her far more on show. Especially dancing with King Niko.

'Everyone is watching you anyway, Princess,' Niko said softly. 'Why not show them how little you care about what has happened?'

Men like Niko and Lucian were not used to being denied. Plus, she *was* a princess. She was supposed to dance at palace balls. And the truth was she never had. She'd never been to a ball like this.

'Thank you, it would be an honour.'

He bowed and led her onto the dance floor. She was aware of most people turning. She knew he was ensuring she was no social outcast—not allowing her to remain an object of pity. She held her head high and suddenly she found she truly no longer cared what any of them thought. Her freedom from all this was imminent and as a result she could actually enjoy it. There was no real pressure. She no longer had any *requirement* to perform. She wasn't going to be a princess for very much longer. She could just relax and, incredibly, she began to enjoy herself. She actually giggled at King Niko's mild joke.

He too was kind and she softened towards him. No wonder he and Lucian were friends.

Afterwards, another man came over to her—a dashing captain from Niko's enormous entourage. He asked her to dance and she hid her reluctance and accepted. As they glided by the group around King Lucian she saw King Niko standing next to him now, watching her with a broad smile on his face. Lucian was also watching. But he looked as emotionless as ever.

'Princess Zara.' Another ultra-polite man from the party from Piri-nu asked her to dance. Then another.

Queen Maia seemed both awed and amused by the whole spectacle. She and King Niko frequently danced—always circling near to where Zara was dancing with yet more officers from Piri-nu. And in the times when they didn't dance, Zara chatted more and more easily with Maia, sipping cool drinks. She discovered Maia shared her sweet tooth so she delighted in telling her which of the delicate cakes were the best—especially the miniature caramel apple tarts. Zara was the only person King Niko danced with aside from his wife and Maia seemed particularly amused by the offers that Zara constantly received. Her dance card was very full indeed. It wasn't long before she didn't want it to be.

'Stop them, please,' Zara muttered in a laughing undertone to Maia. 'My feet are killing me.'

Maia giggled and took her arm. 'Then let's go find some more of those fancy cakes and hide.'

They sat in an alcove that afforded them some privacy while allowing them to watch proceedings. As Zara caught her breath she realised she wanted to savour this last experience. She wanted just a little more—to dance with Lucian. Just the once. She wanted a fairy-tale moment when the long-lost King returned and swept the rejected princess up and away.

But fairy-tales didn't happen in real life. Rejected princesses kept their chins up. They smiled. Even when their hearts were being crushed ever so slowly under the weight of unrequited, impossible affection.

Her only consolation was that Lucian danced with no one. Not once.

She caught his gaze once more from where she sat. Caught it, held it, melted inside. It was only when someone stepped from behind him that he startled and turned quickly away. She too turned, only to realise Maia had been watching that wordless interaction. Maia had *seen*.

Zara felt a flush burnish her cheeks.

'What do you plan to do?' Maia asked softly.

About her future, right? Not about Lucian. There was nothing to be done about him.

'I want to go away,' she muttered.

'Not home?'

'No. I think I'm going to go to England.'

'You have friends there?'

Zara took a breath. 'No, but I need independence anyway.'

Maia had a gleam in her eye. 'You want to work?'

'While I get some formal qualifications.' She nodded. 'I didn't get the greatest education when I was younger.'

'Nor did I,' Maia said quietly. 'So I'm studying a couple of papers in Piri-nu.'

'You are?' Zara was surprised. 'That's great.'

'It's wonderful. I'm loving it.' Maia's smile widened. 'There are lots of courses. You shouldn't go to England. You should come to Piri-nu and train for whatever you want there. We have much better weather.' Enthusiasm made her speak faster. 'We could be study buddies.'

Zara giggled and shook her head. 'I couldn't—'

'Why not?' Maia suddenly took her wrist and pressed it tightly. 'I'm serious. If you need somewhere to go, come to *me*.' She glanced across the room to where Niko was conversing with Lucian and her voice dropped lower still. 'No one else needs to know. We do discretion really well there. I promise. I can help.'

Zara's heart thudded. Her gut told her Maia was genuine and lovely. 'Thank you. I might have to...' She snatched a quick breath as she realised she might have a new plan that was even better. 'I'd pay you back.'

'I know you would.' Maia smiled. 'Just like Lucian.'

Zara's heart constricted.

'Take my private number now,' Maia insisted. 'Before Niko comes back and interferes.'

Zara's giggle was a touch watery, but she pulled herself together. 'Thank you.'

To her amazement, they all stayed at the ball almost until the very end.

'You've been so kind,' Zara said to Niko and Maia as they left the enormous room together. 'It was lovely to meet you both.'

'I wish you the very best, Princess.' Maia pulled her in for a quick hug and muttered into her ear, 'Let's see each other again very *soon*.'

It was very late but Zara opened the window to breathe in the cool winter air. She was horribly torn—partly relieved that the ball was over, yet despairing at the same time. She'd returned to a kind of public life, which meant she would have to leave here soon. It would look odd to all if she were to remain for much longer. She had to move forward with her life and now, thanks to Maia, she had an even better plan crystallising. But she was wide awake—not wanting the evening to end.

She heard the softest knock at her door. She'd known he would come. He stood silent, the heat in his gaze saying it all. She stepped back. In a heartbeat he was inside, quietly closing the door behind him. He scanned the room—assessing the windows. The exits. Checking security, as always. And, as always, she checked him. In his dark suit with the gold detail he looked suave and regal, but still dangerous and edgy. She knew he must be nearing exhaustion.

'You made it through the entire evening.' He spoke bluntly.

'I survived it, yes.' She put a hand on the back of the sofa, her legs weak at the sight of him.

'You didn't enjoy it?' he challenged huskily. 'That wasn't your laughter I heard across the ballroom?'

'It was for show.'

'Not entirely.' He walked towards her. 'I think you enjoyed it.'

Well, how could she not enjoy such an evening in a venue so stunning and the food so sublime? And most of the people—the ones she'd mingled with—had been courteous and kind. It had been a taste of the absolute privilege someone in her position *could* have.

'Maybe it wasn't so bad,' she admitted. 'King Niko and Queen Maia are lovely. And I liked the dancing.' She was surprised when he stiffened. 'Did you enjoy it?'

'Did I enjoy watching you look so beautiful as you danced with other men?' he muttered slowly.

'Well, that's your fault for ordering them all to dance with me,' she said softly, because she was sure that was what he'd done. 'I would have been happy to remain a social outcast. My feet are killing me.'

But he still didn't smile. 'I didn't order anyone to dance with you. I think that was Niko amusing himself at my expense.' His gaze heavy-lidded, he studied her mouth. 'He saw how furious I was when he first danced with you. I was jealous of my best friend. A man I know to be utterly in love with his wife.'

Oh, he was in a dangerous mood. Zara's heart thudded.

His glittering gaze skittered lower, sweeping over her silk gown. 'Will you have trouble getting out of your dress tonight?'

She stilled. 'I don't think I can manage the buttons.'

'I think you'd better or I'll end up shredding yet another of your dresses.'

A firestorm cascaded over her. She lifted shaking fingers and unfastened the first button. Then the next. Then the next.

He watched, utterly motionless, for a moment, only to suddenly shoot her a devastating smile. 'You prefer that I don't wear a jacket, right?'

She couldn't answer as he undid his buttons. And she forgot to finish unfastening her dress. Because he wasn't as butter-fingered as she and in the next moment he stood bare-chested before her. Her pulse quickened. So did her breathing. Because he didn't stop at the jacket and shirt. He toed off his shoes and unfastened the top button of his formal trousers—then somehow slid the zip down despite that bulge.

'You want me, Zara?' he asked huskily when he finally stood before her, fully naked. He was huge all over—tall, broad-shouldered, those large muscles rippling and his massive erection rigid. 'Because I want you.'

She was so relieved her knees went weak. He laughed throatily and caught her, sliding her to the floor, pushing the loosened silk from her body in seconds.

'Kiss me,' she begged.

'I intend to,' he growled. 'I'm going to do everything I've been dreaming of doing all damned night.'

He didn't just kiss her. He consumed her. Everywhere.

'Spread wider.' He pushed her thighs apart with his powerful hands and groaned. 'All mine.' He bent and feasted upon her. 'Only mine.'

'Yes.' She gasped at the rough swipe of his tongue and the silken soft brush of his lips.

'I can't get enough of you, Zara.' His grip on her tightened. 'I need this.'

'So do— *Oh, yes!*' She arched, her eyes almost rolling backwards as the decadent pleasure he gave overwhelmed her. She convulsed uncontrollably, lost in the throes of an orgasm so intense she barely remained conscious through it.

But he stroked her gently, keeping her with him, making her tumble deeper and deeper—because her want for him was endless.

'Zara…' He roused her again with the sexiest whisper. 'It's time for us to dance.'

The sexual smugness in his eyes as he reared above her made her even hotter. But he rose to his feet.

'Please,' she muttered almost inaudibly as he gazed down at her. 'Lucian—'

'We haven't made it to the bed,' he teased.

'I don't care.' She shivered greedily. 'Don't make me wait any longer.'

His body tensed. With a swift move that emphasised his jaw-dropping strength, he stepped between her legs and scooped her up. She immediately wrapped her legs around his hips, moaning at the sensation of having him hold her so completely. He was her iced-up man mountain, but he had a volcano inside him and when he erupted he bathed her in his searing vitality. She adored it when he let himself go like this. He planted his feet wide, anchoring them there in the centre of the room. His arousal pressed against her core. She pressed her hips closer to him as best she could. His gaze smouldered but she was ecstatic. She smiled right at him. He hissed and she saw the sexual restraint in him snap.

'I'm sorry I made you wait.' He slid her onto him in a slick, strong move.

She cried out in relief, in ecstasy, in raw, desperate need. He was so big and he held nothing back and it was *everything*.

'This is what you wanted?' he growled.

'Yes. More. Now.'

It was searingly physical and she relished it. As did he. He wrapped one arm around her hips, his other up her back, his hand spread to support her head. He impaled her onto him, over and over. They were both slick and hot. Both fiery and physical. He balanced her with shattering ease—it was entirely his strength keeping them upright, his strength sealing them together.

He grunted in feral appreciation of his complete domination of her, releasing gusts of hot air that teased her breasts as he thrust into her again and again. She clamped on him the only way she could—where he'd pushed in, gripping hard to lock him, fighting with her hands too—greedily grabbing his slick, strong muscles. He swore then, lifted his head and pulled her to meet his mouth. She moaned as he took her there too. He relentlessly drove deeper and deeper, claiming—*caressing*—her with everything he had.

She would never let him go. *Never.* She wrapped herself even more tightly around him—clinging with every ounce of strength she had. Her body could stand the sensations only for so long. Every muscle screamed in sexual tension as he nailed her to him until she tore her lips free, her head falling back as a high-pitched, keening scream of release was ripped from her.

As she collapsed onto his shoulder she heard his shout echoing within her. She barely had any strength left to cling to him. But somehow he could still move. He carried her to the bedroom and carefully put her down on the bed. She needed more strength to pull him down to the bed with her, but she was too spent and he was too swift. He pulled free. Barely conscious, she whimpered at the loss of contact. She'd wanted to stay like that with him—not just entwined, but locked together. She wanted that always. But that wasn't what Lucian wanted. It wasn't *ever* what he would want. So, for all the bliss she felt, one corner of her heart broke as he pressed a too-gentle kiss to her cheek and whispered, 'Sleep.'

# CHAPTER THIRTEEN

ZARA BARELY SAW Lucian the next day. There was nothing new in that except a melancholy swept over her, a sensation that was at odds with how she'd thought she'd feel. She'd thought she'd be relieved—that she'd cleared that challenging hurdle of the public appearance at the ball and her future would now be free of such things. But she'd actually enjoyed the evening more than she'd ever imagined she would. She'd enjoyed the conclusion of the night more than anything.

While most of the dignitaries had now left, the city was still in party mode. To have arranged something on this level in such a short time was an incredible feat and demonstrated just how completely—and quickly—Lucian had assumed control of the Crown. And how happy the country was to have him back.

She deliberately didn't check the papers. The media could be so fickle—positive one moment, shredding the next, so she knew it wouldn't serve her well. She would keep calm and carry on and quietly make her plans for a private, quiet life. She'd messaged Maia just to double-check she'd meant her offer of help. Maia's reply had been immediate. Zara knew she had her path now. Except there was that twist of yearning inside.

That night there was a dinner for the few dignitaries who'd remained for the extra day. She didn't attend. She hid in the private wing. But she saw him on his way to the banquet hall—clad in another fine woven suit. She stopped as he passed her in the corridor. She saw the exhaustion at the back of his eyes and could feel the strain emanating from him.

This was a man who'd survived a lot—who'd deliberately put himself into punishing, dangerous, demanding situations while working for Niko to strengthen his endurance and resilience—both physical and mental. But she knew his new life here was taking its toll. This was emotional. This was his home. Where he'd been born and raised and his parents had died. Where he'd been most vulnerable. Returning to face all this alone was challenging for him. He had so many memories tangled with contrary emotions. It exhausted her just to think about it, but he was the one *living* it. She knew he had much to do, but there had to come a point where he couldn't go on without decent rest. This constant hyper-alert state—seeking—*expecting*—danger all the time had to be punishing.

'Why aren't you coming to dinner?' he demanded in a low voice.

'Why do you think?' She shook her head at him. But her heart smote and she leaned a little closer. 'You can't go on like this. You're barely sleeping.'

His eyes flared. 'I have a job to do.'

'You can't do it properly without proper rest.'

He shot her a withering glance.

'Oh, please. As if you're not human?' she jeered. 'I know you're *very* human.'

There was a flicker in his eyes but he said nothing more as he walked past her.

It hurt. And it made her angry. He'd said nothing about the previous night. She knew there could be nothing more between them, but that restlessness was brewing again. So powerful, so complete. She was beginning to fear that the ache she felt for him was going to be unending.

So she stayed awake. She heard the bang and ripple of fading fireworks and knew those last guests would retire to bed soon. She knew which was his room. He'd taken the one only a few doors down from hers.

It was very late when she knocked on the door.

He said nothing when he opened it and saw her. But he reached for her wrist and hauled her inside. The suite was smaller than her own. Darker and spartan in its decor. It suited him. But she didn't linger to admire the furnishings. She walked directly to the bedroom.

'What are you doing?' he muttered as he followed her.

'You get to come to my room and take what you want, when you want. Why can't I do the same?'

'I thought I came to your room and gave you what *you* wanted.'

The challenge rippled through her. 'Okay then, what do you want from me?'

He stared at her and she just knew he was battling his self-control, overworked as it was.

She cocked her head and shot him a smile. 'My worst?'

With a groan he capitulated. 'Zara...'

The smile on his face then was so charmingly boyish and devilish it smote her heart. For a second the tortured, burdened man was gone and only humour and heat remained. She wanted to see *him* flushed and sated. She pushed him onto the bed. To her surprise, he actually fell backwards. She smothered a giggle as she knelt astride him. But then her smile faded—she wanted to touch him. To *give* to him.

She caressed the scar, it was a tough cord of gnarled skin, breaking the perfection of his eyebrow. And then she kissed him. His arms lifted—urging her closer. Too quickly. She pulled free and laughed again, before teasing him every way she could think of. Letting instinct—imagination...sheer curiosity—guide her. She swept her hand over his chest—tracing the tattoo, then the scar from the skating accident, the one that had helped identify him to the world. The other scars, the stories she didn't yet know. She wanted to know. Everything. And he lay back and let her—until he was shaking and incoherent and straining in that sweet torture.

'Lucian,' she breathed and bent to him again.

He roared his release and she swallowed the salty heat of him, stretching her hands wide to soothe his shudders, then licked her way back up his body.

'Pleased with yourself?' He held her above him.

She smiled. Then felt him move beneath her. Desire coloured her vision as he took his turn—his time—in teasing her. It was only moments until she couldn't stand any more. She moved quickly to mount him, grinding in absolute, fierce abandonment. Riding him was such pleasure. She gazed into his eyes and moaned as his devilish fingers teased, giving her the slightest of nudges to topple her over the edge.

'Zara.' He pulled her down to rest on him. 'Zara, Zara, Zara...'

His arms were so heavy, trapping her to him. This was what she'd wanted. What she'd ached for all this time. To be held by him—for them to be curled together in a tangle that *couldn't* be undone. With both of *them* undone. Able to rest at last.

Finally, he sank into sleep.

Hours later, Zara paced in the small lounge, silently biting her nails. Finally, she heard stirring from the room next door. A mutter. Then the thud of heavy footsteps.

'What time is it?' Lucian appeared in the doorway, naked save for a towel. He stared at the clock in horror. 'I slept for *nine hours*! I—'

'Clearly needed it.' She held her ground, hiding her knotted fingers behind her back.

His jaw dropped. 'What did you do? Surely Victor knocked?'

'I sent him away.'

'You *what*?' He looked astonished. Then irate.

'You needed sleep. I don't think you've slept for longer than a ninety-minute stretch in days.'

'You had no right.'

'No, but I did it anyway and I'm not sorry.'

'I have people to meet. I have a *country* that I owe—'

'You don't need to feel guilty about what happened.'

'I don't need you to mother me,' he snarled.

'Don't be reductive. I know perfectly well I'm not your mother. But I *am* your friend.'

'No—' he turned cold '—you're not my friend.'

'Suck it up, Lucian,' she flung back, instantly wounded. 'You're not invincible. You look so much better for it.'

That threw him. 'I look better?'

'You're not a machine, you know. You're human. With basic needs.'

*'Needs?'* he echoed and advanced on her.

She'd not seen him like this, his jaw stubbled, his hair slightly in tufts. Why had she ever thought those eyes of his were cold? But she backed up a pace because now he was looking feral.

'I thought you didn't want to be late for your meeting.'

'I'm so bloody late it barely matters now. What does matter is that I remind you who's in charge around here.'

She was suddenly as angry. With him for being angry. With herself for caring when it was so clear he didn't want her to. And how could he be so *useless* in caring for himself while at the same time demanding he meet impossibly perfect standards?

'Would that be you—lord and master?' she snapped. 'The great King himself. You want me on my knees?'

Yes, it was provocative. Deliberate. Dangerous. But she was alight with adrenalin.

'That's a very good idea,' he snapped.

Electricity charged the atmosphere. She wasn't afraid of the seething emotion. It was welcome. With a furious lift of her chin, she lowered first to one knee then the other and leaned back slightly to gaze all the way up to his fiery eyes.

'Drop the towel,' she said.

He froze.

'Drop the towel, Lucian.'

He was hard, proud, fierce. But the very last thing he was right now was in charge.

'Zara—'

She tugged the towel and took him in hand. Quite happy to hold him firmly. Quite happy to revel in the desperation of his gasp. She fluttered her fingers and then held him firm, while teasing the very tip of him with her tongue. Entirely on instinct. Entirely with feverish delight. And as her pleasure rose she moved restlessly, more rapidly, until she felt the vibrations in his muscles and heard the savage edge to his growl of frustration and need. She saw the clenched fists at his sides as he held back. She didn't want him to hold back. Ever. So she pressed closer still. Gripped harder. Rubbed harder. Sucked harder.

His hands thrust in her hair and his hips bucked wildly before he pulled away from her and snarled, '*Stop.*'

She stilled, panting, aching with emptiness.

'*All fours.*'

She looked into his expression and heat swamped her. Control lost to him again. But she gave it so willingly. The truth was *neither* of them were in control now. He had such need for her—for this at least. He dropped to his knees too, behind her. His hands slid, his fingers discovered her slick heat. And then his mouth.

She buckled, bending her head to the ground on a sob of ecstasy at how hot this was between them. Nothing but desire. No shame. No power game. Not any more. This was raw—as it always was because this emotion couldn't be contained and it was everything. It was rough but passionately so—not violent. Never that. The intensity with which he caressed her was stunning, as if he were desperate to drive her to that edge right with him. Reaching forward, he covered her wide-spread hand with his—laced then locked his fingers through hers. His chest was pressed flat along her back. He gripped her tightly, stopping her from being shunted away by his own force. And he didn't hold back. He pounded—deeper, harder, hotter. Owning her. Claiming her until she felt branded as his from the inside out. It was as if he couldn't get deep enough, close enough. As if it were a battle for his very survival—to be with her. It was the most animal of couplings. It would have been brutal if it weren't so beautiful. If there weren't such *feelings*. Desperation. Desire. Domination—yes. All lust—so close to love.

'Zara!' he growled. '*Zara!*'

But he pulled out and spun her over and suddenly was back, right back with her. In her. Only now he was gazing into her eyes and in his she saw that wild emotion. Such devastation. And his hold on her tightened even more as she shook apart and his big body finally quaked too. Until he collapsed over her. Utterly spent.

Such swift pleasure. Such abandonment. Such chaos. She closed her eyes. He was pinning her, but she was already his prisoner—shackled by the unbearable delight he gave.

The silence in the room was heavy, punctuated only by their jerky breathing. But as their rough gasps eased the atmosphere only seemed to sharpen.

'I am too heavy. I apologise.' He didn't even look her in the eyes. 'I had better get to that meeting.'

He took the towel and left the room. Left her there, all but catatonic on the floor. Shattered.

# CHAPTER FOURTEEN

LUCIAN WAS FURIOUS with himself. He'd just exhibited a total loss of control. Again. He'd given in to an absolute emotional response. Again. He felt like a bastard. He'd been rude to her. He'd left her on the *floor*. What kind of human was he? He never should have touched her, never taken everything he wanted. Solace. Pleasure. So selfishly.

It was worsening. Trying to be near her—but not having her—simply caused carnage because, in the end, he lost control. Repeatedly.

He had no recollection of her leaving his bed this morning. Or of anyone knocking on his door. How could he not have woken? He couldn't remember the last time he'd slept as deeply or as soundly. But apparently every one of his senses had been dead to the world this morning. It was shockingly unacceptable—not only because of the risk to his personal safety but because he'd forgotten everything outside of that bedroom. He'd indulged in pure, physical comfort and neglected his work completely. *That* was not good enough.

He struggled to concentrate now. Also not good enough. His country deserved better. Wasn't that why he'd returned?

He'd been determined to step up to the plate. To be the King his people deserved. And he'd known, hadn't he, that this needed his complete and undivided attention. Because when his personal desires were released, his performance dipped. Emotional distraction was utterly destructive.

But, given his failure, the only thing he could think was to switch his plan entirely. Ending this was apparently impossible, but if he could *tame* his own distraction then maybe he'd be better. The fact was they were drawn to each other. Their chemistry *refused* to be denied. So they shouldn't try. Maybe it was that denial that made it worse. So perhaps it needed its own bottle—to be contained and allowed out only at the *appropriate* time. He needed to strategically regain control of this situation. And he knew just how to do it.

'Zara.' He walked into the library with a tray in his hands. An offering. Caramel apple tart and tea.

She realised this was his wordless way of trying to make amends. She didn't want to accept wordless any more. That he'd brought it distressed her even more. Because he *almost* cared enough. He was courteous. Kind. Attentive even. Certainly passionate. But there it ended.

She watched him warily. 'I've written up a list of responses. The books are sorted. My work is done.'

He set the tray down and took the seat opposite, as he always did.

'I want you to marry me.'

Her heart stopped and it took her two tries to get her immediate answer out. 'We've been through this already.'

'I won't take no for an answer this time.'

She stared at him across the table. Trying to keep calm internally. Failing.

'Why?'

'It makes sense. It's the simplest, most effective solution.'

'To what problem?'

'To several problems.' He leaned towards her. 'You were

right. I need an heir of my own and perhaps it needn't be in a decade after all. It would be efficient if I married you now.'

'Efficient? Because I'm already installed in the palace? Because I've already been vetted?'

His nostrils thinned. 'You're better at it than you give yourself credit for. You charm anyone you meet. You know what you're doing. You were beautiful at the ball.'

'Are you saying I could pass as a queen?'

He'd effectively listed some of Garth's reasons. She understood duty. She would be docile. A good enough clothes horse.

'Are there any *personal* reasons why you think this is a good idea?' She barely kept her tone cordial.

'I trust Victor, but I think, after this morning, everyone will know there's something between us. This will leak, Zara. Our marriage will protect you from those complications.'

'Because my reputation needs protecting? Didn't you once ask what century this is?' She glared at him. 'Anything else?'

A muscle in his jaw flexed. 'We're good together.'

'Do you mean in bed? Because we haven't often actually *made* it to a bed.'

Once, in fact. His bed. Where they'd both slept like newborns. But the afterglow this time was now more like an after *burn*. It wasn't the love bites on her breasts or the grazes on her inner thighs from his stubbled jaw this morning causing the sting.

*We're not friends.*

It hurt. Deeply. He wanted her. He liked her. Respected her even. He'd been kind. He wanted her physically. But he *didn't* love her. And she knew he'd fight to keep part of himself separate from her. Always. His heart was out of bounds to everyone.

'Anything else?' she prompted again.

'You don't have anywhere else to go. You have no real plan, Zara.'

Not true, actually. Not any more. But she kept that to herself for now. Because he still wasn't offering the reason she really wanted.

'You were angry with me this morning,' she said. 'I overstepped your mark. What if I overstep it again?'

'I was taken by surprise. If we're married, there won't be the need for secrecy. Nor will there be any uncertainty—'

'You mean you'd know I would be in your bed every night,' she said.

He nodded.

'You want stability and certainty,' she clarified.

In *every* element of his life. She *could* be a convenient wife to him. Useful. Suitable. And perhaps she could support him in the limited ways he could accept. And the thing was, she would have accepted his proposal only weeks ago. It was the kind of marriage she'd thought she would get with Anders. But not now. She wanted more. She wanted unconditional, absolute love. And she wanted it from him. *Only* him.

But *he* didn't want that. Not with her or anyone.

'There's another problem that you haven't factored in,' she said.

'Oh?' He waited.

She was shaking inside. 'You won't like it.'

He waited but she felt horribly tight in the throat.

'I don't usually have to prise information from you, Zara.' He regarded her steadily with those pale blue eyes. 'You can tell me anything.'

'I've fallen in love with you,' she whispered. 'I have. Fallen in love. I realise this wasn't supposed to happen.' Her heart skipped as she watched him. 'And I know it's not what you want in this proposal of yours.'

There was no reaction. None. He was still as stone.

'So I hope you'll understand that it's best that I say no. It's also best that I leave now,' she muttered, quickly standing up.

'Are you going to throw that pertinent fact out and then run away?'

'Don't.' She paused, two steps from the table. 'I'll get angry.'

'Go on then.' He stood too. 'Get angry.'

Fury flared. 'I just told you I'm in love with you and you say nothing, other than to demand *more* from me? When you give me *nothing* at all in response.'

'Because there's nothing I can say to that.'

'Not even a thank you? Not even that you appreciate my honesty?' She was suddenly incandescent. 'Because you obviously can't reciprocate.'

'We're…' He dragged in a breath. 'We're *friends*.'

For a man determined to remain so distant, the acknowledgement of any kind of emotion should be a win, she supposed painfully. But it wasn't.

'Are we? Wow. I thought we were only lovers. Even then barely. I'm merely an uninvited guest who you sometimes have sex with.'

He stared at her rigidly.

'But that you care a little is more than I ever should have expected.'

'From me?'

'*For* me.' She shook her head.

He blanched and took a step towards her. 'Why can't this be enough for you? Why risk…?' He breathed out. 'This is good. This *is*.'

A man who could hardly stand her to stay the whole night with him?

Lucian was everything, except for that block of ice in his heart. That part of him she could never touch. That part he didn't ever want to give her. That part he'd locked away for good.

'You disappeared for the best part of a decade,' she said. 'I'm going to do the same. I'm going to Piri-nu.'

For a full minute he was silent. 'Disappearing isn't all it's made out to be, Zara,' he gritted. 'It's not for you.'

'You don't think I can handle it?'

'Your skin will burn.'

'I'll use sun lotion and cover up.'

'You'll still be too hot.'

'I'll get used to it.'

'You'll miss the snow.'

'I'll get used to missing *many* things. People adjust to new circumstances when they have no choice.'

'It won't be enough.'

'Friends and a warm welcome won't be enough?' she challenged. 'It was for you. Why not me?' She was so hurt. 'I want to go somewhere new. Somewhere where I don't have to be a princess. Where I don't have to be a disappointment and where I don't have to be *disappointed*.'

'You should have more.'

'Then *offer me more*,' she snapped back.

He froze.

'You don't want to,' she said quietly. 'You're *scared*. You're clinging to an impossible ideal of self-control and sacrifice as if it can somehow make you worthy and keep you *safe*. I don't blame you. I can't imagine the pain you've endured. But I can understand the loneliness.' She lifted her head. 'It shouldn't be like that for always. You have too much to give.'

'There's nothing.' He was barely audible.

'Not true.'

'There's nothing I *want* to give.'

And there it was.

'You don't *want* anyone to truly care about you,' she said. 'Because you don't care about yourself.'

He *hated* himself. It wasn't Anders who was his real enemy at all.

'You can carry the Crown, Lucian, but to carry someone's heart… To accept their love? That's impossible for you. You're so guilt-ridden you struggle to accept the respect of your subjects. You can hardly accept tenderness from me. Sex, yes. But an act of caring—of compassion?' She shook her head. 'This is totally the wrong time for you. Totally. You're busy. And you don't want this. And I'm so very sorry for you.'

'So it's pity not love you feel. I thought you were brave,' he snarled. 'Ready to take on the world as you want it.'

'That's exactly what I am doing,' she said. 'I want independence but I don't believe that equates to emotional isolation the way you do. To me they're two very different things. We would want different things in our marriage.'

'What do you think I would want?'

'Stability, security. Everything you've said. Perhaps to protect me, also. Because you pity me and you take on guilt even when you're not responsible. Because we're good in bed together. At least for now. You think you can keep yourself safe for ever. But you can't. It's impossible. You can't even accept a little help.'

He'd just offered her what she desperately wanted and it was the worst feeling ever because it wasn't for the *reasons* she needed.

'I *can* accept help till I get on my feet,' she said proudly. 'I know I can't do everything all on my own, all of the time. You can't either. But you won't admit that. You won't even see it.'

'Don't think you need to fix me.'

'Neither of us need to be *fixed*,' she snapped. 'But you need to *forgive* yourself. You need to heal. I can't do it for you. And you *can't* know what you really want until you've processed that.'

'And how do you know what you really want?' he jeered.

'By knowing what I *don't* want. And I don't want this.' She dragged in a painful breath. 'I actually do need you to be my friend, Lucian. I need you to put *my* wellbeing ahead of your own temporary desires,' she said. 'I know you don't want to hurt me. I know you've *never* wanted to hurt me. And this would.'

'I am not as honourable as you seem to think.' His control slipped. '*This* is not what *I* want, Zara.'

'Well, we don't always get what we want. Not even kings.' She finally lost it. 'Find someone as heartless as yourself,' she said. 'Because that's not me.'

'Zara—'

'I'm being *honest*. Which is more than you can seem to be,' she flared at him. 'I'm in love with you. And I know you feel something for me too. But you can't even admit what that is, let alone embrace it. If it's just lust, that's fine, Lucian. But at least admit it. And if it's lust it will fade. Signing up to a lifetime commitment right now is *madness*. Especially when the truth is you want to be alone. You've made that very clear. I'm not going to live where I'm not loved—I need to be loved, just for myself. My family didn't love me enough like that.'

'You happily accepted a similar offer from Anders only weeks ago, yet somehow I am *worse* than—'

'And I was *wrong* about him. And thank you for stopping it. You've opened my eyes in many ways, Lucian. And now I know that for me to accept *your* proposal is even more wrong. It's *so* different. Knowing you don't feel the same would only destroy me.'

He became a statue once more. 'I do not want to see you destroyed. I'm sorry you feel that is what would happen if you were to accept my proposal,' he said stiffly. 'Piri-nu is a place of sanctuary. I will make the arrangements.'

'How long will that take?'

'You can leave as soon as you would like.'

'I'm already packed.'

'Then I'll get onto it immediately.'

He was true to his word. Zara had been standing, shell-shocked, in her room for only twenty minutes before there was a peremptory knock on her door.

Lucian stood there, the aviator sunglasses back on. 'You'll go by helicopter to a private runway in Austria. An unmarked jet will be there. It will take you direct to Piri-nu.'

He was silent as he carried her bag to the helipad. She didn't know what she'd wanted. What she'd hoped for. He was utterly cold and emotionless. Only that wasn't true. That wasn't the Lucian she knew. *Intimately.*

He faced her, all ice. 'I've used you. Abominably. I apologise. I cannot make amends. I can only apologise.'

She stared at him sadly. 'Are you not angry right now, Lucian?' Because she was furious.

He barely hesitated. 'I'm always angry, Zara.'

Yeah, and he made her even angrier. He still couldn't be vulnerable—or honest.

She stepped right up to him. 'Anger is an expression of *hurt*. Of *other* feelings that have been wounded. Because *you* feel deeply and you feel *lots* of things. Including love. You're just trying far too hard not to.'

He was stuck trying to protect himself—so he wasn't really living at all.

'*I* chose to come here. I chose to stay. I chose to have this affair with you.' She straightened proudly even as her voice shook. 'And now I choose to end it. That's where you can't stand in my way.' But the hurt leaked out in stinging tears that coursed down her cheeks. 'Stay suffering, Lucian. Stay drowning in your unnecessary guilt.' She dragged in a hiccupping breath. 'You know we could have had *everything* but you're too scared.'

He took a half-step nearer before stopping himself. 'Please don't cry, Zara.'

'You might like to mask every emotion,' she cried. 'Pretend like you feel nothing. But I'm not going to. It won't make it go away. It won't just disappear. Loving people and losing them hurts, Lucian. Like this is for me, right now. And not even you can deny it.'

# CHAPTER FIFTEEN

PIRI-NU WAS EVERY bit as hot as Lucian had warned. Every bit as beautiful. Gold-ringed emerald islands, sapphire waters, the widest of skies. It was a paradise, where anything would be possible.

'The air-conditioning is fantastic, isn't it?' Maia smiled as she joined Zara in the beautiful lounge a week after her departure from Monrayne.

'I'll acclimatise.'

'Give it time. It's a big adjustment.'

The croissant Zara had selected for lunch was the lightest, most buttery pastry she'd ever eaten, but she couldn't finish it. Her appetite—so endless back in Monrayne—was deadened here. The heat, she supposed. Heat and heartache. She would get used to both. She would cope. Ultimately, she would thrive.

She finally had the freedom she'd wanted. No title. No expectations. No need to seek impossible approval. Not from her family. Not from Lucian either. She would be herself and she would be okay.

'You and Niko have been so kind.' She gestured towards the campus prospectuses Maia had gathered for her. 'I'm excited to work through these.'

'I'm glad.' But Maia's expression turned cautious as she sat beside Zara. 'Are you okay, though?' she asked quietly. 'Have you been in touch with Lucian?'

Zara's heart skidded. Maia hadn't asked about him until now.

'No.'

Maia nodded but couldn't quite hide her curiosity. 'I had the feeling you were close...'

Zara shook her head. 'Apparently we're *friends*,' she muttered.

But they really weren't.

Sympathy softened Maia's eyes. 'I had no idea of Lucian's past before Niko told me. It must be very complicated for him and he must have so much to deal with,' she said. 'I'm sorry if things haven't worked out the way that *you* wanted. Take the time you need to rest, here. Grieve. Then go on.'

Zara nodded, appreciating Maia's honesty and her restraint. She didn't attempt to make it better and offered no false reassurances. It was what it was. And it was over.

She'd contacted her parents, simply to let them know she was safe and well and hoped they were the same. A small part of her still wanted to please them—her inner child who craved their attention, love and approval. But the adult in her needed this chance to live her life fully and not settle for less.

She didn't try to contact Lucian. She needed a complete break to recover. Because she had been just that distraction—like a balm to help him get through a brutal time. She'd offered physical contact, amusement, maybe the smallest solace. But there wasn't depth to it. She'd overstepped the boundaries he'd tried to keep. Her fault for taking it so seriously and thinking she could get beneath the gnarled, scarred tissue protecting his heart. He didn't want her to do that. And that was fair enough. Who was she to demand more than what he was willing to give? Just as he shouldn't demand she take less than what she wanted too.

They wanted each other, liked each other even. But, ultimately, they wanted different things.

Lucian wished he'd refused Zara when she'd requested to leave just over a week ago. He could have been a demanding dictator but he'd helped her leave instead, making it as swift as possible. Not because he'd been determined to do the right thing but because it was what she'd needed from him. Because he couldn't give her what she'd said she *wanted*.

Because he couldn't believe what she'd said she felt.

Because he couldn't have stood to hear her say it ever again.

He could not be the man for her. He had to be King more than man. Duty had to supersede the personal. What was best for her would never be him—not now, not even in that damned decade he'd banked on. How badly he'd just hurt her proved it, right?

'Zara has settled in well. Maia's enjoying her company very much. They've been spending a lot of time together.'

He really didn't want to listen to Niko right now but he couldn't slam the phone down on his friend.

'That's great,' he said mechanically.

There was a silence then a growl from Niko. 'I know I always beat you in calculus but I didn't realise you were actually *this* unintelligent,' he said.

'You never beat me in calculus. I helped you.'

'That's not how I remember it,' Niko shot back blithely. 'But, either way, you need to sort your head, Lucian.'

'Because...?'

'You know why,' Niko said. 'You've just let the best thing to hit your life leave.'

Lucian gave up any pretence of ignorance. 'What has she told you?'

'Nothing. It was obvious at the ball, Lucian. You couldn't take your eyes off her.'

Yeah, that was part of the problem.

'You know you were going through the motions for years here on Piri-nu. Working hard, building strength, amassing resources, silently seething, barely existing...but you actually smiled when you mentioned her to me when I arrived. Did you even know you did that?'

Lucian closed his eyes. She'd always made him smile.

'It's the most alive I've seen you in *years*,' Niko added brutally. 'Don't sink back into that numb state now—'

'Niko—'

'No, I don't want to hear whatever the excuse is.' Niko spoke over him. 'I know there are issues. We all have them. You damn well know I do. That Maia does. But you also know I'm better when I'm alongside her. Same thing, brother. You'll handle everything better with Zara beside you. So will she. That's how it works.'

'I'm not what she needs—'

'Are you sure about that?' Niko growled. 'Because she looked mighty alive to me that night too. Less so now.'

Lucian tensed. 'You said she was settling in well.'

Niko paused. 'You can't deny you care about her.'

'That isn't the point.'

'Isn't it? Because I think you know she cares about you. And I think that scares you so much you've sent her away.'

Damn Niko. Lucian needed him to back off.

'If the stuff holding you back is heavy, then get help to sort it,' Niko said more gently. 'You can't let the past stop you from being happy—not now you have this chance in front of you. Don't stall out. Don't waste any more *time*, Lucian. It's too precious. I never understood that before…'

Lucian knew Niko was thinking of his wife and his unborn child. He knew how his friend had fought to have them.

'Trust in this,' Niko continued after a beat. 'Let that old stuff go and *trust*. I promise you it'll be worth it.'

Lucian's thoughts inexorably turned back to Zara. To those moments when he'd held her and she'd held him. To that night when he'd slept more peacefully than ever. He'd been safe in her arms and she'd tried to tell him he always would be.

'What's she doing now?' he asked quietly.

'No, I'm not going to be your spy. If you want to know how she is then come and see her for yourself.'

Niko rang off. Lucian gritted his teeth, that old anger flaring. But it wasn't anger. Zara been right about that too. She'd called anger an expression of hurt—of betrayed trust, bruised love, burning regret. So many feelings that he'd hated but couldn't stop. They surged in him now and so many others tumbled in too. He couldn't stand it. Niko was right. He needed help to sort it. Because he couldn't stay as he was—not even stalled but submerged in an emotional mess that he couldn't process.

But he needed to. Wanted to. Now.

Lucian stood at the window and looked out at his city. One time at dinner Zara had described it as 'snow-globe-perfect'. But a snow globe needed a good shake to bring its vibrant beauty forth. Apparently, Lucian needed more than one good shake. He'd needed to hear the plain truth from both Zara and Niko.

The palace was as lifeless as a tomb—mirroring how he felt inside. He hated the emptiness. Hated how he ached inside and out as he acknowledged the truth. He'd been more awfully selfish than ever—asking everything of her and not offering the real truth about himself. He'd given her his body, sure. A place in his palace. But he'd not trusted her to tell her she had his battered heart.

And it was way past time that he did.

# CHAPTER SIXTEEN

ZARA CHECKED THAT she was fully in the shade and then stretched out. She was acclimatising slowly to the temperature and at peak heat she needed to just relax with a book. Only she kept reading the same line over and over.

'Zara?'

Aviator sunglasses. Stubbled jaw. Massive muscles. He had that slightly on-edge aura about him. That element of danger.

Zara sat bolt upright. 'You shouldn't be here. You shouldn't have left Monrayne. It's too soon for you to be away for long.'

'No one knows I'm away and the jet is being refuelled as we speak.'

'You're going straight back?' Her heart lurched. 'How long are you planning to be on the ground?'

'As long as it takes to tell you some things face to face.'

He wanted to talk? Her wariness escalated.

'I guess you're lucky I'm here.' She stood. 'I could've been on a boat. Maia's been taking me around the islands but she was too tired today...'

She trailed off as she saw the glimmer of guilt on Lucian's face. Of *knowledge*. Had Maia known he was coming? She had phoned Zara's suite this morning and insisted on making up for it by arranging for Zara to have a full spa treatment. She'd been so full of apologies Zara hadn't been able to refuse.

As a result, Zara had been pampered all day. That was why she was standing here now feeling like some glamorous nineteen-fifties movie starlet with her hair sleek, skin buffed, toe-nails painted and clad in a pretty silk dress that just brushed her mid-thigh. No one would ever guess she'd been crying her heart out upon waking every morning this last week.

'You look like you're enjoying it here,' he said.

Yes, Maia had conspired against her. But while she might have known Lucian was going to surprise her, she'd also ensured Zara was looking her absolute finest when she faced him. Which made Maia a *true* friend and ally.

'Very much,' she said. 'Niko and Maia have been wonderful to me. I understand why you chose to stay here.'

'You prefer it to Monrayne?'

'It's very different,' she answered noncommittally.

He took a breath and stepped closer. 'When I last left here I thought my future was pretty simple. I'd return to Monrayne, expose Anders, reclaim the throne and do the right thing for my country. I'd strive to be a good King. I would stay focused. Stay selfless. I even made a vow—to do nothing but that for the decade ahead. I promised, Zara. But it was an impossible task. Part of me remains greedy.'

Her heart splintered. 'Because you're a human, not a robot.'

He nodded. 'Right, because I tried to live without half of life's necessities. No rest. No recreation. No intimate relationship.'

He took off his glasses and she saw the emotion warming his eyes.

'You think those are necessities now?' she breathed.

He hesitated a moment. 'I've had a couple sessions with my old therapist because returning was harder to handle than I thought it would be. The panic attack. The sleeplessness…'

'Most people who'd been through what you've been through would be the same. You've lost a lot. But Lucian, I was just…' She cleared her throat. 'I was in the right place and I was convenient. That's all. You don't have to pretend that what happened between us meant anything more than that for you.'

His eyes flared. 'Zara—'

'I'm okay. I'm not destroyed—' she hurriedly interrupted him '—I've got through lots of tough things and I'll get through this. Maybe I just latched onto you too because you made me feel…wanted. Certainly not frigid around you, so thank you for that, I guess.'

'You thank me?' He stepped closer. 'Are you saying it wasn't as precious to you as you said only a few days ago?'

Her heart broke all over again. She couldn't lie to him. She adored him and right now she was both so happy and so sad she lost the power of speech.

'No?' He traced her face softly. 'You can't say that?'

She closed her eyes briefly. This wasn't fair.

'This is not a *convenience*, Zara,' he whispered. 'This is not a distraction. This isn't an alternate kind of comfort-eating through an emotional time. *You* are the emotion—all of them. *You* are the upheaval. You are *everything*. I walked into that damned cathedral, ready to slay the dragon from my past and I took one look at you and promptly forgot who I was and why I was there at all. *Everything* fell away and nothing but you mattered.'

'It was the dress,' she muttered. 'It was blinding. There were so many jewels all over it—'

'It wasn't the damned dress.' He laughed on a breath. 'You turned. Looked at me. You saw me. And I saw you. Here.' He pressed his hand on his heart but his eyes burned bluer with frustration even as his voice grew softer. 'But it was impossible. The *worst* timing. You were wounded by Anders, your family. And I was seeking not revenge, but *redemption*, just as you said. You were right in everything, Zara. I'm trying very hard not to mask my emotions any more. I want to be honest. I need you to believe me. To trust me.'

'Of course I trust you,' she muttered. 'You've always been honest with me—'

'No, I haven't. I lied to you, Zara. Lied by omission when I didn't tell you…'

She stilled. 'Didn't tell me what?'

'That I love being with you. That I love you talking incessantly to me. I love trying to make you laugh. I love it when we're just hanging out. Being with you makes me forget everything bad that ever happened. But the thing is I can't use you like that. You're not my therapy dog, remember? I want to be fully present, to be one hundred percent. For Monrayne, yes, but mostly for you. Can you be patient while I get there, Zara?'

'Are you asking me to wait for you?'

His lips twisted as he shook his head. 'Maybe a better man would. But I waited a decade before taking the throne back from Anders and I'm not waiting a decade before sorting myself enough to be with you. I don't want to miss out on any more *time*. I want you *with* me to do that. I want you to come back with me right now. But I'm going to be working on things for a while. Could you tolerate being around while I do that, do you think?'

He wanted her with him. He wanted to be with her. Because he loved her. And he was still holding himself to overly exacting standards.

'I'm not exactly perfect and whole myself, you know,' she muttered. 'I get nervous in public. I can write, but put me in front of a crowd and I just want to vomit.' She paused. 'Except when I'm with you. I don't feel like throwing up then. I feel courageous around you. After all, I successfully blackmailed you…'

'You did.' He smiled.

'So I guess I used you a little too.'

'You can use me any time, anyhow, you like.'

Her heart raced. 'You want me—'

'Back. Now. Because I'm absolutely and utterly in love with you,' he said huskily.

She stared up at him and those tears filled her eyes.

'You can take time to think about it if you need and fly a bit later. If I'm rushing you—'

'Life with you will always be intense,' she whispered. 'You don't actually do life any other way.'

'I'm trying very hard to hold back now.'

'What would you do if you didn't hold back?'

'I'd pick you up, get you to the jet and take off before you could stop me.'

'And then?'

'Spend the rest of my days serving Monrayne and loving you. I want to do everything with you beside me. And I would never let you go again.'

'Then don't hold back, Lucian. Don't ever hold back with me again.' She launched herself into the arms of her mountain of a man. His ice had melted and the warmth of him was utterly intoxicating. He was big and strong and she just buried herself in his hold as he carried her to the waiting car. They didn't speak a word on the short drive. They were too busy kissing.

But as he led her up the stairs of the jet he smiled. 'What if I told you there's a caramel apple tart on board the jet?'

'Why didn't you say that first up?' she teased. 'We would have been in the air twenty minutes already.'

'Zara…' He laughed.

She'd been too busy crying to pay too much attention to the interior of the private plane the last time she'd flown in it and she was too busy drinking him in this time. The second the jet levelled out after take-off Lucian unfastened his belt and came to her.

But she held him at bay, the practicalities worrying her. 'You're going to smuggle me back into the palace, right? I'll just live there quietly and secretly for—'

'Ever? No way. You've lived like that almost all your life. Not happening. You're going to travel. You're going to study, you're going to manage whatever projects you want, save all Monrayne's old castles if you want—'

'It's going to be weird.'

'It's going to be fine. You just move in. We won't care what anyone has to say on it.'

'I can't just start living at the palace.'

'Why not? Cutting one side of your life out completely isn't healthy and it isn't sustainable. Trust me on that. You've never had the experience of living as an actual Royal. Give it a chance.' He tempted her with the most gorgeous smile. 'Be my date. Dance with me. I'll come see your parents with you. We'll travel together wherever. I want more balance. We'll take weekends. Summer holidays. We can come back here—' He broke off and drew breath. His lips twisted in apology. 'But no pressure for more than that. I've tried to get you to marry me twice recently and I'm not risking rejection again yet. You need time to make sure this is a life you want. Time where you're free to come and go and do whatever you want. Because there will be limitations if you choose to become my wife. I don't want you to miss out on experiencing your full freedom first. So I'm not going to propose again for a year. Three hundred and sixty-five days exactly. I promise. Will you give Monrayne and *me* that chance?'

She stared into his amazing eyes, knowing that there was no disentangling the man from his Crown. And that was as it should be.

'Of course I will.' Her heart thudded. 'Promise you won't ask anyone else in that time either.'

'What? Zara,' he admonished. 'Do you think any other woman would please me?' he said thickly. 'Do you think I want this with anyone else? Only you.' He claimed her intimately. 'Only you will ever do for me.'

Her mouth parted on a wordless sigh as he drew her even closer.

'I know you like that,' he muttered, watching the colour wash over her skin. 'I like it too.'

Pleasure flooded her swiftly. She was so happy, so certain of him that she couldn't resist teasing him. 'It's just that I'm your first.'

'Rubbish.' He nuzzled her neck and laughed. 'You're the only one I've wanted like this. I was waiting. Not for the right moment but for the right person.'

So seductive. So true. For her too. But she couldn't help another smile as she swept her fingers down his sternum. 'I just thought you were hot.'

He narrowed his gaze and moved a little harder, deeper, faster. 'The bare chest?'

'You know I can't see past it,' she sighed.

He chuckled. 'That was my back-up plan in case you weren't willing to listen to me when I got to Piri-nu.'

'That and the caramel apple tart.' She laughed but she spread her palm over his old ice-skating scar and felt the strong thud of his heart. It grounded her in the searing heat between them. 'It's not just the chest,' she whispered.

'I know,' he whispered back. 'You love me.'

'I do.'

'Best thing ever. I'm sorry I pushed you away. Sorry I didn't know how to accept it. That I was too scared to answer honestly at the time.' He cupped her face. 'But I'm getting better at it. I love you too.'

He was brave and strong, loyal and honourable and *hers*. She'd never felt as happy as she did in that moment.

'Take me home, Lucian.'

Her body shook as he unleashed his absolute force on her. '*Yes!*'

# CHAPTER SEVENTEEN

*Three hundred and sixty-four days later*

LUCIAN WAS LATE to dinner.

Zara toyed with the cutlery. Silly nervous. Her brain refused to get off one track. Tomorrow would be a year to the day that he'd found her on Piri-nu and brought her back home to his palace in Monrayne. A year in which he'd promised he wouldn't propose to her. He hadn't said he *would* propose on this day of course, just that he wouldn't propose *before*. Which meant that he might not propose at all. Of course, there'd been nothing stopping her from asking him in all this time, except she'd thought that as he thought she needed time, perhaps *he* really needed time... To be certain that was. Because she already was. She had been from the start.

'Sorry.' He shot her an apologetic smile as he finally walked in. 'Back-to-back meetings. Both ran over.'

'It's okay.'

He'd been oddly preoccupied the last couple of weeks. He probably hadn't even remembered what date it was.

His coronation had occurred seven months after his return and two months before Anders was found at the bottom of a cliff in South America. Apparently he'd accidentally lost control of his motorcycle on a corner, but Lucian had suspicions that he'd crossed swords with career criminals and been chased down. It had been a sad end to an unhappy life. Garth had been fined and retired quietly into the countryside, his time in the palace now consigned to the history books.

But Lucian's reign had simply strengthened from its astonishing start, while Zara's residence in the palace had been accepted with a surprising lack of side-eye. Lucian had offered a short explanation that she was a friend, staying indefinitely. It hadn't taken the media, citizens and rest of the world that long to work out that she was a 'special' friend, given she accompanied him on every evening outing he attended. And any trips he took abroad. That she also went with him on his weekends away and on his summer retreat into the hills...

To *her* astonishment, it seemed they *approved* of her. They liked her honesty, her moments of awkwardness, her appreciation. And they loved the way *he* smiled when he was with her. That he'd stopped her from marrying someone else had been spun into a feted romance—as if it were a fairy-tale.

It wasn't. It was so much better than that. It was funnier, lovelier, hotter. He'd given her a life of luxury, taken her to amazing places she'd never imagined getting to see and introduced her to wonderful people. He'd also supported her as she undertook part-time study in the management and conservation of historic buildings—the part of her previous life that she'd actually loved. Plus she'd kept working on the palace correspondence—they worked on it together now. And with Zara's help he'd opened other parts of the palace to the public. But she liked being here with him in the older, private palace wing best. Working alongside him in the library. Dining with him here in their room. Being held by him in their bed.

'You're not hungry?' Lucian noticed her pushing the food around the plate.

She shrugged and jerked her chin towards his plate. 'You've not done much better.'

He smiled ruefully and pushed back his chair, stepping round to kiss her. Thoroughly.

'Do you know we've made love in every room in the palace, yet not in here,' he muttered. 'How has that happened?'

'We've always been distracted by caramel apple tart,' she murmured.

'Ah. Yes, that's very sweet, but not as sweet as you.' He released her with a groan. 'But we can't tonight because I've still got a million reports to wade through. I'm sorry.'

'And I have reports of my own to write,' she said, though it was going to be a struggle to concentrate. 'I'll do it in bed.'

'I'll join you as soon as I can.'

But a long time later he still hadn't made it up to their suite. She turned the light out yet couldn't sleep. Still nervous. She loved living with him. She would live here for the rest of her days just like this. But she wanted more. She wanted a family with him. She dreamed of the two of them having it *all* together.

'Zara?' She heard his voice in her dreams, husky and loving. 'Are you awake, darling?'

She stirred drowsily. 'What time is it?'

'Just past midnight.'

He sounded very serious and she came fully awake.

'Is something wrong?'

He lit the small lamp on the table and sat on her side of the bed. 'I wanted to keep my promise, but not for a second longer than I have to.'

'Your promise?'

There was the barest hesitation, an indrawn breath. 'Will you marry me, Zara?'

Tears instantly sprang to her eyes, but nothing could hold back her smile. Or her answer. 'You know I will.' Shamelessly joyous, she threw her arms around his neck and tugged him down to her. 'I thought you'd *never* ask again!'

His kiss was hotter than ever—lush and long—and it didn't matter that she was both laughing and crying.

'It's been a very long year biting that question back every bloody day,' he groaned. 'And these last weeks I've been going round the bend, trying to dream up the perfect way to propose. I thought about taking you to Piri-nu. About lighting up the sky with fireworks. I even tried to figure out when and how to bake the engagement ring into a caramel tart…' He shook his head. 'In the end I just couldn't wait.'

'And I'm so glad,' she breathed. 'This is perfect. I'm so glad you didn't wait a second longer. I was working up the courage to ask you—' She broke off and narrowed her gaze on him. 'What engagement ring?'

'Good thing you've stopped biting your nails.' He chuckled but her heart smote as she gazed at the ring he held for her.

It wasn't like any she'd seen before. Set in gold, this was a series of baguette cut sapphires, creating a kaleidoscopic effect. Like a hall of mirrors, the stones shifted from the deep blue stone in the centre to pale at the edges.

'I had it made specially,' he explained huskily. 'It hasn't belonged to anyone else. So there's no baggage or bad memories with it.'

'We can't always escape baggage,' she whispered.

'No. But perhaps we could put the baggage in a cupboard sometimes and unpack it slowly in those moments when we have the strength to bother.' He slid the ring down her finger. 'I don't want to be burdened by the past. By the expectations of others. I don't want that for you either. You'll wear all the family jewels, but this one is just for you from me.' He pointed to the central stone. 'It's the colour of your eyes.'

'And they run all the way down to the colour of yours,' she added, pointing to the palest stones at the edge. 'I love it.'

'Good,' he growled and pushed her back down on the bed. 'Because I love you.'

They were swift then. Whispering words of love and tenderness and relief. Then there were no words, only that delicious tension as sighs quickened and bodies heated.

'You know we'll have to get married in the cathedral,' he said, holding her close after.

'Oh?' She froze.

'But I was thinking we could do it at some ridiculously early hour when everyone else is asleep. If you're very lucky I might even go bare-chested.'

A wave of amusement washed over her.

'Half-naked nuptials?' She giggled and pressed her forehead against his chest. 'Lucian.'

'We can do whatever we want,' he said softly.

'We can*not*,' she said prosaically. 'But I will get into another wedding dress. I'll walk down a long, scary aisle in front of millions. Only for you.'

His arms tightened. 'Thank goodness. I thought I was going to have to kidnap you. But if you like we can have a private wedding ceremony as soon as possible, followed by a public blessing a little later, once the pageant has been organised. A compromise. What do you think?'

'Not having to walk up the aisle, terrified someone might *stop* it actually sounds really good to me,' she admitted.

'No one will be able to stop it,' he promised. 'Because we'll already be married.'

'That sounds perfect.' She smiled.

And it was.

# CHAPTER EIGHTEEN

*Four years after that*

LUCIAN WATCHED IN amusement as Niko walked towards him—one child on his hip, another walking alongside him, holding his hand. Maia was a step in front, holding yet another toddler, while the last was in the arms of a nanny. An entourage of assistants followed.

'Wow.' Lucian removed his sunglasses and smiled broadly as he took in the spectacle. 'How was the flight?'

'Piece of cake.' Niko winked.

The good humour was so very typical of his larger-than-life friend.

'What else is a ten-hour journey with triplet toddlers and a five-year-old?' Lucian stepped forward to scoop up the nearest small person tottering rather unevenly on the frosty path.

'I always forget how cold your country is, Pax.' Niko shivered and wrapped his spare arm around his wife. 'But it's lovely to see your smile.' He cocked his head. 'You are quietly content, I believe.'

'*Ecstatic,*' Lucian corrected. 'And not quietly at all. Shouting from the rooftops, in fact.'

'Where is she?' Niko glanced past him.

'Making sure everything is ready inside.' He'd not wanted her to come out in the cold.

Inside, the palace was decorated in vibrant festive ribbons and bows, while Zara stood by the enormous twinkling tree in the entrance hall—his own sparkling angel. A heavily pregnant angel.

'I wanted to come out to greet you.' Zara hurried forward to hug both Maia and Niko as they walked in. 'But Lucian bullied me into waiting in here.' She shot him a look that was both vexed and flirtatious. His favourite kind.

'I didn't want you to slip on the ice—' Lucian shrugged unashamedly and set Niko's child down.

Niko laughed. 'He's right.'

The children scampered around their feet. His firstborn, Kristyn, was round-eyed at the triplets her own age, while Niko's eldest, Kailani, took the lead. It was all chatter, giggles, full-bore chaos as all the treasure in the world tumbled about right in this room with him.

'Is there caramel apple tart?'

'Are we going to ice-skate?'

'Or ski? Can we ski?'

Protective and possessive, Lucian laughed at the endless excited requests. His daughter had made him a hostage to fortune completely, but she'd enriched his life in ways he'd never imagined possible. He couldn't wait to meet his son.

He felt Zara's arm slip around his waist from behind and turned to draw her closer still. Emotions threatened to momentarily overwhelm him—but he let them wash through. He'd got much better at allowing them, accepting them—welcoming them even. Some emotions more than others—like happiness, amusement, love. He caught Zara's eye and felt even more…bliss, anticipation. *Anticipation* of bliss.

Her hold on him tightened and she smiled. She knew he needed her close—that physical contact had become as essential and as natural to him as breathing.

Life was for living. And the life he'd built with Zara was utterly and imperfectly all.

\* \* \* \* \*

# COMING SOON!

We really hope you enjoyed reading this book. If you're looking for more romance be sure to head to the shops when new books are available on

## Thursday 14th September

MILLS & BOON

# MILLS & BOON®

## Coming next month

### REDEEMED BY MY
### FORBIDDEN HOUSEKEEPER
Heidi Rice

My taste buds were already dancing a jig as Jessie uncovered the feast she had prepared for me.

But as my gaze devoured her lean frame disguised in the baggy T-shirt and scuffed jeans she always wore, and I noticed the flushed dewy skin of her face devoid of makeup as she straightened and grinned at me, the swell of something hot and fluid blossomed in my groin. *Again*.

The irritation twisted into resentment in my gut.

Somehow, the housekeeper I didn't even like had begun to captivate me. I was actually beginning to look forward to seeing her each day, anticipating her arrival like a lovesick teenager.

"I'm sick of always eating vegetables," I added, knowing that my anger had nothing to do with her choice of menu and everything to do with the fact I could not act on my attraction to her, even if I had wanted to.

I did not sleep with my employees. Even ones that fascinated and — *damn it* — excited me.

*Continue reading*
REDEEMED BY MY
FORBIDDEN HOUSEKEEPER
Heidi Rice

*Available next month*
www.millsandboon.co.uk

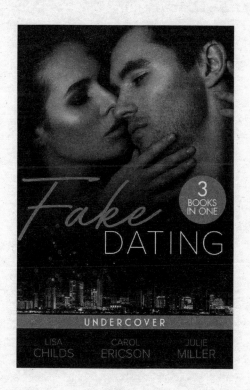

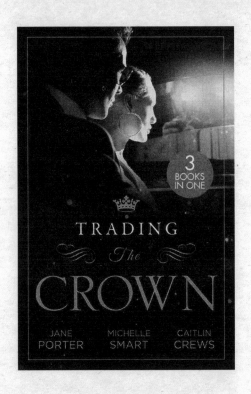

# LET'S TALK
## Romance

For exclusive extracts, competitions
and special offers, find us online:

- **MillsandBoon**
- **@MillsandBoon**
- **@MillsandBoonUK**
- **@MillsandBoonUK**

Get in touch on 01413 063 232